Praise for

Island
of Secrets

'**I was engrossed** and hanging on each and every word. This book
will leave a lasting impression . . . [and is] one that I will find
myself recommending to everyone I meet'
REA'S BOOK REVIEWS

'Raw emotions, family vendettas, hidden secrets and three
very strong women. It's a book I **enjoyed very much**'
THAT THING SHE READS

'A **beautiful, heart-breaking** story of sacrifice and love
in the face of evil'
FOR THE LOVE OF BOOKS

'We raced to the end with our hearts thumping'
LOVE READING

'A **moving, emotional, engrossing** story that was written with such
intensity and honesty . . . **I loved every minute of it**'
SHAZ'S BOOK BLOG

'Attention to detail is second to none . . . I cannot
praise this book enough and just hope that the
author writes another book soon'
BOON'S BOOKCASE

Villa of Secrets

Villa of
Secrets

Patricia Wilson

ZAFFRE

First published in Great Britain in 2018 by
ZAFFRE
80–81 Wimpole St, London W1G 9RE

A CIP catalogue record for this book is
available from the British Library.

ISBN: 978–1–78576–439–4

also available as an ebook

5 7 9 10 8 6

Typeset by IDSUK (Data Connection) Ltd
Printed and bound in Great Britain by Clays Ltd, Elcograf S.p.A.

Zaffre is an imprint of Bonnier Books UK
www.bonnierbooks.co.uk

For Berty, Michelle, and Peter.

PANDORA'S BOX

Hope is the only good spirit left
In the box, swiftly closed by Pandora.
Trust – a mighty value – has gone.
Restraint tramples flora and fauna.
The Graces quickly abandoned us all,
While Vanity makes us much poorer.
Nevertheless, we have Hope, my friend,
Thanks to the deft hand of Pandora.

Chapter 1

Rhodes, Greece, Present day.

Naomi shut the heavy door and slipped through a crumbling archway that spanned the street. She stood for a moment, eyes closed and face turned to the sun. Perhaps she shouldn't leave her grandmother alone, but Bubba was sleeping and Naomi, desperate for some fresh air, would return in twenty minutes.

She tossed her dark hair back and power-walked along the village side road, pumping her arms and heading for the beach. Wild ox-eye daisies, poking from cracked kerbstones, nodded in welcome as she rushed by.

Sandstone walls lined her way, time-worn, dull and dusty. Pastel masonry broken by startling blocks of colour – her neighbours' courtyard doors. Blue, mauve, turquoise, crimson and green.

A motley assortment of pots pinched the road into pedestrian narrowness. The containers housed a riotous collection of flowers: salmon geraniums, cerise dahlias, and top-heavy Easter lilies that exuded an exotic perfume. Vermillion bougainvillea, vivid and impenetrable, reached over a high stone wall halfway down the street, providing a much-needed patch of shade across scorching cobbles.

Nearer the beach, a web of familiar smells surrounded Naomi. She inhaled the scent of summer and the sea, and childhood scenes with their inseparable perfumes rushed into her mind.

She recalled piles of yellow net on the seawall, drying in the noon sun. The cement wharf was spattered with translucent fish scales, glinting harlequin sequins in the harsh light. Weather-worn canvas sails that had scooped endless journeys out of the wind ended their days hanging heavy and exhausted over harbour railings. On her arms, briny crystals sparkled like carnival face paint. When she licked the prickling salt off her skin, she tasted pure Mediterranean and longed to dive into the sea.

When she was five years old, Naomi helped to scrub sacks of blue-black mussels with her mother, on the deck of her father's boat, inspecting each one carefully before dropping it into the bucket. Side-by-side, content and silent, her parents exchanged wide smiles, which only now Naomi realised were full of pride. She recalled leaping off the pier with her school friends, bombing the water, howling with laughter when they broke the surface.

Rowdy birds had screamed and jostled behind her father's laden boat on its return to port each morning. Before school, Naomi would race along the shore parallel to the vessel, waving and calling, 'Papa! Papa!' over the sea.

On the beach, a row of weathered men with their arsenal of long fishing-rods, laughed and encouraged her. 'Run, Naomi, Run!' Papa would sound the foghorn in her honour and wave back.

Ten treasured years of love and laughter with her parents. Then Rebecca was born, and everything changed.

Naomi loved the sea, its sounds and its basic salty shape-shifting aroma – despite all it had taken from her.

She found the beach empty, apart from a lone fisherman who sat on an upturned bucket and stared out over the Mediterranean. Naomi had seen him there before, clean shaven, weathered face, well-worn expensive clothes. She returned his nod as she passed.

Smooth grey stones spliced by veins of white marble, clacked and slipped underfoot. She hurried towards a ribbon of wet sand, skirting the waterline. In the distance, a magnificent cruise ship headed for Kos, and she imagined her husband serving dinner in one of the sumptuous dining rooms.

At dawn, *The Royal Sapphire* had berthed in Rhodes Town. When Costa finished work, he had slipped home.

'Surprise!' he called, barging through the door with a bunch of yellow roses thrust at her.

'Costa! Oh, Costa!' She flung her arms around his neck and kissed him fervently.

Costa, a head taller than Naomi, lifted her off her feet and said, 'You drive me crazy, Naomi love. I had to come.'

She stuffed the bouquet in a jug of water, and then grabbed his hand. With two months catching up to do, they rushed upstairs and spent the entire afternoon between the sheets. Tumbling and fumbling, laughing and loving, never needing to say how much they still cared for each other.

After, they showered together, kisses tasting of toothpaste, bodies slippery with bath foam. Scrubbing each other's backs, they made plans for the winter, talked about their boys at university, the olive harvest, and what type of sofa to buy.

She glanced at the ship. *I love you, Costa.*

The day's boisterous waves had abated and a path of orange light reached across the Mediterranean from the setting sun.

Startled when a white bird darted, arrow-like, from the bamboo thicket, Naomi pulled up. The little egret pursued a dragonfly, then folded its angelic wings and returned to the dense shoreline vegetation.

Stunned by the magical scene, Naomi thought of her sister in London. She longed to share the precious moment and imagined telling Rebecca what she had witnessed. Would Rebecca experience such beauty in the big city? Did Rebecca realise what she was missing and how much she was missed, or had the magic of Rhodes faded from her memory forever? Her life was probably full, with her handsome husband and the chaos of young children.

Naomi recalled Rebecca's giggle whenever they got up to mischief, her self-effacing humour, the playful glint in her eye. The downturn of her mouth when she contemplated the less fortunate. Saddened that her sister was now lost to her, Naomi regretted not knowing her nieces or nephews.

She reached her turning point, a cement bunker in the shallows, remnant of the last war. It faced the Turkish mountains, visible across the sea. Although tilted by shore erosion, the grey pillbox appeared indestructible. Naomi sat on a rock. With her eyes on the cruise ship, her thoughts returned to her only sister.

At least Rebecca wouldn't have money worries. London was a place for the wealthy, where people lived in luxury that they took for granted. Naomi hugged herself, wondering if she would ever see her sister again. She wished old wounds would heal and that they could exchange a few words occasionally.

No one doubted Rebecca and her husband were in love. If only Bubba had explained the reason for her wrath ... perhaps Rebecca wouldn't have retaliated with such vehemence. A decade had passed since Rebecca's departure. Ten years of a crowded house, growing boys, exams and overstretched finances. But now, with Naomi's sons settled at university, and Costa back on *The Royal Sapphire* for the cruising season, her home felt echoingly empty.

She turned and retraced her steps. On the way, she peered into the bamboo. The egret had vanished. Such a beautiful bird, yet there was no sign it had ever existed. Just like Rebecca, she thought.

4

Ten years was a long time, and Naomi and her sister used to be so close. Naomi could start peace talks, why not? Someone had to try and bring the family back together.

Yet Rebecca's fair-haired Austrian husband was the problem. No, that wasn't quite true. Naomi's grandmother had caused the split. Naomi suspected that Bubba, who was Jewish, had too many wartime memories buried in the recesses of her mind. If she was right and those recollections resurfaced now in Bubba's feeble state after the stroke, Naomi didn't want to contemplate the consequences.

A wave broke over her trainers. Naomi stared at her wet shoes and, for the first time in many years, found herself hurled back in time to that same beach on the worst day of her life.

* * *

Rhodes, Greece, November 1984.

Bubba yelled up the stairs, 'Put your coat on, Naomi. Let's go before it gets worse. I can't sit here feeling useless. I have to look myself!'

Naomi, ten years old, ran down the stone steps as her grandmother, with Rebecca bundled in a shawl and clutched to her chest, called out, 'I'm taking the baby across the road, child.'

'I'm coming, Bubba.' Naomi followed her grandmother into the blustery street. Her red coat danced around like a gleeful puppy but Naomi was in no mood for games. She struggled to get her arms into the sleeves.

Bubba passed the infant to the priest's wife, promising to return soon. The priest, Papas Yiannis Voskos, came to the door. He dropped to his knees and fastened Naomi's buttons. She had never seen him look so downcast, his eyes bloodshot and restless in his hirsute face. He would usually grin and say, 'How's my big girl today?' and in a flash, produce a sweet or a cent from behind her ear. On the day of the storm, fun had abandoned him.

'Any news?' he said to Bubba, gripping the wooden crucifix that hung against his chest.

Bubba shook her head. In a voice shrill with worry she said, 'I can't stand the wait. It's driving me to madness.'

Papas Yiannis glared at the black thunderous clouds. 'God, keep them safe.' He rested his hand on Bubba's shoulder. 'Be careful on the beach, woman. It's dangerous down there.'

Bubba and Naomi leaned into the wind and hurried towards the shore. The roar of the sea met their ears long before the water came into view.

They rounded the corner, hammered back by the gale as huge waves rode on the shoulders of a fearsome swell. Tumultuous foam crashed onto the sand, terrifying Naomi. She clutched her grandmother's hand and stumbled along the slope of pebbles. They stayed high on the slippery stones, yet her shoes were soon soaked through.

The squall whipped Naomi's clothes around her almost knocking her off balance. She tried to yell, 'I'm scared, Bubba!' but the wind stole the words from her mouth. In the racket made by rolling pebbles, roaring breakers, and the gale howling in her ears, she peered out to sea.

Although barely five o'clock, black clouds scudded across a full, December moon, throwing the scene into eerie darkness. Then, shafts of brilliant moonlight broke through and illuminated the tempest.

Naomi thought of her grandmother as a bucket of hugs and kisses waiting to be delivered. But the gentle expression had gone, leaving Bubba's face pinched and bitter. Her eyes narrowed to slits and her jaw thrust forward as they peered through spume and spray, desperate for a glimpse of *Elevtheria*, her parents' boat. The sea kept coming at them, driving them even higher up the wet stones.

Mama and Papa should have sailed home that morning after a night's fishing.

'They'll be all right, Bubba,' Naomi tried to say. Papa was the perfect sailor and she never doubted his sea-faring skills. He'd told her many exciting stories that involved stormy nights on the boat. Tales of waves as high as the house, mermaids, and sea monsters, and she would glance sideways at him, unsure which parts of his story were fact and which were fiction.

Bubba, stick thin but strong as a mule and just as stubborn, was beaten back by tiredness and gale-force winds. They returned home reluctantly. Papas Yiannis said he would pray for them. Bubba's tears ran like red rivers on her pale, salt-dried face. At first, Naomi thought they were tears of blood.

Embarrassed to see her grandmother weep, she didn't know where to look. Bubba sat next to Rebecca's wooden cradle, rocking the newborn and staring at nothing. Every once in a while, her chin shivered with a fresh bout of crying. She placed her hand on Naomi's cheek and said, 'Child, you're so like your mother. My poor, sweet, Sonia. Pray to God she's safe.'

Even now, when Naomi looked in the mirror, she saw the classic Greek features of her mother and, she guessed, of her grandmother too when she was young. Small in stature, olive skin, brown eyes, and a thick tumble of dark curls.

She tried to make Bubba feel better, brushing her tears away, hugging her and kissing her cheeks, exactly as Mama did when Naomi grazed her knees.

The show of affection only made Bubba worse.

Naomi was more worried about Bubba than her own parents. Her father was the best sailor in the world. He would have found a safe haven somewhere. She knew all about 'safe havens' because they featured in most of his bedtime stories.

'Remember, Naomi, no matter how bad the storm, you can always find a safe haven, a calm place to shelter until things settle and it's safe to go on.'

Later that evening Bubba crept out of the house. Naomi, mature for her years but still not realising the seriousness of the situation, worried when she didn't return. Remembering Bubba's earlier distress, she suspected the old lady had returned to the beach. She checked on baby Rebecca, who was sleeping in her cot, then followed her grandmother to the shore.

The storm had abated. The moon slid behind thick clouds, and the wind complained moodily. Alone in the dark, Naomi grew scared, sensing evil in the night, but then Bubba's shriek ripped through the darkness. For a moment, afraid of the Bogeyman, Naomi shouted, 'Bubba!' into the stiff breeze, desperate for her grandmother to hear her.

Bubba's wailing made Naomi think the Bogeyman had her. She didn't know what to do. What if Bubba had fallen, broken a leg, and lay screaming in agony? Naomi had to help but her trepidation mounted. Monsters and demons returned to her imagination and dampened her bravery once more.

'Bubba!' she shouted again, running across slippery stones, fast as she could, because everyone knew the Bogyman couldn't run very well. 'Bubba, where are you?' She stopped, enveloped by the night, twirling around because the Bogeyman was always behind you . . . or under your bed . . . or wherever you could not see him. But he looked for you, and you daren't even breathe in case he heard you and pounced. Now he was on the beach, in the dark. She sensed his presence, looming.

A shape lurched out of the night. Naomi squealed and cowered, unable to move her feet. Bubba staggered towards her, clutching a splintered plank that Naomi recognised as part of a wrecked fishing boat.

'Are they home, Naomi? Are they safe?' the old woman wailed.

'No, I haven't heard, Bubba, but they'll be all right. Papa's a good sailor.' Overcome with relief, she was ready to deny, even to herself, she had been scared.

Naomi took Bubba's gnarled hand and led her back to the house. 'Shush, you'll wake the baby,' she said, quite the grown-up one. Her parents would be proud. When they returned, she might receive a pocket-money rise. 'You dry your eyes and wash your hands, and I'll make you some cocoa,' she told her grandmother, because that was what her mother would say when Naomi got upset about anything.

The next morning, haggard and red-eyed, Bubba rocked Rebecca to quieten her crying.

'Get dressed, Naomi. We must go to the chemist for baby formula,' she said.

* * *

Naomi flung a flat stone across the water and counted four bounces before it disappeared. Although her memories were painful, there was something pure and cleansing about them.

The fisherman was re-baiting his hook. 'Any luck?' she called.

He shook his head. 'Nothing.'

'Perhaps tomorrow,' she said encouragingly.

He smiled, eyes crinkling in the corners, rugged features lifting. She had the impression he didn't smile often enough.

Naomi arrived home, pushed open the blue front door, and stopped dead.

Sweet old Bubba sat on the edge of the bed, crying, struggling with a gun in her good hand.

Naomi leapt forward. 'No!'

In a flash, she imagined a deafening explosion with grotesque consequences. Everything frothed up inside her like milk on the boil and she almost vomited on the pebble mosaic floor.

She lunged, desperate to grab the weapon before her grandmother could pull the trigger.

Chapter 2

Bromley, London.

Rebecca came out of the gym honed, toned, and looking good. She pushed herself through a thorough workout at least twice a week to prepare her body for pregnancy, and had never been in better shape. The last of the sunlight streamed through the kerbside trees, throwing mottled shadows onto the pavement. The air was sweet and fresh after a recent shower, and the world sparkled with the vibrancy of late summer.

A man walked towards her and she sensed his appraisal of her body. Her skinny jeans and skimpy white t-shirt revealed a sliver of tight abs, and at thirty-three her breasts were still firm enough to allow her to go braless occasionally. She avoided his eyes as he passed.

Such moments made her feel good ... yet she knew she wasn't perfect, and her buoyant mood plummeted. Just a glitch, she thought, as if God had decided to hold back on something. But these days what nature wouldn't bestow, technology delivered for a price – that was where her hopes and dreams lay. Over the course of a decade these thoughts had become her constant mantra. They kept Rebecca sane in her darkest hours.

In vitro fertilisation was constantly improving, and the clinic Rebecca and Fritz attended had all the latest equipment. One day she would have her family.

Up ahead, a woman at the bus shelter stuck her hand out. Rebecca could have jogged to catch her ride, but she decided to walk to the next stop, passing the gorgeous baby boutique on the way. Her little boy would be a blue-eyed blond, just like Fritz, and her daughter would have wild dark hair and the olive complexion of the Cohen family.

She stopped at the shop front, disappointed to see a woman at work and the space a disorganised jumble of clothes, toys, and a wigless mannequin. The window dresser dragged an antique rocking horse, dappled grey with a real-hair mane and tail, across the floor. Rebecca wondered how many toddlers had settled in that leather saddle over the years, and the ghost of their laughter rang in her ears. She was smiling when the naked mannequin toppled towards the glass.

Instinctively, Rebecca threw her hands up and gasped. The dummy hit the window with such a crash she was surprised the glass didn't crack. The window dresser lunged and caught the sliding dummy before it reached the floor. Rebecca's palms were still against the window when the young woman looked up and mouthed, 'Sorry!'

She shook her head and, slightly nauseous, turned away. The sun disappeared for the day and a few spots of rain plopped onto the pavement.

Chapter 3

Rhodes, Greece.

Papas Yiannis, an overweight Moses with tortoiseshell glasses, unruly hair, and a long beard the colour of damp cigarette ash, had walked over from his house across the road. He and Bubba had hatched a plan and wanted Naomi to take care of it.

'We're depending on you to do this,' he said earnestly.

'But why? It won't work!' Naomi said. 'You can't just post a gun to England. And what's Rebecca going to think when she receives it? I'm astounded that my own grandmother and you, Papas, a man of God, have thought up this crazy idea. Have either of you considered the possible repercussions?'

They both pulled in their chins and blinked. She continued. 'Where did it come from, and why is it in our house – our *home*?'

'Naomi, your grandmother will explain the whole thing when she's stronger. Trust her.'

'After everything I've done for you and your sister.' Bubba's one drooping eye appeared emotionless, the other overcompensated and glared angry daggers.

Instantly, Naomi felt the presence of Rebecca; this was about her and, for a second, she resented it.

Now, beyond the striped rug hanging over an archway, Bubba was asleep in her bedroom that used to be their lounge. Papas Yiannis had gone back home across the street. Naomi stared at the gun on the table and tried to rationalise what had happened, but her thoughts were far from clear. She was overwhelmed by relief, grief, and an odd sensation that had made her insides quake the moment she had returned from the beach and saw her grandmother with a gun.

So much could have changed in the seconds after she walked into the cottage. How was she supposed to know Bubba was trying to dismantle the gun? Naomi had thought her grandmother was going to kill herself. The weight of her own emotions pulled at her jaw, turning her mouth down, and aching in her neck. Tears of relief rolled down her face. She found it impossible to imagine life without Bubba.

The weapon lay disassembled and inert on the time-worn kitchen table.

What was her grandmother doing with an old gun? Where had it come from? What awful deeds were attached to its past? Naomi knew the Jews of Rhodes had a disturbing history. As a child, she had visited the museum at the Kahal Shalom Synagogue in Rhodes Old Town with her sister and grandmother. But young Naomi was more interested in the prospect of an ice cream in the square. Impatiently, she had watched Bubba scrutinise faded photographs of skinny men in baggy suits. The old lady often nodded and muttered, sometimes dabbing her eyes or shaking her head.

Naomi took a calming breath. The tension of the evening made her body clammy, like waking from a nightmare. Her white tank top and khaki shorts hung damp and heavy against her skin. She needed a cool bath, perhaps a fresh bar of her latest Parma violet soap, or her homemade honeysuckle shower foam. Sometimes, the only place she could relax or work on her business plan was in the tub.

She stared at the five pieces of gunmetal that made up the pistol. Despite the weapon being dismantled, her heart continued to thud. Reluctant to touch it, she covered the parts with a tray cloth.

The contrast of a cold metal killing machine and the embroidered pink flowers seemed ludicrous.

Guns N' Roses, she thought playfully, recalling her youth. Half-forgotten nights with Costa came rushing back. Loud pop songs blaring from an evil cassette player notorious for chewing their favourite music tapes. They were sitting on a blanket on the roof in the light of a full moon when Costa asked her to marry him. They toasted each other and their future with cheap beer and sang their anthem, *Knockin' on Heaven's Door*, until Bubba banged her broom handle on the ceiling under their feet, telling them to turn it down.

At times, their passion for each other would become so intense they wanted to get under that old blanket, but they had feared the priest could see them from his darkened window.

Naomi started up to her bedroom, the stone steps cool underfoot. Shortly after, wearing nothing but the scent of honeysuckle and a bath-robe with *Costa Cruises* embroidered over her heart, she returned downstairs and rummaged in the kitchen drawer.

Where was the wretched door key?

She glanced around the small room that was desperate for a lick of paint, unable to remember ever locking the cottage, but a gun in her home changed everything. Although the pistol was disassembled, she recalled a film where Al Pacino snapped his weapon together in seconds, and he was blind!

There was a sense of urgency in the night, and she had no chance of sleeping until the house was secure.

Realising the futility of securing the door when the window catch was broken, she leaned out and hauled the louvres closed. Old paint crackled and flaked as rust broke its grip on the hinges.

After bolting the shutters, Naomi spotted the big iron key peeking from behind a length of crocheted curtain. The lock mechanism, also rusted, proved difficult but after a drip of olive oil, the stubborn contraption turned.

Sleep came in fits and starts. She woke in a sweat under the faded patchwork Bubba had sewn together decades back. At four thirty, Naomi abandoned her bed.

In the kitchen, she lit one of her vanilla candles. Released by the flame, the fragrance filled the room along with a glow of soft yellow light. She closed her eyes and inhaled gently.

Ice cream; fudge; Mama's hair.

Her tentative relaxation shattered when she found herself staring once more at the tray cloth covering the gun. Naomi yanked the kitchen drawer open and swept the offending pistol into it. The clatter made her jump. She glanced at the woven rug separating the kitchen from Bubba's room. Had she woken her grandmother with the dramatics? She stilled and listened. The gentle snoring paused.

'Help me . . . help,' Bubba whimpered.

Naomi's heart leapt. She pushed the rug aside, turned on the light, and hurried to Bubba's side. 'Sorry, did I wake you?' She rescued a pillow from the floor, plumped it and wedged it behind her grandmother. 'Do you need anything? Some tea?'

'Tea, yes. What time is it?' Her eyes, huge and slow-blinking, appeared alien-like in her thin face.

'Early.' Naomi sat on the bed and rubbed cream into Bubba's dry hands. 'I'll run you a bath later. You can try my jasmine shower foam, then sit outside for some fresh air while I do your room.'

They exchanged a glance. 'Sorry,' Bubba slurred.

Naomi recognised the honesty in her word and she filled with tenderness.

'Don't be silly. You've nothing to apologise for. Try and get another hour, then I'll bring you a nice mug of mountain tea, okay?' She smoothed a strand of silver-white hair away from Bubba's cheek.

'Will you take me to the hairdresser's sometime this week?' the old lady asked.

Speechless for a moment, Naomi lay her hand protectively over the thick braid that snaked across Bubba's pillow. 'But you've never been to the salon in your life. What's brought this on?'

'I want it cut off. Short and spiky like that TV woman. It'll knock years off me and be easier to manage.' She smiled at Naomi, her mouth pulling up on the good side of her face. 'No need to look so shocked, child. It's only a haircut I'm asking for, not Botox and a boob-job.'

Naomi giggled, glanced at the small flat screen on the opposite wall and said, 'You've been watching too much American TV. Don't ever change, darling Bubba.' She kissed her grandmother's forehead but, as she stood, Bubba snatched her hand.

'You will do it, won't you?'

Instantly, Naomi knew she wasn't referring to the hair appointment. Her voice hardened. 'I said I would, didn't I?' She tugged her hand from Bubba's grasp and moved to the door. 'Have I ever let you down, Bubba?' The words came out harder than she intended as she left the room.

'I said words I regret . . . to Rebecca,' Bubba cried. 'They've haunted me every day since.'

'Sleep now . . . Sleep.' Naomi allowed the rug to fall behind her.

She needed to put her mind to work. The fact that Naomi felt she could rightfully call it 'work' was an achievement in itself. A landmark in her business' progress, and she was obviously grateful for the extra cash. Her last batch of candles and beauty products had made her fifty-three euros. A turning point. Earnings of less than two euros an hour, but that didn't matter. She had a profit margin. The recent rise in electricity, water and phone prices strained her finances, and she considered every cent that came in and went out.

Naomi longed to have her own shop, with her products artistically displayed on glass shelves. When things got tough, it was this dream that kept her going. She would mix creams and perfumes for her loyal customers, and always have fresh wild flowers on the counter.

The window over the sink drew her attention. Above it, a bare plank fixed by three cheap brackets supported decades of her grandmother's writing. Greek, Italian, and kosher cookery books, volumes of handwritten lotion and potion recipes, and several hard-backed notebooks containing Bubba's perfume formulas. A burgundy silk-bound book labelled THE POEMS AND SONGS OF PANDORA COHEN also stood on the shelf. Naomi smiled at reading her grandmother's beautiful name on the spine and promised herself she would find the time to study the verses. At the opposite end of the bookshelf was the only ornament in the room: the china figure of a singing girl.

She flung the cobalt shutters open, allowing a cool draft to enter the stuffy kitchen. A sudden gust extinguished the candle, leaving a thin wisp of smoke coiling and rising for a moment . . . like a smoking gun. She glanced at the drawer, reached for the light switch, but hesitated when a window across the street lit up. Papas Yiannis was making his early-morning coffee before he left for church.

Movement on the priest's flat roof caught her attention. Silhouetted by fading moonlight, his granddaughter Marina kissed her boyfriend goodnight, one floor above Papas Yiannis's head. From the darkness of her kitchen, Naomi watched them and recalled the magic of romance. He lifted a simple ladder and lowered it onto Marina's balcony. After another hurried embrace, Marina slipped off her high-heels, hitched her short skirt even higher and climbed down to her room.

The two were in love, Naomi knew it. Since his wife and daughter had died, Papas Yiannis, who was already an old man, had become overprotective of his teenage granddaughter.

The boyfriend hauled up the ladder, lay it out of sight, and crossed the rooftops like a cat burglar making his escape.

Naomi recalled the breathless passion between her and Costa when they'd met in Crete. Nothing would have stopped her from seeing the athletic brown-eyed man she'd fallen for and then married. Time proved the strength of their love with two fine sons at university and a husband that she missed terribly throughout the summer season. She turned on the kitchen light and headed for the coffee pot.

Despite his bullying her about the gun the night before, Naomi was fond of Papas Yiannis. His offer to look in on Bubba this morning was a kindness in itself. Since the stroke, Naomi had little time for herself. She mused over what she could fit into her upcoming hour of freedom. Before she left, there were Bubba's ablutions to deal with, and breakfast . . . then the pistol. She shivered, wondering once again if dreadful deeds were connected to the weapon. Surely not. Nevertheless, the sooner she got rid of it, the better for everyone.

She filled an enamel jug and stepped outside to water the geraniums. The lingering night air cooled her damp skin. She studied the fading stars, glum for a moment as Bubba's emotional outburst came back to her: *after everything I've done for you and your sister*. So out of character. She didn't understand what had upset the feisty old woman. The stroke? These days most patients made a reasonable recovery. Bubba knew that.

Strokes were common in Paradissi Village. People blamed the airport, the planes, something to do with exhaust fumes or jet vibrations.

Just a month ago life had been normal, calm and organised. Naomi had ambitions and a modest business plan. Her routine teetered on the brink of change and a tinge of excitement hung in the air.

After many years of putting others first, her days had become her own once more. An adventure. She wore makeup, painted her toenails, and socialised in a quiet way. The girls' poker night was the highlight of her month. She regarded her occasional lunch at a beachside taverna and her fortnightly trip to the hair-dresser's as pure luxury.

How short-lived that precious interlude had been. Now she had a bedridden grandmother in the living room, and a gun stashed in the kitchen drawer.

There was no doubting that the stroke had been severe. Naomi wondered how she would cope if, after living an active life, she was so cruelly poleaxed. To lie on a bed with nothing but a sponge ball to squeeze and a lifetime of memories to contemplate must be torture.

The illness brought on a type of dementia that triggered Bubba's maudlin recollections, especially when she was tired. One moment she was fine, her old self; the next she would slip into a time of danger and sorrow, and relive her darkest hours. A single word could flip a switch and send her hurtling into a past that Naomi knew nothing about. Bizarrely, she found herself fascinated by these ramblings, although they seldom made sense.

Bubba claimed her old life was nobody's business but her own. However, when these moments took her, she returned to an era of emotional turmoil; her eyes glazed, tears welled, and she often called out for her father.

Chapter 4

Bromley, London.

Rebecca put the toilet seat down and sat with her back against the cistern. She popped the syringe out of its packet, and took a breath. This awful moment made her stomach churn. Her heart thudded and her mouth felt dry. The loneliest minutes of her life. She thought of Naomi, a trained nurse. Naomi must have done this a hundred times, to others of course. She chewed her lip, wishing her sister was here right now to take care of the injection for her. God, how she missed Naomi, and Bubba, although the resentment at their split had never quite gone away.

She put the point of the needle against her skin, her head swimming. Quickly, or she would faint. With a whimper, she pushed it into her flesh and shoved the plunger all the way down. She couldn't look at it now, so she threw her shoulders back and stared at the ceiling, waiting a moment before withdrawing the needle.

The syringe and the packaging fell to the floor and Rebecca blinked back her tears. Blowing her cheeks out, she remembered she only had one more injection to go.

She cradled her arms and looked down, imagining the infant that she prayed would be the result of this fertility treatment.

'I hope you appreciate what I'm going through for you, baby,' she whispered.

She tidied up, straightened her clothes, and went into Fritz's office.

'Am I interrupting anything? I need a hug,' she said quietly.

'Hello, beautiful.' Fritz swivelled his chair around and pulled her onto his knee. 'Are you all right? You look a little ruffled.'

'Just my jab. Last one tomorrow, thank God.'

'I could have done it for you. Wouldn't that feel better?'

She shook her head. 'What are you up to?'

He beamed. 'We've received an offer for the company, from America. They want to amalgamate.'

'That sounds exciting.'

'It is, more than I ever dreamed. There's a mountain of work to get through over the next month, but we've signed their contract to meet the deadline. The deal with Aloe Cosmetics clinched it. A huge effort, but it paid off in the end.' His excitement was contagious.

'I'm thrilled, Fritz. You've worked incredibly hard. You deserve this success.'

'I'll take you out this evening, a champagne dinner to celebrate!'

Rebecca's mood dampened. She smoothed his pale blond hair that he had a habit of pushing back. 'Oh, Fritz, I'd love to, but like I said, it's my last jab tomorrow. You know how it is. I wouldn't want to jeopardise anything at this stage, sweetheart. I'll cook you a super steak, how's that?'

'Lovely,' he said, but she could see he was crestfallen. He placed his hands on her tummy. 'You've got your own priorities to take care of, I do understand, darling. It's important, and I appreciate all you're going through for us.' He kissed her cheek. 'Now, off to the kitchen, woman! I've work to do.'

They both laughed, and Rebecca left him at his desk.

Chapter 5

Rhodes, Greece.

Naomi caught Bubba's whimper and rushed into the room. Her grandmother cowered against the pillow, her eyes wide, glazed, afraid.

'They're going to hang me! Help me, please. I have to escape,' she slurred. 'Papa! I can't see him. Where is he? Don't let them kill my Papa, I'm begging you!'

Naomi held her grandmother. 'Come on, Bubba. It's just a bad dream. You're safe with me.' She found it heartbreaking to see the old lady like this. Whatever was going on in her mind was very real to her grandmother.

Bubba thumped herself in the chest. 'I loved her, and because of me she's dead too. Please, bring her back!'

'Who, Bubba? Who did you love?' Naomi asked, cooling her grandmother's forehead with a damp facecloth, but Bubba had purged herself of the memory. Exhausted, she returned to sleep. Naomi watched her eyes flutter behind thin lids, and the occasional twitch of her body with a half-started word on her lips.

Despite these anxiety attacks, the last thing Naomi expected was Bubba's strange request: to post a gun to Rebecca.

Dragged away from her thoughts by more movement across the road, Naomi saw Papas Yiannis in his striped pyjamas ambling onto his front porch. He pushed his fingers behind his glasses and rubbed his eyes. Above him, Marina's bedroom light went out. The priest placed his tiny coffee cup on the tin table and pulled out a rickety chair.

Reluctant to break the peace of the hour, Naomi gave him a wave.

He nodded before sucking the froth off his drink.

Naomi returned indoors and tried to block thoughts of the gun by concentrating on a fresh batch of hand cream. She gathered the ingredients from memory, no longer needing Bubba's recipe.

2 cups of olive oil.

1 cup of coconut oil.

1 cup of beeswax.

8 drops of lemon essential oil.

She'd forgotten something . . . honey, that was it. She pulled the kitchen cupboard open and reached for the jar. The cruise calendar and a photo of Costa and her boys were taped inside the cream-painted door.

Uplifted by thoughts of her husband, she placed a hand on her cheek the way he did when he said, 'I love you, Naomi.'

Costa would be prepping breakfast for the rich and lonely, before they disembarked at the port of Kos.

Naomi recalled the time she had sailed to that island on the fast-cat ferry and met Costa at the port. They dashed about the town where he showed her the ancient plane-tree under which Hippocrates had taught his disciples of medicine. Like tourists, they scrambled through the town's archaeological site in the blazing sun, and admired antique mosaics underfoot. Eating cheap ice cream from McDonald's, they wandered about in Freedom Square, taking in the mosque, the museum, the spice market, and then the castle.

Naomi kissed her finger and touched Costa's photo.

She scooped ingredients into a jar that stood in a pan of hot water. The fragrant tang of lemon flooded the room. In a short time, the components would meld together, ready to be whipped, potted, and labelled.

If only life were that simple.

She reached into the kitchen drawer, withdrew the gun barrel, and prepared to wrap it. First, she polished her prints off the metal. You couldn't be too careful with a lethal weapon. So that Rebecca wouldn't recognise her handwriting, Papas Yiannis had written a note to go with the parcel. The only words were: INSTRUCTIONS TO FOLLOW.

* * *

Naomi power-walked through Paradissi Village, striding towards the airport. A favourite exercise route. Perhaps subconsciously, she wished to greet her boys home from university, or her husband at the end of the season, or one day, her sister. In fact, the walk had no other purpose than to burn a few calories and calm her nerves before she faced the post office.

She passed the infamous sex shop, currently the talk of the village, and longed to go in and investigate. Costa would be shocked but thrilled, if she surprised him in something red, and flimsy, and outrageous. Naomi shook her head and walked on. She was saving for a new sofa.

Orange butterflies flitted between roadside blooms of tansy and yellow tobacco blossoms, stealing their nectar. The dawn air, getting warmer by the second, was laden with fragrances: jasmine, honeysuckle, and night-flowering cactus. She sniffed, and analysed, and considered how to reproduce the perfumes using essential oils.

Somewhere, a caged canary trilled. Naomi wondered if birds enjoyed the wonderful scent of flora at daybreak. Few people realise the power of scent, how it prompts our hunger or satisfaction, and can make us hot with desire, or recoil in revulsion.

The edge of a distant cloud sizzled gold like a firework fuse, warning Naomi she hadn't long to reach her turning point before sunrise. The small knapsack tapped a steady rhythm on her back, spurring her onward.

She wondered why Rebecca couldn't respond to Bubba's correspondence and save Naomi from all this melodrama. Naomi understood her sister not answering the first letters, when tempers were still frayed, but years passed before Bubba wrote again. The outcome remained the same. No reply. She found it difficult to believe Rebecca would hold a grudge for so long.

Naomi doubted the conspirators would get the reaction they hoped for. Yet, she hadn't the heart to go against them. Since the night of the hurricane, Bubba had dedicated her life to Rebecca and herself, and Papas Yiannis had always been ready to offer support.

She recalled the day they delivered the bad news, two days after the storm.

'Take your sister for some fresh air,' Bubba said, placing baby Rebecca in the pram. 'Don't forget to use the brake when you stop.'

Naomi, proud of her baby sister, didn't need telling twice.

When she returned, the priest was in the house. He and Bubba were red-eyed and oddly breathless.

When Papas Yiannis told her the news, he held Bubba's hand, squeezing it until his knuckles turned white.

Odd the things that stay in a child's mind.

'Naomi, I'm sorry, but we think your father had a problem with *Elevtheria*,' he said, gulping between words. 'Your parents are lost at sea, *koritsie*.' Even now, he still called her *koritsie*, my girl, occasionally and it always reminded her of that day.

She accepted the information as she accepted everything adults told her.

That Mama and Papa never said goodbye made her unreasonably angry. Furious with the world, she had punched a girl in class who called her a liar and said her parents were dead. Naomi found it impossible to say why she'd behaved so badly, and it got her into awful trouble.

She couldn't grasp the situation, and didn't know how to deal with the information she'd been given. As the days passed, Naomi came to realise Mama and Papa really weren't coming home any time soon. Splinter by crack, her heart slowly shattered. She wouldn't talk to anybody about it because, secretly, she expected her parents to walk through the door at any moment. She truly believed Papa had found that *safe haven* he talked about. How could anyone be sure he hadn't?

A globe the size of a football stood in the corner of Naomi's classroom. At the end of the lessons, she would look at it and study how much sea there was to get lost in. Her father had to be out there, she convinced herself, lost because of the storm. After all, there were no road signs in the ocean. He'd be desperate to bring Mama back to his girls and Bubba. Papa was certain to find the way home eventually. He was very special, amazingly strong, and *always* right.

One windless day, when the sea was flat as glass and sound carried for many kilometres over the water, she heard the motor of an old fishing boat that was too far away to be seen.

It must be them!

She rushed into the shallows, cupped her hands around her mouth, and shouted as hard as she could, 'Papa, Mama! This way! I am Naomi! I'm here!' Over and over she repeated herself, jumping up and waving her arms above her head because grown-ups probably saw further than children. They'd realise the island they were sailing past was Rhodes, and they would recognise her and be filled with joy at seeing her. She imagined them so full of laughter they'd rock the boat, glad they weren't lost at sea any more.

Her father would push the long, wooden tiller and turn *Elevtheria* towards land, happy to return from their safe haven after such a lengthy journey.

A neighbour must have caught her racket and told Bubba. The old lady scurried down the shore, straight into the water. 'It's not them, Naomi. It's not your Mama and Papa.'

'Listen, Bubba! It's Papa's boat. The priest said Mama and Papa were lost at sea. They're trying to come back from their safe haven, but they don't know the way. If they don't hear us, they'll sail right past. Shout, Bubba. Please! Shout!'

Slowly, Bubba shook her head.

'Please, Bubba! Please! They're going past. They'll be gone soon. They might end up on the other side of the world. Shout as loud as you can! They *have* to hear us, I want them to come back . . . to return home! I've been waiting so long, Bubba . . . I miss them so much.'

'Oh, you poor child,' Bubba said gently. 'Your parents are in Heaven, Naomi.'

'No, Bubba, no! They're lost at sea. Papas Yiannis said so. Please don't say those things. I've been looking out for them, listening, every single day after school. No, no, you're wrong!'

Bubba wrapped Naomi in a tight hug and they both cried hard, their bodies shaking against each other. Then, when their tears were spent. Bubba took Naomi's hand and said, 'Let's shout one last time, on three.'

They stood in the water, holding hands, their faces turned to the sky. Together they shouted with every bit of strength. 'MAMA! PAPA!'

'I think they heard us in Heaven,' Bubba said. 'Come on, give them a smile and a wave, and then we'll go on home.'

They waved, smiled through their tears, then returned to the cottage in silence.

And all through that time, Naomi now presumed, Bubba had this pistol hidden in the house.

According to Bubba and Papas Yiannis, taking the gun apart and posting the parts separately would not only instigate Rebecca's curiosity, but also avoid flouting the laws about shipping a firearm. Not that either of them understood exactly what those regulations were.

She wondered how long it had taken them to hatch this crazy plan, and what the hell was Bubba doing with a pistol hidden away. What if her own boys had found it when they were young? She shuddered.

A coach of tourists turned into the airport. The soft light strengthened around her, pale shafts fanning across the sky. Feeling the burn of lactic acid in her thighs, she pushed on.

A *Tui* plane, wheels down, headlights blazing, seemed to skim the distant treetops on its runway approach. The noise filled the air. Naomi reached the traffic lights, turned, and headed back to Paradissi. At this rate, she'd get to the post office before it opened.

The sun rose above the horizon and glittered off cars and windows. Naomi's shoulders warmed and her elongated shadow undulated over the tarmac before her. At least her silhouette appeared tall and slim with long, long legs. She watched her shadow, swinging her hips a little and rejoicing in the illusion of a model-like figure, until she almost bumped into a lamppost.

'Look out!' Manno shouted, raising his fat arms. He shook his head and turned to unlock his *kafenion* door.

'Morning, Manno!' Naomi replied, laughing at her own stupidity. 'Nice shirt!' she said, nodding at the garish parakeets and palm trees that covered his mammoth belly.

She took a turn around the village square while Manno gathered scattered chairs and tucked them neatly under his pavement tables. 'Come for coffee,' he called.

'Later!' She grinned and waved.

'I've another bag of ouzo bottles for you.'

'Bravo, thanks again!' The small, retro carafes were perfect for her witch-hazel toner, and they were free.

Opposite the *kafenion*, the grocer's door opened. Stick-thin Savvas stretched his neck and peered around the square. Gangling and mantis-like in his leaf-green overalls and thick round glasses, he threw a wink at Naomi before pulling hessian sacks off crates of fruit and veg.

Both men stopped to watch Katarina come out of the hair salon and clean her window. They exchanged a glance before continuing to study the shimmy of her buttocks as she buffed.

'You're being admired,' Naomi said, marching past.

'Same every morning,' the hairstylist replied. 'I polish my glass; they ogle my ass.'

'Pure poetry!' Naomi called over her shoulder. They both laughed. Ahead, a taxi pulled up beneath a peeling blue and yellow sign: RENT ROOMS IN PARADISE. A couple in party gear tumbled out of the car, paid their fare, and wilted into the apartment. Naomi remembered Marina's tryst and tried to recall if she had ever stayed out until sunrise with Costa.

Passing Naomi, the taxi driver beeped his horn. She lifted her chin, turned her head away, and flat-lined a smile. *Cheeky devil.*

She marched down the shopping street and headed for the post office, hoping for a letter from England. Then, she wouldn't have to post the bloody gun.

A queue of elderly people reminded her it was pension day. Two yellow sacks stood on the kerb, confirming the mail van hadn't arrived yet.

She slumped at a café table under a frangipani tree, pulled a magazine from her rucksack, and stared at the page, but her mind was lost in questions about the blasted gun.

'Naomi!' The urgent voice made her jump.

Her neighbour, Heleny, a large Greek woman with Italian roots, dropped into a white plastic chair that appeared alarmingly inadequate for her hips. She glanced about and whispered, 'You remember that perfume you gave me?' Naomi nodded. 'You won't believe the weird effect it's having!'

'In what way? Perhaps you're allergic to something.'

'No, nothing like that. It's . . . well . . .' She gulped and widened her eyes. 'It's *men*. They keep looking at me and, you know, paying attention.'

'I see. Best not wear it then.'

Heleny shook her head. 'No, you don't understand. I want more. That perfume is amazing, makes me feel . . . *hot*! I was just—'

Georgia rushed up to the table and interrupted. 'Girls, I've brought the latest gossip. A *sex* shop has opened in the village!'

Naomi needed a lift and couldn't resist a little fun. 'That's interesting. Do they need any staff, Georgia? I'm looking for a part-time job.'

Heleny tried to hide a chuckle but her chest bounced and quivered.

Georgia stared at Naomi, her mouth hanging open for a moment. 'You wouldn't! It's disgusting. Children might go in. They're selling all sorts of erotica.'

'What, the children?' Heleny said, losing the struggle to keep a straight face.

Georgia huffed. 'You can laugh, but never mind that. What about the secret door, the documents, the historian investigating? I've just come from the church. They're saying it's a real genuine miracle.'

'What's a miracle?' Naomi asked sitting up, snapping her mind away from the parcel in her bag.

'They say God was searching for someone pure, a man that wasn't corrupt, to get the door in the police station opened. And it took Our Lord Himself seventy years to find an honest man in Greece.'

Naomi hooted with laughter, and then saw her friend was deadly serious and slightly offended.

'Georgia, get your facts straight,' Heleny said. 'Firstly, the historian isn't Greek; he's Italian. Secondly, the Italians are even more corrupt than the Greeks. Who do you think invented the mafia?'

'They can't all be corrupted. Isn't the Pope Italian?' Georgia said flatly.

'No, he just lives there,' Heleny retorted. 'Free accommodation, a perk of the Pope job. The Vatican's probably a registered charity, tax deductible too. Anyway, it's got nothing to do with God. He's too busy causing wars, and cancer, and starving children.'

Georgia's pinched face blanched. With her slender, long-fingered hand, she crossed herself three times before sitting at their table. She turned to Naomi.

'It'll bring trouble, you'll see. No good ever came from poking around in the past.' The words rushed out. 'My man says it was all the Italians' fault.'

Heleny glared. 'Don't blame the Italians! They're the ones who brought tourism to Rhodes. If it wasn't for the Italians, you'd be in the fields picking olives right now.'

'No, it's far too early; they're not ready.'

'You know exactly what I mean, Georgia.'

Naomi supressed another giggle. She loved her friends.

'The point is,' Georgia continued, scratching her nose and talking from behind her hand, 'someone didn't want the contents of that room discovered, but they hadn't the guts to burn the lot. Isn't that right? My husband says it's dangerous, we shouldn't talk about it. He says there'll be important people who don't want questions asked.'

Heleny shook her head. 'You always do what your man says?'

'Don't be stupid. Am I actually talking about it or what?'

Naomi stared into her magazine. 'Cut the dramatics, you two. What door? What trouble?'

'The mysterious door in the police station. Seventy years locked and the key tossed aside. Secret information concerning the dead . . . Ouch!' She reached down and rubbed her shin while glaring at Heleny.

Heleny turned to Naomi. 'Those poor people. Obviously the *malákas* were hoping the room full of war-time statistics would rot to nothing. Nobody wants to remember those times, do they?'

Georgia narrowed her eyes. 'I wish you wouldn't swear.'

Naomi turned a magazine page with no awareness of the article she'd stared at. 'I still don't understand what you're talking about. Anyway, I'd rather not talk about the war thank you very much. I'm not in the mood.'

A frangipani flower floated down and landed on the table. Naomi picked up the waxy blossom, sniffed it, and tucked it behind her ear.

Heleny turned her head dismissively. 'Will you stop blaming the Italians, just because Rhodes was under Italian rule? The Italian army were all murdered by the Nazis, or sunk by the British, in forty-three. It was the Greeks that hated the Jews as much as the Germans. *They* wanted rid so they could steal everything the poor Jews owned. Hypocrites!'

'Poor Jews?' Georgia retorted. 'I've never seen a poor Jew in my life!'

Naomi's anger rose. 'Well, look this way, why don't you?'

Georgia blinked. 'But *you're* not Jewish.'

'Well, my mother was Jewish, and my grandmother is Jewish. My father was Greek Orthodox, like his father before him. So I'm half Jewish . . . but I'm not half rich.'

'And as for the Italians,' Heleny continued, 'they were pawns in a game between the British and the Germans. Cast aside by one lot, and gathered up and murdered by the others.'

'You're talking rubbish, Heleny. The Italians had changed sides, *again*! Like in the other big war,' Georgia retorted.

'Girls, stop it!' Naomi said. 'It was a long time ago, and I doubt anyone here will have their facts straight. Why are we bickering about it now?'

'Because' – Georgia drew the word out for effect – 'behind the door at the police station they found a census the Italians did before . . . you know . . .' She lowered her voice further. 'Auschwitz.'

Naomi supressed a shiver. She didn't want this conversation outside the post office when she had a gun in her bag. 'Look at that cake,' she said, focusing on the magazine. 'We're getting too Americanised. It's just a multi-coloured sugar bomb.'

Georgia nodded at her phone. 'I'm addicted to Candy Crush. That's got multi-coloured sugar bombs.'

Naomi blinked at her. 'You've completely lost me.'

Heleny leaned in and poked the glossy magazine picture. 'It's for Mother's Day. Why don't we all make a cake, and have one of those "bake-off" things? Let our mothers judge them.' She stopped and her eyes turned to the floor. 'Sorry, Naomi, tactless of me. I always think of Bubba as your mother.'

'Bubba is an old *Jewish* term for grandmother,' Naomi said pointedly, her eyes fixed on the page as she scored a point.

Georgia broke an awkward silence. 'That cake recipe's a bit out of date, isn't it?'

'Costa came home yesterday, brought me a stack of mags off the cruiser. They're like new. Where's the post?' Naomi peered up the street. 'Bubba's on her own. I've got to get back.'

'On her own?' Heleny sounded alarmed.

'Well, not exactly. Papas Yiannis is there, but if she needs the bathroom . . .' Naomi shrugged. She had no intention of telling them about the gun, but she couldn't think of anything else.

'Go,' Georgia said. 'If there's any mail, I'll text you.'

'Is that thing glued to your hand?' Heleny quipped.

Naomi nodded at her backpack. 'Thanks, Georgia, but I've a parcel for London and I want to see it go into the last sack. I'll wait.'

'Why the last sack?' Georgia asked.

'Stands to reason. If it's the last sack into the van, it'll be the first out, won't it? Sorted and sent off right away,' Naomi said.

Heleny stretched her neck. 'A parcel? I thought you and Rebecca weren't speaking. What's brought on this sisterly love?'

Naomi blinked and turned away. Heleny hadn't a sarcastic bone in her body yet the thoughtless words stung her. She ignored the question, peered up the street, and saw Elias step into the bakery. 'I need to buy bread before old dirty-fingers squeezes every loaf in the shop. I haven't time to bake today. I'll catch you later.' She stood and slung her backpack over her shoulder.

'Wait! I nearly forgot,' Georgia said. 'I've three orders for the lemon and honey hand cream.'

Naomi grinned. 'Great, thanks. I'm just making a fresh batch. Text me.'

'Just bring it to poker night, okay? It's brilliant for age spots. Mine have almost gone.' She turned the back of her hand for Naomi to inspect. 'Better bring a few extra jars. Word gets around.'

'I hope to . . . but I'm not sure I'll make cards night,' Naomi said.

''Course you can,' Heleny replied. 'I'll sit with Bubba for a couple of hours. You need a break. What's in the parcel?'

'I'll tell you later,' Naomi lied. 'Got to run!'

Halfway to the bakery, she spotted the mail van coming towards her, turned, and marched back to the post office.

Chapter 6

Bromley, London.

Rebecca took the parcel into her white gloss and black granite kitchen. She almost broke a nail extension getting through the swaddle of brown paper and layers of tape. Frowning, she stared at the tube-shaped black metal.

It must be a car part for Fritz.

The old MG Midget had stood in the garage for five years. Fritz's enthusiasm for its restoration was periodic. Sometimes, when parts arrived, she hardly saw him all weekend and in desperation had placed a table and two chairs in the garage. She would take a drink and have a sandwich with him rather than sit alone in the kitchen. But why didn't this package contain an invoice, and why was it addressed to her?

'Nothing to do with me,' Fritz said when she placed it before him that evening.

Perhaps the garage had made a mistake. A computer error. *Papagopoulos Autos* were the only Greeks Rebecca had any contact with. Even so, it didn't make any sense. She studied the stamps. How long since she'd stood inside a Greek post office? Over ten years?

* * *

The next morning, Rebecca turned the page of her kitchen calendar and stared at the first of the month. Her stomach flipped, jumpy as a bag of frogs. A spiral of red Biro surrounded the first, and even more scribbling around the fifth. For a second, she recognised a couple of red-rimmed eyes with black numerical pupils, glaring at her.

She closed her eyes and imagined herself in the cellar of her marriage: a small dark place surrounded by cold grey concrete, impossible to go any lower, or be any more alone. Ten years and still no children. Time was stealing Rebecca's childbearing years, and the walls were closing in. Her only window of escape was the round glass Petri dish in the IVF clinic.

Her last chance loomed ever closer. *Please, God, let the procedure be successful.* Third time lucky, they say. . . but it wasn't. Now, about to embark on her last try at in vitro fertilisation, Rebecca was afraid. Whatever the outcome, they decided this would be their final attempt, and then forget it. As if 'forgetting' was simple.

Rebecca shoved the mystery parcel on the hall dresser, ready to give to the postman if she should catch him. She glanced at the dresser mirror, noticed the fine lines around her eyes and between her brows, clearly visible in the morning light. As a wedding photographer, she was expected to pay attention to aesthetics, and look the part. The last thing a bride wanted was to see worry lines on the photographer's face.

Fritz bounded down the stairs and grabbed his briefcase off the hall stand.

'Morning, handsome,' she said, slipping her arms around his waist. 'Coffee? Toast?'

'Late. Got to run.' He broke free, pecked her cheek and reached for the front door.

'Don't forget we're at the clinic at six, darling,' she said, the waver in her voice hardly noticeable.

Fritz stopped, his hand on the latch. 'Damn . . .' he said under his breath. Still for a moment, then turning to come back to her.

After ten years, Rebecca's heart still skipped when her tall blue-eyed blond husband approached. But when their eyes met, a stab of panic caught her.

He took her slender frame into his arms, pulling her close. The scent of freshly applied aftershave zinged about him.

'Sweetheart, I'm terribly sorry, but you'll have to cancel,' he said. 'I've a shareholders' meeting that'll probably overrun. Crucial that I'm there.' He pushed her auburn hair back and kissed her forehead. 'Don't look so worried; you'll get lines. Just reschedule for next week.' He sighed, peppermint mouthwash clouding his breath. 'I didn't realise; the month's raced by.'

Rebecca peered into his eyes. They dulled as his emotions shut down and her dreams imploded right there in his arms. She forced a smile and nodded, the lump in her throat hard and painful.

'Don't worry, darling. It can't be helped, I guess,' she managed.

She was ovulating *now*. Not something to be rescheduled for next week, but she would gain nothing by pointing this out. Fritz had so much going on, he needed to stay focused on the business. She slipped her arms inside his jacket, around his waist, and squeezed. She knew how much Fritz hated the IVF clinic.

'Right, then,' he said, pulling away and forcing a boardroom smile. 'You'll make me even later, Mrs Neumanner. Don't wait up, I've no idea what time we'll finish.'

* * *

Rebecca decided to take the four-thirty bus into town. She enjoyed people-watching on public transport, and it took her mind off the clinic. The passengers were a mixed bunch. Junior

40

school children chatted to their mothers, and older girls whispered and giggled, flicking their hair and glancing around, while teenage boys talked too loudly.

Was she doing the right thing? Yes, yes, of course.

Last time, after she'd miscarried, Rebecca buried herself in photography. Insane with grief, she trekked the parks and city streets through rain, sleet and snow. She tried to find the meaning of life through a Canon lens, tried to focus, tried to zoom in on the beauty of it all.

Rebecca hoped for a girl and, although they never talked about it, fearing a jinx, she suspected Fritz would prefer a boy. There was something not right about going to get pregnant without your man. But, despite her phobia of needles, she'd braved two weeks of fertility injections to increase her egg production. Exactly thirty-four hours ago, she had suffered an injection of something she didn't remember the name of but was nicknamed 'the hormone of pregnancy'. This caused her eggs to mature and loosen from their ovary walls.

The treatment was precise.

'You'll ovulate thirty-six hours from now,' the doctor said as the needle plunged into her flesh.

She nodded, winced, and stifled a cry of pain.

The medical staff scheduled her egg retrieval for thirty-five hours after that jab. To re-schedule, as Fritz suggested, was impossible, but perhaps he had too much on his mind to think it through.

Everything had changed a little since their last attempt at IVF, which failed after only two weeks. She'd started to bleed, her emotions plummeting. This time it *would* work. She refused to consider failure again. All that self-blame . . . hysterical crying, the feeling of worthlessness.

41

Rebecca got off the bus. The IVF clinic was a hundred metres from the stop. Her boot caught a broken curb. She stumbled, lurched and almost fell. Calm down, she told herself. What difference did it make that she was alone? She could do this … yes, she could! Yet her quaking insides did nothing to boost her confidence.

Her thoughts were all questions. Would it work? Would she tell Fritz immediately, or wait until she was sure? Would she hold a perfect baby in her arms in nine months' time? There lay her greatest nightmare: what would she do if she learned her baby wasn't perfect? The very thought made her ill. 'Usually, nature aborts if the foetus isn't developing perfectly,' the specialist had said. What if it didn't, and she gave birth to a grossly deformed child. She'd wanted to ask, yet hadn't, oddly superstitious about tempting fate.

The building loomed before her. She stared at the double doors. Time to turn back? Phone and cancel? She'd paid up front and prepared. Wouldn't it be foolish to walk away now? But her feet wouldn't move forward.

'Mrs Neumanner, how nice!' A cheery voice to her left. Her heart thudding with indecision.

She forced herself to turn, smile, and say, 'Hello' to her middle-aged gynaecologist, Quentin Alsop.

'Come, I'll walk with you. A big day today, yes?' he said.

She swallowed hard. 'I'm a little nervous.'

'You'll be fine. Don't worry.' He cupped her elbow and steered her towards the doors; an action Rebecca hated but she resisted a petulant urge to pull away. *Get used to being manhandled*, she told herself.

Come on, Rebecca, woman up!

They would put her to sleep and, guided by ultrasound, push a hollow needle through her vagina wall into her ovaries, to suck out the liquid. The embryologist would then search the fluid for eggs.

Please, let there be an egg.

* * *

Rebecca awoke bleary-eyed and dry-mouthed. A nurse entered.

'How are you, Rebecca?'

'Groggy,' she said. 'Is there any news?' There was no need to expand.

The nurse beamed. 'Ten eggs. Well done, you!'

Rebecca gasped. Ten possibilities of fertilisation in the Petri dish. Ten chances of a perfect child. Ten chances of her dreams finally coming true.

* * *

Rebecca woke in the night, squinted at the bedside clock, 3 a.m. She turned, slid her hand between the sheets and found a cold empty space where she hoped to find the man she loved. Her other hand lay flat on her belly, another cold empty place where she longed to nurture a tiny life that she would also love. She stared towards the ceiling and allowed tears to spring free and slide into her hair.

* * *

The next morning, Fritz phoned. 'Sorry, darling. It turned into a late night so I booked into the hotel rather than disturb you. How was your day?'

'Good, yes, very good actually,' she said. 'I went to the clinic. I've to go back in four days.'

Somebody was speaking to Fritz. 'Sorry, darling, I missed that,' he said to Rebecca, and then, 'Can you *please* give me a minute?' to somebody who was vying for his attention. He came back to her. 'Sweetheart, it's manic here. I'll speak to you this evening, okay?'

Rebecca found it hard to think of anything but the clinic.

How many of the ten eggs were successfully fertilised? Fritz's sperm, 'harvested' and banked a month back, had saved Rebecca having to go through the fertility injections all over again because Fritz hadn't been able to keep their appointment.

'Just in case,' they'd told Fritz as they handed him the plastic beaker and ushered him into *The Men's Room*. 'Always best to freeze a quantity of sperm.'

The clinic told Rebecca they'd phone with the result the moment they had news. The day ticked by. Rebecca's hopes descended a little further with each minute, until she resigned herself to failure.

She thought of Naomi. Her sister only had to look at Costa to get pregnant, even before they were married. Her first, Angelos, was born six months after the wedding. Her next, Konstantinos, had made an appearance almost exactly a year after Angelos. Rebecca was jealous. She recalled her nephews when they were toddlers: Angelos and Konstantinos were adorable.

Through the kitchen window, she gazed at her garden of empty dreams and decided to get some fresh air. Plant some bulbs, bring new life to the borders.

Her phone rang as she settled on the kneeler. She dropped the trowel and snatched her mobile from the trug of mixed bulbs.

'Mrs Neumanner?' Quentin Alsop, the specialist.

Rebecca's heart hammered. 'Yes, that's me, Rebecca Neumanner.'

Chapter 7

Rhodes, Greece.

Papas Yiannis had rushed to church the moment Naomi arrived home, but that evening he looked in again while she slipped to the supermarket.

'Bubba's taking a nap,' he said when Naomi returned. 'She's had a glass of milk with her pills and settled down to sleep.' He folded his arms across his wide chest and dropped his head to one side. 'The past week's been a great strain, Naomi, but now that you've agreed to her wishes, I'm sure you'll see an improvement in her health.'

'Thanks for this morning. I appreciated the break,' Naomi said as she loaded cheese and eggs into the fridge. Turning to face him, she took in the dark grey cassock that he still wore, although officially retired. As usual, the priest had unbuttoned the skirt and tucked the corners into his leather belt. His long grey beard was gathered into an elastic, and his shoulder-length frizzy hair caught-up and tied in a neat knot on the nape of his neck.

Naomi realised everything about Papas Yiannis was grey, yet he was the most colourful character she had ever come across. A modern-day icon of the traditional Orthodox priest. Picture-postcard perfect.

'Apologies for dashing off this morning,' he said. 'The last rights, a dear old friend.'

'Sorry for your loss. It must have been difficult.'

'Did you post the parcel, Naomi?'

She nodded.

'Any problems?' Naomi shook her head. 'Good. I didn't think so. Encourage Bubba to talk. It will help relieve the burden of her past.'

Burden of her past? What burden? What past? She nodded again but he recognised her puzzled look.

'Don't worry. You'll understand when you read the diaries.'

'Thank goodness for that,' Naomi said before she found herself bewildered again. 'Just a moment . . . what diaries?'

Papas Yiannis wagged his silver-topped walking stick. 'It's a big story. Be patient. She always wanted to tell you but, well, you'll understand soon enough.'

'Will you have a coffee?' Naomi asked. 'I've some questions if you can spare me a moment.'

'Coffee, lovely . . . but it's no good quizzing me. It's Bubba's responsibility to enlighten you.'

'No, it's not about Bubba.' She made the coffee as she talked. 'Do you have any information about a door at the police station? This is probably just gossip, but my friends are asking me questions and I don't have a clue. I've been too busy making my creams, and what with Bubba's stroke, I seem to have missed the local news.'

Papas Yiannis stared. 'Naomi, why do you think we're going through this business with the gun?'

'Bubba wants to make peace with Rebecca?'

'Well, yes, there's that; but the main reason is your family property.'

'Family property? What family property?'

The priest's jaw dropped. 'Are you saying you have no idea?'

'About what?'

He stared for a couple of beats. 'Sorry, I didn't realise.' He scratched his head. 'Your great-grandfather had a tailor's shop in

46

the centre of the town. In fact, he owned the entire block of six premises. You really didn't know?'

'Papas, what do *you* know about *your* great-grandparents?' Although the priest's hair always hung heavy over his eyebrows, she realised he was frowning.

'Point taken,' he said after a moment. 'Even before the war ended in forty-five the people of Rhodes the town council . . . how shall we say . . . absorbed the Jewish property and belongings. Document names were changed when Nazi Germany stated that the Jews weren't allowed to own businesses. Deeds were retitled and the land registry, rewritten.'

'You're not telling me we still own the buildings in the city?' She placed the small Greek coffee in front of him.

'Well, morally, yes. Your great-grandfather bought and paid for the building with honest money, and the building was taken from him for no other reason than his religion. Now there's a chance to claim it back. But, the municipality of the Dodecanese insist that every living beneficiary must attend the court in person to make their case.'

Naomi's jaw dropped. 'But it's a world heritage site!'

'Indeed, and a very valuable one too. As you know, Bubba has written many letters to Rebecca. She wanted to ask her forgiveness, but Rebecca never answered. Just before her stroke, when Bubba learned of the chance to get her father's property back, she wrote again to explain, but didn't received a reply.

'As you say, your great-grandfather's building is part of the UNESCO world heritage site. The property must be worth a million.'

Naomi's eyes widened. 'A million?'

'If not more. We're sure if Rebecca had read the letter, she'd have responded. Now, time's running out. There are only a couple of months left to stake a claim. Posting the gun's a desperate effort to make Rebecca sit up and pay attention.'

Naomi felt oddly abandoned. 'Why didn't Bubba tell me? Didn't she believe I had a right to know? Didn't she realise I'd probably hear it from someone else and feel hurt and ignored?'

Papas Yiannis smiled softly and patted the back of her hand. 'She wanted to protect you from disappointment. Without Rebecca, you've no hope of getting anything.'

'Much as I hate flying, why don't I simply go to London and get Rebecca to come home?'

'We've considered that, but peak season prices make it impossible. We checked with the booking office. In July and August, you're looking at a thousand euros for flights plus everything you'd need for a week in London. The court is scheduled for October. Neither of us has that sort of money. My pension's meagre and I believe the boys' university fees and accommodation in Cyprus demolished your savings.'

'Wow, I didn't realise things had gone up that much. So, you anticipate that sending Rebecca the pistol will do what?'

'As she can't be sure it came from her grandmother, the gun parts are bound to arouse her curiosity, at least that's what we hope. After the last part, Rebecca will be expecting instructions, but she'll get Bubba's diaries from the war.'

'Diaries?' Naomi huffed and half grinned. 'You mean like how to make tasty potato-peeling soup?'

The priest's expression changed: a flash of bitterness, confusion, and then humility. He placed his big gnarled hand on Naomi's shoulder and peered into her face while he gathered his thoughts. 'Naomi, there's a lot you don't understand.'

Bewildered by this reaction and the seriousness of his voice, she said, 'I'm sorry. I can see I've offended you.' She lowered her eyes. 'To be honest, you're right. I didn't know anything about the gun or our property. I know zilch about my grandmother's past or her war experiences.'

Naomi suspected something had upset Bubba just before the stroke. Why hadn't she seen this coming? Shamefully, she realised, she had been too busy with her lotions and potions to sit and talk to her grandmother.

'I understand they rounded up the Jews, a couple of thousand I believe, and shipped them to Auschwitz. It's awful . . . *awful!* On occasion, I've asked Bubba how she survived, but she refuses to talk about it. I presume her memories are too painful to relive.'

'More than painful, Naomi.' He dropped into Bubba's armchair, took his glasses off and rubbed his eyes.

Naomi suspected she was on the verge of facts that would change her perception of Bubba for ever. She hesitated. *What had happened?*

'In the Second World War, when she was sixteen, your grandmother wasn't the woman you know.' The old priest faltered, his eyes searched the floor and then returned to her.

Naomi sat on the stool at the side of Bubba's armchair and took his hand. 'Go on,' she said. 'Tell me.'

He bowed his head. The room was silent, the air still. Outside, cicadas sawed through the peace, building to a crescendo before a sudden, heat-heavy silence. Naomi waited, shocked when a tear splashed onto the back of her hand.

'Oh, Papas, are you all right?'

The priest nodded at the bookshelf and the china ornament. 'Pass me that last book, will you?'

She did.

He read the spine. 'Pandora, what a lovely name.' He allowed the book to fall open and peered at the words. 'Bubba could have been a great singer. She had an amazing voice.' He hummed a vaguely familiar tune. 'She sang at your mother's wedding. I've never heard anything like it. There wasn't a dry eye. Some months later she got an offer to go to Italy, but she wouldn't leave your mother. Sonia was pregnant with you at the time.'

'I didn't know.' Naomi's heart swelled with love for her grandmother. What a huge sacrifice she had made. 'You were going to tell me about the war.'

The old priest took a breath and swallowed hard. 'Yes . . . the war. Pandora Cohen was . . .' he hesitated, gulped, and started again. 'In the war, Pandora Cohen was a freedom fighter for Greece. A terrorist and an assassin. Even though the Rhodians were responsible for the murder of her family and almost the entire Jewish population of this island, she risked her life fighting for them and their country.'

Assassin? A killer? Naomi shook her head. Whatever she expected, it wasn't this. 'Sorry, you mean . . . she *killed* people?'

'Hard to accept, but I promise it's true.' He paused while she digested the information. 'She was little more than a child, very immature to start with, but she grew up hard and fast, and she suffered such appalling pain and loss. Pandora Cohen is the bravest person I've ever met. You can't imagine how many lives she took or how many she saved, or the incredible danger she put herself in for others. I couldn't have done it.' His voice dropped. 'You'll understand *everything* when you read her journals.'

Naomi repeated herself. 'I can't . . . you're saying she actually took people's lives – *killed* them? My own grandmother?'

'She was an assassin.'

Naomi thought about the gun and wiped her hands down her thighs, suddenly angry although she couldn't say why. 'Where are they, her diaries?'

'Shhh,' the priest said, glancing at the archway. 'She gave them to me for safekeeping after Rebecca was born. The gun also. Originally, she instructed me to hand them over to you when she died, as anything else was too difficult for her to bear. But now, everything's changed.' He nodded, anticipating her next question. 'Yes, I think the decision to reveal her past brought on the stroke. As if her brain shut down at the thought of revisiting that time. I'll give you the first diary in a moment. It would be better if she didn't see you reading it. I don't want her getting upset. It may knock her back . . . or worse.'

'You're fond of her, aren't you? I've always felt it.' Horrified, she saw tears rise again in the old priest's eyes.

He nodded, pulled a huge hankie from his cassock, and blew his nose. A smile trembled on his lips and Naomi sensed his emotional struggle. 'You'll understand.' With a groan, he pulled himself out of the chair. 'Now, walk over the road with me and I'll give you the first diary.'

Naomi switched off the light and followed Papas Yiannis across the road. He had aged quite severely lately. She guessed him to be in his eighties, like her grandmother.

The sun had set and the street emptied. He pulled a second chair up to the tin table, invited her to sit, and then disappeared indoors.

Naomi listened to the sounds of the evening. Somewhere in the village above, a woman laughed, her voice merry and tinkling. Down towards the shore, a frog croaked and the sea rushed and shushed against the pebbles. She glanced up at the pink-grey sky where the first stars twinkled faintly. A plane rose from the airport, its roar breaking the silence, lights flashing from its wings and its vibration palpable in the still air. A thrill

51

raced through her, as it always did at such a massive display of power and technology. Then, the peace returned.

The priest came with cans of iced tea and straws, and an exercise book covered in brown paper. 'This one's only half full,' he said. 'She had to leave it behind for Evangelisa, but she started another diary the very next day.'

Naomi stared at the book. 'Who's Evangelisa?'

Papas Yiannis blinked at her for a moment. 'She hasn't told you anything at all, has she?'

Naomi shook her head and then looked up. Something caught her attention across the street. She peered at her own window, worried about Bubba being alone. Then she realised, what she saw was the reflection of Papa Yiannis's house in her glass.

The boyfriend was lowering a ladder for the priest's granddaughter. Naomi glanced at the priest. He calmly watched the reflections.

'I'm at a loss, Naomi. It's been going on for a month,' he said quietly. 'I was in my sixties when she was born. Now I'm too old and tired to deal with a teenager in love.' He sighed, watching the reflection of Marina come onto the balcony and climb the ladder. 'She needs her mother to talk to, and so do I. I'm out of my mind with worry.'

The lovers kissed and then, hand in hand, disappeared across the rooftops.

'I've been in love,' he said. 'In a way I still am, so I understand Marina wants to be with her boyfriend, but I also realise she's not going to tell an old man she has a lover.'

'Would you like me to have a word? Make sure she's being sensible?'

'I'd appreciate it. Meanwhile, I'll watch out for her safe return at dawn. Tell them they should use the front door. They think they're being quiet, but dragging that ladder above my bedroom ceiling makes an awful racket at four in the morning when I'm trying to sleep.'

They exchanged a smile and drank their tea in silence. Naomi picked up the exercise book. The journal seemed oddly heavy considering the size of it and she wondered at the weight of the revelations that lay inside. 'Thanks for this,' she said staring at the name, Pandora, ornately written on the cover.

Back home, Naomi looked in on Bubba who slept soundly. She settled in her grandmother's chair, opened the faded diary and studied the neat handwriting before starting to read.

Chapter 8

This book belongs to Dora Cohen.

!!!PRIVATE!!!

Sunday, 16 July 1944

Paradissi Village, Area of the Butterflies, Rhodes, Dodecanese Islands of Italy, Europe, The World.

Today is my sixteenth birthday. After breakfast, my mother gifted me this book to celebrate. My father has given me the pen I'm writing with, which is a new invention. I don't have to dip it into an inkwell, like at school. It's called a fountain pen and has a black rubber tube inside, and a little gold lever on the outside. I must place the nib in the ink bottle and pump the lever a few times to suck ink into the tube.

The pen is marvellous and I believe I'm the first person in Rhodes to have one. Danial, the eldest of my brothers, gave me three bottles of ink: black, blue, and red.

I received a box of six bath cubes from my grandparents. They look so pretty through the cellophane window, each wrapped in gold foil and a band of flowery paper. I took the lid off, closed my eyes, and inhaled the beautiful smells. Lily of the valley, roses, honeysuckle, and jasmine. My senses drifted in a fragrant jungle, bumping into one perfume, then another. I'll never use them because they're too lovely to disappear in our tin bath.

Mama made a birthday cake with candles, but when I blew them out, I couldn't think of anything to wish for. I'm always wishing for something: to be pretty, to have a larger bust, to be in the choir.

I also wish Mama hadn't written 'Pandora' on the front of my book. Everyone calls me Dora, even my teacher. I like Dora. I've decided the diary will be my secret friend. I'll tell her everything, all my confidences and imaginings, which I shall write down every day, starting now.

I am exactly sixteen years old and I'm in love. I don't know his name, so I refer to him as the Curly Haired Boy. He looked at me today and nearly smiled. I can hardly explain how that made me feel, except like my blood rushed through my veins at a thousand kilometres an hour and my heart couldn't keep up. I can't stop dreaming about him. I want to go and talk to him, but that's not the way to behave. My father would be disappointed.

My schoolbooks are spread over the bed because I should be doing homework, but I'm not. I am drawing hearts with our initials scrolled in the centre, and an arrow piercing through. D.C. & C.H.B. I'm also trying hard to look pretty. I brush my hair until it shines, and wear my whitest socks. I smear a little olive oil on my eyebrows and lips, and stuff my second-best socks inside my new brassiere.

I hope nobody else (especially Mama) notices my sudden bust development. Curly Haired Boy sings with the Italian choir. I wonder what it would be like to kiss him. Being a good kisser is important because if I don't get it right first time, he may never want to kiss me again.

My best friend Irini, who's one week older than me, said she's heard you can get pregnant from kissing, but I don't think that's true. I am not sure how you do get pregnant, or how the baby gets out. Irini says it must come out of your belly button. Otherwise, what's the point of a belly button?

We made round dolly-bags in sewing class at school and they close by pulling a cord threaded through the top. Irini says your belly button probably works like that because she has been told that when the baby's born, they tie the cord in a knot and cut it off. So, we guess that after the baby's out, they pull the cord to

55

shut the belly button, tie it and cut it off. Then I imagine it sort of heals over until it's needed again.

My mother has told me about periods, which I've been having for two years now. Mama promised to tell me more about the facts of life when I need to know, which isn't yet, she said. And I'm forbidden to talk to anyone about these things because they're completely private.

Growing up is a weird business. I constantly feel I'm on the edge of some huge revelation that will change my life. Yesterday, Irini asked me if I've got any hairs you-know-where yet, and I felt really stupid because I didn't understand what she was talking about. We did an inspection of my legs and under my arms, and Irini told me they were coming. She said her sister has great bushes under hers and we laughed a lot, but then I was ashamed of being childish and found I was blushing. It's all very confusing.

I've tried to ask Mama about these things, but she gets flustered and tells me I will find out soon enough. I think there should be a book, *How to Become an Adult on your Sixteenth Birthday*. When I understand everything, I might write it myself to help others in my predicament. One thing is for sure, when I have a daughter and she is sixteen I will tell her everything, or perhaps I'll just give her the book I am going to write.

Irini received a pair of fully fashioned nylons and a suspender belt for her birthday. I longed for the same, but they don't make them in my size.

Being very small for my age has always been a problem for me. People treat me like I am a child. Once, someone called me 'Titch' at school and I was so upset I sat under the table when I got home and cried my eyes out. Papa coaxed me out and made me sit next to him on the sofa. He put his arm around me and told me I'm small for my age because my mother had me very early, seven and a half months, instead of nine. He said I should have died, being so small, but I didn't because I'm a born fighter. Although I didn't die, I've never actually caught up in size.

I've always remembered that, and when anyone teases me about being small I tell them, 'I may be small, but I'm a born fighter, so watch out!' and I'm tempted to give them a punch. Twice, I got into big trouble because I really did clout somebody, and I had to promise Papa I'd never do it again.

The worst thing was, I had to apologise to the pig who had tripped Irini up and laughed at her sprawled on the ground. I punched him hard under his ribs, and for a horrible minute I thought he was going to die. He doubled up, fell to his knees, and made awful noises like he couldn't breathe in. Still, after that incident, the teasing stopped.

When Irini and I dress up, she's promised to draw a line up the backs of my legs with her sister's eyebrow pencil, so it looks as though I'm wearing nylons too.

On the day the Athens ferry comes in, Irini and I go to the port. It's against the law to kiss in public, but people don't seem to care when the person they love is boarding the Athens ferry. It's the only place we can study people kissing.

When I get home, I rush to my bedroom and practise kissing on the back of my hand. I look forward to having a real boyfriend, and I want to be prepared and get everything right when I do find my special person. Papa says preparation is everything. He's the best tailor on the island and he taught me the saying, 'Measure twice and cut once'. This is to avoid mistakes, and I think it's a good rule to live by.

* * *

Naomi smiled at Dora's honesty. The priest was right: her grandmother had been a very young sixteen-year-old. But this often happens when a girl is born into a houseful of boys. She recalled being around thirteen when she and Heleny learned how babies were made. At that time, Naomi had her first kiss. Costa and his friend had followed Naomi and Heleny for weeks. Eventually, one Saturday evening, she had allowed him to kiss her behind the church.

Rebecca was even younger when her curiosity arose, and although biology was newly taught in secondary school, her question was almost the same as Dora's. She came stomping home and got Naomi on her own.

'Naomi, Alexa says you can become pregnant from kissing boys. It's not true, is it? She's just saying that because Michalis wants to kiss me and she's jealous.' Naomi laughed and shook her head. 'Well, how do babies get made, then?' Rebecca persisted.

That had wiped the smile off Naomi's face. She said Rebecca would learn everything in her biology class. Reading about Dora's mother now, Naomi realised things hadn't changed that much over the decades.

She remembered Costa taking the boys aside 'for a quiet chat,' when they were thirteen and fourteen. He came back flustered and red-faced. 'They know more about sex than I do, Naomi!'

How she had laughed.

She got up, opened the kitchen cupboard, and ran her finger down his roster. *The Royal Sapphire* was heading for Piraeus, Athens's port. Soon, he'd be home for winter and she couldn't wait.

She returned to Bubba's chair and the diary.

Until recently, I lived in Spartili Street, Paradissi Village, which is about fourteen kilometres along the coast from Rhodes Old Town, the capital of Rhodes. This island is very beautiful. Over the centuries, many nations have claimed it: Greeks, Venetians, Knights of Saint

John, then the Turks, and now the Italians. My village, Paradissi, is the best one on the island because we have the most flowers.

Last month, we had to move from Paradissi, down to my father's shop in the Jewish quarter of Rhodes Old Town because of an order from the Germans. Jewish people can only live in certain areas. Paradissi Village, where our home is, is allowed, but my aunts, uncles and cousins are living in our Paradissi house because they had to leave their homes in villages where Jews are no longer permitted.

Papa says it's only temporary. Some people say Rome is liberated and the war is close to ending. Others claim Italy's surrendered to the enemy, like they did in the last war, and we should be ashamed. I listen to everyone, but I don't really understand the politics.

Although we're Jewish, we didn't have a problem with the Germans until now. However, some Jewish families left the Jewish quarter in Rhodes Town, and moved to the mountains because they're afraid of bombing raids executed by the British.

The Juderia is near the city walls, in the area of the deep harbour. The British are trying to destroy this port, along with any German ships moored there. They often hit the Jewish quarter instead, and several houses have been bombed and our neighbours killed. One bomb landed on our shelter, and it was lucky we weren't inside. Many of our friends died horribly and in excruciating pain. Crushed to death, or burned alive because of the British bombs. Everyone wishes they'd leave us in peace.

Mama wants to pack up and go. We were told of a fishing boat taking people to Turkey tomorrow night, but Papa says it's too dangerous. The British do their bombing after dark and Papa says they don't care who they hit as long as they frighten the Germans.

They frighten us all.

The last boatful of Jews departed in the night, but no one's heard of it since. We wonder what happened. The moment war broke out, many of our friends set out for America, and others for Rhodesia.

Rhodes is Italian, it has been since the Great War. Until now, we Rhodians fought alongside the Germans against many European countries; but then we changed sides. Germany became our enemy. Now, people say Germany and the Axis are winning, and the conflict will soon be over. I get confused. Why did Italy join the British, whose bombs have been killing us in our beds? Germany's our enemy now, and they occupy the island. The Germans were fine at first, apart from murdering all the Italian soldiers. But these past few weeks, things have become difficult. The Germans have changed.

I don't like them much. They're not as friendly as the Italians, and they can't sing either.

Captain Vittorio, the Italian who ruled us, ran to hide in the mountains with his soldiers. The Nazis found them and took them to a hill overlooking Faliraki. Captain Vittorio and his men were offloaded from the truck, lined up, and shot in the head.

I've tried to imagine how it would feel to be shot in the head. Sometimes we hear distant shooting and wonder if it's the Germans executing more people.

I know all this because now I'm sixteen my parents talk more openly in front of me. Papa says I should understand what's happening in the world, but Mama claims I'm still too young. I don't like to pick sides, but I believe Papa is right. How can I understand the situation and make decisions for myself, if I don't know what's going on in the world?

I'd better explain the situation in case, one day our – my and Curly Haired Boy's great-grandchildren – get to read this. In 1912, Italy seized Rhodes from the Turks who they were at war with. After the 1914–18 war, Rhodes and the rest of the Dodecanese Islands were assigned to Italy. Some people speak Greek, some Italian, and many use both languages. The Jewish community speak Ladino, which is a sort of Spanish-Italian-Hebrew.

There is censorship here and, since last year when the Germans took over, we Jews are forbidden to have a wireless in the house.

Chapter 9

Naomi closed the diary while she thought. This was written in 1944. Could the Jews of Rhodes really not have known the horrors that were happening in the concentration camps, the brutal extermination of Jews? Wouldn't their Rabbi have warned people? She tried to imagine what life must have been like for the Jewish population of Rhodes in 1944: being forced to live only in certain areas; seeing their property confiscated; being forbidden to employ non-Jews. Their children were forbidden to attend normal schools; they couldn't even keep a radio.

Didn't they realise they were being segregated? Yet now that she thought about it, the Greeks had a hard time too. Ruled by the Italians since the First World War, the Greeks were forbidden by the Italians to speak Greek, and unlike the Jews and Muslims, they were not even allowed to live in Rhodes Old Town. It was no wonder the modern Greek population of Rhodes clung to their deep rooted resentment of Italians, Jews, and Turks.

She decided she'd try to get to Rhodes Old Town and visit the Jewish Museum, if Heleny or Georgia would sit in with Bubba for a couple of hours. She wondered if she could find her great-grandfather's property. How amazing it would be to stand in the place where her ancestors lived and worked.

'Naomi, child . . .'

Pulled out of her thoughts and slightly alarmed as she always was when Bubba called, Naomi dropped the diary and went into the next room.

My father gets news of the outside world from his custom[ers].
People have heard whispers of atrocious happenings to Jews [in]
distant countries, but everyone agrees such things would nev[er]
happen here.

Monday, 17 July 1944

My father's a tailor. His shop's in the centre of Rhodes Old Town.
I say *his* shop, but the building has been taken from us and given
to the city for the duration of the war. I don't believe Papa had
any choice, but he won't talk about it.

I started a new school when we moved to Papa's shop in
the Jewish quarter of Rhodes Old Town. It's a school for Jewish
children. We're not allowed to attend the town school anymore,
because of our religion. Mama said this was an ominous sign, but
Papa said it was nothing to worry about. Mama gets worked up
about everything. Our new school was busy at first, as there were
over four thousand Jewish people in Rhodes, but half have left,
and even more are waiting to have their applications for visas to
other countries approved.

I wonder if we should leave too. It's difficult trying to imagine
starting a new life far away from home.

61

'Are you all right? Can I get you something?'

'Sorry to be a pest. I know it's late, but could I sit at the kitchen table for a while?'

Naomi smiled. 'Of course. I was getting a bit lonely by myself.' After a short struggle with Bubba's arm around Naomi's neck and Naomi's arm around Bubba's waist, they got into the next room.

Bubba's eyes fixed on the diary. 'So, you're reading it.' She gulped and her hand slid over her mouth for a moment. 'I can't remember much of what I wrote, nor do I want to. But don't take it the wrong way, child; I would do it all again – give it all up for you and Rebecca. You've been worth every sacrifice, every moment.' She paused, staring at the cover. 'I only wish I could have given you a better life, a bigger house, and not become such a burden.'

'Bubba! You're no trouble at all! Don't be silly. I'm starting my business because of your lotions and potions book. Who else could give me such a wonderful gift? Your recipes are priceless.' She put the kettle on and then reached for her lemon and honey hand cream. 'Here, what do you think of this?' Bursting with pride, she held out the small white jar.

Bubba pulled her chin in and squinted at the green and gold label. 'Oh!' She chuckled. 'I'm famous! *Pandora's Hand Cream*.' She glanced up, and Naomi's heart soared to see such pleasure shine from her grandmother's face.

The old lady held the jar further away to read the smaller print. 'ORIGINAL RECIPE. NO ADDITIVES. GUARANTEED TO FADE AGE SPOTS AND IMPROVE SUN-DAMAGED SKIN.' Bubba's crooked grin said everything.

'I ordered the labels online. Heleny helped me with the design. It's called branding, when you choose a style for your product. I'm so excited about it all.'

'Me too, child.' Bubba's eyes sparkled. 'When I first made it, I just dropped a dollop into whatever container people brought, be it a little jam jar or a cracked cup. One of the women I cleaned for, the mayor's wife, liked to use Simpson's Salmon Spread and, before I put her kitchen rubbish out, I'd search for empty jars.' She dropped her head to one side. 'Squat white glass things, they were, and I'd cut wax-paper circles for the top.'

'I think I remember them. Didn't you use pinking shears and yellow gingham to cover them . . . and an elastic band?'

'I did. The fabric was from a dress with a very full skirt. The material lasted me years.' She giggled. 'Did you know, that hand cream bought our first TV? I was very proud of myself.'

'So you should be.' Naomi opened the jar and rubbed a little cream into Bubba's lame hand. 'I remember when Mrs Voskos allowed me to watch her new TV. It didn't come on until half past five with children's programs. I was so excited I couldn't sleep through siesta. She made me sit on the floor, and I wasn't allowed to speak! Very difficult for me.' Naomi laughed. 'When she went out of the room, I'd run to the little screen and put my face right up to the thick glass. I was sure if the people in the TV studio looked into the camera, they'd be able to see me.'

They smiled at each other, then Bubba's eyes returned to the diary. 'I meant what I said. Apart from what happened to Evangelisa, Irini, and of course my darling family, I wouldn't change a thing. In the end, everything's been okay. You and your boys, and Rebecca, have been compensation enough for the dreams I sacrificed. I wanted to say that, in case I die in the night.'

'Bubba! Don't talk stupid now!' Naomi wondered who Evangelisa was, and found herself impatient to read more. They chatted for a while, drank their mountain tea, and then Naomi returned Bubba to her bed.

She picked up the journal with renewed curiosity.

My father's famous in Rhodes for his beautiful suits. Now, we are forbidden to employ non-Jews, so Mama and my brother Danial have to help Papa in the shop.

I've three brothers, Danial, Samuel, and Jacob, who are all older than me. I also have a sister, Evangelisa, who's eighteen months younger than me. We're not alike. She is taller than me and has Mama's looks. She's so pretty, everyone loves her. I'm like Papa, except I hate sewing. Although I'm small for my age, on account of being born early, I'm strong as any boy.

I'll never be extremely clever, but I try my best and I am sensible, everybody says so. I love writing. My teacher says I have talent, and she has high hopes for me. She told me to write every day and use as many different words as possible, so that's what I shall do in this diary. When I start work, I'd like to be a newspaper reporter and travel the world. To do this, Papa says I must achieve higher exam results. I've six months to go, then I leave school and have to find a job.

The truth is, I want to be a singer more than anything. That's my dream. Aunt Martha says I should train to be a reporter, in case I don't make it as a singer. She says you never know how your voice will turn out, but reading and writing is always reliable, so I read my father's newspaper from front to back every day and look up new words in our dictionary.

Mama says singing, sketching, and writing are all a waste. I should learn to sew and bake; and being a reporter is no job for a woman. Nice women don't work after they are married, and I shouldn't get ideas above my station. If I can't sew, I should become a teacher or a nurse. They're respectable jobs that I will be able to go back to when my children are grown.

Papa smiles and says I should hang on to my dreams.

According to my music teacher, my ear's good but my voice needs work. She gave me vocal exercises, scales, but when I practise, Mama tells me to hush. I've tried sewing, but although I can write neatly and draw people's faces well enough, my hands are clumsy with a needle, and the touch of some material gives me goosepimples.

I'd love to join the choir and sing with the Curly Haired Boy, but girls aren't allowed.

My brothers like to hear me sing. They encourage me and I try to impress them. The Italians all sing well. When the choir practises in the square, opposite my father's shop, I offer to clean outside.

I sweep the pavement and polish the glass and the brass door handle, but mostly I'm watching the choir's reflection in the window and listening. The Curly Haired Boy is with them, but he's not singing.

I told my best friend, Irini, that I thought the Curly Haired Boy had a cold, because he didn't sing. This meant I'd have to postpone our first kiss. Irini said it was probably because his voice was changing into a man's and he had to rest it. Irini knows a lot because her older sister tells her everything.

I can't explain how I feel when the choir sings, except to say my skin tingles. All I want is to fill my lungs and hold an A sharp forever.

Yesterday, they sang *O Mio Babbino Caro*, and I almost cried with the beauty of it. I stood outside to listen and I'm not exactly sure what happened. I was singing along in my head as I polished the glass, and I closed my eyes for a moment to concentrate on the song. Then, before I could do anything about it, I was holding the last note with every ounce of energy I had. It poured from me, long, even, and powerful. I thought I'd suffocate with the need to breathe in before I got all of the note out.

When I opened my eyes, it seemed everything had come to a halt. Shoppers, walking through the square, stopped to gawp at me. The choir, silent, stared in my direction. I turned to run into the shop and bumped into my father who stood behind me. He appeared astonished.

Everyone thinks I'm mad.

Then, *snap!* People laughed and clapped, and I loved it. The world sparkled and apart from when the Curly Haired Boy nearly smiled at me, that clapping was the most special moment of my life!

Next time the British bomb us, and we sit in the shelter, I'm going to sing that song. Usually we sing hymns, which is a bit morbid because it's as if everyone expects to die. The point of being in the shelter is that we're safe, unless there's a direct hit, then we are dead.

Chapter 10

Naomi cooked a rabbit casserole and baked a crusty loaf. The cottage filled with the aroma of fresh bread and of the cinnamon, orange, and savoury herbs in the stew. She took a substantial bowl of it and a chunk off the warm brown loaf across the road.

The priest's eyes lit up. 'My absolute favourite meal. Thank you, Naomi.'

Bubba, who made a slight improvement each day, also enjoyed the food. Propped by a few cushions, the old lady sat at the table for the first time since her stroke. She managed to feed herself, flashing her crooked smile at Naomi.

'This is delicious, child.'

'It should be. I used your recipe.' Naomi nodded at the bookshelf over the sink.

Naomi had just finished eating when a knock sounded on the door and Marina stuck her head in. 'Hi. I've brought your dishes back, Naomi,' she said. 'Grandpa really enjoyed the food. He said you cook every bit as well as Bubba.'

The old lady grinned and dribbled stew down her chin.

Marina was clearly embarrassed, not having seen Bubba since the stroke.

Naomi mopped her grandmother's face.

'You look nice,' Bubba slurred, taking in Marina's skimpy black shorts and red crop-top. 'But you forgot to put your dress on.'

'Bubba!' Naomi exclaimed. 'She looks absolutely lovely. That's what young people wear to party these days.' She turned to the priest's granddaughter. 'Take no notice. You're as perfect as a top model. Where are you off to?'

Marina grinned and wiggled her hips. 'Jason and I are going to DJ at an eighties disco in town.'

'An eighties disco sounds like fun,' Bubba said. 'I wouldn't mind attending that myself. You'd never catch me dancing in my underwear though.'

Naomi had a quick flash of Bubba cavorting in her big pants, knee-highs, and cross-your-heart bra, and she giggled.

Marina's eyes widened and she took a step towards the door.

Bubba continued. 'Do many eighty-year-olds go to these discos then? Are there any men there? Would you two give me a lift?'

Marina, clearly horrified, glanced at Naomi. 'Ah, sorry! It's booked up, Bubba. Oh, listen, Grandpa's calling.' She spun around and flew out of the cottage.

Naomi chuckled. 'She means eighties music, Bubba, not a disco for eighty-year-olds.' She paused to let the information sink in. 'I've booked your hair appointment for next Wednesday,' she said stacking the dishes in the sink. 'Katarina offered to come to the house, but I said it'll be nice for us to get out for an hour. Heleny will move her plant pots, so the taxi can get to the door. What do you think?'

'Thanks,' Bubba said. 'I wish I could help you clear up, but I'm very tired.' Her eyes twinkled. 'I guess I'll have to give the disco a miss this week.'

Naomi blinked at her. 'You devil! You knew exactly what she meant, didn't you?'

'Tee-hee, did you catch the look of pure horror on her face?' Bubba's shoulders jigged up and down.

Naomi laughed too. 'Good to see your old sense of humour is back. Doctor Despina's pleased with your progress too. She's booking you in for physio at the hospital, now that you're strong enough to travel.'

With Bubba settled and the dishes washed, Naomi moved to the patio with half a glass of red. The air, still warm after a sunny day, hung motionless in the quiet street. She could hear faint whispers from the shore and knew from its sound, the sea was flat as oil. The deep throaty chug of an old fishing boat meant it was heavily laden, returning to the local harbour where restaurateurs, and chefs, would be waiting to have the pick of the catch.

Naomi swished her hand through a knee-high pot of basil, closed her eyes, and inhaled the minty-liquorice scent. Her mother taught her to do the same after cleaning shellfish, to remove the stench of fish from her hands and clothes.

Despite her financial difficulties, her sick grandmother, her darling boys residing in distant Cyprus, her husband away on a floating palace with the rich and lonely, and her estranged sister not speaking to her, Naomi found it hard to imagine anything but peace and tranquillity in the narrow street of Spartili, in Paradissi Village.

Apart from a few years spent at Heraklion's University Hospital in Crete where she studied nursing, Naomi had lived her entire life in the little house. Memories of Crete came tumbling back. Costa was heading to Heraklion now, waiting on passengers in the cruiser's fine-dining room.

Naomi closed her eyes and evoked the city. Lion Square with its magnificent fountain, bustling coffee shops and tavernas, The Venetian castle on the long sea wall that dog-legged into the Aegean Sea. Cardiac Avenue, as they called the harbour wall at the hospital, because every patient with a heart problem was ordered to walk to the end and back once a day.

After her first schoolgirl kiss, Naomi hardly saw Costa. Then, as if fate was waiting for the right moment, she came across him in Crete, Lion Square, on New Year's Eve. She'd gone with a gaggle of student nurses, drinking and dancing at the public party in the city centre. As church bells chimed midnight, people leapt into the fountain. Someone grabbed her hand and said, 'Come on, Naomi. Let's do it!' They jumped in together and, under a torrent of water at midnight, she and Costa kissed.

'Make a wish,' Costa said, and then he kissed her again.

Two days later, they had their first date. Costa, who studied at Heraklion's Hotel Leisure and Tourism College, took her to Knossos archaeological site. Thrilled by the ruins of the Minoan palace, she gazed at dark red pillars, sacred bull horns, and colourful frescoes. He entranced her with stories of King Minos, the Labyrinth, and the Minotaur.

They had been together ever since.

With a smile on her lips, Naomi opened the diary and started reading.

Tuesday, 18 July 1944

Because I am sixteen, I have new responsibilities. My mother says that at first light I'm to go up the mountain of Filerimos with Evangelisa and Irini to collect our flock from the shepherd, and herd them to our pen behind the convent so the sheep can be shorn.

I've done this job before with my brothers. When I say, 'done this job' I actually mean that I took a book and let the boys do the work. This time Danial was supposed to come with us, but he must have a tooth out. Samuel has to help Father in the shop, and Jacob has a violin lesson. The shearer won't wait another day. If I'd known herding would be my job at some point, I would

71

have paid more attention. Evangelisa's worried we can't do it, but I convinced her (and myself) we can.

I am actually looking forward to the challenge. It's a chance for me to prove myself as an adult and I'm determined to do a good job.

Irini arrived with long staffs of mulberry for guiding the sheep. We have a seven-kilometre walk to the shepherd, and five more to our pen. Papa has a wooden hut next to the sheep fold where we'll sleep for three nights, while the shearer does his job.

Danial will come on horseback later to drive the flock back. I'm pretending to be full of confidence for the sake of Mama, whose legs are swollen and painful, and also to stop Evangelisa fretting.

Papa says we should set out before sunrise, so I must stop writing now. I've packed a bag with a change of clothes, some rusks and honey, and I'll take my writing things of course.

I just peeked out of my bedroom window, which overlooks the square. The choir's gathering. I saw the Curly Haired Boy peer at the shop. He's really dreamy. I wanted to open my window and wave, but I ducked behind the curtain instead.

That's when I thought, *Why can't I be bolder?* At that moment I made my birthday wish.

I wish I was really, really courageous!

A spark of bravery seemed to ignite and grow inside me right then and there. I lifted my hand to wave, stuck on a smile, and stepped into the centre of the window.

The Curly Haired Boy had turned away, but his friend, Carlo, who Irini adores, saw me and waved back. Pure embarrassment! I yanked the curtain closed.

Wednesday, 19 July 1944

I begged Evangelisa to stop fretting. We'd be fine. Papa told us there was no time for breakfast, we should take the boiled eggs and bread to eat later. He seemed anxious. I hoped he wasn't having second thoughts about putting me in charge.

We slung our bags on our backs, grasped our mulberry staffs, and said goodbye to everyone. The sun rose over the horizon. Yellow light sliced between dark pines and threw broad stripes across the Mount Filerimos road. The air smelled rich and damp and wonderful.

After walking the steady slope for an hour, we came to a roadside spring and stopped to drink cold mountain water. We sat on the lower branch of a wind-bent pine. I wanted to write in my diary, but Irini and Evangelisa kept bobbing up and down and laughing at me, so I gave up.

Irini threw me a smile, then turned to my sister. 'Let's collect pine nuts. Look, I'll show you how,' she said, jumping down. She picked up a fat, newly fallen cone and cracked it open with a stone, then she popped the kernel into Evangelisa's mouth. 'Tasty, hey? You'll find two under each scale, Lisa. Mind your fingers now.'

Evangelisa hopped off the bough, which swung a little higher. Irini glanced my way again, her wonderful smile wide and her eyes bright in the dappled light. Something passed between us that made me warm in the pit of my stomach, and I found myself squirming with pleasure against the rough branch. I wished Irini was my sister.

Thursday, 20 July 1944

Danial didn't turn up yesterday, which is a problem because Evangelisa's shoe has come away from the sole. My parents are proud that we've never gone barefoot, but it's made our feet tender and walking any distance is impossible for Evangelisa. I have no choice but to trek home and get my old shoes for her. I'll take my diary and update it as soon as I have an opportunity.

*　*　*

What a terrible day this has turned out to be! On the way back, long before I reached the city, the haunting sound of a *tsambouna*

73

drifted through the bushes. I peered through a gap in the shrubbery and saw a sun-browned boy sitting on a rock under a gnarled but magnificent holm oak. Surrounded by sheep and engrossed in his music, he squeezed the *tsambouna*'s goatskin bag under his arm while his fingers raced over the bamboo pipe. His clothes were in a poor state of repair, and he sported an oversized black leather cap at a jaunty angle.

The area was grazed bare apart from hundreds of mauve globe thistles that stood a metre tall. The wild flowers surrounded boy and sheep. Regal, silver-green stems held their perfectly round flower heads still, like an enchanted audience listening to his music,

The sun, blindingly bright, made me squint. I watched him through half-closed eyes. There seemed something almost biblical about the scene and I wished I had my watercolours with me.

I had to overcome my shyness and tell the boy we would be late collecting the sheep. When I stood tall and waved my arms to attract him, he jumped off the rock, left his *tsambouna* behind, and pushed through the flock towards me. He was around my age, much taller than me, but very dirty and rough-looking. It occurred to me he would be an interesting character to write about, and I wondered what sort of life he lived, alone on the mountainside with his sheep.

The moment our eyes met, I felt the heat of a blush in my cheeks and forgot what I was going to say. I looked away quickly and stared at his bare feet while I composed myself. As my courage grew, I studied him carefully, inch by inch, and by the time my attention had returned to his face, he looked blatantly contemptuous.

'You just going to stare at me all day or something? Forgot your manners, have you?'

Indignant, I put on my best voice and said, 'I am the tailor's daughter. Please inform your master we'll not be collecting our flock until later this afternoon.'

'Oooh, later this afternoon,' he sneered, his wide Mediterranean face mocking me. He pulled off his cap and made a sweeping bow. As he stood, his dark curly hair fell to his shoulders and although it was difficult to believe, I realised in an instant, this unkempt youth was the smartly dressed young man who had stolen my heart when he sang in the choir. The person I had dreamed about. The one whose arms I wanted around me more than any other's.

I couldn't speak, and hated myself for blushing in front of him. My pulse was thrumming in my ears, and I felt my fingernails digging into the palms of my hands. Thoughts became a confused jumble and I didn't know if I was pleased to be this close to him, or disgusted that he was so dirty. I wanted to say something clever to hide my insecurity, but before I had a chance, he grabbed my shoulders and kissed me hard on the mouth. Our teeth clashed. It happened so fast I retaliated without thinking. I bashed him hard on the side of his head, and struggled free.

This wasn't how it should happen! A woman's first kiss was supposed to be the most special moment in her whole life. The start of a beautiful romance, true love, marriage, a home, perfect children. And now, he'd ruined it all! For a moment I couldn't speak, couldn't even think, then I exploded with embarrassment and anger,

'How dare you!' I yelled, the words almost strangled by fury. I wanted to punch him and yell; *Watch out, stupid shepherd boy, I'm a born fighter!* but I didn't. I spun away from him so fast everything went off-kilter. I staggered a few steps, pulled myself together, and then marched away. A first kiss was a first kiss, it couldn't be taken again, and he had turned mine into something snatched and sordid. The entire experience was horrible! I hated him for destroying a magical moment in my life that I had looked forward to for so long.

The urge to run was difficult to resist, but I clenched my teeth and walked tall, like an adult. As I travelled down the road, towards the city, I decided not to tell my parents, or anyone else except for you, dear diary. My parents have enough worries without me adding to them. I ordered myself to shut up and stop snivelling. I was sixteen! The time had come for Pandora Cohen to grow up.

* * *

I arrived home three hours later and found Mama distraught.

'Dora, why are you here? You're supposed to be taking care of Evangelisa on the mountain. Where's Irini? You haven't left your sister alone on Filerimos, have you?'

'Irini's with her. Don't worry, Mama. Evangelisa's shoe's broken. I've come to get my old pair. But what's the matter? Why are you crying?' I asked.

She blew her nose, stared at me for a moment, then said, 'You may as well know the truth. Your father and the boys . . . they've gone. The Nazis have them. What am I going to do, Dora? Why wouldn't he listen to me? We could've been in Turkey by now.' She hugged herself, then me. 'I kept saying we should leave, but nobody listened!'

'Where are they, Mama? Tell me! What happened?'

'Oh, my dear Dora, there was gossip that no one wanted to believe. That's why I persuaded your father to send you up Filerimos. Thank the Almighty he heeded me for once, but now, here you are again! You must go back and stay out of sight. Don't let them get you too!'

Panic swelled in my chest and throat until I couldn't speak or even think straight. I stared at Mama and waited for an explanation.

Her crying went on for what seemed like forever. Eventually she lowered her hands, blew her nose, and stared as if surprised to see me.

'Mama, tell me what's going on. Stop treating me like a child!' I've never spoken to either parent like that before, but she seemed hysterical.

76

Mama jerked her head back, as if slapped. 'Sorry,' I said. 'But tell me what's happening, please.'

She nodded. 'It started the day before yesterday, we heard gossip about the Nazis that worried your father. I persuaded him that you two should go up the mountain. I knew you'd be safer there. Oh, why didn't I send your brothers too?! Your father was trying to get us all on a boat to Turkey but . . .' She broke down again, this time sobbing uncontrollably. 'Too late. He's gone, Dora! And the boys! What's going to happen?'

'How do you mean, "Gone"? Where are they, exactly?'

'After you'd left for Filerimos, Gestapo soldiers with megaphones came into the Juderia.' Her eyes stared wildly ahead as she recalled. 'Oh, Dora, we were about to face the moment we'd refused to believe would ever occur in Rhodes. The Nazis ordered all men and boys, fourteen and over, to present themselves at L'Aeronautica.

I knew this building, just outside Rhodes Old Town. It was the Italian Aero-Nautical offices, now taken over by the Germans.

Mama was still talking. 'The Germans threaten severe reprisals if anyone disobeys.'

'Reprisals?'

She shook her head. 'Your father started packing and said we must go to the mountains. He planned to collect you and Evangelisa on the way.'

Mama buried her face in one of Papa's big white handkerchiefs and sobbed some more.

'He wouldn't listen! You might as well know. There's talk of appalling things the Nazis are doing to Jews. Everyone else seems to think it wouldn't happen here. They tell me I'm wrong to worry, but how could they know? For the past year, I've been begging him to take us to Turkey to start afresh! There are Jewish communities there. They'd have helped us. But he insisted we wouldn't run. He applied for a visa to move to Cyprus, more than a year ago. Every day we've waited for that document, but it never came. Now look at the mess we're in!'

I absorbed all this information. It didn't seem real, and Mama was a great one for doom and drama. Yet the shop was closed and my father and brothers, gone.

A tap on the window drew my attention. An excited sparrow hopped up and down on the windowsill, pecking at a column of ants that marched across the glass. Each insect followed the other. Systematically, the bird annihilated the entire tribe.

I went to investigate.

'Leave it!' Mama shouted. 'It's getting rid of the ants. I hate those things.'

'What shall we do, Mama? We have to get Papa and the boys out of there.'

'We can't. The Nazis said ten people will be shot for every one not turning up.'

'How would they know if anyone was missing? Surely some could escape.'

Her face became bitter. 'Because, Dora, our fellow Rhodians sold us out!'

'What do you mean?'

She looked at me as if I was stupid, then folded her arms around me in a tight embrace. 'That's why Rabbi Asher brought us the newspaper. It said the Rhodes Town Council handed the last census to the Nazis. They have the names, ages, and addresses of every Jew on the island.'

'But, why?'

'For the same reason they confiscated all the Jewish property, invented a land registry, and changed the ownership deeds to suit themselves. Because they are greedy and jealous.'

'Is that why they took Papa's shop, yet allowed us to continue as if we still owned it?'

She nodded. 'They were planning for this day.'

'But they'll have to return everything after the war, won't they?'

'Don't be naive, Dora. We won't get anything back! We've been robbed by people who make their own laws. Laws that have nothing to do with justice.'

I had never seen Mama so bitter.

'Nobody wants to endanger the lives of their friends and neighbours, so everyone obeyed the order. Your Papa said I shouldn't worry, that the Germans were going to put them to work. Why else should they take their papers? He's a fool! Why couldn't he see? Why wouldn't he listen? Stupid, stupid man!' Then she completely broke down. 'If anything happens to him or my boys, I'll die!'

'Papa must be frantic with worry,' I said. 'We must find a way to help them.'

'Wait for news. That's all we can do. If we run and hide, God knows what the Nazis will do.'

Neighbours came to our house. A lot of whispering took place on the doorstep. I don't think Mama or her friends have a plan. Nothing like this has ever happened before. While Mama is occupied by her neighbours I'm taking the opportunity to update my diary. I suspect Mama is going to demand a lot of my attention until all this is sorted out.

* * *

In the afternoon, police knocked on every door in the Juderia. The women were ordered to present themselves, their children, all their papers and any valuables they have, at L'Aeronautica at 7 p.m. that evening.

'Mama, why do we have to take our valuables? And what about Evangelisa and Irini?' I asked.

'Leave the girls where they are. They're safer up Filerimos.'

'And our valuables?'

'If the men are going to work on another island, perhaps the German base on Kos, our Rhodian banknotes will be worthless. Gold and silver are the next best thing.'

At 6 p.m., the Greeks and Italians disappeared from sight, doors and shutters closed. Jewish grandmothers, children, and babies in their mother's arms, came together in the square. We walked as one body of misery, passing through empty streets. Outside the city walls, groups from other villages including our relations from Paradissi, joined the throng. More than a thousand women and children gathered at L'Aeronautica. Silently as souls entering Hades, we filed into the building.

Before we were all inside, the Germans changed their minds and ordered us home again, instructing everyone to return tomorrow morning with food and clothes for ten days. If we don't, the men will be shot. What if they notice Evangelisa and Irini are missing? I am afraid.

* * *

Dear diary, I am writing this by candlelight. It's the middle of the night and our house is full of my relations, but everyone is asleep now. All our Paradissi aunts and cousins are staying with us in the city. Our house at the back of the shop is crammed, but it takes the pressure off me a little as Mama is occupied by my relations. For once I am glad they leave me out of the conversation.

My aunty and two cousins went to sleep in my small bed. I slept at the bottom of my parent's bed with Mama and my grandmother at the top end. My grandmother's feet smell. Everyone else slept in the boys' room. Grandmother's snoring woke me in the night and I worried about my father and brothers, and Irini and Evangelisa. If somebody didn't follow orders, would the Nazis really shoot the men? Would they realise my sister and my friend were missing? Could they force me to tell them where they are?

I wondered if they'd heard the news on Mount Filerimos? If we were moving to another island, they should come with us. I have decided to write all this information in my diary and then hide it under Evangelisa's dresses, so that if we have to leave Rhodes, she will find it if she should return home before us. I really don't want her to read about the shepherd boy kissing me, but

I don't have time to change anything. I will pack my new school exercise books in my duffel bag and start a fresh journal tomorrow. Also, I've written Evangelisa a letter, just in case things don't go to plan.

Thursday, 20 July 1944

Dear, Evangelisa,

I'm sorry I left you on Mount Filerimos with Irini, but I didn't know, when I returned home to fetch some shoes for you, what was taking place. You will have read the diary, and know the awful things that have happened to everyone, so far. I might be sent to Kos with Mama, Papa, and the boys, and if so, I know you will be fine with Irini. Stay hidden from the Germans, be brave, and do whatever Irini tells you.

I am sure we will be reunited soon, but until that day, remember we are thinking about you, and missing you. And Irini also. We all love you very much, and we are sorry to leave you behind, but Mama says you are much safer hidden away on Mount Filerimos with Irini, than under German eyes, on Kos.

Lots of love from your sister, Dora and all you family, XXXXX

Chapter 11

Bromley, London.

Rebecca held the phone to her ear. This was it, the news she's been waiting for.

'Hi there. I'm calling with your results, Rebecca.' Quentin Alsop said.

'Yes, go on.'

'First, I should tell you that the chromosomal abnormalities that affect at least half of the human embryos created for in vitro fertilisation . . .'

What? What was that? Abnormalities!

'. . . can now be predicted within the second day of development, long before we need to transfer the embryos to your womb.'

'Sorry, I'm not grasping what you're saying.' Rebecca couldn't disguise the alarm in her voice. She wasn't able to make sense of the specialist's words. 'Will you run that by me again? Is something wrong?'

'No, no, Rebecca. Just the opposite. The bottom line is that we have four eggs positively fertilised into embryos. Everything looks good. We'll select the strongest two for transfer on Wednesday. I've booked you in for 3 p.m.' There was a lengthy pause. 'Is that all right, Rebecca?'

* * *

Fritz was in Earl's Court for a three-day exhibition. Rebecca didn't understand exactly what it was about, having hardly seen him all week. His advertising agency – amalgamating with one of the largest companies in America – kept him at the office far too long.

She recalled a time, after their wedding, when life was full of laughter, dinner parties, and plans. At weekends, they'd take a champagne hamper to a car rally, buff paintwork and polish chrome alongside their fellow enthusiasts. Fritz, manly and proud; she, pretty in flouncy Monsoon dresses and wide-brimmed hats.

'Let's make the most of our time alone, before the babies arrive,' he would say, holding the door of his latest vintage auto open, and bowing slightly. She would primp and flirt and play the part.

Now, when he was home, he paced, hypothesised, phoned, analysed. Over breakfast, he spouted figures and expansion plans. She tried to rustle up interest, but in truth she hardly cared. All she thought about was the small, round Petri dish that contained her eggs and his sperm – *their babies* – in the clinic, fifteen miles away. It wasn't what they'd envisioned all those years ago, but the IVF clinic served as a means to an end. They *would* have their perfect family.

The morning after Fritz returned from Earl's Court, she asked if he could take a few hours away from the office. He swung around and looked her in the eye, and in a heartbeat of confusion she turned and fiddled with a flower arrangement on the table.

'No way, darling. This week's manic. Why? Was there something important?' he said.

She recognised a glimmer of panic so slight no one else would notice. Fritz could hide his emotions behind a boardroom exterior. Nevertheless, he was astute. He'd guessed she wanted him to attend the clinic with her. Surely he had an obligation to hold her hand while the fertilised eggs were returned to her womb.

She shook her head. 'No, nothing I can't deal with,' she said lightly. She wrapped her arms around him wanting to bind him to her. 'I love you,' she whispered.

His shoulders relaxed, confirming her suspicion. 'I've a presentation this afternoon. Their director's organised dinner to celebrate our new partnership. Sorry, darling. I doubt I'll be home before ten.'

* * *

Five days after having her eggs taken, Rebecca found herself back in the IVF waiting room, slightly embarrassed to find it busy. A middle-aged man in white dungarees, up a ladder, fitted what appeared to be a smoke alarm. She caught a curious glance from him. An attractive couple's body language opposite made it clear they were deeply in love. They sat close, touching hands, peering into each other's eyes. Rebecca had an urge to explain why she was alone, but what would they care?

The man up the ladder started whistling an Adele tune. Rebecca studied the young couple and guessed this was their first or second visit.

'That's done it,' the workman said, climbing down the ladder and dragging it into the corridor.

The nurse came into the waiting room. 'We're ready for you,' she said to the couple, holding the door open. She nodded at Rebecca. 'I'll be back in a moment.'

The workman came back for his tool bag. 'One more to fit, a quick test, then I'm done,' he said grinning. 'Nothing to be alarmed about, people.'

The nurse rolled her eyes.

The workman also gave Rebecca a look, one that said, 'I'm yours whenever you want.'

She turned her back on him and gazed out through the fine lace curtains.

On her own, she thought about her eggs, the cells dividing and multiplying into what would become her baby. Today, they'd place them in her womb. Last time, she'd miscarried six weeks after the transfer, but two years had passed, and science had improved a lot since.

Now she was healthier, fitter. She didn't smoke or drink alcohol, she jogged, and only ate organic food. She *deserved* a successful pregnancy.

The nurse returned. 'Hello, Rebecca. We're ready for you.' She smiled. 'No need to be anxious; the egg transfer's quite painless.'

Rebecca nodded.

The nurse continued as they walked down the hall together. 'It's an exciting day, don't you think?'

Rebecca nodded again. She hung her clothes in the changing cubicle and put on the blue clinic gown before the nurse helped her onto the examination couch.

The specialist, Alsop, joined them, followed by a nurse. 'Hello again, Rebecca,' he said placing a clipboard on top of the screen. 'This won't take long. I'm going to transfer the two strongest embryos into your uterus. Do you understand?'

Rebecca said, 'I've had this done before.'

'So you know the procedure. Draw your heels up, and let your knees fall apart—'

Before he could say any more, a screeching fire alarm went off. Rebecca abandoned her position. A nurse stuck her head into the room. 'Don't panic, it's just a test,' she yelled. 'There's no fire. Sorry.'

Alsop stared at the door. 'What the *hell's* going on?!' When the racket stopped, he regained his composure. 'I do apologise, Rebecca. It's a simple fire drill.'

'No need. I saw the worker fitting an alarm when I arrived.'

The door opened again and the embryologist entered, a beautiful woman with coffee skin and raven hair. The nurse, pushing a trolley, followed. They appeared flustered, no doubt startled by the alarm. The embryologist smiled at Rebecca and nodded at the specialist.

Alsop took a breath and said, 'Let's get on then, shall we? Sorry about this contraption, Rebecca. It always feels cold. Try and relax.'

She concentrated on her breathing and hardly flinched when the stainless steel entered her. She imagined Fritz holding her hand.

'Very good,' the specialist said. 'Now this may be a little uncomfortable, I'm going to stretch your vagina until I can see your cervix, the neck of your womb. If you experience any serious discomfort, tell me.'

'Okay.'

The nurse took her hand and Rebecca realised she was clenching her fist. 'Relax. You're doing fine,' the nurse said.

'Enough!' Rebecca cried, wondering if he intended to use a forklift truck to deliver the embryos.

'Perfect,' Alsop said. 'Now the part you've been waiting for, Rebecca: you are about to get pregnant. This won't take a moment and, once again, if you feel any discomfort, let me know.' He glanced at the monitor. 'We have the most up-to-date ultrasound here. You'll be able to observe exactly what's going on.' The nurse smeared gel on Rebecca's belly and slid the rectangular sensor back and forth.

Rebecca saw a speckled picture of her womb, a light triangle on the dark screen.

'Now, here we go,' the specialist said. 'I'm inserting a very fine catheter, with your eggs held at the end, into your uterus . . . there, see?'

Rebecca watched the thin white line with a dot on the end move towards the centre of the screen.

'I'm about to manoeuvre them into position.' He squinted at the monitor. 'There we are, perfect.'

Rebecca glanced at the specialist; his eyes sparkled. She twisted her neck and stared at the monitor again.

'Now, here's an amazing fact,' he said. 'Let's zoom in. I want you to watch the screen very carefully. When I let the embryos go, you'll notice a minute, but very distinct, flash come from the eggs.' She heard the excitement in his voice. 'So you see, Rebecca, sparks really do fly when a miracle happens.'

And then she saw it. The tiniest flash.

Chapter 12

Rhodes, Greece.

A noise distracted Naomi. She looked up and saw Heleny scuttling down the street, towards her. Reluctantly, she closed the diary and slipped it behind the pot of basil.

'Naomi, I hope you don't mind me interrupting you at this time of night, but I've been trying to catch you alone. You know you're my best friend, and I wondered . . . well . . . I need some advice.'

Surprised to see Heleny wearing full makeup, elegantly coiffured, and dressed in a red shift that revealed her heavy curves with startling frankness, Naomi patted the empty seat next to her. ''Course I don't mind, Heleny. You look glamorous . . . and pleased with yourself. What's going on?'

Naomi's friend batted mascaraed eyelashes and grinned. 'I have a lover,' she whispered, her smile radiant. 'He can't get enough of me and I feel wonderful! It's that perfume you gave me, I swear.' She sniffed her wrist. 'It makes me feel so womanly.' She did a kind of slow wiggle in which every part of her moved in one direction or another. 'At first, I just dabbed it on my neck. That's when he became interested. So, I splashed a little here.' She stuck her finger between her voluptuous breasts. 'We went to the pictures, and he had his face in my chest before the end of the film.'

Naomi laughed. 'You don't think it might be because he's attracted to you and your bosom?'

'No, I can *prove* it's the perfume working. I invited him to try my moussaka last night, but before he arrived, only in the name of science of course, I put a few drops in my pants, you know, on my . . . unmentionables.' Her eyes widened and she pointed, as if Naomi wouldn't understand. 'Down there.'

Naomi struggled to keep a straight face. 'And?'

'Fannes and I were at it like rabbits all last night.'

Suddenly, Naomi realised how insecure and lonely her neighbour had been, and felt slightly ashamed that she hadn't been a better friend. She remembered how Rebecca would always come to her whenever she had a problem, asking about boys as if Naomi was an expert. But surely Rebecca's life was perfect now, with her rich husband and her house in the glamorous city of London.

She took Heleny's hand and said, 'Well, let me tell you something about Fannes: he's a very lucky man.'

Heleny's face flushed. 'The thing is I used too much perfume. Now I've run out and I'm afraid the magic will fade if I don't wear it. Only . . . it's been a difficult month and—'

Naomi clicked. Heleny survived on a part-time cleaning job at the school and never usually indulged herself. She must have spent a fortune on the dress and makeup.

'Sorry to interrupt but you've reminded me, I need some of those delicious melt-in-the-mouth shortbreads you make.'

'*Kourabiéthes*?'

'That's the ones. With Bubba to care for, and my lotions and potions, I haven't had a moment to bake. I realise it's a terrible cheek, Heleny, but if I give you the ingredients, would you do me a huge favour and knock a batch up, in return for a couple of bottles of perfume?'

Heleny's smile widened. 'You don't have to pay me, Naomi. I'm happy to help.'

'You're very kind, but I'd hate to take advantage. Would you mind? I understand if you're too busy with Fannes.'

'No, no, I love baking. It'll be a pleasure.'

'Then sit tight while I get the stuff you need.'

Naomi slipped indoors, grabbed a carrier and threw packets of icing sugar, flour, butter, and the other staples that made the snowy-white sugar-coated biscuits. On top of the ingredients she placed two bottles of perfume. When she returned to the patio, her friend had opened the diary near the end and was reading.

'Heleny, that's private.'

'Sorry, it'd fallen behind the plant pot. What powerful writing,' she said prodding the page. 'It's true then . . . Bubba, and the war?'

Naomi stuttered, 'I don't know what you're talking about.'

'Mama once told me Bubba was a wartime hero. A legend. But nobody talked about it, or recognised her bravery.'

'But why?'

Heleny dropped her head to one side, gauging how frank she could be, then she lowered her eyes. 'Because she was Jewish of course,' she said sadly. 'Sorry, but it's a fact, and also because, you know how it was in those days . . . a baby out of wedlock?'

Naomi nodded. 'That child was my mother.' She tried to keep the animosity out of her voice. 'Anyway, I'm not even halfway through yet, so please don't say any more. Perhaps when I've read the diary, and you have a little time, you can tell me what else your Mama told you?'

'Glad to. I'd better get on and leave you in peace.' She picked up the carrier, glanced inside and grinned. 'Thank you, this means so much to me.'

Naomi watched Heleny's wide hips as she returned to her house up the street. She recalled the evening Rebecca left, walking up to a taxi on the main road. They'd wanted to hug, say goodbye properly, but racked by tears and steaming angry, they didn't.

Heleny turned and waved, but Rebecca had never looked back.

Naomi picked up the diary. Resisting the urge to read the page that had grabbed Heleny, she continued where she'd left off.

Friday, 21 July 1944

Diary number two.

I'm very tired, and it has been a terrible day, but I want to write all this down before I go to sleep, because who knows when I will ever get the chance to update my diary again. As planned, I left the first diary at home, under my sister's frocks. Now, I'm sitting on the concrete floor of L'Aeronautica and it's difficult to stay awake. We are worn out by worry.

This morning, we gathered bundles of clothes and food together. Afraid of what lay ahead, we all put on a brave face. The women led their children out of the Jewish quarter and, once again, the streets were peculiarly empty.

Outside L'Aeronautica, the German soldiers told us to line up. A man that I guessed to be a little younger than my mother, began talking to the women quite urgently. I couldn't hear what he said, but everyone became agitated and some mothers started crying.

A shiny black car with two German flags on the front stopped in front of the building. The driver emerged and opened the door for a tall, fair man with a stern pale face. He wore a smart, charcoal suit with a grey coat draped over his shoulders, and he had a silver-topped walking stick under his arm. A person of importance. The German soldiers immediately faced him and stood to attention.

I saw an opportunity for us all to run away, but then what would they do to the men?

A high-ranking officer came out of L'Aeronautica and saluted. They spoke quietly, then the well-dressed man returned to his car and the chauffeur drove him away.

'Who was that, Mama?'

'Frick Hendrick Nüller.' She spat on the pavement, cleansing her mouth of the name.

Guards grabbed the man that had agitated the women with his quiet words and marched him off.

'And that?' I asked Mama.

'The Turkish Consul-General, Selahattin Ulkumen,' my mother replied. 'He was begging us not to enter the building, but we must. Now stop asking questions, Dora.'

Once inside, we searched for my father and the boys. We found them with Uncle Levi, my grandfather, and our cousins.

'Papa!' I rushed into his arms. He held me tightly, yet didn't seem pleased to see me.

They hadn't eaten since leaving home, and my brothers were starving. We shared the food with them.

Some people insisted we were about to be relocated to mountain villages; others said we were going to be put to work as labourers and cooks for the Germans.

That evening, we received orders to hand over matches, candles, cigarettes, scissors, knives and many other things. Some adults wept, but most seemed numb, staring, hugging their children.

This was an important event in my life, a chance to try my reporting skills and interview people, but they didn't want to talk. I found Carlo, the boy Irini liked, and sat with him.

'Where's your friend?' he said, looking past me.

'Up Filerimos with my sister. What's happening? Where are we going?'

'Nobody knows. Yesterday, they kept us in the yard. We were baking, and had nothing to drink. We could hear someone over the wall using a hose, so we shouted for him to give us water.'

He shook his head disbelievingly. 'He threw the end of the pipe over, but before we could all get a drink, we heard gunfire.'

'What? You don't mean they shot him?!'

'I think so. A woman screamed hysterically, then the hose disappeared back over the other side.'

'They shot him . . . they really shot him . . . for giving you water?'

Carlo shrugged. 'We should try to escape. There must be two thousand of us, and about a hundred of them.'

Before I could learn any more, Mama called me over and told me to be quiet and stay still.

The room became morbidly silent, but as evening fell, a ruckus sounded outside. I moved to the window and listened. From his accent, I guessed it to be the Turkish man again.

'You have no right to hold my people!' he shouted.

'They're not "your people",' a German yelled back. 'They're Jews! All Jews are Jews, and all Jews go to the camp by order of Mein Führer!'

The Consul-General persisted. 'Their religion is beside the point. It's their nationality that is the issue. These are Turkish citizens.' He waved a sheet of paper. You are in danger of breaking Turkey's neutrality agreement with Germany! Do you want us to join the Allies?'

After a beat, Ulkumen continued. 'According to our law, all Turks are equal, regardless of gender or religious beliefs, be they Jewish, Muslim, or Christian – men or women! I have the papers of my people here, and I *demand* you release them immediately. If you don't, you'll instigate an international incident. I've warned you where that will lead.'

The door opened and two SS officers came into the room. They stood either side of the Consul-General while he read out a list of names. His eyes flicked up and skimmed our faces after each one. In the following few minutes, a total of forty-three Rhodian Jews, supposedly with Turkish ancestry, were allowed to leave the building.

The tension was palpable. Some were panting, others chewed their lip, or squeezed their children too hard. A woman sobbed loudly. Someone else repeated the word 'Please' over and over.

A thin, middle-aged man with big eyes and a hooked nose pushed to the front and fell to his knees before Ulkumen. I recognised our maths teacher from Jewish school. A very strict and proud person. I felt ashamed to see him on the floor, begging.

'Sir!' he implored the Turkish consul. 'I have five children in here! My wife's pregnant. Please save us. I know where we're going. I've heard about the death camps. Don't let it happen!' He reached out and grabbed Ulkumen's trouser leg and then pressed his forehead against his knee in a gesture of supplication. 'Send one of the Greek or Italian officials to plead for our release as you so nobly did for your people. I'm begging you!'

The SS officer lifted his boot and, smiling, kicked the teacher in the face with terrific force. The teacher cried out. His head whipped back and blood gushed from his face. The officer checked his trousers for blood spatter, and then gracelessly shoved the Turkish Consul-General out of the room.

Alone again. Abandoned in our misery. Women fussed about the man, mopping his face and crying. His nose was clearly broken, and he had a deep gash across his cheekbone.

I kept hearing the teacher's words in my head. The death camps? What could *they* be? I wished people would share what information they had. I found Carlo and asked him, 'What's a death camp?'

He swallowed and frowned. 'Nobody wants to say. Sounds like a nightmare, doesn't it?'

'I'm afraid.'

'Me too,' he said.

* * *

It's dark outside now. We don't know what time it is because the Germans have taken our watches. Everyone is tired and I fear

I will fall asleep soon, so I have written down all that I have seen. I studied the adults' faces and saw real fear, which I'd mistaken for confusion earlier. Our worlds have been turned upside down, and the prospect of internment in some kind of camp seems to be the fate that awaits us.

Saturday, 22 July 1944

We lay on the floor all Friday night, hardly sleeping. The poor man with the broken nose had two black eyes by this morning. I took charge of the younger children, gathered them together and played quiet games. Cat's cradle, jackstones, I spy. I tried to catch the words whispered between adults, but whatever they knew was kept from me and the other teenagers.

We remained locked in the building through Saturday; tired, hungry, and anguished.

As I write this, I look around and try to share with my diary all that I see. Parents stare into each other's eyes, some weep, others clutch their children and pray. Most sit on the floor and gaze into space. An atmosphere of desolation has settled on us, as the inevitable looms. Yet, I still don't understand. I remember my teacher telling me to record *who, what, where* and *why* when I write a story, but in this situation, I only know the *who and the where*.

Earlier, I found Irini's mother and father and informed them that Irini remained up Filerimos with Evangelisa. They said, 'Good.' However, Irini's mother, white-faced with worry, cried. Was she sad because Irini wasn't with them? I asked Mama, but she told me to be quiet and stop asking questions.

How can I be a reporter if I don't make enquiries? I sense a historical moment that begs to be recorded. The mothers with young children or babies have gathered in one corner to breast-feed, while the men huddle together at the other end of the room and talk quietly. Old couples lay side by side on the floor, holding hands, using their bundles as pillows.

I found my oldest brother and sat cross-legged beside him. 'What's going to happen, Danial? Please don't treat me like a child, I have a right to know.'

He put his arms around my shoulders and squeezed. 'Nobody knows for sure. It's all speculation, Dora.'

'Why are they treating us badly, all of a sudden? And what's a death camp?'

His face paled. 'An awful nickname for the German work camps.'

We sat next to each other, silent with our thoughts.

After a while he said quietly, 'All we have is hope, Pandora. Pray that the war ends soon, for all our sakes.' He took my hand. 'Meanwhile, I've a new riddle for you.'

Overwhelmed by sadness I replied, 'Go on then.'

'What falls into the sea every day, but never gets wet?' He turned and although he smiled, his eyes remained dull. 'A bag of caramels when you tell me the answer.'

Unable to come up with anything, I said, 'I'll get it, don't you worry, Danial.'

We shared out the last of our food while Rabbi Asher quoted the Torah.

Chapter 13

Bromley, London.

Exactly one week later, a second package arrived from Greece. Rebecca tried to explain to the postman that the first parcel was not for her, but he replied that he was new and would she hold on to it for a few days until the regular postman came back? He pointed out it did have her name on it, and it couldn't be particularly important as it hadn't been sent by registered mail, and there was no return address.

She opened the package to see if an invoice with a contact number lay inside, but it didn't. This parcel was a mismatch of smaller parts including a largish spring. Mystified, she placed it alongside the other, in the dresser drawer. Perhaps someone would discover where their mail had gone and come knocking on her door. More important things weighed on her mind.

The local mechanic knew nothing about the packages. She checked they still held her phone number on file, in case anything turned up.

The Greek stamps brought Bubba and Naomi and the island of Rhodes into her thoughts. She frowned; what if they had something to do with it? But that didn't make sense, not after almost ten years of silence.

She missed them both, yet the resentment of a decade ago still hurt. She remembered the terrible fight that had caused her to leave. They'd forced her to choose: them or Fritz. An unfair position to put her in. She chose Fritz and although she never regretted the decision, her heart still ached when she thought of her family.

Somewhere across town, a vintage-car enthusiast was probably frantic after ordering hand-tooled parts for his precious vehicle, and for some reason they were misdirected to Rebecca. But how her name came to be on the packet was a mystery. She ticked off all the things she had bought on eBay, but nothing made sense.

In the conservatory, she photographed a bunch of tulips for a greeting card company, losing herself in her work. The light was perfect, but she needed a fresh angle. She set the camera on her heaviest tripod, gripped the lever and turned it, locking the gears. Suddenly, she realised the parcel was more likely to be part of a robust professional tripod. There were many different kinds, with levers and gismos. Later she would call the online store where she bought her photography equipment and see if they knew anything about it.

* * *

The following Friday, when another package arrived, she was strangely pleased to see it. A puzzle to take her mind away from her womb and what might be living or dying inside her.

She placed the third parcel on the lounge coffee table, and then brought the first two packets and put the contents side by side, before unwrapping the latest arrival, her logic being that if she saw the parts together there was a chance she would recognise something.

The moment she laid eyes on the contents, she realised her mistake.

Wrong, wrong, wrong!

This piece was without doubt a pistol grip and trigger. *A gun,* she thought, suddenly recognising the first part as the barrel.

A bloody gun! The first real gun she had ever seen in her life. Who the hell would send her a gun, and why?

She nudged the parts into position on the solid oak coffee table. The barrel, the bits and pieces of a firing mechanism, and the grip and trigger. *A bloody gun!* She peered at the fancy initials embossed into the metal above the grip, F N. Who was F N? Fritz Neumanner? Who'd sent a gun bearing her husband's initials to her home?

Perhaps the pistol belonged to Fritz. A shiver ran through her. But the stamps were Greek and Fritz knew nothing about the first parcel. Could Bubba have been right all along? The thought was shocking. Bubba always maintained that Fritz Neumanner was the grandson of Frick Nüller. The war criminal responsible for indefensible crimes against humanity. The man who organised the displacement of the Jews of Rhodes to Auschwitz, the concentration camp. Frick Nüller, judged, convicted and sentenced to death in his absence. But this was pure fabrication on Bubba's part. The old lady believes every blue-eyed blond was a Nazi, and she has no right to dump her hatred of an entire race on the man Rebecca loved.

Tears pricked her eyes. This was just the sort of quiet way Bubba would use to prove her point. Rebecca missed her grandmother and her sister terribly. Two people she treasured most dearly, but if they refused to accept the man she had married, she had no choice but to break away from them.

This gun turning up from Greece, with her husband's initials on the side, meant what? Rebecca recalled the letter she received from Rhodes after leaving to live in London with Fritz. She hadn't opened it, still broken-hearted that Bubba had forced her to make a choice: her family, or Fritz.

She left the pistol on the table and went into the kitchen to think.

* * *

The kettle switched itself off. Rebecca hadn't moved from the window where raindrops trickled down the other side of the glass. She stared out at the long lawn surrounded by a thick, high hedge. The perfect playground for her children.

There would be swings, a pool in the summer, a trampoline. Perhaps a set of small goalposts where their little boy would learn to kick a football with Fritz's guidance. Rebecca pictured a quaint Wendy house with a picket fence, where she'd sit with her young daughter and sip tea from tiny china cups. 'Pass the Iced Gems, please.'

If she listened hard, she could hear the laughter of her unborn children.

The apple tree sapling she and Fritz had planted in anticipation of their family, was now heavy with fruit. She placed her hand on her belly and wished.

After three years of marriage with no pregnancy, her narrow fallopian tubes and Fritz's low sperm count were diagnosed as responsible. For the following seven years, they'd sought clinical help to produce a family, but each effort ended in heart-breaking failure. After all the pain and expense, they were right to agree that this would be their final try at IVF.

Poor Fritz. He hated the clinic. He hated having to masturbate on demand. He hated ejaculating into a beaker. And he hated handing it over to a nurse.

Harvested, such a pleasant word. Harvest time brought images of impressionist paintings, plough horses, haystacks, autumn sunshine; skeins of migrating geese, shifting their V formations as they honked and flapped overhead; baskets of sweet grapes, pumpkins, chestnuts and apple picking. The bounty of life.

Nothing like the degradation Fritz felt having his semen 'harvested', frozen, and stored. Rebecca thanked God her husband had agreed and obliged, because that stored semen meant the possibility of getting pregnant without him.

The staff were very sympathetic and supportive, but so they should be for the money it cost. Rebecca had her own demons to conquer: her fear of needles. She hated injecting herself, but if supressing hormones and then stimulating ovulation paved the road to a family, she would do it.

Surely the inconvenience and embarrassment, and the pain they both endured was worth it? Everyone seemed determined they would have their children to love and cherish in the end.

This time, she made up her mind not to visit baby shops, or buy mother-and-baby magazines, or redecorate the nursery. This time she would accept the result. This time she would not go to pieces at the first spot of blood in her underwear.

So far so good. The pregnancy confirmed. She decided to wait until she was twelve weeks before she told Fritz. Mainly because they had agreed on one more try at IVF *together*. She reckoned that as he was hardly involved in this attempt, it didn't count, and if it should fail, at least she had another chance.

Rebecca peered at the sky and blew her cheeks out. The rain stopped and the sun broke through, the garden sparkling fresh. Perfect weather and nobody to enjoy it with. She made herself a camomile tea, returned to the lounge, and stared at the gun.

Chapter 14

Sunday, 23 July 1944

I am afraid, really afraid! Those who slept were woken by shouting Germans. Before sunrise, they started herding us out of L'Aeronautica in rows of five. I don't know where we're going. I'm scribbling this down, quickly as I can, as we shuffle forward, because I have no idea when I'll get another chance to update my journal. Babies are crying with hunger. I can see through the doorway as they march the first captives out. Police and soldiers line the street pointing their guns at our friends and neighbours. Three wagons carried the aged and infirm away. Black exhaust smoke drifted in as they passed by the entrance. Our group is close to the doors now.

Papa has just tapped me on the shoulder and said, 'Be a good girl and put the diary away, Dora.' His voice is odd, sort of scratched, like I remember the wireless when someone had knocked the aerial. I want to hug him, and I want him to tell me everything will be all right. I just stash the diary in my duffel instead.

*　*　*

It is night now, and this has been the worst day of my life! Why didn't I hug Papa when I had a chance?! Now it's too late, *too late*! So much has happened since we left L'Aeronautica this morning, I'm in a rush to write it all down, right now, while it's still fresh in my head.

Before daylight, we were forced to walk towards the harbour.

Air-raid sirens wailed, making communication impossible. Dawn pushed back the night as we approached the quayside. Three rusting ships tied up to port. Some of the adults muttered prayers. Others put on a brave face for the sake of their children, saying everything would be fine once we had left the island.

I became separated from my family and tried to spot them amongst the hundreds of sorry captives, but the man at my side threw an urgent punch at my arm. 'Keep your head down, child. Don't look around.' His tone, flat and lifeless, frightened me. Anguish filled my chest and made my throat ache.

I stared at the ground as we walked, noting small obscure details and filing them away. Suddenly, everything seemed important. Two flattened cigarette ends in the gutter, one with dark pink lipstick. A burst balloon. A short length of yellow party streamer, coiled and trodden on. The remains of someone's celebration, a party. I imagined the day we would all return to our island and celebrate – me and every member of my family.

A hand touched mine, fingers tangling. I glanced sideways. Carlo. I squeezed his hand but didn't speak in case the Nazis pointed their guns at us. The walk to the harbour didn't seem as bad with my hand in his. I imagined telling Irini when I got back . . . because I *would* return to my friend, somehow. Also, Evangelisa needed me. I worried about her. Mama and Papa had depended on me to take care of her.

In that moment these thoughts were an escape from the trudge. I fantasised about the Curly Haired Boy, getting married, building a house in Paradissi and having lots of beautiful children. Mama and Papa would come for coffee and cake. Him not being Jewish might be a problem, but I wasn't sure because nobody ever talked about such things.

German guns pointed at us from all directions. We turned into the port. The air raid siren deafened us. The three cargo vessels were moored to my right. To my left, the lorry transport

103

for the old and sick pulled to a halt. As the sun rose, that sorry human freight disembarked. Just before we reached the huge wheels and dull grey-green paintwork, I glanced over my shoulder, searching for my family. I caught sight of Papa and, as our eyes met, he flicked a rapid glance to the vehicles. I understood and made a quick nod.

'Oy! No turning around!' a soldier yelled, jerking his gun at me.

I cowered, afraid of being shot right there and then, and of disappointing Papa. I tugged at Carlo's hand. Irini would love me forever if I managed to save Carlo from the Nazis and bring him up to Filerimos.

A hullabaloo kicked off behind me and I heard Papa's voice. 'Walk tall, children! Be proud of who you are. They can't take that away from us!' He started singing and despite the bravery of his words, the distress in his voice broke my heart.

Carlo let go of my hand and a sense of hopelessness overcame me. Perhaps nine metres separated me from my father, yet it seemed like an abyss. I longed for his arms around me. The safest place in the world was inside one of Papa's hugs.

Others joined in the song, but the guards blew their whistles or yelled. I flinched, terrified, when a shot fired. Someone screamed. Behind me, people shouted but I dared not look back again.

* * *

I have to stop for a moment. I'm crying as I write about these events that took place only this morning. It seems like a lifetime ago. I must try and be objective, unemotional, and record the facts as they happened. That's what journalists do. . . stay true to the story, but it's difficult when the facts concern your family and friends – the people you love. Yet now, more than ever, I owe it to my family to keep up this journal.

* * *

As the commotion took place behind me, we drew alongside the biggest truck. With one long sideways step, I slipped under the vehicle and hid in the dark shadow between the rear wheels.

Because of my small size, I discovered I could almost stand upright. I pressed myself against an inner tyre, watched the feet of my friends, neighbours, and family trudge past. Hot metal from part of the wheel dug into my back, and I feared it would burn through my dress. The sirens howled. Confused emotions rose inside me, but with the sound of the air-raid warning, came hope.

I searched the distant sky for bombers heading our way. The British had inadvertently destroyed much of our synagogues and Rhodes Old Town, attempting to score points against the Germans. Would they come now, bomb the Nazis to death and save us all?

Clearly, the Jews of Rhodes didn't want to leave the island. Distraught women wept against the chests of their husbands. Men with their chins thrust forward held their weeping wives, mothers, and children.

The stench of rubber from the tyres burned my throat. I squeezed my eyes closed to calm myself and get rid of the tears, then I peered at what I could see of the sky from under the truck, searching for planes.

What if the soldiers found me? Papa would be disappointed that I hadn't managed to escape. He relied on me to take care of Evangelisa and the sheep.

Air-raid sirens continued. The shiny black car with German flags up front, drove onto the quayside. Because the people in the car were lower than the soldiers and captives, I feared they'd see me. I flattened myself against an inner wheel. Suddenly engulfed in exhaust fumes, I realised the vehicle had reversed and its back end almost touched the lorry, giving me more cover.

When the fumes cleared, I slid to the edge of the wheel and stared at the ships. The scene that met my eyes branded itself into my mind and I knew it would stay with me for the rest of my life. I dropped to my knees and peered from behind the car. Joined by an officer, Frick Hendrik Nüller strutted along the quayside. He pointed his baton at the ships and laughed. Then he stood tall and arrogant, his eyes narrow and the smile of satisfaction clear on his face.

All he had to do, to change everything, was lift his stick and order everyone off the boats.

Do it! Set my family free!

He didn't. He gloated. He talked loudly with the officer in charge, saluted, and then returned to his vehicle.

There had to be something I could do. But a cold feeling in my stomach told me the situation might worsen.

Until that moment, I had never truly hated anyone before. I stared at that man's face, determined to remember every feature, and I swore to myself that if ever I got the chance I would send Frick Nüller straight to hell for what he had done to my loved ones.

One day, Frick Hendrick Nüller, I will find your family and I will take them from you.

Why didn't Papa want me with them? To tell the truth, I would rather work for the Germans and leave Evangelisa and the sheep with Irini if it meant being able to stay with my family. *What a shameful thing to think!* Evangelisa is my family too. Her family is on that ship and she doesn't even know what's happening. Horrible as the time has been, at least I had experienced another two days with them all. I had to have something ready to tell my sister when I got back to the hut; but what? My mind was all over the place.

I tried to calm down by thinking about my brothers. Jacob, who's seventeen, was nowhere to be seen. Samuel, twenty last Thursday, and Danial, twenty-one, stood with Papa.

Danial spoils me. Sometimes, very late at night, he brings me a glass of Mama's lemon and barley. He sits on my bed and tells me where he's been and who with. There's a curfew, so he's not supposed to be out after dark, but on Saturday evenings he meets his girlfriend and a few others. I'm thrilled to hear of his adventures. Once, they put a trip wire across the street and a German soldier fell over it. I told Irini and she said she could fall in love with Danial.

He goes to amazing parties where they play music and dance the jive and jitterbug. Each week, his girlfriend writes down the latest popular song and Danial brings it home for me and Irini to memorise the words. I don't know why that memory made me want to cry right then.

I stared at the ship. My brothers stood at the rails peering over the quayside. I longed to run out, waving my arms, so the Nazis could put me on the boat with everyone else. But my family expected me to take responsibility for Evangelisa. Being grown up isn't all I imagined.

I wanted to be with them. Better to be in their midst than under a German truck, but Papa had his reason for making me hide, and I trust him completely. I wonder if they're really going to Kos, they say it's a beautiful island. I could take the ferry and visit them if I had the money. Then I remember the Russian dolls.

On our bureau stands a brightly painted babushka doll into which Papa empties the small change from his pockets each evening. He wouldn't mind if I borrowed a little to buy me and Evangelisa a ticket to Kos. Aunt Martha bought the dolls for Mama years ago. There are seven pieces and, over time, each of us have claimed a doll, Papa has the largest; Evangelisa, the smallest.

Thinking about the dolls, fitting together as perfectly as my family, calms me down. We all belong together.

I caught sight of Aunt Martha. She dabbed her face with a lace handkerchief. Her other hand on the shoulder of my Uncle Levi. She wore her usual red lipstick and, around her neck, the fox stole with ruby-glass eyes bit its own tail. Although impossible to see from that distance, I knew an extra fine hairnet kept her freshly permed curls in place. She always appeared perfectly groomed, even after the torment of L'Aeronautica.

Aunt Martha's daughters, Sadie and Purl, hugged their parents. They wore their Friday best. My dear granny, one of the first on the ship, gripped the rails, stretching her neck and peering up and down the quay. She's not good on her feet, but far too proud to use sticks. Her pale face and sunken eyes worried me. She didn't look well and I wanted to hold her hand.

Papa must have told everyone I'd escaped and I sensed their thoughts were with me, each of them silently wishing me luck. I longed for the moment I would be able to hug each of them again.

A starved dog with protruding ribs and short hair the colour of toffee, bounded towards the truck. I tried to shoo it with my hands but, persistent and playful, he wouldn't leave. The creature cowered at my ankles, submissive, turning its great brown eyes to meet mine. 'Go away!' I whispered, but he licked my feet and whimpered. The soldiers were only metres from me. I ducked, and quickly dodged around the truck's front tyre, but the dog persisted, so excited at this new game he stopped to cock his leg against the tyre.

A little river of urine snaked behind the wheel, followed by the dog's nose.

'Oi!' a soldier shouted, marching over.

I pressed myself into the hollow of the metal wheel, terrified I'd be seen. From the corner of my eye, I watched the soldier's hand come down and grab the pup by his tail just centimetres from me. He dragged the wriggling dog from under the truck, put his foot under its ribs and flicked it off the quayside into the sea.

Oh!

I almost cried out. The soldiers laughed and moved towards the ships. I searched the ghostly faces of the captives. At least my family were all on the one ship, except I hadn't seen Jacob or Mama. They couldn't be going far, not packed together like that with the strengthening sun beating down.

Where was Mama? My mind screamed her name in the hope that she'd respond and I'd get a bearing.

I know this sort of thing works because once, when I thought about Irini, she knocked on our door less than a minute later, and many times I have heard people say, 'I was just thinking about you.' Another time, when Evangelisa's cat had disappeared, I really focused on telling Cleo how much she was missed. That very afternoon, the cat returned.

Mama! It's me, your Dora. I'm under the lorry! Look this way, I want to see you!

My father had blood in his white hair. He gazed over his shoulder to the quayside and then struggled to turn around in the tightly packed bodies. Although a distance away, I knew he searched for me. As I stared at him, he lifted two fingers over each ear and wiggled them.

Little rabbit, run, little rabbit!

I felt the ghost of his fingers racing up my ribs when I was younger, tickling my armpits until I screamed for him to stop.

Oh, Papa!

In seconds, he was gone. Pushed back by the surge of more people being forced onto his ship.

I understood that Papa was telling me to run. I dragged my eyes from the vessel to take stock, and crouched to get a better view of my surroundings. The sun was up, bathing everything in harsh light.

Fifty metres of quayside lay between me and a ferry ticket stand, my only cover. Nine exposed metres between me and the dockside. I was a good swimmer. I could hang on to a tyre dangling to protect the ships' paintwork until the coast was clear, then swim for shore.

When the British bombs started falling, I'd be safer in the sea than under a Nazi truck.

I stared at the horizon. Where were the planes of our new allies? Though the British were always bombing us and had killed many of my friends, they would make a great diversion for my escape. A splash on the water distracted me. A seagull landed, and another, then even more. This was not my day. If I jumped into the sea now, the rising birds were sure to attract attention.

I stared at the ships again. My father peered in my direction. I stuck one arm out and gave a quick wave, before retreating behind the rear wheel.

Please, please, please let him see me.

When I peeked out again, Papa had one arm horizontally across the front of his chest, and the other behind it making a rabbit shape, like when he used to make shadows on the wall for me and Evangelisa, years ago. My heart melted. Papa forgets I'm a woman now.

The siren continued to howl, but apart from enemy soldiers, a couple of dock workers, and the entire Jewish community, there wasn't a soul to be seen. Then I had a frightening thought. If the British bombers came, they'd surely blow the ships, and the people, and my truck to pieces! Horrified, I stared at the sky.

Chapter 15

Rhodes, Greece.

Naomi's elbow slid off the arm of the chair. She woke with a start, her heart racing. The day had fallen into darkness, the diary open in her lap.

She pulled herself up and went inside for a coffee. Rebecca would have received the gun by now. If she still lived at the same address, that is. The thought worried Naomi: her sister could have moved over the years. Why hadn't she thought of that before? A total stranger may have received the gun parts, and, even worse, handed them to the police. The whole idea had been ludicrous, and she deeply regretted giving in to Bubba and Papas Yiannis's plan.

The following hour drifted by in a breathless haze filled with words never said, questions never asked, and hope that all of this would sort itself out. She had tried to phone Rebecca's old mobile, but found it unavailable. She phoned directory enquiries, gave Rebecca's address, and scribbled down the number.

Why hadn't that occurred to her sooner, too?

Naomi keyed in the number. The phone, an old-fashioned affair, needed a good clean. Not long ago her house had been spotless. Lately, she had let things slide a little, not finding enough hours in a day for everything.

Knowing she was about to open old wounds, her trepidation rose. If she didn't handle this right, it might turn nasty and rip them all further apart.

Would Rebecca realise something important must have happened for her sister to call? Naomi longed to hear her voice. She punched in the long number, misdialled, and started again. Her heart thudded and her fingernails drummed on the worktop as she waited for her sister to pick up; then she realised she had no idea what to say. She hung up.

Best to write a few things down, prompts in case she got stuck for words.

* * *

Bromley, London.

From her home office, Rebecca cancelled wedding photography bookings. Brides-to-be pleaded with her, but when she told them why, they offered their best wishes.

While in the middle of returning a booking deposit, the phone interrupted her. She didn't recognise the number, picked up, and said, 'Rebecca Neumanner.'

'Rebecca, it's Naomi.'

Rebecca's stomach lurched. She stabbed the red button. End call. *Bloody hell.* Then she regretted it. How did Naomi get her number? She stroked her belly. The last thing she wanted was stress. Perhaps – oh please God – perhaps she would hang on to her baby this time. Her hand shook as she turned the phone to voicemail. Was it bad news? Bubba?

Don't think about it.

She would be devastated if her grandmother died and they hadn't spoken since falling out. Rebecca closed her eyes and hugged herself, desperate to nurture the spark of life that nestled in her womb. Would her body keep it safe for nine whole months? She imagined the scrunched-up face of her infant, moments after birth. How she would love her child. She had read every book on parenting, determined to be the perfect mother.

112

Her phone rang again. *What the hell?* She walked out of the office, glancing back, undecided. Should she answer? She stared at the floor, willing the phone to kick into voicemail.

Her sister sounded different, older, nervous. Or was she upset? Rebecca turned the coffee machine on, then off. She shouldn't drink coffee. In the lounge, small and alone in the spacious room, she curled foetus-like on the expensive cream sofa. The soft leather cooled her skin. The phone rang again, redirected to voicemail.

She pulled a cushion under her head, closed her eyes and concentrated on her breathing. The doorbell caused her to flinch. Friday, the day of the gun parcels. What was this now? Instructions to follow? She felt herself living in some weird screenplay and imagined the postman would turn out to be Alfred Hitchcock.

'Be calm,' she whispered before concentrating on deep even breaths. She could ignore the postman; however, if it was another parcel he would leave it next door. She hurried down the hall, recognising the yellow GPO jacket through her stained-glass window.

* * * *

Rebecca dropped the chunky brown envelope on the kitchen worktop and stared at the phone. She should check the voice-mail . . . she should. What was the point of fretting? She picked up and listened.

'Rebecca, I need to speak to you, urgently. I'll call back in ten minutes.'

She sat there, staring at the phone and then the envelope. Absolutely no stress, they'd said at the clinic. 'Take yoga classes if it helps, but we need you to keep your blood pressure down.'

The phone rang again. Voicemail. She placed her hand flat over the envelope. *No stress.* She marched across the kitchen, toed the pedal bin, and dropped the envelope into the rubbish. The steel lid fell with a clatter. Nothing in the world was more important to Rebecca than her pregnancy.

The phone rang again. *That's Naomi, determined as always.* Perhaps it *was* about Bubba. Dear Bubba. She needed to know. Her hand trembled as she picked up. If there were any dramatics from Naomi, she'd hang up immediately.

'You have to read it,' Naomi said. 'I don't know if it's arrived yet, but it's important. I'm not trying to make trouble, Rebecca. I miss you more than you can imagine. Goodbye.'

'Wait! Bubba? Is she . . .?'

'She's suffered a stroke. Read the diary. I'll call you tomorrow.' And with that, she ended the call.

Bubba, a stroke, how awful. How was she? She recalled Bubba's last words. 'I never want to see you again, Rebecca. You're no longer part of this family!'

Rebecca had screamed back that she didn't want to be part of a family that included a bitter old Jewish bigot. She remembered the instant shock on Bubba's face. Why had she said such a disgraceful thing? Bubba was a kind old lady who wouldn't hurt a fly, and Rebecca regretted those cruel words, but there was no going back on all that now. The damage was done, and 'sorry' wouldn't heal such deep wounds on either side.

She glanced at the pedal bin. What was so important about a diary? She retrieved the envelope, opened it, and started reading.

Chapter 16

Rhodes, Greece.

Naomi returned to the second diary, recalling where she was up to. She had to remind herself that Dora was Bubba, a concept she found difficult to accept. The only thing they seemed to have in common was their diminutive size. The diary showed her grandmother in an entirely new light.

Poor Dora, afraid and alone, parted from those she loved and hiding under the Nazi truck on the quayside. Air-raid sirens blared in her ears. Her family imprisoned on the rusting ships, and she could do nothing.

More activity on the quayside drew my attention. Gangplanks were hoisted and dock workers hefted rope loops off mooring stanchions, taut on their anchor chains. The three vessels pulled away from the quayside.

Please don't sail away! I don't want you to go!

Seagulls took to the air. No time to fret or speculate; I had to dive into the sea.

Mama, Papa, I will find you! Send me some good luck! Here I go, on three; run for the edge and jump into the sea. One, two—

My plan was scuppered before I'd set foot out of the truck's shadow. Two Nazis came around to the blind side of the vehicle and spoke in German. A match fell to the floor in front of me and I caught a whiff of sulphur. I hardly dared breathe; their thick-soled boots stood less than a metre from where I crouched.

Two minutes later, they crushed their cigarettes. One soldier marched away. I recognised the metallic squeak of the wagon door opening. Too late to make a run for the dockside.

A boot disappeared towards the driver's footplate.

I jumped away from the wheel, afraid it would catch my dress and drag me to a horrific death. I'd been so busy observing the ships and the officers, I hadn't noticed the troops assembling at the port entrance, ready to march back to the barracks.

When the lorry drove away, I would be left alone, exposed on the quayside with nowhere to hide. The sea was my only option.

The siren stopped. My heart sank. No bombs. The silence meant everyone would hear the splash as I hit the water, a metre below the dock. I wish I'd learned to dive properly, like Danial. He pierced the surface like an arrow, hardly a sound, barely a ripple. Jacob and I hugged our knees and bombed the water, competing to make the biggest waves.

Two trucks drove away. I watched the driver's feet. He changed his mind, walked to the passenger door and opened it. Probably too hot in the cab, I thought. He moved towards the truck's tailgate. I turned too.

Then, I realised what my father had tried to tell me. The little rabbit's shadow!

Low sun shone under the lorry, sending my elongated shadow out from the rear of the vehicle like a cat's tail. I dropped onto all fours and, with my eyes fixed on my shadow, I crawled backwards until it disappeared into the shadow of the truck.

My knees were stinging and bloody, and I realised I had scraped my skin on the concrete. This wasn't the time to start crying, but I couldn't help it.

Papa! Somebody! Help me!

I had to get into the sea. Salt water purified wounds; Mama taught me that. I turned towards the quayside and stuck my head from under the bumper, ready to lunge forward and leap into the Sea; but then – intense pain.

The soilder grabbed my hair and swung me from under the lorry.

'Please . . .' I sobbed violently. 'You're hurting me.'

Pain burned my scalp. The soldier's sour breath stank of cigarettes. The Nazis shot people. Would he execute me? Bang. Dead. Beads of sweat glistened on his face. His eyes narrowed and he muttered something guttural.

I'm a fighter, I reminded myself, *I survived because I'm a fighter!* But there was no fight in me, just the jangled nerves of a coward.

'You've got so much to live for,' my granny had said when we talked about my future. I want to sing. I want to write. I trembled violently.

'*Verdammt!*' the soldier spat when my feet were off the ground. I didn't struggle. His eyes met mine and narrowed.

I stared at him, my eyes wide and pleading, the puppy-dog look that sometimes got me out of trouble.

He glanced around. The ships were inaccessible, anchored offshore. I thought my hair was coming out by the roots. It took everything I had not to scream. He threw me into the lorry's passenger side and slammed the door so hard my brains rattled.

I scrambled across the cab, frantic to leap from the driver's side and run away before he reached the front. He got there before me and shoved me back into the passenger's footwell. I cowered into the corner, making myself small, shaking like a kicked dog.

He started the truck with a jolt.

Trapped, I swiped my tears away and stared at him. My knees hurt. His pale skin glowed pink from too much sun, his nose was peeling. His eyes were pale and cold in his fine-boned face. He glanced at me, a tic twitching the corner of his mouth.

'*Bitte, bitte,*' I pleaded.

He poked a finger towards the floor and ordered, '*Sei still,*' followed by something I didn't understand.

I couldn't see where we were going and with each bump on the uneven road, grit on the floor dug into my shins and my bleeding knees. Oddly, I became deathly calm. The soldier appeared worried. His eyebrows bunched as he chewed his lip and squinted about. After a few minutes, he took his hand away from the wheel and patted the passenger seat. I understood and scrambled up, peering at our whereabouts.

We travelled uphill, through an area of olive groves and vineyards, green and linear in the red earth. They soon gave way to overgrazed scrubland crisscrossed by goat-tracks. Above, Cyprus trees that loomed dark in the shadow of Filerimos Mountain appeared menacing, like black dragon's teeth. I realised we were on the road to the army camp near the airport viewing tower.

Sickened, I realised the soldier intended to hand me over. They would shoot me!

The truck slowed for a hairpin bend in the mountain road. I pushed down on the metal door handle with all my strength, and as soon as it gave way I threw all my weight against it. At the same moment, he made a grab for me while still navigating the sharp bend and simultaneously braking hard. The jolt of brakes swung the door open. I tumbled out, somersaulting down the steep slope.

It's odd how a single second can stick in your head forever, like falling through the air. I don't remember experiencing any pain when I hit the ground, nor when I came to a halt in the thorn bushes. A moment later, unbearable burning sensations travelled from my wrist to my shoulder. The pain was pure agony, worse than anything I'd ever experienced. I screamed. My scraped hands and knees stung, and bits of twig, dried grass, and hair lay over my face.

The truck stopped. The soldier, silhouetted against the cobalt sky, stood at the edge of the road above, peering down. I froze, wishing the dragon's teeth would snap closed and devour him. He placed his hands on his hips and stared into the scrubland. Could he see me in the brush? Perhaps he thought I'd broken my neck. He stood for a minute, scratched his head, then returned to his cab and drove away.

118

I whimpered as the lorry disappeared over the hill leaving nothing but a cloud of dust on the ridge and a whiff of diesel in the air. Perhaps the German thought I wasn't worth the bother. Blinded by the pain in my arm, I thought about my parents and wished I was with them.

My throat burned, and my body was weak from dehydration and lack of food. But fate was my tormentor that day and only minutes later the sounds of a convoy registered. The first jeep appeared over that same ridge. Surely, I'd be seen when they neared.

I tried to crawl through the scrub, but the pain in my wrist was too intense and I could not put it down. The tears returned and I cursed them, vowing never, ever, to cry again. The 'tring, tring, tring' of a bicycle bell caught my attention and I dared to lift my head high enough to see down the road.

Standing on his pedals, his bike tilting violently from side to side with the effort of coming uphill, was the ragged shepherd boy. He wore nothing but frayed trousers cut off at the knees, a dirty vest, and a pair of large boots laced with string. A crudely whittled catapult was caught in the leather belt of his pants.

I wanted to cry for help, but a glance in the opposite direction stopped me. The German convoy approached.

The boy leapt off his rusted bike, letting it clatter onto the road.

Horrified when he raced towards me, I yelled, 'Go away!' as loud as I dared.

He plucked a sage bush from the ground, metres from where I lay, and then thrust it over me.

'Don't move!' he whispered.

The overpowering scent of the herb filled my nostrils, making my eyes water and my nose itch. The sound of army vehicles grew louder until it drowned out my thudding heartbeat. I closed my eyes, desperate to halt an oncoming sneeze. Sage always had that effect on me. With a squeal of brakes and the stench of diesel, the convoy stopped only metres from where I lay.

The shepherd boy ran in a zig-zag pattern through the scrub, away from me.

What was he doing?

In the jeep that led four covered wagons, one of the soldiers stood and shouted. 'Boy! Is this your bicycle? Get it off the road, NOW!'

The shepherd boy came running, his heavy boots thumping. He pulled up, standing stiffly at the side of the road where he executed an exaggerated German salute.

I wanted to pinch my nose to kill the gathering sneeze, but I dared not move my hand.

The soldiers laughed at the boy. 'What are you doing?!' the leader yelled.

'Sir, I'm saluting you, sir!' the boy shouted, standing to attention with his chin up and his skinny chest thrust out. This brought more hilarity from the men.

'Why's your bike in the road, and why are you running about like a lunatic, boy?'

'I saw a hare, sir. I was trying to catch it for my father, the shepherd, sir!'

'Move the bike. Next time we'll drive over it. Got that?'

'Yes, sir! Thank you, sir!'

I realised the boy was putting on a performance for the soldiers in order to draw their attention away from the spot where I lay. He was doing such a good job of behaving like a half-wit, if it wasn't for the pain in my arm and the danger of the situation, I'd have laughed out loud. Like me, he knew the advantage to be gained by behaving childishly, however, I had my small size to help me in my deception, the shepherd boy was almost adult in size, so this boyish behaviour made him appear slightly ridiculous.

He came running to his bike. I must have relaxed a little thinking I had avoided being discovered, because just as he lifted the bicycle I sneezed.

The Germans *must* have heard me!

The soldier tilted his head to look past the shepherd boy. 'What was that?'

'Me, sir! Sorry, sir! It's the pollen. Permission to wipe my nose, sir!' He swiped the back of his hand under his nose, and then down the side of his pants, before he saluted again.

The occupants of the jeep were laughing. The leader glanced at his watch, flapped his hand at the driver, and the convoy continued.

'Don't move, they're watching,' the boy said from the corner of his mouth, before dashing about like a dog with fleas again.

When the vehicles were out of sight, he returned, shifted his bike and lifted the sage brush. 'You okay?' he asked softly, dropping to his knees at my side. 'I saw you fall from the truck.' He slipped his arm under my shoulders and tried to help me sit up, but I cried out with pain. 'Were you one of the Jews from the ships?' He plucked a twig from my hair, tossed it away, and peered into my eyes as if seeing me for the first time.

Chapter 17

Naomi rubbed her eyes, surprised to find it was almost midnight. Heat rose in her cheeks after reading that last line. The fatal evening her parents left for their fishing boat came rushing back. She recalled sitting on the kerb, playing jackstones with Heleny after a game of hide-and-seek in the dry river bed. Her father came over, his smile wide and his eyes crinkling in the corners, 'Be good for Bubba, will you? And help her with the baby.' He pulled a twig out of her hair and absently put it in his pocket. She jumped up and hugged him, and he kissed the top of her head.

Mama appeared at his side. 'You're growing so fast, Naomi. We're very proud of you. And she stooped and kissed her cheeks. 'See you after school tomorrow. Be good, bye now.' And they continued hand in hand down Spartili Street. Naomi closed her eyes and could see the backs of them as they walked away, the sky turning red.

All the years since Papas Yiannis told her they were lost at sea, she'd been angry that they had never said goodbye, but all the anger that came *after* the night of the storm had blanked out the previous evening.

They had said goodbye.

She sobbed, her tears breaking free. Why hadn't she remembered all that when she was a child so cruelly orphaned? For a moment, her anger surged. She sensed her mind had played a cruel trick, and she understood a little of Bubba's pain when her deeply buried memories surfaced.

She wiped her eyes, wondering if Sonia and Zorba had said goodbye to Bubba, and she guessed that they had. But perhaps the shock of their deaths had also wiped that last memory from Bubba's mind? Naomi imagined she would come across the answer later in the diary. A diary that closed the divide between innocent sixteen-year-old Pandora and grandmother Bubba, a stalwart woman and tower of strength before the stroke.

* * *

Mid-morning the next day, Naomi nipped up the road for a carton of milk. Activity in the tiny shop on the corner of Spartili and the main village road drew her attention. They were moving out, hefting boxes and chairs into a van that blocked half the narrow street.

Her chest tightened with hope and excitement. How often she had dreamed of having a shop.

She stood in the village supermarket, staring at the shelves, imagining what it would be like to own business premises. That place was tiny, and right at the end of her street, perfect. At the counter, she paid for the milk and asked what they knew.

'They've moved to the car showroom that's been empty a while. Now, the Lotto's a big posh place with sports TVs and a coffee shop of its own.'

Uplifted to hear the Lotto shop had done that well, she returned to the top of Spartili Street. When she had time, she would work out how much money she would need to get the place up and running. Then she scolded herself for having ambitions beyond her reach. But one could dream.

She peered through the dusty glass that made two walls of the three-by-four space. The removals had gone and the door was locked. Her heart thumped so hard she told herself to calm down.

The empty shop had white shelves on two walls, and a counter. She imagined her jars of cream displayed in little pyramids, with the prices painted onto pretty pebbles she'd collect from the beach. A jug on the counter stuffed with fresh wild flowers, or lavender and myrtle from her back yard. She would stand behind the counter wearing a new dress, something floral, and a touch of makeup, and she would dab her customers' wrists with a sample of her latest scent.

She blinked the illusion away and looked again. A broken chair lay on its side, the floor was scattered with scratched tickets and torn football-coupons, and phone wires hung out of the wall. How many people had entered the betting shop with hope in their eyes and left with the dull look of disappointment. The Lotto shop had been a roaring success because get-rich-quick was the national sport of Greece.

Back home, Naomi wondered what a licence to sell perfume and cosmetics would cost? Although Greece was in dire financial trouble, the government did everything it could to stamp out the entrepreneurial spirit. She sighed.

'It can't be that bad!' Heleny's voice made her jump.

'Sorry, I was daydreaming.'

'Tell me about it.'

'That little shop on the corner.' She nodded towards the village road. 'I can't get it out of my head, but I can't come up with a way to obtain the premises on my meagre finances.'

'Brainstorming, that's what you need,' Heleny said with glee. 'Let's do it. I'll call Georgia, and we'll get Bubba, Pappas Yiannis, and young Marina on it too.'

'I don't know . . . I'm being stupid, daydreaming. I don't have any money, and they'll all think I'm mad. Delusions of grandeur.'

'Nonsense! Anyway, what harm can it do if your friends give you their honest opinion?' Heleny dropped a huge carrier of *kourabiéthes* into Naomi's lap and plopped into the chair next to her. 'Three o'clock this afternoon okay?'

Naomi chewed her lip for a moment and then shrugged. 'What've I got to lose?' Yet she had already resigned herself to disappointment.

'That's the spirit.' Heleny grinned.

'Thanks for the shortbreads. How's it going with Fannes?'

Heleny's face fell. 'He's married . . . the bastard!'

'Oh, I'm sorry. How did you find out?'

'Credit card under my bed. Must have fallen out of his pocket when he tore his clothes off in a mad frenzy of lust and passion.'

Naomi bit hard on her lip.

'Same name on the card, but Mrs. It had to be the wife's. He denied it at first. Keeps calling me. I'm not wearing the perfume again until he gives up.'

'Look, Heleny, all things have their opposite. Why don't I mix you a different perfume that will stop his advances?'

Heleny appeared alarmed. 'I don't want to smell like shit,' she cried.

Naomi laughed. 'You won't, trust me.'

Heleny looked sceptical. 'If you're sure.' Her grin returned. 'Anyway, I'd better go and organise the brainstorming meeting. Brilliant! See you at three.'

Inside, Naomi made four litres of lemon tea, stacked it in the fridge, and filled all the ice-cube trays, while her hopes and dreams soared and plummeted.

Who do I think I am . . . my own shop? It will never happen.

'Come on, Bubba, darling. Breakfast outside today while I do your room,' she said cheerfully, manoeuvring her grandmother onto the patio and into the chair.

'You're very perky today. What's going on?' Bubba asked.

'Brainstorming lotions and potions this afternoon. We're having a meeting with our friends, Bubba, so please try and come up with ideas to boost the business.'

'Sounds like fun,' she said. 'Give me the recipe books. I might think of something useful, but don't be disappointed if I can't.'

Naomi stood back and looked at her. 'Do you know, I'm seeing a huge improvement in you every day.'

Bubba frowned. 'My mind seems good and strong after sleeping, but when I get tired, it's as if I get jumbled . . . wires crossed. I see things from the past that have been buried for years. They come back so real that I think I'm there, living it all over again.' She stared at the floor. 'I'm afraid I'll get stuck in one of those dark places, and never return.'

Naomi's heart went out to her. 'Oh, Bubba, you *are* getting better. Don't worry.'

'I wonder if, when my mind is stronger, I should read a little of the diaries, just a page or two, remember, and then come back to now – if you know what I mean. That way, I reckon the old grey matter would get stronger and sort itself out.'

'Like a mental exercise?'

Bubba nodded. 'Also, I want to say this: I don't want to be a burden. When my time comes, Naomi, promise me you won't let them keep my old heart going. No tubes and wires and bleeps. I want to leave with dignity, in my best nighty.'

Naomi swallowed hard. 'You have my word. It will be difficult, because I love you so much, Pandora Cohen.' She pulled in a shaky breath. 'Is there anything else?'

'Yes. Every Clean Monday, when the Christians celebrate the start of Lent, go up Mount Filerimos, fly your kites and remember me . . . and Giovanni, Sonia, Irini and Evangelisa. Take some rose petals down to the harbour and throw them on the water, for Papa and all my family. They never had a funeral, even that was taken from them.'

Naomi nodded, unable to speak.

'And fireworks . . . I'd like to go out with a bang.'

* * *

Naomi bustled all morning. She tried to concentrate on the brainstorming session, but her mind returned to Bubba's words again and again. There was so much she didn't know about her grandmother. Who was Giovanni, and what other secrets from the past would come to light?

After changing Bubba's sheets and dusting her room, Naomi settled her grandmother down for a nap and then started mixing a new perfume for her friend. She leafed through Bubba's book, studied scents she hadn't considered before, and came across one titled *Time to Say Goodbye*. She read through the ingredients.

Powdered Iris: for its lack of warmth.

Ground anis: for its antiseptic qualities.

Oil of grapefruit: for its Alpha male scent.

Aldehydes: that give No. 5 its blast of lioness-danger.

She turned the page for the recipe and found an envelope taped to the paper. Inside was a yellowing cutting from a magazine.

CHANEL No. 5

Pierre and Paul Wertheimer, brothers and directors of the Bourjois perfume house, joined with Chanel in 1924. While the new corporation name – Parfums Chanel – implied a fifty-fifty split in ownership, the Wertheimers in reality retained the rights to marketing, distribution, and – in return for full financial backing – seventy percent ownership.

With the onslaught of World War II and the seizure of all Jewish property, Coco Chanel saw an opportunity. Parfums Chanel had been operating with great financial gain, and Chanel used her Aryan heritage as leverage to petition for sole ownership. This petition was ultimately successful and cemented Coco Chanel as the sole owner of Parfums Chanel, leaving the Wertheimer brothers with nothing of the company they had built.

Naomi would never buy a bottle of Chanel again, then she realised she never had anyway. Far too expensive. She replaced the cutting and set about mixing Heleny's perfume.

With the task completed and Bubba still sleeping, Naomi snatched ten minutes for herself. She sat outside with the diary, eager to discover if this Giovanni was the shepherd boy, and what put him in the same league as Bubba's friend, sister, and daughter.

Chapter 18

Prostrate in the thorn bushes, I nodded at the shepherd boy. 'Yes, I was supposed to be on the ship with my family, but I escaped.'

I caught a glimmer of admiration in his big brown eyes. 'You hurt?' he asked.

'My wrist . . .' Trying to lift it was excruciating. 'I think it's broken.'

'Look at that. Broke as sure as eggshells. You want me to fix it, Jew Girl?'

I didn't believe this shepherd had the knowledge to set bones. 'I should go to the hospital.' The pain made me gulp between words.

'You do and they'll just stick you on the ships with all the other Jews, see. I heard they's killin' them all.' He nodded over his shoulder towards the distant sea.

'What do you mean? How do you know about anything like that? You're making it up to scare me. Well, it's not working, Shepherd Boy. I'm not scared. Not at all!'

'I saw the procession at sunrise, down to the harbour. I got a hammock in the tree up there, guarding your father's sheep against feral dogs. I can see all the way out to sea from that tree.' He lifted his chin towards a gnarled old carob on a rocky promontory above.

The horror of what he said welled up and filled by brain. 'You liar! Why are you saying such things? My family's on that ship! Mama, Papa, my brothers, and all my relations too.'

'Just be glad you're not.'

'If it's true, why didn't you *do* something to stop the soldiers? Somebody should have *done* something! Where are they going?

I can't accept that you actually had that information and we didn't.'

'Of course I knew. Everybody knows. They're shipping them to the prison camp. No one comes out of them places alive. We was told, "look the other way or you'll be next", so everyone did.'

'You're lying! How could people know and do nothing? If our neighbours had been taken away, we'd have fought for them! There must be a hundred Rhodians for every German.' If it wasn't for the pain in my wrist, I'd have hit him.

'Ask yourself: why did they take your wireless? So you wouldn't hear what's happening overseas.' He pulled the catapult out of his belt and laid it next to my arm. 'This'll hurt, but if you scream we'll be in trouble. I need some material to tie your arm to my 'pult before we move.'

I hardly listened to him. My family were heading for an awful prison camp? It couldn't be true!

'Jew Girl!' He pulled me from my thoughts. 'What shall I use for strapping your wrist to the splint?'

Unable to concentrate on anything but my loved ones, I said, 'We have to stop the ships! The Germans told everyone they were going to work on another island.'

'We can't do a thing until your wrist's bound. Shall I rip a strip off your frock?'

'No, take it off my petticoat.' I was trying not to cry.

The shepherd boy's words hurt as much as my wrist. How could they put my family in a prison, and where was this place? Would there be a doctor to care for my mother's bad legs? Would there be a comfortable bed for my grandfather and his crooked back? Had Mama packed the hot water bottle for when Sammie got earache? My head was full of questions.

'Stay still. I'll get it off you,' he said.

The pain increased, throbbing knives that slashed right up to the backs of my eyes. Every movement made it worse. I lay almost face down in the scrub. He moved around to my feet and his hand slid up my leg. 'Touch anything you're not supposed to and I'll scream my head off.'

'Full of gratitude, aren't you, Jew Girl?' He tugged at my petticoat.

'Can't you just tear a strip off the bottom?' I squeezed back tears and bit my lip.

He did, then he pulled the rubber sling off his catapult and pocketed it. I suspected he'd cut it from an inner tube.

While he strapped my wrist to the catapult, his great mop of dark hair hung over my face. It had a strong herby smell that I was trying to place when he said, 'What you sniffin' me like a dog for?'

My cheeks burned. 'Sorry. Your hair's very shiny, but it smells . . . unusual.'

He put his arms around me and helped me to sit, answering my question as he did so. His mouth was next to my ear and, as he spoke, strange tingling sensations passed through me and my heart raced. For a moment, I felt safe in his embrace, and then oddly excited. I put my shivery feelings down to delayed shock, from the fall.

'It's rosemary. Stops me gettin' nits off the sheep, see?'

'Nits!' That brought me back to reality. My head itched at the mention and I pulled away from him.

'You're brave, Jew Girl,' he said breathily. I saw a glimmer of admiration in his eyes, but there again, perhaps it was annoyance. 'We must get away from here, this place is too close to the Axis camp.'

He frowned and squinted into the sun, towards Filerimos, where I hoped Irini and Evangelisa were still waiting for me. But what if they had been captured? What if the Germans had put Irini and Evangelisa straight onto a boat – a different boat from Mama and Papa? Were they safer on a ship than here? Was the shepherd boy telling the truth? He looked like a liar and a thief, and how could I know he wasn't?

All kinds of horrors raced through my mind.

'I have to get to our sheep hut, I've been away three days. My sister—' I stopped myself. What if the business with the bike was all an act? The shepherd boy might be a traitor.

'You've got a sister?'

Could I trust him? I peered into his eyes and decided I had no choice. 'My sister and friend are alone, waiting for me. They've no notion of what's happened in town.'

He made a sling from another strip of material and knotted it behind my neck. I got to my feet and crouched in the undergrowth while he hid his bicycle in the bushes.

We both listened for army traffic, deciding when it was safe to follow the sheep track to the monastery.

'Now!' the shepherd boy exclaimed. 'Stay low, and when I say, "down!" drop into the scrub, right?'

'Right.'

We ran uphill, towards the monastery. My arm seemed to explode with every step and, in less than a hundred metres, I had to walk.

'What's your name, Shepherd Boy?'

'Giovanni Pastore, shepherd. My family have been shepherds since Byzantium. What's yours, Jew Girl?' he said sarcastically.

'Pandora Cohen. Why did you kiss me like that?!'

''Cause I wanted to. My father says you should do what you want with women, so I did. You're the first woman I got a chance to kiss. You objectin' or somethin'?'

A weird little spark of pride went off inside me at being referred to as a woman. 'Yes, I'm objecting! You so much as smile at my sister or my friend and I'll make you sorry you ever did.' I stammered.

'You talk a lot, Jew Girl.'

'And stop calling me that. It's not polite!'

'Why? You ashamed, or what?'

'No. What have I got to be ashamed about?'

'The weird things you lot do. I'd be ashamed.'

I pulled my chin in and stared at him. 'You're talking rubbish, Shepherd Boy!' Then I had to ask, 'What weird things?'

'Killing babies and drinking their blood, for a start.'

'*What?!* What a preposterous thing to say. Why would anyone invent horrible stories like that?'

'Because it's true, I've been told.'

'Do you believe everything you're told, boy? Because if you do, you set yourself up for pure ridicule. There'll be lots of people laughing behind your back.'

He stopped in his tracks and frowned. After a moment he said, 'So it's not true? You don't drink their blood?'

'Of course it's not true!' Then I couldn't help myself. 'We roast them on a spit,' I said quietly. He looked absolutely horrified. Unable to keep my face straight a moment longer, I burst out laughing.

He appeared confused, but then understood the joke.

'All right, you got me. To be honest, I never believed it anyway.' The vegetation grew higher as we approached the woodland.

We continued in silence and eventually pushed through the trees that surrounded our hut.

'Dora!' Evangelisa cried, running to meet us. 'What happened to you?'

Relieved that they weren't on the ship, I introduced Irini and my sister to Giovanni before telling them I had fallen and broken my wrist.

'Is there any water in the hut, Irini? I'm terribly thirsty.'

She nodded and fetched me a glass, which I gulped down before even saying thanks.

Evangelisa started crying, 'I want to go home! You left us all alone for days, Dora. I was scared you wouldn't come back.'

I put my arm around her shoulders. 'Look, we'll return home soon. Mama and Papa have gone to work on another island for a few days, so we'll have an adventure living in the sheep hut while they're away. It'll be fun, you'll see.'

Irini told the shepherd boy, 'We've no food left, even the pine nuts are finished, and Evangelisa's only got one shoe.'

Giovanni promised to bring us something to eat in the morning, and he took my sister's broken shoe with him. He jerked his head sideways at Irini and said, 'Come with me, we'll get some wild pears and pomegranates.'

I had the measure of him straightaway. I wasn't going to let the shepherd boy kiss my friend. 'You stay here, Irini. I'll go,' I said squinting at Giovanni.

He scowled.

'But what about your arm?' Irini looked disappointed. 'You should rest it. Besides, I've been cooped up for days, Dora.' She glanced at Evangelisa. 'I *really* need a break.' She took the contents of my bag into the hut, slung the duffel onto her back, and then followed Giovanni.

'Don't you dare try anything, Shepherd Boy!' I called after them.

Frantic about Mama and Papa and, also, in severe pain, I went to lie down. I must have fallen asleep immediately. Evangelisa woke me.

'Dora, I'm hungry.'

'Evangelisa! My wrist's broken and it hurts a lot, our family are on a ship bound for God knows where, and my friend's just gone into the woods with an uncouth shepherd boy. I'm shocked that all you can think about is your belly!' I snapped, instantly regretting my outburst.

Evangelisa's lip curled. 'There's no need to be nasty. I want my Mama!' she wailed.

'I'm sorry. Please don't cry.' My own emotions bubbled to the surface. Starving and in pain, my own tears were dangerously close. I took Evangelisa into my arms and hugged her. 'Come on now, be a big girl. We're going to be fine.'

Irini returned alone. She gripped the hem of her skirt which contained a mound of small green pears and one large shiny pomegranate.

'Where's my duffel, Irini?'

'Giovanni's taken it to fill with things for us.'

We ate until stuffed and, as we lay on the bed, we listened to our stomachs gurgling from all the fruit.

I decided to wait until Evangelisa was asleep before I told Irini what had happened. Poor Mama and Papa. I wondered where they were right at that moment.

The candle flickered and shadows danced around the room before the flame gutted. Plunged into darkness, we snuggled up together under an old woollen blanket on the big bed.

Evangelisa squeezed my hand. 'I'm scared, Dora. I can hear strange noises. Perhaps there's a wild animal outside, or really bad people.'

'Don't be silly. It's your imagination playing tricks,' I said calmly. 'Now go to sleep. I'll be right beside you all night.'

Irini had her back to me. When Evangelisa was asleep, I turned over, rested my broken wrist on her waist and whispered, 'Did Giovanni try to kiss you, Irini?'

'Yes, but he asked me not to tell. But we'll never have secrets, will we, Dora?'

I told her about him kissing me, and how I hated it when our teeth clashed together. 'I've decided I don't want to kiss another boy. I found it quite horrible.'

She turned over and gently stroked my face. 'You're doing it wrong, Dora. Be soft and gentle, like this.'

Irini kissed me delicately on the lips. Her breath like a hundred butterflies dancing over my face. I found her mouth much more pleasurable than anything else I had experienced. Then she kissed me a little longer and held me against her.

Before a minute had passed, I was kissing her back and I sensed she enjoyed the practice as much as I did. Comfortable in Irini's embrace, with my body pressed against hers, I relaxed and allowed my mind to drift over all that had happened that day.

I thought about Papa, and my brothers, and poor Mama and her bad legs. Proud Granny with her mischievous smile. Grandpa and his painful lumbago, and Aunt Martha with her perfect makeup and her fine hairnet. Misery and despair filled

every part of my body and I found myself crying for all those that
I loved so much.

'I'm afraid, Irini.'

She held me tightly while I sobbed into the crook of her neck.

'It will be all right,' she whispered. 'I promise. Don't fret now.'

In the darkness of that awful night, I wondered if the shepherd
boy was correct, and my loving family were in for a horrible time.
Were they really gone from my life forever? I refused to accept
they'd be killed. Giovanni was a liar. Oh, Papa, what shall I do?
My tears rose again and I sobbed in Irini's arms.

'What's the matter? Is your arm hurting a lot?' she asked
gently.

I whispered my worst thoughts, that our families might be put
to death in a Nazi prison. She started crying for her parents and
her sister, Eva, too. She pleaded with me to tell her everything
I'd experienced, and all about her family as I'd seen them in
L'Aeronautica. She even made me describe what they wore,
right down to her mother's shoes.

I woke in the night with my arms around Irini. We fit together
like two spoons. I felt I was holding my entire family and I recalled
each in turn, the unique things about them, individual qualities,
and special moments we had shared. How could I get used to
the idea that I'd never see them again? Giovanni was wrong. I
kissed Irini between her shoulder blades and pressed my cheek
against her back. My loved ones would return – they had to.

* * *

This night seems endless. I clung to my friend and stared into the
dark for a long time, afraid of all that the dawn might bring for
those I loved. Unable to go back to sleep, I slipped out of bed,
lit the oil lamp, and finished writing the events of this terrible day.
I have to find a way to help my family. I don't know how, but
there must be something I can do.

Chapter 19

'Yoo-hoo!' Heleny hurried down the street.

Naomi stood and shoved the diary under her seat cushion.

'Is anyone here yet? Am I late?'

'No, you're fine. I've put paper and pencils on the table. I've made iced tea and plated your lovely shortbreads for refreshments; have I forgotten anything?' A Shiver of excitement raced through her. Where would this lead? Then the futility of it all took over. 'Heleny, I'm wasting everyone's time. The truth is I haven't the money to start a business.'

'Well, in that case, you'll just have to go after that job in the sex shop.'

They looked at each other and laughed.

'Poor Georgia, I simply can't help winding her up,' Naomi said.

'Poor nothing, she loves it. Why don't you put your products out, samples for everyone to try?'

'Good idea. By the way, here's your new perfume. *No Man's Land.*' She dabbed a little on Heleny's wrist. 'What do you think?'

Heleny sniffed, frowned, and smiled. 'Unusual, but not unpleasant. I'll give it a go and let you know the result.' She reached out and touched Naomi's arm. 'Thank you.'

'It's me who owes you thanks for organising this brainstorming. I'm quite nervous about it.'

'Naomi!' Bubba, who had slept most of the day, started giving orders. 'Get me into that nice cardigan you bought me for Hanukkah. I want to look good for your business meeting.'

Naomi and Heleny exchanged a grin. They rushed into Bubba's room and smartened her up.

'Lipstick!' Bubba cried.

Naomi applied her peach lip balm.

'Heleny, pass the scissors,' Bubba said. 'Now, cut this bloody plait off! Chop it straight along the back of my neck, I can't wait for the hairdresser's.'

When the deed was done, she asked for a mirror and nodded at her reflection, fluffing her hair with her good hand. 'Smashing! Get me to the table before anyone else comes. I don't want to come across as an invalid. Let's have a splash of your sexy perfume, child, and a large glug of wine to start the ideas flowing.'

Naomi blinked at her. 'Sometimes you astound me.' Minutes later they raised their glasses in a toast.

'To Pandora's Box,' Heleny said, and they chinked.

Papas Yiannis and Marina arrived, followed by Georgia. They gathered around the table and Naomi explained the reason for the meeting. Heleny said they should do it properly and she would keep the minutes. The priest asked about finances. Georgia suggested household products that Naomi should consider, such as lavender pillows and wardrobe sachets to repel moths.

'Can I say something else?' Georgia picked up a pot of cream. 'Pandora's products, shouldn't they be in a square container? Like Pandora's Box?'

'Good point,' Naomi said. 'What do you think, Marina?'

The priest's granddaughter seemed slightly startled. She shrugged. 'I don't know . . .'

'You mustn't be shy,' Heleny said. 'You're young, and you took business studies, so your thoughts will interest us all.'

138

'I . . . I don't like to say.' She stared at the table top. 'I love the perfume and the idea, but it all seems old fashioned and a bit boring, actually. Sorry.'

Everyone blinked at her, slightly embarrassed.

Naomi broke the silence. 'No, that's great. Exactly what we need to hear.' She patted Marina's hand. 'Keep going. What would you do if it was your business?' She glanced around the table. 'It's the young that have money to spend, so we have to recognise what appeals to them.'

Marina nodded. 'I don't understand why you want a shop. It seems mad. You should have a website, and a blog, and do makeup videos for YouTube. You could have online launch parties for new products, record wild flower walks and talk about essential oils, and get your range into the local chemists. Or consider direct selling on a large scale, like to some cosmetic companies. Why restrict yourself with the work, expense, and limited location of physical premises?'

They all stared at her.

'Sorry . . . sorry,' she muttered.

'No, that's great!' Naomi noticed a flash of pride in the priest's eyes. 'But I'm not sure I'd be able to cope with the Internet stuff.'

'Why not take on a partner who's good at that sort of thing?' Marina said. 'That would leave you free to continue with what you excel at: the products. I'd work full time for forty per cent of the net.'

Naomi's mouth fell open.

'Think of it like this,' Marina carried on, bolder now. 'The more we earn, the more I make. It would be in my interest to do everything I can to boost the business. The first thing I'd do is go to the bee museum, get them to display your products, and cut a deal for beeswax and honey, and anything else you use that comes out of the hive. It's all very well using the broken church candles, but you need to be able to cost a product properly in order to price it correctly.' She glanced around the table and, seeing she had everyone's attention, she continued. 'On the downside, there is a lot to be paid for in advance to set up any business.'

Naomi absorbed all this and could see Marina was right. 'How do you mean, that last point about money?'

'Well, if you wish to expand outside Rhodes and your local friends, there's testing, shelf life, and patenting to deal with, all essential, expensive, but necessary to get your range into the big stores. You need a certified accountant to set up a limited company, and he'll want paying. The biggest money eater of all is advertising.'

Naomi's hopes plummeted.

'No, don't be disheartened,' Marina continued. 'You have the most important thing, the first line of products. It's just a case of taking one hurdle at a time. There's no timescale for going global is there? It is simply the ultimate goal.' They all stared at her and she faltered. 'Naomi, I may have a degree in Business Studies, but I can't advise you on everything. I'm only a shop girl selling shoes to earn a monthly wage. But I'm sure of this, we need money, a backer. There are people out there looking for new lines, and there's funding on the Internet.' She picked up a little pot of lip gloss. 'Did you know that Greek women spend more on cosmetics than any other country in Europe?'

They all shook their heads.

'Anyway, in my opinion the name is brilliant. It covers all angles.'

'How do you mean?' Naomi asked.

'Well, Pandora's Box, the whole mythology thing, gives you the perfect titles for various categories. The Graces, there's a tag for your mature skin range. Perfume, Aphrodite. Aftershave, Zeus. Helios, sun creams and lotions. Evil *has* to be the young makeup line – black eyes and dark lipstick. You don't have to stick to the actual legend, just hint at it.'

'But I can't produce things like mascara,' Naomi said.

'No, but the Chinese can. We have a lot to talk about, and even more to research, but first, I'd like to suggest a target: five years to get Pandora's Box into a major supermarket.' She looked at each in turn. 'What do you think?' Stunned silence filled the room.

A thrill raced through Naomi.

The old lady was the first to speak. She nodded at Pappas Yiannis. 'This granddaughter of yours isn't just a pretty face. She's got a brain too.'

Naomi tried to consider all that Marina had suggested. 'But what on earth could I blog about? I've lived here all my life. I'm not in the least bit interesting.'

'Sorry, but you're wrong, Naomi,' Marina said. She glanced around the table again, and seeing all eyes on her she seemed to grow a little. 'Actually, you're *amazing*. I'd be fascinated to hear how you started, where your recipes came from, what improvement certain ingredients bring about. What's behind the name "Pandora"? I want to know everything, and others will too. Using basic and pure ingredients is a bonus; people don't like chemicals on their skin. You've got heaps going for you.'

Naomi felt a spark of hope. 'Thirty-five per cent, and you have yourself a deal, Marina!' she said.

They shook hands across the table.

Everyone clapped and nodded, and Marina beamed at her new partner.

'Contract!' Bubba said, primping her hair. 'As the founder of this business, before anything goes any further, I insist all agreements are put down in writing by Heleny, signed and witnessed.'

Heleny turned to the back of her minutes notebook and started scribbling.

Marina said, 'Let's get the ball rolling right now. Open a Facebook page for Pandora's Box.'

'I'm not on Facebook.'

Georgia got up and collected Naomi's laptop from the kitchen counter. 'You'll have one in five shakes, Naomi. Budge up so I can sit beside you.'

'I seem to be redundant,' the priest said. 'Shall I pour everyone a drink before I go?'

'Just a moment, Grandpa. We need two witnesses for the contract, and there's only you and Georgia that aren't involved.'

The meeting went on until evening. When the brainstormers had returned to their homes, Naomi and Bubba were peculiarly quiet, each with her thoughts. Once Naomi had put her grandmother to bed, she experienced a wave of exhaustion and decided on an early night herself.

She woke at dawn and, as had become a habit, made her coffee and sat outside with the diary, eager to see the sunrise and learn more about Bubba's life.

Chapter 20

Monday, 24 July 1944

It has been another difficult day but, thanks to the shepherd boy, I may be able to help my family. I woke from a deep sleep at daybreak. The hut was in darkness and, for a moment, I was confused with no memory of where I was or who I was with. Filled with panic that the knowledge I needed might somehow be kept from me, or that I had lost my mind, I bolted upright. Sweat dampened my face and my heart pounded against my ribs.

The pain in my wrist brought the horrible events of Sunday back to me.

I slid out from between the warm bodies of Irini and Evangelisa and saw the diary still lay on the table next to the oil lamp, after my midnight scribblings. Not wanting Evangelisa to read what had happened to our family, I slid the journal under the mattress before I crept outside the hut.

The atmosphere was moist and fresh, heavy with the perfume of pine, as if the island had been disinfected overnight. Dew covered the ground and hung like glass beads from the tips of leaves and wild flowers. I sat on the log, watching the forest wake. The air filled with birdsong. Insects with iridescent wings buzzed sleepily from one blossom to another hunting for nectar.

The sky became a watercolour of peach and pale grey. The sun and the Turkish mountains peeked over a ghostly veil of morning mist. The breeze shifted, the air suddenly drenched in the perfume from the crimson rose bush that rambled over our front door. The blooms hung, full and heavy, against dull, weathered planks. A recent fall of petals, fat and bright as fresh blood, covered the ground. They would soon shrivel, fade, and blow away. Forgotten.

I recalled planting that shrub with Mama; one of my earliest memories.

The rose bush had been little more than a twig. While I helped her stuff soil around its roots, Papa and Danial roasted a lamb over a pit. Mama glanced at them and laughed. 'There's something about men and fire, Dora. Look at those two, in their element. It doesn't matter how advanced man gets; that bit of caveman never leaves.'

Daydreaming about it, I could smell the roasting meat, the oregano, and the pungent charcoal. Such a glorious day. Mama hasn't laughed like that for a long time.

Sammie and Jacob collected snails, placing them in an old orange crate filled with sage. They'd feed on the herb for a week, before Mama cooked them. My brothers were teasing each other, Sammie trying to get a small snail to balance on Jacob's nose. Jacob laughing and going cross-eyed watching it. Papa caught my eye, smiled broadly and winked. Even when I was that young, I loved him more than anybody.

As I reminisced, the sun appeared through the mist. A huge yellow ball that silhouetted a couple of hooded crows, croaking untunefully. I promised myself that when my family comes back, we'll return to the hut, enjoy the scent of roses, roast a lamb, and eat together.

Giovanni and his dog broke through the bushes. *How dare he kiss Irini?!* I wasn't sure if I wanted to speak to him.

'I've brought you a lump of boiled mutton and half a loaf of heavy bread,' he called holding out the bulging duffel. My resolution to be horrible waivered. I was so hungry my stomach gnawed at my ribs. The dog was huge. A comical short-haired creature, buttery yellow with black extremities. It seemed to be wearing an oversized head and paws, which suggested it was a pup. It loped around the shepherd boy, its tail curled along its back, and its wide face turned up, waiting for a command.

Giovanni drew a line in the air with his finger, and the dog immediately sat at his feet.

144

'She's Kopay, a Turkish sheepdog,' he said. 'Only a year old, so I have to be strict with her, see.' He grabbed a handful of loose skin on Kopay's neck. 'Come forward and let her sniff your hand.'

I went to go down on my knees. 'No! Always be above your dog, right? She could kill you in a moment. In Turkey, they protect the flock from bears three times your size.'

'A real beast, then.' I held out my arm, calmly. Animals sense fear, I understood that. Kopay snuffled my palm, dropped her head to one side and fidgeted back a step.

'She respects you,' Giovanni said.

'That pleases me. What would I have done if she hadn't?'

'Climb the nearest tree.' He laughed. 'You should have a dog up here to warn you if anyone's about.'

'We haven't enough food for ourselves. How would we manage an extra mouth to feed?'

I entered the hut and woke Irini and Evangelisa. Together, we pulled a small table to the edge of the bed and put knives, forks, and plates out as Mama would have done.

The shepherd boy produced a saddle needle and some gut and began fixing Evangelisa's footwear. 'I didn't have time last night,' he explained. 'Had another flock to deliver.' He set the shoe on a log in the hearth and used a flat stone to knock the needle through the leather. Evangelisa watched him, admiration shining from her eyes.

Frantic about my family, I kept seeing that picture of them in my head, crammed onto the dreadful ship.

'Giovanni, are the ships still in the port? Is it possible to stop them leaving and set our families free?'

He shook his head, avoiding my eyes. 'They've gone to Simi or Kos. They're not coming back, get used to it,' he said quietly, out of Evangelisa's earshot.

'No, I refuse to accept it. There must be something I can do!' Poor Mama and Papa. At least my brothers were with them. I was confident Danial and Papa would take care of everyone. Hopefully, they'd find a way to escape together.

Evangelisa gawped at Giovanni with her cow eyes. She might be taller, and far more beautiful than me, but she can be very shallow and it's embarrassing. Still, I must remember she's only a girl, so I forgive her.

I glanced at Irini and, as if reading my thoughts, she rolled her eyes and said to Giovanni, 'How do you know where the ships are going?'

'One of the *Andartes* told me.'

'You're friends with the rebels?' Irini stared at him, then turned to me and made an O with her mouth.

'Outside, please, Giovanni. I need to speak to you.' I nodded at Irini and Evangelisa and said with authority, 'Stay here, I'll be back in a moment.' I didn't wait for a response, and marched past Giovanni and out of the hut.

My insides quaked, but I had to establish myself as leader. On my birthday, Papa told me there were two kinds of people: those who let things happen and those who make things happen, and I had to decide as an adult which one of those I would be.

I was born a fighter, so the decision had been made with my first breath. I would make things happen.

My music teacher told me timing was as important as pitch. I recalled the conductor of the choir that sang outside my father's shop, a very small man who demanded everyone's obedience. The choir, most of whom were head and shoulders taller, respected him. When he lifted his baton, talking stopped, people stood taller, all eyes were on him.

I admired that man and decided that I would take his example. Nobody would see me acting silly, degrading myself or anyone else. I would give credit where it was due, put others before myself, and not give in to false flattery. I would be as self-confident and respected as the choirmaster.

I waited on the log. The cabin door squeaked. I sat taller. A moment later Giovanni was beside me.

I took a breath, the new adult growing inside me. After a short silence I said, 'I want to thank you for fixing my wrist. You did a good job.'

'I've fixed many a broken leg before.'

I figured he was lying and wanted to say so, but that would be childish. I squared my shoulders and turned to face him.

'On the sheep,' he said, reading my disbelief.

I nodded, surprised my restraint had brought the truth rather than a squabble. 'I have to see the *Andartes*. Can you fix that too?'

'What for? They can't make it no better.' He nodded at my wrist.

'I believe you're right, but I want to speak to them about my family on the ship; ask if they can do anything or if they've heard where the boats are going.'

'I told you: they're being taken to the prison camps. Get used to it. You won't see them again.'

His words cut into me like knives fresh off the grinder. My fists clenched. A bolt of pure agony shot from my broken bone to my shoulder. I whimpered, yet welcomed the pain. That mind-numbing feeling annihilated my grief and helplessness. I screwed my eyes closed, grabbed my wrist, and held it to my chest.

'It's bad, isn't it?' Giovanni said. 'Here, have a go at this. It'll help.'

I opened my eyes as he pulled a bent, hand-rolled cigarette from his pants pocket and lit it with a greasy lighter.

I shook my head. 'No, thanks.'

'Really, this isn't ordinary tobacco, it's herbal. Dried basil, hemp, and a little cinnamon. My father grows it, a recipe guaranteed to stop pain.'

He held the cigarette towards me and I sucked on the end, exhaling immediately. Smoke stung my eyes and I ended up sniffing back tears and coughing.

'You're doing it wrong. Look. Breathe out, suck air in through the cigarette, and hold the smoke for as long as possible.' He passed it to me. 'It'll make you dizzy, but the pain will ease.'

I tried again. For a moment everything receded and my head spun, before a coughing fit took over.

'Disgusting!' The word came out half swallowed. I handed it back and pulled in a few deep breaths.

'Yeah, but the pain's going, eh?'

I nodded. 'What's that writing on the paper?' Braver now, I plucked the cigarette from his fingers and gave it another try.

'Holy stuff. My dad don't have fag papers, but the Bible pages in church are perfect for rollin', real thin and shiny like. I takes a few every time I go into Agios Marinos church, and I use a bit of tree resin for the glue.'

'You take them from the church? Bible pages? But . . .' I couldn't believe that I'd helped to burn Bible pages to ash. The Christian Bible in Agios Marinos was not exactly my religion, but burning any religious book had to be a big sin. 'Oh dear, what about God?' I whispered, almost afraid I'd be struck down right there.

Giovanni shrugged. 'God don't smoke, far as I know.'

I had to think about that. My brain had gone to sleep, lulled, I guess, by the dubious cigarette, but a moment later I found myself giggling uncontrollably. 'God don't smoke!' I repeated, finding the words inexplicably funny.

Giovanni beamed at me.

'It's working then?' he said. 'I always smoke when things get too bad. It helps. What do you do?'

'What do you mean: when things get bad?'

'Sometimes my dad gets drunk and gives me a clout. Hit me with a plank once; broke my arm, so I understand what you're going through.' He nodded at my wrist. 'What do you do to cope with pain?'

'Things never got this awful before.' I thought for a moment. 'Once, I had appalling toothache. It nearly drove me insane, so I sang until it went away.'

'You sing when you're hurtin'? That's weird, singing's for being happy, see. I get to sing with the choir sometimes. Papa makes me scrub up till my skin's stingin', and I have to wear my best clothes, but I don't mind because I like singing. You don't sing when you're hurtin' though. Least, I don't.'

'I do.'

He stared at me for a moment. 'I've just realised who you are, the girl with perfect pitch, from the shop in town.' I smiled, pleased he remembered me. 'Sing something now,' he said.

'Can't. I'm not in the mood. Will you teach me some choir things, voice exercises?'

He nodded, our eyes met and for a moment I forgot everything. I found his company calming one minute and exciting the next. 'What did you want to talk about?' he said.

'About the bandits. Do you really know them?'

'Sure. They rely on shepherds to pass information. Same on all the islands.'

'Will you take me to meet them, the *Andartes*?'

'They'd kill me.'

I tutted. 'You're lying about knowing them, aren't you?'

His head snapped round. 'No! But I'd get into trouble if I brought a group of girls to their hideout. Anyway, they wouldn't want to speak to strangers, would they?'

'Then they'd be stupid. I could give them information about what went on at L'Aeronautica. But if they're not interested, fine!'

'What happened?'

'Do you think I'm that unwise, Shepherd Boy? Take me to meet them and I'll tell the leader of the rebels, nobody else.'

After a long silence he said, 'All right, I'll talk to them later, ask if they'll see you.'

'Do that, and hey, guess what? I'm not a girl, I'm a woman, so get used to it!' Sometimes, I got sick of having to shout about my age to be taken seriously.

He huffed. 'We must get the sheep. Your flock's on the other side of the woods; it'll take all morning to fetch them uphill.' He

149

put his hands on his hips and stared at the sheering pens. 'Got to repair that fence first. The shearers leave soon, so we'd better move ourselves.'

'You're not listening; I need to speak with the *Andartes!*' I yelled, standing up.

'You all right?' Irini's voice came from behind me.

'No, I'm not! This stupid . . .' I bit my lip. Childish behaviour wouldn't get me anywhere. 'Sorry, Giovanni,' I said. 'I *am* grateful, but I feel so helpless.'

He nodded. 'Let's go and eat. Don't know about you, but I'm starved.'

We returned to the hut where Evangelisa sat at the table gazing at the hunk of boiled mutton.

'Look, Giovanni,' I continued, 'I'm in charge of the sheep. They're my responsibility, so don't worry about them. Get me to the *Andartes*. That's all I ask.'

Irini's eyes flicked to mine and widened. I gave her a nod. She returned to preparing the food, breaking bread into chunks, adding a sprinkle of oregano and salt followed by a drizzle of olive oil.

My stomach growled. Giovanni reached for the bread.

'Wait!' Evangelisa cried. 'We must say the *Hamotzi.*'

'What?' Giovanni said.

'Wash your hands.' She nodded at the bucket of water by the table.

He dropped the bread, looked at his hands and said, 'They's clean.'

'You can't eat with us if you don't,' she said, shocking us all with her authority. 'Dora, please say the *Hamotzi.*'

I grinned at Irini. This was a new side of my sister, and I liked it. '*Blessed are You, O Lord our God, King of the universe, who has sanctified us with his commandments and commanded us on the washing of hands.*'

150

We took it in turns to dip our hands into the bucket and then dry them on an old towel folded on the table. Everyone watched me. I nodded, and we started on the bread.

'Wait!' Giovanni said arrogantly. 'We can't start until we've said Grace.'

We stared at him. He touched his forehead, chest, and each shoulder, put his hands together, and said, '*For what we are about to receive, may The Lord make us truly grateful.*' He looked at us in turn and said, 'Say, Amen.' We did. 'What are you waiting for? Eat!' he said.

We ate ravenously, stuffing meat and bread in our mouths and gulping cold water collected from the nearby spring.

We'd barely satisfied ourselves when Giovanni sighed, looking from Irini to me. 'You'll have to pay me. One ewe and two lambs, right?'

'One ewe, and we'll shear the sheep ourselves,' I said.

'Ha! You've no idea how to shear.'

'We'll learn, don't fret. You can have a lamb in exchange for three sets of shears.'

'Three lambs for three shears,' he replied.

'You get two lambs and a ewe. I get three shears, and you show me how to use them. That's it. Deal?' I asked.

'One ewe and two lambs in exchange for a meeting with the *Andartes* and three sets of shears, okay, and I'll give you a hand to round up the sheep.'

I nodded once.

He spat on his palm, wiped it down his trouser leg, and held out his hand.

I did the same. We shook hands and Giovanni stood to leave.

'Wait!' Evangelisa cried again. 'Dora, prayers please.'

Giovanni rolled his eyes. 'Not again . . .'

'It would be nice if Irini did the honours; what do you say, Evangelisa?' I asked. She nodded.

151

Irini said, 'Blessed art thou, O Lord our God, King of the universe, who feeds the whole world with thy goodness, with grace, with loving kindness and tender mercy. Thy great goodness food hath never failed us. O may it never fail us for ever and ever for thy great name's sake, since thou nourishes and sustains all beings and does good unto all, and provides food for all thy creatures whom thou hast created. Blessed art thou, O Lord, who gives food unto all.'

'Grief!' Giovanni exclaimed. 'You Jews are a long-winded lot. My turn now.'

He crossed himself again, put his hands together and said, 'Thank God for a good meal, Amen.' He glanced at each of us and said, 'You may leave the table.' He turned to me. 'Right, I'll talk to the Andartes, then I'll help get the sheep up.'

* * *

When Giovanni returned he had a swagger in his walk. 'Nathanial, the Andartes leader, will see you at noon tomorrow.' He stuck his chest out and did a head waggle. When he grinned, an odd little spark exploded inside me and I realised I was grinning back.

It seemed a long wait, but I had no choice.

'Let's get the sheep,' Giovanni said. 'You'll need sticks. Hold your arms out to herd them. Don't chase sheep that break away; the dog'll bring them back, right?'

Excited by the challenge, I thought herding couldn't be too difficult, could it?

Giovanni strolled to the pens and threw a sack down. 'That's your shears. I'll give you a lesson later.'

Chapter 21

Bromley, London.

Rebecca listened to the ringtone and knew that it would be Naomi. Her sister was waiting for her to pick up. She'd rehearsed what to say when they spoke next: that she didn't want to get involved. What was the point? The Greeks weren't going to give the Jewish population their belongings back. She hovered, hesitated, and finally picked up. The call had timed out.

Why was all this happening now? Rebecca was six weeks pregnant for the first time in her life. At the clinic, they told her all the signs were good. Each day, each hour, was lived on the knife edge of hope. She decided to tell Fritz the brilliant news that evening, unable to keep it from him any longer.

The phone rang again. She picked up immediately.

'Rebecca, please don't hang up,' Naomi said breathlessly, nerves still apparent in her voice. 'The court case has been brought forward. We've only got a short time left to prepare. Please say you'll come over.'

'Naomi, it's difficult.' She paused for a beat. 'I don't think—'

'I realise I'm asking a lot after all that happened,' Naomi interrupted. 'I understand that, but this is very important, not only to us, but to the entire diaspora of the Rhodes Juderia. People are coming from all over the world – Canada, Australia, Israel – in the hope they will get their property back.'

Rebecca hesitated.

'And Bubba's desperate to make peace with you. Rebecca, I don't know anything about your life. You've probably got kids, and it's school-term time.' Naomi's words sliced through

Rebecca like a knife. 'Perhaps you have a job and it's difficult to get leave. I understand all that. I've been there myself, but a lot of people are depending on the result of this case. It will set a precedent for the thousands that were mercilessly robbed, not only of their loved ones, but also of every stick of their possessions.'

'I want to help, Naomi, I really do, but—'

'Please, Rebecca. I'm begging you,' Naomi said. 'What could be more important?'

'I, oh, Naomi . . .' Rebecca choked on rising tears. 'There's a lot you don't know.'

She heard Naomi gasp. 'Good God, Rebecca! What's the matter? What's going on?'

Rebecca swallowed hard and found herself lost for words. Silence hung between them.

Naomi tried again. 'Tell me, Rebecca. Something's awfully wrong . . . I feel it. I'm sorry; I always imagined your life in London was how you always wanted it.'

Too anguished to speak, Rebecca took a breath. 'I can't talk about it right now.' Suddenly, she wished Naomi was with her. She wanted to explain everything to her sister. Ten years of trying to conceive. The pain and the heartbreak of her miscarriages. The hope and the fragility of her current situation.

Naomi would understand. Again, she faltered, telling herself to keep calm. *Breathe.* 'I'll speak to Fritz and give you a definite answer tomorrow morning,' she said before ending the call. She made a mental note to ask Naomi for her email address next time they spoke.

She decided to nail Fritz down, tell him she was pregnant at last. He seemed to be avoiding her, or was her imagination working overtime? Her hormones were all over the place, and he was still up to his eyes in the business. Things would calm down soon, he had promised, and then she hoped they'd take a holiday together.

Rebecca needed time alone with him, although if she were honest, she didn't see a vacation happening in the near future. She had to tell Fritz, but it was like a jinx. She feared that when she told him, she would miscarry. There was no logical reason for her to think that way, but she couldn't help it.

Her home life had become chaotic. She couldn't concentrate. Each day she remained pregnant was an achievement and strengthened her chances of going full term, but also multiplied her anxiety. Her superstitions reached new heights. She wouldn't open the nursery door or glance at the window of a Mothércare shop. Visiting the bathroom was an anxious necessity; she checked for signs of a miscarriage on every occasion.

Mealtimes became disastrous. Unable to concentrate on the simplest food, she double salted potatoes, or forgot the salt altogether. She had taken up yoga, spent hours doing gentle exercises, walking, or resting. Everything was connected to her state of health and her pregnancy.

To make life easier, she ordered meals online and had them delivered. She set the table with her best china, added a centrepiece of red roses, and made an effort with her hair and makeup.

Fritz arrived home that night with stress written all over him. Things hadn't gone well at the office. His mood worsened when he discovered she hadn't collected his suits from the cleaners.

'Make sure you get them in the morning,' he said at the dinner table. 'We've got the reception to launch our advertising campaign tomorrow afternoon.'

'Reception?' Rebecca cried. 'Oh Fritz, I'd forgotten!'

'Rebecca, I just don't believe it. You've nothing to do all day. I depend on you to take care of a few simple things,' he said angrily as she served him Marks & Spencer's moussaka.

'Fritz, I'm sorry, really. The thing is . . .' she hesitated, watched his eyes. He was bound to be thrilled. She blurted her news out, breathless and excited. 'The thing is I'm pregnant, six weeks, and for some insane reason I can't concentrate on anything.'

'Pregnant?' He dropped his cutlery and stared across the table, his anger giving way to disbelief. 'What? I don't understand. How did that happen?'

He didn't appear thrilled at all.

She tried to talk about it but the right words escaped her and eventually she cried, 'You're always too busy . . . You've no idea how painful those hormone injections were, and everything was set up at the IVF, but you're too busy to spend a little time with me these days. You couldn't even spare me one hour of your precious life for such an important thing as having our own baby.'

He continued to stare at her. 'But, we haven't . . . Who's the father?'

She tutted and huffed. 'You're not serious?! *You're* the father, of course. You banked sperm, remember? Or is your head so full of the company merger that it slipped your mind?' Her voice was corrosive and, too late, she regretted the sarcasm.

'Rebecca, stop it,' he cried. 'You have no idea how impossible you've become! You're obsessed with having a baby. The woman I married was fun to be with. She was glamorous, adventurous. She kicked off her heels and danced all night. People loved to come here, to dinner. You were the perfect host.' He pushed his plate away. 'Yesterday, a colleague asked if we're still together. Can you believe that? It made me realise how much we've changed. It's like we're leading separate lives.'

'But I'm six weeks pregnant, Fritz. Listen to me. You're supposed to be thrilled and *still*, all you can do is talk about work! You don't realise how much *you've* changed either.'

He put his elbows on the table and dropped his head into his hands. 'How can I be thrilled when I'm afraid to come home because your dreams might have ended? How can I get excited when I dread the thought of you crying all night after you've miscarried?

'Since we started the IVF treatment I've done everything I can to make life run smoothly for you. I've done my best to remove every element of stress from your day. I don't know what else I can do. Yet all the time, that terrible feeling of failure is hanging over me. The fear that you will go through the trauma of a miscarriage again simply breaks me up, Rebecca. It's more than I can bear. And I'll tell you now: I'm never setting foot in that fucking IVF clinic again!'

Rebecca's heart shattered. She couldn't speak for the pain. Where had all this anger come from? 'But our plans, a family, our children,' she whispered. 'What happened, Fritz? We were so happy.'

'I'm sorry, Rebecca, I really am, but I just can't do this anymore.' He pushed his blond hair back, shook his head, and then dropped it into his hands again. After a long silence, he said, 'I wasn't going to tell you this yet, but I must go to America for a month, soon. I was planning on taking you with me, but I think it might be good for us to spend a little time apart. Decide on our priorities, what we want most out of life.'

'Fritz! Fritz, what are you saying? Are you asking for a separation? Is there somebody else?' Horrified, she stared at him. He didn't answer. 'Please, don't do this to me, please. I love you. I'm pregnant. I'm having our baby!'

A pained look spread over his face. 'No, of course I don't *want* us to be apart, Rebecca. I love you too, more than you know. But I think we need a little time to consider our life goals.' He turned away, staring into the distance. 'I have to go on this trip anyway, so perhaps now's the best moment for some breathing space.'

'But I'm pregnant, Fritz.'

'How many times have you said that? I've come to hate those words because they always lead to heartache. I can only believe the worst. You're going to lose it again and it will tear you apart. I never want to see you so emotionally wrecked as you were last time, Rebecca. I can't stand being so helpless while you go through hell.' He sighed and looked her in the eyes. 'I want to give up the idea of having children. Think about it while I'm away. Learn to accept it.'

Rebecca felt hollow and cold. He simply wasn't getting it. She *was* pregnant, but he was devoid of joy or excitement, or even the hope that she would go full term. She hadn't realised what she'd put him through, or how badly the IVF and her distress had affected him.

'Actually, Naomi's been calling from Greece,' she said quietly. 'She wants me to go home for a week or two.'

Fritz looked up. 'Naomi? Your sister?' His face hardened.

Rebecca glanced towards the window, longing to be in the garden. 'Yes, Bubba's had a stroke, and there's a court case coming up about our family property in the city.'

'Can I do anything? We have a great legal team.'

Rebecca shook her head. 'Thank you. Considering how they treated you, it's noble to offer, but I doubt it. She wants me beside her for the case.'

Fritz stood behind Rebecca's chair and massaged her shoulders. 'A stroke? I am sorry. How is she?'

'I don't know, but I'm worried. We didn't part on the best of terms.' Suddenly, she didn't want him touching her and shrugged from under his hands, instantly regretting it. How could she explain? Whatever happened to Bubba's family wasn't Fritz's fault; it all happened before he was even born. Nor was there any proof that his father or grandfather was an evil Nazi involved in the extermination of the Jews of Rhodes, or any Jews for that matter. Bubba's accusations were a figment of her imagination. She needed to place blame, but had no right to pick on the man Rebecca loved.

'In my opinion, you should go to Rhodes, darling. We both need a break – think things through. You can't put our lives on hold every time you might be pregnant.'

Calmer now, she considered his suggestion. 'Perhaps. You do mean it though, don't you, Fritz? You do still love me? You're my world. I didn't realise all this had been so difficult for you. I'm terribly sorry.' Rebecca stood, and moved into his arms. 'I do love you, Fritz. I could never love anyone the way I love you.' She kissed him.

'And I love you, darling,' he murmured, pulling her to him, and then he kissed her passionately and slid his hands up the inside of her sweater, cupping her bare breasts.

She struggled from his arms. 'I can't, Fritz. I don't want to take a chance.'

'For God's sake, Rebecca! I'm a man. It's been almost two months!'

'I'm sorry, I know, but . . .' Her emotions welled up and tears broke free. 'I'm sorry, so sorry, darling.'

He sighed. 'Me too,' he said softly, taking her into his arms again. 'Like I say, we've become obsessed. I'm as much to blame. Let's try and get back to how we were, shall we?'

She nodded and pressed against his chest. 'I'll go to Rhodes,' she said. 'Naomi's been sending me Bubba's diaries from the war. They're fascinating, and tragic.'

'Really.' His voice hardened again. 'Your grandmother still believes my family's personally responsible for the murder of her family and millions of other Jews? Even if they were, she's grossly unfair pinning that on me.'

Rebecca thought about what she'd read in the diary. 'You'd understand if you knew what happened to her. That's why she sent me the gun.'

'*Gun?!* What gun?'

'Those parcels, they weren't car parts. It was a gun, Bubba's pistol.'

'Good God! What do you mean, Bubba's gun?'

'She was a freedom fighter, an assassin, in the war.'

'Bubba, the old lady?'

Rebecca nodded.

After a moment, Fritz said, 'Can I read the diary?'

'That's the exact reaction they hoped to get from me when they sent the weapon,' Rebecca said.

Chapter 22

Rhodes, Greece.

The receiver rattled in the cradle when Naomi hung up. Why she got herself into such a state about phoning her sister, she didn't know. Yet she sensed something was terribly wrong in London. Her heart went out to Rebecca, practically all alone with problems that she was reluctant to talk about, even to her sister. She probably had lots of friends to offer her support, but there was nothing like family, everyone recognised that. Naomi scribbled on a post-it note: *get Rebecca's email address.*

Bubba's voice came from the next room. 'Plato, not Shakespeare, you fool!' the old lady yelled at the TV quiz.

Naomi smiled. Her grandmother's recovery was gaining momentum. Her delusions were less frequent, and she persevered with her exercises, building strength in her affected limbs.

The young always think they're capable of anything, she thought, but they have no concept of what the elderly can overcome. She thought about Marina. Would this partnership work? With maturity, Naomi had come to realise that most challenges weren't as easy as you first perceive. But she had made a commitment and told herself – as she so often had when unsavoury nursing tasks revolted her – she would just have to get on with it.

She picked up the diary, stared at the brown paper cover spattered with water stains, and traced them with her finger. Had

Dora cried over the journal? Where was she and what was on her mind when those tears fell?

Her thoughts returned to her sister. How was life in London, she wondered. Was she happy? Did she have children? Did she ever think about Naomi and their childhood?

Bubba had always struggled for money, accepting any work that came her way, often leaving Naomi in charge of her sister in the afternoons. Every spare moment of Bubba's day was taken by cooking, cleaning, sewing and knitting.

She recalled the shiny yellow dresses with stiff net petticoats, and red hand-knitted twinsets with mother-of-pearl buttons. Bobble hats and mittens for the winter. Bubba dressed her and Rebecca the same, but it was Rebecca who received the compliments. 'She's so pretty!' people would say. And she was.

When Naomi was thirteen, Bubba, who already had a part-time job at the school, got a couple of hours' employment at the grocer's every afternoon. Their lives changed for the better. Bubba wore her best clothes to work, and put on powder and red lipstick. Naomi was so proud of her.

'You look like a film star, Bubba,' she said, and her grandmother preened.

A few weeks into the shop job, Rebecca, who was nearly four years old, fell down the stone steps. When Bubba saw the huge egg-shaped lump on Rebecca's forehead she went crazy.

'What on earth were you doing, Naomi? You were supposed to be watching her! Can't I trust you with anything?' she shouted.

'I was on the toilet, Bubba.' Naomi had put a cold flannel on the bump, hoping it would go down before Bubba's return, and she had given Rebecca a teaspoon of honey to shut up her wailing. Obviously, her efforts where not good enough. Stung by Bubba's words, Naomi rushed outside, sat on the ground in Spartili Street and cried.

She drew her knees up, rested her head on them, and gave her tears and sobs full reign. Presently, a giant-like figure sat next to her, his heavy arm slid around her shoulders. Papas Yiannis pulled her to him and said, 'She loves you, you know? Only, things are hard for her right now.'

'I did my best, but it's never good enough. I want Mama and Papa! They *really* loved me . . .'

After a short silence he said, 'One day, when you're much older, you will understand just how much your grandmother loves you. But for now, you'll have to take my word for it. So, come on, big girl, I think Mrs Voskos has some spoon sweet. Let's go and find out, shall we?'

He never explained. With the memory, Naomi's curiosity was reignited. She opened the diary again.

The shearing was a catastrophe. Giovanni sheared one sheep, talking his way through it.

'Right, push her rump down, girls, turn her onto her back, and keep her feet off the floor. Then snip down her belly, careful not to cut her teats.'

It seemed easy. He snipped away while the sheep appeared docile in his hands.

'Have you got it?' Giovanni asked, holding the creature still with no apparent effort. The sheep wasn't distressed, and appeared clean and tidy when he released it. 'I must leave. I've work to do,' he said.

'We'll be fine, don't worry,' I assured him.

We only managed a total of three sheep all afternoon, and they looked nothing like sheep when we'd finished with them. Great tufts of fleece dangled from half-shorn beasts, and we were black and blue from struggling to turn the wriggling kickers that weighed more than the three of us together.

I found it impossible to shear with my broken wrist, so I helped Evangelisa. Irini struggled on her own.

Irini's sheep succeeded in spinning itself upright, and engaged Irini in a wrestling match that ended up with Irini rolling on the ground with the creature. In the scrabble, the sheep scraped his hoof down her hip and got its hind leg stuck down the side of her knickers. The ewe did a three-legged race towards the woods, hauling flailing Irini with it.

Evangelisa and I grabbed Irini's arms. Unfortunately, the lunatic sheep continued to gallop, dragging Irini's pants off, and also one shoe, which we found later.

The three of us gave up, exhausted and disappointed. We had failed at what appeared to be a reasonably simple task.

I gave Irini my spare underwear. We fell into bed, too tired to wash or eat. Our muscles burned, our bruises hurt, and Irini had a nasty friction burn on the back of one thigh. We decided to try and get someone else to shear, like Giovanni. It would cost a couple of ewes, and I know he would make us eat humble pie.

* * *

The hut is silent now, apart from the occasional dream-drenched mutterings from Irini and Evangelisa who are both sleeping restlessly in the bed. I am so tired my head is buzzing, and I have to make a real effort to keep my eyes open, but I want to get the day's events into the diary while they are still fresh in my mind. Tomorrow, I hope to find a way to stop the ships and rescue our families.

I want to say how proud I feel. My sister and my best friend do everything I ask of them, without question, regardless of how difficult the task. I am filled with gratitude. I can't think of anything else to write, so I will hide the diary once again, and bring it up to date as soon as Evangelisa is asleep tomorrow evening.

Tuesday, 25 July, 1944

This morning, Giovanni arrived waving Irini's underwear and dragging the ewe on a rope. 'Funniest thing I ever saw!' he called out waving the knickers over his head. 'A demented sheep with women's pants around one leg.'

'They're not mine!' I said, aghast, holding my hands up.

He looked at Irini and Evangelisa. They both shook their heads vigorously.

'Fine, then I'll keep them.' He stuffed the briefs into his pocket and marched to the sheep pen with a real swagger to his step.

His hysterical laughter when he saw the state of our flock made me hate him. I'd never heard Evangelisa use bad language before, but she cursed Giovanni for his mockery, swearing like a sailor, which only made him laugh more.

We were stiff, sore, and famished. The only good thing about his arrival was the food he brought: a rabbit.

Evangelisa cried, 'I can't eat a poor little bunny.'

Irini rolled her eyes and Giovanni grinned. 'You will when you're starving,' he said.

We followed him into the hut and watched him skin and gut the creature. The dead rabbit was far easier to handle than a live sheep. I noted that we had olive oil, honey, onions, and other ingredients in the hut, but I needed fresh oranges and cinnamon to make a proper stew.

'There's a cinnamon tree,' Giovanni said. 'Follow me, Dora.' He walked towards the forest. 'We'll gather oranges on the way back.'

When his back was turned, Irini rolled her eyes and puckered her mouth, clearly understanding the shepherd's intentions. I lifted and dropped my shoulders as if I had no idea what she meant, then we grinned at each other. I love Irini so much. 'Be careful,' she mouthed silently. I nodded and followed Giovanni.

In the woods, he said, 'What will you pay to learn the whereabouts of a cinnamon tree, and for the rabbit, of course?'

'You expect me to pay?'

He nodded. 'Cinnamon trees are rare as angels, and nothing's free, unless you find it yourself.'

'What do you want? Please don't ask for any more lambs.'

He stopped walking and turned to me. 'I want a proper kiss on the mouth.' He said it boldly and without emotion, the way some customers spoke to my father in the shop; *I want turnups, and wide lapels with a buttonhole.*

I stared at the ground, unsure of myself, trying not to think about my father at that moment. Perhaps if I closed my eyes and imagined Giovanni was Irini, I'd be all right. The situation was ridiculous. How often had I watched him at choir practice and dreamed of kissing him? Now I had the chance . . . and just because he was dirty and dressed in rags, I hesitated. Was I mad? *Grow up, Dora!*

I put my hands over his ears, pulled his head forward, and kissed him hard, holding my breath. Then I let him go and stepped back.

He blinked slowly. 'Wow, you're a good kisser!'

'And you're average,' I said, staring at the sky and tapping my foot in a bored manner, secretly thrilled I'd been so bold. 'Now, where's the cinnamon?'

We traipsed to a clearing. In the centre stood a magnificent tree with spreading branches and leathery leaves like bright-green teardrops. The atmosphere around the tree seemed magical, almost surreal. The sun bounced off the shiny foliage and threw dappled light over encircling pines, creating an illusion that they were dancing, or at least shifting, around the cinnamon tree.

I gasped at the sheer beauty of it.

'What?' Giovanni said, standing beside me.

'It's so . . . amazing.'

He nodded. 'My grandfather claimed it was planted by Dionysus himself.' He stood next to me, staring at the tree.

'Dionysus, the god of wine?' I realised my hand was in his and started to pull away, but he held fast, and turned to face me.

He peered from under his long lashes. 'Dionysus, the god of fertility,' he whispered taking a step closer so we were almost against each other. His breath caressed my face and I wanted something more from him, but I wasn't sure what. I loved it when our eyes met, yet at the same time, I felt shy and embarrassed, and had to look away.

Annoyed with myself for being indecisive, I pulled my hand from his. 'Behave yourself!' I remembered all the help he had given us. He pretended to be hard and all knowledgeable, yet underneath I felt he was a very special person. I could feel the beating of my pulse as he took my hand again, his face serious, his eyes the colour of dark chocolate.

'Just a hug then?' He drew me to him, and instinctively I closed my eyes. With my face against his chest, I felt the rise and fall of his ribs, and heard his heartbeat. I put my arms around him and wanted to stay there forever, content and safe – but I had responsibilities back at the hut.

'I should leave soon,' I whispered easing myself out of his embrace.

Giovanni turned his mouth down in mock disappointment, but his eyes continued to glimmer hopefully. He pulled the hunting knife from his belt.

'What are you going to do?' I asked, nervous of the glinting blade.

'I'm about to get your cinnamon, but this tree is rare, my father says there isn't another in all Greece, so I have to be careful I don't kill it.' He moved towards the trunk and started patting and stroking it quite tenderly. 'This is important, see.'

'Why? Shall I do it too?' I looked up into the dense foliage.

'Like this,' he said standing behind me. He took my hand and stroked the bark. 'I want to kiss you again,' he whispered against the nape of my neck. 'I want you to be my girlfriend.'

Shivers of delight raced down my spine. I'd never experienced such feelings before. A thousand butterflies caressed every part of my body as he kissed me gently below my ear. I wanted him to kiss me on the mouth, the way Irini did, but when I turned around we just held each other for a long time, and it was enough.

'I feel safe in your arms,' I whispered. 'I wish I could always feel like this, but most of the time I'm so afraid for my family, I can't think of anything else. If I believed what you said, about what will happen to them, I would go crazy. It's heartbreakingly cruel, and I can't imagine what that news would do to Evangelisa.'

He stroked my face. 'Don't waste your energy fretting about stuff you can't change, Dora. It's better to concentrate on the things that will make a difference in the end. He held me tightly.'

I nodded, happy to be in his embrace. He held me tightly until I turned my face up to his and he kissed me again. I don't know how we came to be on the ground, under the cinnamon tree, but we kissed each other on every exposed place. The sensations were so wonderful, his caresses made my skin tingle, and for those moments everything was forgotten. I wanted to stay in his arms, in that safe place without worries or fears, but his breath became laboured and I sensed a change in him so I pulled away.

'Please, Dora. I only want to kiss you . . . that's all. Nothing else, I promise. I want to kiss you here,' he said, quickly sliding his hand up my inner thighs and cupping my secret place.

I was so excited and at the same time shocked that I pulled my hand back and gave him a hefty whack, completely forgetting about my broken wrist and the catapult.

We both cried out in pain. My whole arm seemed on fire. His cheekbone turned dark red.

'Sorry, I . . .' I stammered.

'No, me . . . truth is, I got carried away.'

After a few calming breaths, Giovanni whispered, 'Wow!' and glanced sideways at me. 'We'd better get the cinnamon and go back, okay?' I nodded and he stroked the tree trunk again.

'Why are you doing that?' I asked.

'I want a piece of her heart, and to get it I have to cut deep. Under this rough bark lies the sweetest spice. If I do it properly . . .' He continued to pat and stroke down the trunk. 'If I treat her gently, she'll give it up, her inner layer. The bark lets go of the cinnamon, so I can take what I want.' His eyes flicked to mine and he seemed to smile right into my soul.

After a moment, he stopped patting, gripped his knife, and stabbed hard into the tree.

I flinched, and perhaps whimpered.

He removed a rectangle of bark, then a second one from the fine, inner layer, which he gave me to hold.

'It's red,' I whispered.

'That's because of the phoenix,' he said. 'She builds her nest with branches from the cinnamon tree.'

'The phoenix bird?'

He nodded. 'Dies in flames, and rises again from the ashes.'

'Do you really believe there is such a thing?' I don't know why I thought about my family at that moment.

'Got to be. Stands to reason. When something's destroyed, then it's always a better thing that takes its place, right? I mean, look when there's a fire. Everything's charred, all the trees and grazing burnt to ash, but six months later the pasture's stronger and lusher than ever.'

The shepherds were often blamed for fires on the island, and Giovanni's words made me wonder if those suspicions were correct. I held the sliver of cinnamon to my nose and inhaled its intoxicating scent while he slotted the rectangle of bark back into the tree.

'There,' he said. 'The scars will heal over and nobody will ever know I've taken a piece of her heart.'

Our eyes met and, suddenly shy, I felt the heat of a blush. Giovanni the poet. Too much time on his own, I thought.

At the hut, we placed the rabbit and all the other ingredients into a cauldron on the fire. I washed myself, brushed my hair, and then followed Giovanni through the woods. At a point that looked like everywhere else, he told me to stop, and he disappeared into the trees.

Moments later, two rough-looking men appeared and led us down a steep track. We emerged in a small clearing surrounded by dense woodland. A band of men seemed gathered for the meeting.

'Wait here!' our escorts ordered Giovanni.

They ushered me towards the group, which parted to reveal a mountain of a man wearing a black shirt and beige jodhpurs. Everything about him was big. Huge hands, and long hair almost touching his collar. He had a neat, dark beard and strong even teeth, rather like our horse. I noticed a muscular Alsatian tied to a tree behind him.

The *Andartes* leader balanced a frying pan and a chunk of bread on his knee, and I guessed he had just finished eating. He put the pan aside and asked my name and where I lived. I did the same, which clearly surprised him.

'Not information for you,' he said. 'So, why are you here, little one?' He seemed impatient.

'I want you to stop the ships leaving and set my family free.'

'Ha! Such a small thing.' He smiled and tossed the bread to his dog.

'You are my only hope!' I cried. 'You're the *Andartes*, the secret army. You must help them. Get the boats to turn around!' I grabbed his sleeve and tried to pull him up.

170

He didn't budge. 'I can't. It's impossible.' He grinned at me. 'Who do you think we are?' Then he laughed as if I'd made a huge joke and everyone joined in.

How dare he! My temper boiled until I was so furious I snatched the big frying pan with two hands and with all my strength, whacked him over the side of his head.

'You've got to help them!' I shouted. Shocking pain raced up my arm when the pan connected.

'Hell!' he yelled, cradling his face. 'You little rat!'

'Aaah!' I cried, dropping the pan and hugging my wrist to my chest. Although I knew I'd hurt him, he roared with laughter. I lunged for the pan again.

Somebody grabbed my collar and lifted me off the ground. Blinded by fury, I fought like a tomcat, scratching and spitting, then I swung my leg forward and back with all my strength. My heel whammed into soft flesh and a howl sounded in my ear. The bandit let go of me.

The scruffy rebels, red-faced and hysterical with laughter, only made me madder. Another reached for my hair, but I snatched his hand and bit as hard as I could. He yelped, slung his other arm around my waist and lifted me off my feet. Clutched under his arm, I was helpless.

They dropped me into an olive sack. I was petrified they'd put rocks in and drop me into the sea, which was how locals got rid of kittens. I kicked and writhed, but it was no good. They closed the top and hung me up, probably from a tree branch.

Trapped in the mouldy olive sack, my broken wrist on fire, pain throbbed up to my shoulder. I thought about all the people squashed together on the ship, suffering the July sun. I had to do better. I had to get out of there.

I wailed as pitifully as I could. Nobody likes to hear a child cry.

'Please!' I sobbed, 'my arm hurts too much and my hair's caught in the top. I'll behave, I swear!' Someone pushed the sack and it swung violently. 'No! I'm going to be sick. I was just crazy with worry about my parents. I miss them . . .' I felt ashamed of using my parents, considering their predicament was far worse than mine.

The laughter died and I heard the leader's voice. 'Will you behave, little girl?'

Little girl! I hate being called that. I've been teased and bullied all my life because of my size, and before I could stop myself anger overcame me.

'I'm not a little girl! I'm a woman, and I'll thank you for treating me like one!' Then I remembered I wanted their sympathy, so I shut up.

'Really, how old are you, little one?'

'I'm sixteen! And I'm a born fighter! I can fight as well as any man so you'd better watch out!' I yelled through the hessian. The rough cloth chafed my skin, and I could hardly think for the pain in my wrist.

'Sixteen, that's interesting. When she stops kicking, get her down, tie her wrists, string her ankles, and bring her to me.'

172

Chapter 23

At the sink, Naomi reached up for *The Songs & Poems of Pandora Cohen* to read with her morning coffee.

The stiff pages were almost stuck together, and blue-grey spots of mildew framed each one with a musty smell rising from the paper. The handwriting was as neat as the diary, but song titles were flamboyantly scrolled and decorated. Bubba had been quite the artist.

Naomi recognised some of the titles: *Lili Marleen, Oh Mio Babbino Caro, One Day When We Were Young.* One cluster of songs had been written by Bubba; some were duets marked 'Me', and then 'Giovanni' on alternate lines, and dated at the bottom. Naomi smiled to herself. Had her grandmother and the shepherd boy sung their duets on the Filerimos mountainside?

Bubba ate on the patio while Naomi cleaned her room.

'Come and sit with me for five minutes,' Bubba said quietly. 'I wonder where you are up to in the diary? I can't stop thinking about it now, and it's troubling me.'

Naomi dropped into the plastic chair. They both stared across the road at the priest's house. 'I'm reading about how the *Andartes* put you in a sack and hung you from the tree.' She took Bubba's hand. 'If you'd rather I didn't read them, I'll put them away. It's not a problem.'

Bubba shook her head. 'Best to read them now, perhaps, while I'm still with you.'

'I wish you wouldn't talk like that. It's not as if you're going anywhere soon, is it?'

'We have to accept things, Naomi. Let me tell you: there are far worse things than dying, I know.' After a moment's silence, she nodded. 'Ah, yes, the sack. I was furious.' She huffed and shrugged. 'Mad as a flea-ridden dog. But it was a difficult time. I felt helpless and desperate.'

Naomi nodded. 'I think you were very brave to take on the leader like that.'

'No, I was foolish, but I became brave. Desperation does that. I matured quicker than any child ever should.'

'I was just looking at your song book. The words are beautiful, especially the ones you wrote yourself, the duets.'

Bubba smiled softly. 'I was falling in love with the shepherd boy. I wanted to be with him all the time. He felt the same way too. We made plans and dreamed of spending the rest of our lives together. We talked about where we would live, what we would call our children, and so on. He was a small reprieve in all the horror that I was experiencing, and all that lay ahead.'

'When Costa gets home, I'm going to ask him to move that shelf. It's no good having your books over the sink, the pages are spotted with mildew.'

Bubba's shoulders dropped. 'I was always writing, or singing with . . .' She halted, gulped, and then said, 'Giovanni.'

'You hesitated. Was there somebody else in your life?' Naomi asked.

Bubba turned to face her, and Naomi saw her eyes mist over as she reminisced. After a long silence she said, 'Somebody else? You'll have to read on if you want the answer to that question, child. But love is a wonderful thing, you know that, don't you?'

* * *

174

Naomi made two mugs of tea, prepared some food, and went in to see Bubba who had returned to bed for a nap.

'Would you like to sit outside again, Bubba? Get some fresh air?'

'I'm tired, child. Must have been all that brainstorming,' the old lady slurred. 'I'll have another sleep when I've eaten. Have you heard from Rebecca?'

'Not yet. But don't worry, she's bound to get in touch.' Best not mention the phone calls and get her hopes up, Naomi thought.

Later, Papas Yiannis brought Naomi's dishes back. 'Another delicious meal, thank you,' he said. 'I've brought the next diary so you can read it before you post it.' He held out another exercise book.

Naomi noticed how badly his hand shook. 'Are you all right, Papas? Sit down.' She indicated Bubba's armchair.

He lowered his eyes and sat. 'Thank you. Old age catching up, Naomi. Everything seems to take a little more effort these days, and I'm so tired all the time. Deprived of sleep by the 4 a.m. ladder.' He smiled. 'But nothing to worry about. What do you think of Bubba's writing?'

Naomi pulled out a kitchen chair. 'Tragic . . .' She focused on the empty seat for a moment before sitting. 'Difficult . . . and startlingly honest. Dora grew up so fast, didn't she? Bubba wanted to talk about it this morning; she told me how much she loved the shepherd boy.'

'Love is a wonderful thing,' he said quietly.

'It seems most of the Jews had no idea of what was going on in mainland Europe, or even Greece.' She met the priest's eyes. 'I actually shed a tear, imagining Costa and my boys sailing away like that. How dreadful.'

'The last Jews to be transported from Greece, only ten months before the war ended.'

'Ten months ... so did they survive and return?' Naomi asked.

'Not for me to say. You have to continue with this monumental history lesson, Naomi.'

As soon as the old priest had gone, Naomi picked up the diary and started reading.

Chapter 24

By time the *Andartes* lowered the sack and let me out, I was exhausted. I ached all over and struggled to hide my anxiety. I've been bullied in the past because of my size, and I know I have to give in to those stronger than me.

'Are you going to behave, little girl?' Nathanial asked. Although he sounded angry, I caught a sympathetic glimmer in his eye.

I nodded quickly, not trusting my voice. Although I'm now grown-up, there's still a lot of the child inside me – and that child wanted to cry. My heart was pounding, and I felt an urge to run. However, I stood firm and made myself as tall as possible, determined to appear calm and sensible.

'Giovanni told me you have information about what happened at L'Aeronautica?' As he spoke, a black cloud rolled over the sun and huge drops of rain fell from a windless sky.

'*Malaka!*' he boomed, making me jump. 'Bring her to the villa.' He turned and disappeared through the dense wall of vegetation behind him.

Two of the bandits lifted me by the armpits. They dragged me through trees that grew so close together, we had to turn sideways to squeeze between the trunks.

On the other side, I could hardly believe my eyes.

The forest had encroached on a magnificent Venetian villa, a sea captain's residence. Tall dark pines surrounded the building like a huddle of witches around the prettiest cauldron.

The deep rose-pink exterior had faded to a pleasing, dusty, hue. Tall columns stood either side of a heavy carved door, and above the imposing entrance, a Juliet balcony supported voluptuous cream balustrades. The roof had Italian terracotta tiles streaked pale yellow and orange. Enormous sandstone quoins framed the delicate blush of the facia and gave it a solid, impenetrable appearance.

The windows, tall and narrow, were covered by louvre shutters on grey marble sills. The place appeared as secure as it could be. Although the entire structure appeared neglected, shabby to say the least, it still had an imposing majesty; magical and overpowering. A building that once seen would not be forgotten.

The men rushed me inside where the *Andartes* leader sat on a dilapidated sofa of huge proportions. The floor was dark red marble, the colour of raw meat, which continued up a sweeping staircase with more balustrades that matched the ones outside. I stood with my mouth hanging open, taking in the wonderful architecture, and wishing I had my watercolours with me.

Someone closed the front door, shutting out the thrum of heavy rain on the trees.

'Bring her here!' Nathanial shouted, clearly annoyed.

The men deposited me before their leader.

'You ever tell anyone about this place and *I* will kill you, *they* will cook you, and *we* will all eat you! Do you understand?'

Unable to speak, I nodded emphatically.

He reached over the arm of the chair and raised a long, plaited whip, which he cracked like a bolt of lightning centimetres from me. 'I will find whoever you told, and I will flay every strip of skin from their body, then I'll cut their head off and feed it to the dogs! Do you understand me?'

I trembled violently and whimpered.

Satisfied that he had frightened the life out of me, he dropped the whip and folded his arms across his barrel chest. 'Now, tell me about L'Aeronautica.'

I took a deep breath, my mouth so dry the first words came out with a croak. 'I was there. All of us were, for three days.' I tried to sound grown-up, and used some of the long words I'd learned recently. 'The situation was unjustifiable. What was the point of it all? They could have left us at home for those three days.' I dared to meet Nathanial's eyes. 'I suspect the Germans are not as organised as they pretend to be.'

At this the *Andartes* leader guffawed. 'Go on,' he said.

'The very old and the sick found our circumstances particularly difficult.' I stared at the ground for a moment, recalling the awful scene. 'We slept on the hard floor without food or water. We got so desperate, we drank from the toilet, but then it blocked and the Nazis cut the water supply.'

'Why aren't you on the ship with the rest?'

'I escaped,' I said simply, lifting my injured arm. 'Broke my wrist in the process. Can you save my family? Are they really going to some awful prison camp?' I chewed my lip, wondering if I should ask a question to which I did not want to hear the answer. I took a breath and lowered my voice. 'Is it true they'll be killed by the Nazis?'

He shrugged. 'Possibly. How can we know?' I saw the regret on his face. 'We only hear rumours.'

'Can't you help them escape?' I asked quietly. 'Please. They're my parents, my grandmother and grandpa, and my brothers and just everyone. Even my school friends were taken. I'm desperate.' My insides were shaking again. 'Why is this happening? What reason could they have for taking my family away? We never hurt anybody. I have to bring them home.'

He shook his head. 'Sorry for your loss, but the situation's impossible. Look at us. We are a few men with a few guns. There's little we can do.' He frowned. 'Consider this. Let's say the enemy are a big ship that we don't want in port. We're not strong enough to push the vessel away. Nevertheless, we sneak along the quayside like mice in the night and gnaw at the ropes. And that's what we do. We find their weak point, and we destroy as much as we can.'

179

'Can't you get more men? There must be a hundred Rhodians for every German.'

'Ha! You think they're going to fight the Germans to save the Jews of Rhodes? The Rhodians are not warriors like the Cretans. Right at this moment, the locals are pillaging your people's houses, smashing the floors and ripping out cupboards, greedily searching for the mythical cache of Jewish wealth.'

'What wealth? We struggled; like everyone else.'

'Try telling that to the locals. Some had their belongings packed in anticipation of the Jewish procession to L'Aeronautica. They moved into the Jewish houses even before the ships had left the island. You'll find few Rhodians among the partisans here. Most of the *Andartes*, including myself, their *capitano*, are remnants of the Italian army who escaped the Nazi bullet. We're alone in our fight against the Axis.'

Drenched in an awful feeling of despair, I stared at Nathanial.

'Little one, I'm especially interested in anything you heard from the Nazis.' He stared at me, his eyes cold and hard again.

I told him about the Turkish Consulate-General, what I'd observed.

'A brave man,' Nathanial said. 'He risked his life to save those forty-something souls.'

'The worst thing was when they took the old ones into another room and pulled their gold teeth out. When the grandmothers and grandfathers rejoined us, their mouths swollen and bleeding, people changed. Adults started crying. Everyone acted strangely, hugging each other.'

I stopped to recall my family, grouped together, pale-faced and silent. 'I didn't realise at the time, but I think the adults knew at that point what was going to happen.'

'Go on,' he said.

'At first, most believed we were being sent to work on another island, a better place. The Nazis had shown the elders a movie about the work camps. In the film, there were nice houses, happy people, and lots of food on the table. Some of our neighbours were excited at the prospect of moving, but not my mother. She was one of the few who didn't believe what they saw on the big screen. She guessed it was a trick, but nobody would listen, not even my father.

'When we got to L'Aeronautica, they took our possessions: money, jewellery, everything. The adults started whispering to each other. Some put their sovereigns and jewellery down the toilet, rather than let the SS have them, but then the toilets blocked, making our situation even worse because the water was turned off. But taking the old people's gold teeth, that changed everything. My father will be proud that I escaped. He didn't want me to get on the ship. When he caused a distraction, I ducked under a truck and hid behind the wheels.'

'You were brave, and quick-thinking.'

I shook my head. 'What's brave about running away?'

'Sometimes it's the bravest thing you can do. Your father gave an order and, even though you didn't understand why and didn't want to execute that order, you did it without question. I wish I had more men with that attitude. Where are your sister and friend now?'

I stood tall. 'I'm not saying. They're my responsibility. I must think about their safety. I'm all they have to protect them now.'

'We'll protect them; you have my word.' I felt him scrutinising me. 'Are you really sixteen?'

'Yes, why?'

'You look younger. You could be useful. If you give us your help, we'll give you our protection. What do you think?'

I considered his words. 'Depends what you want.'

He smiled. 'You're not afraid of us?'

'Should I be? We're on the same side, aren't we? They call you a rebel, but I've also heard you're a respected leader.'

'My God, you're a cocky little madam.' He laughed uproariously, and his men, who stood a respectful distance away, joined in. 'I can't stop the ships, but I believe they're in Kos now and I'll let you know what I hear. Don't lose hope.' He pointed a finger at me. 'With an early end to the conflict, your family may never reach camp. We're doing all we can to crush the Nazis on Rhodes, and you can help us.'

My world collapsed. An ache that started in my heart seemed to spread through my body and I struggled not to cry in front of the *Andartes* leader.

I had to show I could be respectful and act like an adult. 'Sir, can I have your permission to go back to my sister and my friend? They'll be worried.'

He nodded, eyes serious but mouth smiling. 'Remember what I said. You are sworn to secrecy about this place. Come back tomorrow, little one. We'll talk some more.' He nodded at Giovanni who was sitting on his haunches by the door, watching.

The shepherd boy jerked his head sideways. One of the bandits untied my hands and feet. I looked at each man in turn, determined to remember their faces in case I met them under different circumstances. I made a swift nod at *Capitano* Nathanial and then followed Giovanni.

Halfway back, the shepherd boy pulled to a halt and faced me. 'You were brave. A bit stupid at first, attacking the leader of the *Andartes* like that, but after the sack business, yes, very brave.' His eyes narrowed. 'You'll have to keep control of your temper, but that aside, I think you'll make a good rebel.'

His words thrilled me. Proud and honoured, I felt my confidence grow a little. He stepped forward, took me in his arms and kissed me tenderly. His mouth was soft and warm, and his hands pressed in the small of my back. My body melted in his embrace and I wanted the moment to last forever.

We broke apart and continued in silence.

Back at the hut, Irini ran to greet us. 'Dora! I was worried.' She eyed Giovanni. 'You all right? How did it go with the *Andartes*?'

I told her what had happened. Evangelisa was quarrelsome, and I both despaired at her constant complaining and regretted that I couldn't make her feel better.

'I want to go home, Dora! I need a bath and I have to change my clothes.'

'We can't go back right now, Evangelisa,' I said, not wanting to tell her the reason, that we might be captured and deported too. Nathanial might have been exaggerating about the locals behaving like vultures, but still, I had a suspicion there were enemies in the city.

'Mama and Papa left instructions that we stay up here. I don't know why, but I'm sure they had good cause. We must trust them and do as we're told, right?'

Evangelisa stuck her lip out. Her selfishness should irritate me, but it doesn't. Who could help loving my sister? She is so pretty; and because she's the baby of the family, she is spoilt by us all. Although Evangelisa is less than two years younger than me, they're the all-important years that separate child from adult. They also make me responsible for her safety.

'Tell you what,' I said. 'What if Irini and I sneak back to the house and get your things, if you're not afraid of being on your own for a few hours?' I was concerned about the diary and letter I had left under Evangelisa's dresses. Anyone reading the diary would realise Irini and Evangelisa were hiding up on Filerimos Mountain.

'Why would Mama and Papa go off and leave us like this? They haven't even said goodbye. It's as if they sent us here deliberately, to stop us going with them.'

I hadn't considered that angle before Mama had mentioned it, and I had to give Evangelisa credit for hitting on the truth.

She looked miserable and stared at the floor. 'Perhaps I upset them? I keep asking myself. I know I'm selfish, but I swear I won't be, not ever again. I just want them to come back.' She fisted her eyes. 'How can I tell them, Dora? Do you think we'll be able to send them a letter? I promise I'll try harder in everything I do. I love Mama more than anybody in the world, and I want her to be proud of me, even though I'm not as clever as you.'

My heart went out to her. 'They do love you, silly!' I said. 'Don't you know you're their absolute favourite? They didn't say goodbye because they're coming back soon. They didn't want to worry you.' I sat next to her on the bed. 'And you're not alone, are you? You have Irini and me, and we'll be perfectly fine until they return.' I put my arms around her, holding her close. 'Why not write your letter to Mama? She'll like that. Start tomorrow and then, when we know their address, we can post it.'

She seemed happier with this suggestion. I realised we couldn't simply return home and collect our belongings. If we went at night and managed to carry our things to Danial's horse, we could load them on Zeus's back and lead him up Mount Filerimos.

A sensible plan, I thought. We needed food too. Though times were hard, Mama kept a good store. Even if we only rescued the dried peas and beans harvested from our plot, we'd have enough to keep us for a month.

Chapter 25

Engrossed in the diary, Naomi was fretting about the teenagers when an almighty hammering on the door made her jump. She slammed her hand against her chest as if to stop her heart leaping right out.

'Who is it?' she called as she moved to the door. Nobody replied, so she unlatched the top half and pulled it open. Two men in suits, each with a briefcase, stood on her doorstep.

'We've come to speak to Pandora Cohen,' the taller man said.

'She's poorly, recovering from a stroke.'

The younger one dropped his shoulders and sounded sympathetic. 'Sorry, lady. We're here about the court case.'

The other stood firm, chin thrust forward, staring eyes.

'Ah, I see. I'm her granddaughter. Can I help?'

'May we come in?' the first one asked.

Naomi nodded and opened the door.

They introduced themselves. Mr Gianakopulos, tall, very overweight, flabby-faced, perhaps in his sixties; the other, Mr Despotakis, half Mr Gianakopulos' age, neat, clean-shaven and ordinary. Naomi indicated for them to sit at the kitchen table, telling herself she really must try to save the money for a sofa.

Despotakis pulled a sheaf of forms from his briefcase. 'We need some details. First, Mrs Cohen's birth certificate, ID, and deeds for the property you're claiming.'

Naomi shook her head, remembering the diary. 'I don't think she has any documents. The Nazis confiscated our family papers in L'Aeronautica, many decades ago, before they transported everyone to Auschwitz.'

The two officials glanced at each other.

Gianakopulos, dark circles under his eyes and several warts on his face and neck, frowned and then smiled, snake-like despite his fatness. 'No papers, no claim,' he said brusquely. 'No point in going any further. Nothing we can do.'

Naomi clenched her fists. *Who did he think he was?*

'Are there any living relatives besides yourself and Mrs Cohen?' Despotakis persisted.

Naomi dragged her eyes away from the fat bastard. 'I have a younger sister. I think Pandora Cohen was the only survivor of all my ancestors. The rest were transported to the death camps, Bergen-Belsen and Auschwitz. As far as I understand, nobody else survived.'

The fat man turned his eyes towards the ceiling like he'd heard it all before.

Naomi, seething, squinted at him as she continued. 'You know what I mean, Mr Gianakopulos, after being handed over to the Nazis by Rhodians who then looked the other way.'

Gianakopulos's eyes flicked up from the forms and glared at her before playing his spiteful card. 'And Mrs Cohen's daughter, father *unknown*, it says in our records.' The words came with a sneer.

'Then I'm sure it also says "in your records" that my mother, maiden name Sonia Phoenix Cohen, died in 1980, when I was ten years old.' Naomi matched his glare. 'And my Uncle, Jacob Cohen, one of the few survivors of that hell-hole called Auschwitz, died in Italy ten years after my mother, and his wife followed him some months later.' Naomi thought it best not to mention her nieces, as they had long lost touch.

Despotakis lowered his eyes. 'I'm sorry. How come Mrs Cohen . . .' he glanced at the forms, 'Pandora, wasn't taken to Auschwitz too?'

Naomi took a breath, pushing back her frustration and concentrating on Despotakis. She exhaled and said, quietly but forcefully, 'Because my grandmother escaped deportation on those disgraceful ships, the vessels that took all the Jews from this island. I'm proud to say my grandmother joined the *Andartes* and risked her life for the liberation of Rhodes and her people.' Her words were choked with emotion. She stared from one to the other, taking a moment to recompose. 'Pandora Cohen fought for a country that didn't fight for her. The least Rhodes can do is give back what's rightfully hers.'

Gianakopulos snorted. 'You mean her boyfriend was hiding with the bandits and draft dodgers in the mountains? That's more like the truth.'

His mockery was galvanising, and for a moment it left her speechless. But Gianakopulos had pushed her over the edge. She banged her clenched fists on the wooden table top.

'No, I do not mean that! My grandmother was an assassin who executed Nazi informers. Countless Rhodian lives were saved through her actions, possibly the lives of your parents and grandparents too. And while she fought and risked her life for the island of Rhodes, the local thieves and cowards trembled behind their closed shutters! Or should I say, the shutters of the Jewish homes they stole hoping and praying the true owner didn't escape the gas chamber or crematorium, and return!'

She'd gone too far, she knew it. The men looked past her, and Naomi turned to see Bubba in her socks, nighty, and cardigan, standing in the doorway looking bewildered.

Naomi stood and pointed a stiff finger at Gianakopulos's face. 'Don't *ever* let me hear you speak disrespectfully of Pandora Cohen again, or you'll have me to deal with. Now, *get out of my house!*'

Gianakopulos narrowed his eyes and Naomi knew she had an enemy before her.

The door opened and Papas Yiannis rushed in. 'What's going on?' he asked, looking from one to the other. 'I could hear the shouting across the street.'

Naomi didn't take her eyes off Gianakopulos. 'Leave! Get out of my house before I reward your ignorance with words I might regret!'

Gianakopulos looked smug. 'Your house . . . I don't think so, madam.' He hauled his bulk out of the chair.

Papas Yiannis stepped forward. 'Actually, it's my house. You can check your records: Papas Yiannis Voskos, Orthodox priest of Paradissi. Now I think you had better leave the building, as this lady requested.'

Despotakis cleared his throat and handed Naomi a card. 'If you find any papers, would you contact me?'

Naomi nodded.

* * *

'Sorry,' Naomi said when the officials had gone and Bubba returned to her room. 'He was rude and insulting, that Gianakopulos. A horrible man. Still, I shouldn't have lost my temper. He's the type that will make me pay for my words.'

'Never worry about what's said in haste, Naomi,' the priest said. 'There's no point. Now, what will we do about Rebecca? Have you heard from her?'

'Actually, I phoned her.' She told him her concerns about the diary being destroyed. 'She promised to read it, then post it back.'

'Good. I came over because I believe they're bringing the court case forward, again.' He shook his head. 'A little devious, as people living in distant lands, Canada, Australia, and so on, have already bought their expensive plane tickets and booked time off work.'

'What can we do?'

'There's the European Parliament, but time's a problem. Perhaps we can lobby the press. At least that would publicise your situation. Most people have no idea what really happened, and it may harm the lucrative tourist industry of this island if they did.'

He folded his arms across his broad chest and thought for a moment. 'Your case will set a precedent. I suspect they've chosen you because they know you don't have the finances to hire substantial legal aid. The whole thing's devious and underhanded, and now I'm retired, I have nothing to lose by supporting your cause.'

'You're an incredibly kind man, Papas Yiannis. I wonder if any rabbi or imam would support a poor Christian woman against their own people.'

'I'm sure they would. You read about the Turkish consulate. He was certainly a Muslim, and he risked his life for the Jews, far beyond the call of duty. There are good people everywhere, Naomi. Anyway, it doesn't do to analyse people or religions too deeply. It simply comes down to justice and respect.'

'Papas, what did you mean when you told them it's your house?'

He smiled. 'The day I took over this parish, the old priest, the one who sheltered Dora when she returned from Filerimos, gave

189

me the deeds to this place. When your family and all the others were taken, the locals were moving into the Jewish houses, even before the ships had left port. The old papas went straight to the records office that had been set up to register property and had your house put in his name. He hoped your family would return.'

He lowered himself into Bubba's armchair. 'When he retired, he made me swear to make a will that on my death the property would return to your family.' The priest lowered his head and pinched the bridge of his nose. After an emotional moment, he drew a shuddering breath and continued. 'He hoped by the time *he* reached retirement age, there'd be tolerance between religions. Unfortunately, the bigotry and narrow-mindedness are worse than ever.'

'What a kind man,' Naomi said.

'A saint, in my opinion.' He tilted his head back and sniffed. 'What's that delicious smell?'

Naomi smiled. 'Lamb with beans. Can I interest you in some for supper?'

His eyes twinkled. 'Oh, before I forget, I'm sprucing up the house, hoping Marina will bring her boyfriend home.'

'Sounds like a plan.'

'I bought a new sofa, very modern. They're delivering it tomorrow, but the painters can't start until next week. I wondered if you'd allow it to stand on your patio, until the decorating is done. My front terrace isn't deep enough.'

Naomi recalled his traditional wooden-back sofa. 'On condition I can have your old one?' she said, grinning.

'Of course. How's the diary going? I can't help wondering where you got to.'

'Dora and Irini are going into town for Evangelisa's things.'

'A brave thing to do for her sister, don't you think? Shows how much Dora loved Evangelisa, something that didn't always come across in their day-to-day life.' He paused. 'But that's quite common among siblings, isn't it?'

Naomi felt the priest was telling her something important. 'It's obvious there was a strong bond between them,' she said absently, thinking of Rebecca.

The old priest nodded, seeming content that Naomi understood Dora's situation. The moment he had gone, she picked up the diary.

Chapter 26

Late at night, Tuesday, 25 July 1944

Evangelisa has agreed to stay behind and Irini and I will wait until she is asleep before we go back into the city for our things. Irini is also catching a few hours before we go, but I can't, there's too much going on in my head, I have brought my diary up to date, and I will wake Irini soon. I guess it's around midnight, but as we don't have a watch or clock between us, I can't be sure. I hope our plan works, because I can't imagine what will happen to my sister, alone on the mountain, if we get caught. I hope Giovanni would look after her.

Dear Diary, it's time to wake Irini and set out for Rhodes Old Town. I hope I have lots of good news to tell you when I return. Until then, I'll stuff you back under the mattress and hope Evangelisa doesn't find you. With luck, we will be back before she wakes.

Wednesday, 26 July 1944

We made it back, but we are both exhausted and emotionally drained. I am writing this while Evangelisa boils some oatmeal for our breakfast. Who'd believe we would resort to eating horse fodder? Real hunger brings out the worst in a person.

I think about my family, and refuse to accept the rumours. Why would the Jews be rounded up, if not to labour for the Germans? Logically, they had to be well fed in order to work hard.

However, the night's adventure has made me see my neighbours in a new, disturbing light. I have been naive. How can people I respected change so much? I have come to the conclusion that just because people appear to be respectable, and they smile and say the right things, does not mean they are good people.

What horrors awaited us in town! We are lucky to be alive. I think, in hindsight, making a special trip back, for Evangelisa's dresses and a few possessions, was a childish and reckless thing to do.

Our journey started when Irini and I hurried out of the pine forest. We were relatively safe on the long trek back into town, knowing we'd see hooded lights, or at least hear engine noises if any vehicles approached.

Nevertheless, we were spooked, jumping at every rustle that came from the roadside scrub. The night seemed full of strange, scurrying noises and damp, earthy, smells. A barn owl flew straight at us, ghostly, skimming over our heads, its face flat and white with big black eyes, like a child's drawing.

'You scared?' Irini said.

'Of course not,' I replied defiantly although my insides trembled. 'Just being careful, ready to run if anyone comes.'

'Same here,' she whispered.

'Truth is, I'm actually terrified. Wetting my knickers.'

'I'm wetting your knickers too,' she quipped and we both giggled nervously.

We arrived at the city walls hoping we could get through the maze of narrow streets unseen.

Faint music and laughter drifted down the road. A door opened, and the sounds of a party escaped into the night. I thought of Danial. Life went on without him. We dived under a bougainvillea that reached the ground. A couple came into the street. The man pressed the woman against the wall and kissed her. They were canoodling for ages, then I realised they were speaking German! I squeezed Irini's hand. She whimpered.

The woman slapped the German and then stomped back into the party.

'*Warte ab!*' he called, and followed her.

Trembling and afraid, we scrambled from the foliage and hurried onward, leaving a trail of papery bougainvillea bracts, like confetti in our wake. After dodging from doorway to doorway, huddling in narrow recesses, we neared the Jewish quarter.

We only saw one patrolling soldier. He walked across the end of our alleyway just as we approached. Terrified, we flattened ourselves behind a protrusion that supported an overhead arch. There were many flying buttresses in the side streets of Rhodes Old Town.

The soldier stopped. Footsteps came closer. My heart thumped with fear. We peered through a gap in the masonry. He stared up the alley, then drew his pistol and continued towards us. We had nowhere to go! When he was almost upon us, the sound of shattering glass reached us from the main street. The Nazi spun around and ran back the way he'd come.

We scooted out of the passageway and straight up the next one.

Eventually, we reached the Juderia and crouched behind the rubble of a bombed dwelling.

I recollected the night that the Levis's home collapsed. The air-raid siren, the odd whistling noise, the moment of silence when we waited for the explosion that left our ears ringing. My brothers and I dived under the table, clutching each other. The ground shook so hard we realised it was near. Everyone dreaded a second bomb that would kill us all. We waited, breathless, but it didn't come.

A British bomb, they said after the all-clear.

The most appalling screams came from the Levis's demolished home.

'God take her! God take her!' my mother muttered between sobs. And eventually He did. Poor Mrs Levi. She died with her husband and four children. They were blown to bits or crushed to death by heavy sandstone blocks. Not a stick of furniture could be seen – only piles of earth, masonry, and beams. Six bodies

194

were recovered and there were probably more buried. Neighbours' homes were made uninhabitable, and many more had their windows destroyed.

With these thoughts going through my head I dreaded another raid. Also, I wondered if the Germans would be watching the houses that belonged to us.

Everywhere seemed deathly quiet, but then it did just before that bomb fell on the Levis's home. I strained my ears for the drone of an aircraft, but the only noise came from a couple of cats in an ally, then silence.

I didn't have a key for our house, Mama had it in her bag, but we had a spare, hidden behind a broken brick in the courtyard wall.

Irini kept watch. I got the loose brick out and fumbled in the space behind it, dislodging snails and a clump of moss before I found the key. The door scraped the cobbles, the noise scaring us both. I used all my strength to lift the door as I closed it, so it hardly made a sound. We stood still, breathing quietly, listening for Nazi footsteps that thankfully never came.

The same key unlocked the front door; in fact it probably opened half the doors in the city. People borrowed each other's keys if they shut themselves out. The lock rasped and clunked, but the moment it released we scuttled inside.

Because the shutters were closed, the room was pitch-black. I reached for the light switch but bumped into a solid object and nearly fell over. Something was wrong. I stretched out my arms and touched an unfamiliar thing that made me jump before I realised it was glass. It toppled. I tried to grab it, but it smashed on the stone floor. My skin seemed to shrink over my body.

'Who's there?' a man yelled.

Irini moaned.

My first thought was that we'd entered someone else's house. 'Sorry! Sorry!' I called out.

A woman's voice. 'Who is it? Petro?'

The flare of a match. A glimmer of candle flame lit the stairway. The faces were grotesque in the flickering illumination. Then, I recognised the conductor from the choir.

'It's me, Dora, from the tailor's shop,' I said. 'Sorry, we must have made a mistake.'

He came downstairs and turned on the light. 'What are you doing here? They told us you were gone – away on the ships.'

His wife blew out the candle and followed him.

I looked around, confused. I hadn't been wrong; it was our house, our home, but everything was different. Many things that didn't belong to us cluttered the place. Cushions, pictures, ornaments. I felt myself in a nightmare where nothing was as it seemed. Irini came to my side, held my hand but didn't speak. We both stared at the room.

The choirmaster spoke again. 'Child, what are you doing here? You must leave. Go! Now! Or I'll call the Nazis.'

'It's my house. I live here.' I wanted to ask what he was doing in my home, but I was so afraid at the mention of Nazis that I couldn't speak.

His wife, wearing a long cotton nightdress and a pink knitted bed jacket, scurried down the stairs and stared at the door. 'Where are your parents?' she said kindly, patting her pin curls and fiddling with the hairnet strap that cut into her double chin.

'They were taken away on the ship. Everyone was but I escaped.' I sniffed, near to tears again. 'Mama, Papa, my brothers, grandparents, all my cousins, aunts, uncles. I don't understand why. Do you know why? I miss them. And I'm scared.'

The choirmaster grabbed me by the shoulders. 'Where is it, your father's gold?' he said. 'Where's it hidden?'

'Gold? We don't have any,' I said, suddenly noticing a hole into the floor where we had replaced some broken tiles.

'It's here somewhere. I know it,' he snarled, staring about the room. His fingers dug into my shoulders and he shook me. 'Tell me where it is or I'll call the Nazis!'

How often I'd watched this man from my bedroom window, admired him, thought he was the sort of person I would like to model myself on. At that moment, I recognised nothing but a greedy rodent.

His wife said, 'Now, now, Petro. Let's feed these children and see what we can do for them. Poor girls.'

'We can't harbour Jews! They'll kill us, you stupid woman!' He jerked his chin towards us. 'Get them out of here, or I'll summon the patrol and hand them over.'

'Stop it!' she said harshly. 'Keep your voice down. Poor child,' she said, turning to me, glancing at my wrist and the crude splint. 'Sit down and tell me all about it. There's chickpea soup in the pan. Would you like some?'

I nodded frantically. 'Starving.'

The woman looked at Irini, who also nodded eagerly. 'Eat a small donkey, mane and tail too,' she said, which made the woman smile.

She fed us dishes of thick soup, drizzled with olive oil and a squirt of lemon juice and accompanied by hunks of fresh wholemeal bread. A simple, yet amazing meal that I will never forget.

I told her I'd come to get our possessions and provisions, and would she mind?

She helped us collect things, including the Babushka dolls. Although Papa's small-change had gone, the dolls were nestled together and I knew Evangelisa would love them.

The choirmaster grumbled and said if we ever returned, he'd hand us over.

'Petro! Stop behaving like the backside of a mule!' his wife exclaimed. 'Or you'll feel the sting of my carpet beater!'

Clearly, the choirmaster's wife was the boss in that marriage, and also on our side. Strangely, I didn't mind that they were looking after our house. It seemed better to leave it with people taking care of things until my family came back. Which I knew they would.

With our stuff bundled into two blankets, we crept into the courtyard. The choirmaster's wife followed. 'Now, Dora, tell me: is there any treasure, or savings, hidden in the house? I can keep it safe for you, out of my husband's greedy clutches.' Her face pinched and her eyes narrowed keenly, glinting over a tight-lipped smile.

She appeared snakelike in the moonlight and I couldn't look away. I shook my head. 'Honestly, we had to take all our valuables to L'Aeronautica. The Nazis took everything and they searched us all, even the children. Nobody has left anything of worth behind.'

'So, the SS have it all, yes?' Her face relaxed and her kindness returned.

We thanked the woman, before I followed Irini towards the city walls and the bastion gate of Saint John.

We stopped many times to rest our arms, aware that a Nazi patrol might discover us at any moment. To be caught out after curfew carried the penalty of death. Shot on the spot. At least everywhere was in darkness, in case the British bombers came over again.

Our horse was stabled five hundred metres from the entrance into the Old Town. As we approached the gate of Saint John, we heard men talking and realised there were sentries posted on the fortifications.

How could we get over the bridge that spanned the moat without being seen? The moon was up, spreading a moody, gangrenous light over the island. We crouched low and scooted across the moat.

As we approached the shack, Zeus nickered and whinnied. The top of the stable door was open, and the moment I reached our horse I shushed him. Irini rubbed his nose and I patted his neck before we opened the bottom of the stable door and slipped in.

Exhausted, we dumped the heavy bundles in the shack, glad to stop for a well-deserved rest.

The moon was high and our eyes had their night vision, but hardly any light reached inside the stable. I saddled Zeus, fumbling, unsure of what I was doing. Danial had tried to teach me to ride, but my heart wasn't in it, I was happy to muck out for him. Now I wished I'd paid attention.

When Danial started helping in Papa's shop, after his work at the port, he gave a little money each month to a young Albanian who cared for Zeus. The boy had done a good job; the stable was tidy and the horse, well kept.

In the silence of the night, we heard a vehicle approaching. A Nazi patrol.

Chapter 27

Bromley, London.

Standing in the kitchen in her white silk pyjamas, Rebecca stared at the calendar. Seven weeks. One more and she had made it to two months pregnant. Life could not be better, and she wanted to put her arms around Fritz and tell him how happy she was. But on the first Monday of the month, Fritz would leave for work at dawn and not return until after nine, tired, worried, and restless.

'An early start to set the month ahead,' he would say.

She decided to phone him at ten and tell him how much she loved him. Before that, she would shower, wear something nice, and do her hair in case he wanted to video call.

After making herself a green tea, she sauntered into the living room to reread some of the diary. Dora's story amazed her. She saw in the two sisters similarities between Naomi and herself. Naomi had always taken care of her. In the minimalist lounge she stared at the driftwood coffee table, sure that was where she had left the diary the night before. Perhaps Fritz took it to work; she'd ask him when she phoned.

By ten o'clock, she looked her best. She called his mobile but it was turned off. He must be in a meeting. She called the office to see what time he would be free.

'Can I take a message?' the woman said. 'Mr Neumanner doesn't work on the first Monday of the month. I'll get him to call you back tomorrow.'

Rebecca frowned. 'Sorry . . . Mr Neumanner, Fritz Neumanner doesn't work on the first Monday of the month? Since when?' she asked.

'Three months or so. Can I take your name, madam?'

'No, it's fine. I'll call his mobile, thank you.' With that, she hung up. What was going on? Fritz never had a day off work. There must be a simple explanation, but she couldn't think of one. She hunted around for the diary again. As if on cue, the post came, and as soon as she saw the envelope she knew another diary had arrived.

This was turning into a very strange day.

Where was Fritz on a Monday? Why hadn't he mentioned taking the day off? Perhaps he was ill, going for treatment and didn't want to worry her. She searched her mind for anything unusual the previous first Mondays of the month, but came up with nothing apart from his extremely long day and his excessive tension when he eventually arrived home.

In his home office, she glanced over the desk and found it neat and tidy with no clues to the mystery. She opened drawers and searched through the contents, until she came across his diary. After a moment of hesitation she sat in the swivel chair, licked her forefinger, and flicked through pages of business appointments and notes, until she came to the previous month and stared at a blank Monday. Four weeks before that, another vacant page.

Pensive, she spent the rest of the day in a daze, analysing Fritz, their relationship, and this mystery. In the end she asked herself if she trusted him, and she answered herself with a resounding yes, *totally*. Whatever was going on, she believed he kept it to himself for her sake, and she didn't doubt he would tell her in his own good time. Best to have faith in him and put the whole thing out of her mind.

She looked at the kitchen calendar once more. The next first Monday fell on the day he flew to America, and she would be almost three months pregnant and packing her case for Rhodes. How would Bubba and Naomi receive her? She didn't doubt there would be tension on all sides, but they had to work things out and grow back together. She picked up the brown envelope slathered in Greek stamps and tore it open.

As she expected, another diary slipped out.

* * *

Rebecca lost track of time. Curled on the sofa with the diary, she raced through the pages, horrified to discover what Bubba had been through. The stories were simply written and moving, and Rebecca saw a new side of her grandmother. She wished she had inherited some of Bubba's bravery, and she understood how lonely young Dora must have been without her family around her.

When Rebecca stopped reading, in order to make a herbal tea, she thought about how much Dora cared for Evangelisa. Although Dora had put herself in terrible danger for the sake of a few dresses, Evangelisa seemed to have no notion of her sister's selflessness.

Rebecca considered how Naomi had looked after her when they were younger. A devotion that she had always taken for granted, she realised shamefully. But now she could repay Naomi by helping with the court case. Satisfied with herself, she settled on the sofa and returned to the diary.

Dora and Irini were trapped in the stable. Imagining their fear, Rebecca continued reading.

Chapter 28

'They're coming!' Irini whispered urgently. I closed and bolted the stable door, and we scurried into the hay pile, burying ourselves. The scent of damp grass enveloped us.

Zeus continued to snort and grumble. If we were shot for defying the curfew, our bodies would be left to bloat in the sun, as a warning to others. Would the soldiers see the horse was saddled and come into the shack to investigate? Thank goodness I hadn't put the bridle on first as they would be sure to notice that.

The vehicle stopped and doors slammed. German voices approached. Two Nazis seemed to be right outside the stable. I remembered the pitchfork and its slim, sharp tines near the door. If they probed the hay pile we would be speared, and I wouldn't be able to endure such a thing in silence.

We clung to each other under the itchy mound, hardly daring to breathe. Something tickly crawled up my leg. I clenched everything. Footsteps and German voices came closer. My heart was pounding so hard I could hear it in my ears.

'Shush!' I said, as loud as I dared to Zeus.

Through the straw, I saw the Nazis' torchlight dance around the inside walls. The narrow beam hit our bundles in the back corner. The soldiers seemed to be discussing the situation.

Zeus was panicky, making exaggerated nods and snorting. A hand reached over the half-door, groping for the bolt.

Zeus lunged forward and nipped the intruder's fingers.

The German withdrew. *'Was zur Hölle?!'* he yelled, cursing the horse.

We were terrified but, perhaps due to nerves or exhaustion, Irini started giggling silently as the Nazis stomped away. Hugging each other with our heads pressed together, we vibrated with contained laughter. Moments later, when the jeep engine sprung to life and the soldiers continued their patrol around the city perimeter, our brave charade disintegrated. Our mirth turned to misery. Wracked by sobs of both terror and relief, we cried into the crook of each other's neck, gulping for air, clinging to one another, tears raging.

'I want my mother,' Irini said.

'Me too,' I sobbed back. 'Papa would know what to do. I miss him so much.'

'We should imagine they are here. What would your father expect us to do now?'

But thinking about Papa only made me more upset. I wondered if the Germans would check the stable again on their next round and, if they did, what would happen when they discovered the horse had gone?

We untangled our limbs, climbed out of the itchy hay, and hugged for a moment.

'Without you, Dora, I'd go mad.'

'Don't think about it,' I whispered. 'We'll always be together, Irini. Nobody can take away what we have.'

She nodded and squeezed me hard. 'Let's tie the bundles and sling them over the horse's back.' Luckily, they weighed almost the same, so it wasn't difficult to balance them.

We bridled Zeus. Irini sat upfront and took the reins. Her parents had a mule, which she rode competently. I got behind her and hung on.

Afraid and vulnerable, we listened for soldiers and then walked Zeus towards Filerimos. We gave the city a wide birth, keeping to the shadows and soft ground.

Once we were clear of the suburbs, the view from Zeus's back took my breath away. Now I understood why Danial loved riding.

Poor Danial. When he comes home, I will show him what good care I have taken of Zeus. I'll learn to ride, too. That will please him. I wish I had left a note for the stable boy. He's bound to worry when he finds his precious horse gone.

Halfway up the mountain, a gap in the trees appeared. Irini stopped so we could look down over Rhodes Town.

Beyond the city, the sea was the colour of liquid silver and the bright moonlight danced over its gently rippling surface. In a landscape of dull mauve and dark blue, the island of Simi was nothing but a careless smudge above a veil of mist on the horizon. No sign of the three old ships. Where were they?

I patted the horse. *Can you see further than me, Zeus? Can you see the ship that carried your Danial away?*

I squeezed my eyes closed and whispered, 'I'm thinking about you all. Can you hear me? Papa? Anybody? My spirit's with you. Come back safe.' Desperate for them to know they were in my heart, I pleaded, 'Whatever happens, don't any of you ever give up. Irini and I are doing all we can to help end the war. Hang on, please, just hang on.' I listened intensely, trying to hear Papa's thoughts, but my head was dark and empty.

I had my arm around Irini. She sniffed hard, and I guessed she was evoking her parents and her older sister too. Her body shuddered and she sobbed, and I longed to make her feel better but couldn't think of anything to say.

'Do you believe they're okay, Dora?' she whispered. 'I'm afraid Giovanni might be right, that our families are being killed because they are Jewish.'

'What can we do? I'm scared for them too. We *must* try to stop the war, then they'll come home and everything will be as it was.'

We sat in silence for several minutes, praying for our loved ones, then without speaking Irini nudged the horse on.

* * *

We were sleeping when Giovanni turned up this morning. 'Get ready for a meeting with the *Andartes*,' he said, dropping a bulging sack near the fireplace. 'They want to speak to you again.'

'What do they want?' I slid out of bed and left Irini and Evangelisa to sleep. 'Let's go outside.'

He led the way. 'Not for me to ask, is it? Where'd the horse come from?'

'Zeus, he's ours. Irini and I crept home last night to fetch our things.'

Giovanni blinked. 'You went into town? That was bloody stupid.' He took me by the shoulders and shook me gently. 'You could've been shot!'

His eyes sparked with alarm and I wanted to fall into his arms. Instead I shrugged. 'We needed stuff. How are we supposed to live without clothes and food? What time will we go to the rebels?'

'Noon. I brought potatoes for your pot.' He nodded at the hut. 'Wasn't sure if you had any rabbit left.'

'Thanks. Appreciated.'

'You owe me.' His stern face softened and my heart melted. I gazed into his big brown eyes and wondered if this was love. 'One of the *Andartes* will come here tomorrow. He'll take you to their headquarters again.'

'Here?! But I don't want anyone knowing where we are.' I thought of Nathanial's unruly rebels, horrified that they would learn where we slept.

'They already know where you are. They know everything. I'll bet they know you went into town last night.'

'Not possible. We only decided ourselves late yesterday afternoon.' I hesitated, remembering the sound of breaking glass that saved us from being caught. 'Will this rebel want to eat? Is that why you brought potatoes?' He nodded. I put my hands on my hips and informed him, 'Then you, Giovanni, can tell Evangelisa to peel them, because I'm not.'

'They're fresh. Don't need peeling. I just pulled them up. Stolen, so they'll taste all the sweeter. Scrub them, cut them, and shove them in with the leftover rabbit. They'll be delicious.' He stared at me for a moment. 'You ever shot a gun?'

'Do I look like I ever shot a gun?'

'Only askin', calm down. If Nathanial wants, will you learn?'

'I'll do anything to help stop the war before my family get to the prison camp.'

'Good answer. It's not difficult; just takes practice to hit a target.'

'What about Irini? Will he ask her to learn too?'

'Not sure, we'll see. He might have other plans for Irini and your sister, or he may want you to teach Irini, once you've got the hang of it.'

Thursday, 27 July 1944

I have hardly had time for my diary, not that there have been developments worth writing about since our trip into the city. Evangelisa has tried on every one of her dresses. It is uplifting to see her so happy. I rescued the first diary, and the letter I'd written and hidden under her clothes. There's no point in worrying her.

When I returned from the *Andartes'* villa, Irini rushed out of the hut to greet me.

'Dora! 'she cried clearly delighted, taking my hand and leading me into the hut. 'Come and eat. I was afraid the rebels would scoff all our stew so I saved us a bowl.'

'Thanks.' While we ate, she was talking to me about Evangelisa's frocks, but I hardly heard her. My mind was full of the war and the rebels, and our families. Once I had taken the edge off my hunger, I asked her, 'What do you think, Irini? Can we help the *Andartes* disrupt the enemy? Help end the war before anything bad happens to our parents?'

'Why not?' she said quickly. 'When you dress younger, no one will suspect what you're capable of. It's not as if we can do anything else, is it?'

'Right, but will they treat Evangelisa with respect? She can be a bit naive, and we were exaggerating when we claimed she could cook. All her total culinary skill amounts to right now is washing a few potatoes.'

Irini raised her eyebrows. 'If they don't treat her right, they'll have us to deal with, won't they?!'

'I'll bet the very thought has them terrified,' I said.

Saturday, 29 July 1944

My first *Andartes* job is to sabotage a load of pumpernickel headed for the army barracks. I have to damage as many packets as possible. Nathanial said the foil wrapping kept the bread fresh for years, but once air got inside, it soon perished.

Giovanni has untied my wrist and replaced his catapult with four short lengths of split bamboo and a tight bandage. It feels so much lighter, and he is glad to get his beloved catapult back. I washed my hair yesterday and Irini tied it in rags, so I have a head of stupid ringlets this morning. Evangelisa has lent me one of her frilly party frocks and a pair of white ankle socks that we'd brought from our house in the city.

Armed with a skipping rope with two sharp pins sticking through the handles, I am about to travel to the port on the crossbar of Giovanni's bicycle. If luck is on my side, I will update my journal, with all that has taken place, when I return.

* * *

Dear Diary, what a day this has been! Once again, I found myself in the clutches of a German soldier. A terrifying moment, but I have come to realise that each time I survive being horribly frightened, the event leaves me a little stronger. I conclude that this is how you become brave. You get to realise that you will survive if you are calm, and strong willed, and determined enough.

I know my family will be very determined to survive. They overcame many problems in the past, like having to move from our lovely village of Paradissi, to the Jewish quarter in Rhodes Old Town. This has made them strong enough to deal with anything the Germans throw at them. But let me tell you how my first day as a member of the *Andartes* went.

I travelled to the port balanced on the crossbar of Giovanni's bike. My tension mounted as we neared the town. Giovanni seemed unconcerned.

'How will you pay for this?' he said pulling harder on the brakes as we rolled downhill.

'You're going to charge me?' *Déjà vu*, Giovanni the mercenary, I thought.

'You owe me for the potatoes too,' he said. 'Three kisses wherever I want, and not a cent less.'

This game of his, charging with kisses, had become a joke between us, but in my mood I struggled to respond with a quip that would hide my anxiety.

I'd hardly slept, worried I might fail and let everyone down. Now, my darling Giovanni had sensed my unease and was trying to take my mind away from the assignment. I appreciated the gesture. On the bicycle's crossbar, between his arms, I turned to look at his face.

His eyes flicked to mine and then returned to the road. He whispered, 'Don't worry, you'll be fine.' Then he carried on with the distraction, 'What about you kissing me somewhere that *is* normally covered with clothes?'

'I'm not even going to answer!' My tension continued to build until I noticed him grinning like a madman and I laughed too.

'That's better,' he said pulling up near the port. I practised a little skipping on the side of the road, careful not to stab myself with the pins. The ringlets danced and my skirt flounced as I jumped the rope.

'Definitely ten years old.' His smile fell as he took my hand and placed it on his heart. 'Stay safe, Dora Cohen,' he whispered seriously.

'Will you wait for me, Giovanni?'

We gazed into each other's eyes for a moment before he nodded once, and I skipped away.

* * *

At the port, I spotted the pallet with the pumpernickel packets near the edge of the quay. I hopped along, slowly getting closer to the bread while singing skipping songs. Once behind the pallet, I tapped my rope handle down the rows of aluminium foil, piercing each packet. I skipped about once more, then did the same on the side facing the ferry boat.

The remaining sides were not so easy. Anyone could see me. I looked around and caught sight of Nathanial watching me from a dockside kafenion.

With my arms out, I twirled. Behaving like a child wasn't difficult. Two German soldiers came and stood next to the pallet. I glanced at Nathanial and saw him make a sideways nod, telling me to leave.

I skipped up to the soldiers, then stood on one leg with my hands behind my back. They smiled at me. I mimicked the irritating adulation thing Evangelisa did, swinging from side to side and gazing at them.

'I can count to five hundred,' I said childishly. 'Can you?'

One of the Germans flicked the backs of his fingers at me and they carried on talking.

I turned to face the pallet. Pointing at them and counting loudly. Then, pretending to have lost my place, I tapped each packet with the handle of my skipping rope and started again. It worked. The soldiers laughed, and I had almost finished when another German joined them. The first two stood to attention and saluted.

I had one row left, so I stuck at it, pricking every packet while calling out the numbers.

'Oi!' the officer yelled, grabbing my arm and pulling me away. '*Weggehen!*' he shouted. 'Go!'

I appeared upset by the soldier's rough handling, gathered my skipping rope, and ran off the pier.

'Well done!' Nathanial said at the villa. 'You've impressed me, little one.'

Bursting with pride, I nodded respectfully. My first assignment in a plan to end the war. 'I can do much more if you give me the opportunity, sir.'

Wednesday, 2 August 1944

Dear Diary, once again, I have been too busy to keep up with you on a daily basis. Nathanial assigned various acts of sabotage to me. Irini has been my lookout and helper, and I depended on her for my safety. This has further tightened the bond between us.

We put sugar in army petrol tanks, jammed wood up exhaust pipes, and wedged sharpened metal brackets behind the tyres of stationary jeeps.

After every job, Irini and I have a ritual of mutual appreciation. We shake hands vigorously, step back, and while saluting each other we chant, 'Another job well done, corporal!'

The euphoria of success helps numb our deepest fears. At the same time, we grow even closer, protecting Evangelisa from any information that might cause her distress, and praising everything she does.

Thursday, 3 August 1944

Once again, I am summoned to the villa. Giovanni will come to the hut to fetch me, and I long to fall into his arms when we get into the woods. For now, I must put my diary away, and wait for

211

him. I will record the day's events, whatever they may be, when Evangelisa is asleep this evening.

* * *

Giovanni and I arrived at the villa flushed and breathless, I stood before Nathanial in the lobby and he gave me a knowing look before he spoke.

'Be careful, little one, you'll burn your fingers,' he said nodding towards the door where Giovanni waited. He allowed the words to sink in before he continued. 'Tomorrow, I'm sending you to our mud tunnels to learn to shoot.'

'Mud tunnels? Why? Where are they?'

'In the bamboo groves. The mud dulls the sound of the gun. It's the only suitable location that isn't too far away. There's an old man there, Kapitanos Nikos, who knows every nook and stream of the place. He's the best shot on the island too. You'll be safe with him, and he'll teach you well.'

Time had passed quickly since my family departed on the rusty ships. I wondered where they were and what was happening. 'If it will help end the war, I'll become your best shot,' I said.

'You're a true freedom fighter, little one. I'm going to give you help. Xanthi's just joined us. She's older than you, but like Irini and Evangelisa, she'll be under your command. Once I see you work well together, you can have more helpers and larger tasks to accomplish. Do you understand?'

Although thrilled that he trusted me with my own band of freedom fighters, I was also anxious about the consequences if I messed up. 'I look forward to my next orders, sir.'

He laughed. 'You've got spirit. I like it.' He became serious. 'You remember, everything that's passed between us is confidential. Never repeat anything to anyone. Understand? I meant what I said the first time you came here.'

'Yes, sir. Not to the shepherd, my friend, and especially not my sister, right?'

He nodded. 'If you do, you *will* be killed, along with the person you pass the information to. These rules apply to everyone in the *Andartes*. Now, I've important cargo for the Kapitanos.' He raised his arm and clicked his fingers. A rebel approached with a brown leather satchel and a wooden crate, and then moved away.

Chapter 29

Rhodes, Greece.

In the airport lobby, Naomi stretched her neck, trying to see past the stream of excited holidaymakers who trundled trollies and tired children through the sliding glass doors. She glimpsed anxious travellers crowded around a luggage carousel in the distance.

Where's Rebecca?

The monitor claimed Rebecca's flight had landed. Grinning tourists jostled and shoved, eager to greet the sunshine. A youth texting on his iPhone bumped into her. Despite the air con, the lobby smelled of body odour and cigarette smoke. She decided to wait outside.

On the forecourt, taxi drivers raised cards bearing their passenger's name. Uniformed tour operators ticked clients off their clipboards, while others led tourists to their coaches.

Perhaps Rebecca had changed her mind. Naomi scanned the crowd once more. All the anger and bitterness at her sister's departure came back. The shouting, door slamming, Bubba's tears, Rebecca's face white with rage. And all the time Naomi was caught between the two people she loved. The situation had spiralled out of control and neither Rebecca nor Bubba would consider the other's feelings. She glanced at the arrivals monitor again and tried to swallow her trepidation.

'Naomi!' A woman's voice called from behind. Her heart lifted. She spun around and saw her sister for the first time in a decade.

'Rebecca!' They both froze for a moment, separated by their past yet drawn together at the same time. Naomi felt detached, as if seeing Rebecca through a sheet of glass: cold and untouchable with emotional baggage far greater than the two cerise suitcases on her trolley. After a frigid few seconds, the barriers shattered and they rushed towards each other, sniffing back tears as they hugged.

'My God, it's been so long!' Naomi said stepping away, ridiculously shy. 'Look at you, auburn hair, and not a day older than when you left. All by yourself?' She glanced about, anxious that Fritz might be there.

Rebecca smiled nervously. 'He's in New York. Anyway, better if he didn't come, you know?' She placed her hand on Naomi's shoulder. 'I wanted to say . . . well, I don't want any problems, okay? If Bubba starts getting upset, I'll simply go and stay in a hotel. How is Bubba?' Her voice was breathy, panicky.

'Good. Picked up a lot since you agreed to return home, but a little worried too. Try to be gentle with her, will you? She's longing to explain how sorry she is for what was said.'

Rebecca stared at the ground for a moment. 'I'm quite ashamed of the way I behaved, but she hurt me terribly, Naomi. I find it difficult to believe either of you realised how much. I love you both, you know?'

Well, why didn't you answer the bloody letters then?

Breaking Naomi's thought, Rebecca continued. 'Anyway, water under the bridge.' The tension melted from her face, but Naomi recognised pain in her eyes. 'How're the boys, and Costa? I've missed them too.'

'They're good.' Naomi swelled with pride. 'They'll be back for the court case. We'll all be home for a while.' She wondered about Rebecca's children, but suspected her sister would go on and on about how perfectly charming they were, so she decided to save that question for later. She grabbed the biggest suitcase and walked towards the taxi rank. An awkward silence built, then they both started to speak.

'What's life like in—'

'There's so much I want—'

'Sorry. You first,' Naomi said.

Rebecca nodded. 'I wondered about Bubba's stroke. How's she coping? How're you managing?'

'Every day's a struggle for us both.' Naomi sighed. 'The physical side's tough, but she's improving, and that's the main thing. What wore me down was the severe effect it had on her mental faculties.' Naomi stopped walking and shrugged. 'It was as if her lively, intelligent mind had left home, moved in next door, and she had become an entirely different person. As she began to recover, she'd sort of come back for more frequent visits.'

'Poor you. Must have been hell,' Rebecca said lightly. 'You should have written, or phoned sooner.'

Naomi dowsed a spark of anger and started walking again. 'Not hell exactly, but I've never felt quite so alone. I thought about you often.' She touched Rebecca's arm. 'If I'd been able to pick the phone up and share stuff, it would have helped a lot.'

Rebecca lowered her eyes and after a beat said, 'Look, I'm sorry. It didn't occur to me that anything could be wrong. Only after you phoned and told me about the stroke did I started to worry about Bubba. Selfish of me really.'

'My friends rallied around. Still, I wished I'd had Costa home, not that Bubba's his responsibility.' Perhaps that was a bit bitchy, Naomi thought. The last thing she wanted to do was alienate Rebecca now, yet a certain resentment that she couldn't explain seemed to be building inside her. 'But enough of this. Come on, I'll bring you up to date in the taxi.'

'Before we get there, I wanted to say ... I remembered you were nuts about scents and creams, so I bought you a lovely bottle of perfume in London.'

Naomi experienced a twinge of guilt. 'Very kind, but you needn't have. It's sufficient that you came back.' She wanted it to be true, yet feared her words sounded insincere.

'He can't help having blond hair and blue eyes, you know? It doesn't make him a monster,' Rebecca said flatly. 'He loves me, and I love him, despite all that our love for each other has taken from us.' She sighed. 'Saying "it's not fair", sounds childish, but I don't know any other words that explain how we feel.'

Naomi nodded. 'The whole thing got out of hand, didn't it? We shouldn't have allowed the situation to continue for so long.'

Rebecca dropped the suitcase. 'Can I hug you again? There've been moments when I've missed you so badly.' They embraced. 'You'd never imagine how many times I started to dial your number. Anyway, enough about me. I want to tell you about the scent.'

Naomi nodded. 'Go on.'

'Before I left, I read about the spice tree in the diary. They say life's full of coincidences.' She smiled, her eyes sparkling, reminding Naomi of the fun person her sister was. 'I mean, can you imagine it? An hour before, I'd bought this perfume to bring to Rhodes. The bottle was on the table in front of me when I opened the diary and read about Dora and Giovanni going to collect cinnamon and oranges in the woods. It's an orange and cinnamon perfume. The bottle's even got a little cinnamon stick attached by a ribbon. I know this sounds stupid, Naomi, but I was very nervous about coming back here. When that happened – reading about the cinnamon tree in the diary – it was like a sign that I was doing the right thing. Sounds mad, I know. So although I bought the perfume for you, I hope you understand that I simply *have* to give it to Bubba.'

'Of course you do. That's a really nice gesture.' She paused for a moment. 'I wonder if Bubba remembers everything she wrote. I mean, if Papas Yiannis has had the diaries for over thirty years, I bet she's forgotten how much she revealed.'

'They're so sad. Fritz is reading them too. He took the first one to work with him and read it cover to cover. Couldn't put it down.' Rebecca stared straight ahead for a moment, her face stony.

Naomi touched her sleeve. 'Is everything all right?'

'Yes,' she replied too quickly. 'Everything's fine. He was shocked by Bubba's experiences.'

Rebecca sounded nervous when she talked about Fritz. Naomi wondered if things really were okay between them.

'He's taken the second diary to read on his way to America. Also, he asked if the pistol could be donated to the London gun museum. What do you think?'

'Ah, the beautiful Naomi!' Taxi driver Stelios grinned a set of tobacco-stained teeth. He turned to Rebecca, 'Your sister is back!? The gods smile on me today! Get in, lovely ladies, while I take care of the suitcases.'

Rebecca giggled. 'I'd forgotten what they're like,' she said quietly.

As the cab pulled way, Naomi asked, 'Why do you imagine the gun's got Fritz's initials embossed on the side? I'm confused. Obviously, it's a lot older than Fritz, so I wondered if it really did belong to someone in his family. I don't want to dig up the past, but I can't help wondering how Bubba came to have that particular pistol? To be honest, it's been playing on my mind, Rebecca. It's such a sensitive matter as far as Bubba's concerned, so I wanted to ask you what you know about it before we get home.'

'It bothered me at first but, as I said, life's full of coincidences.' Rebecca glanced out of the taxi window and her eyes widened. 'My God! This place hasn't altered in ten years! I'm so happy to be back.'

Naomi was uplifted to hear the pleasure in Rebecca's voice. 'You're right: nothing's changed, but go on about the gun, before we get home.'

'Ah yes. F.N. is the manufacturer's logo. I googled it. A Browning pistol manufactured by Fabrique Nationale of Belgium. Absolutely nothing to do with Fritz Neumanner of Austria, or Frick Nüller of Nazi Germany.'

'Wow, that's a relief!'

'I know. I also became suspicious when I read those initials. I started imagining all sorts. Then the diaries arrived and I couldn't stop reading.'

'A cunning plan by Bubba. She suspected curiosity would get the better of us. Changing the subject, what about children? I seem to remember you were going to have a netball team.' She laughed kindly until she saw her sister's face and realised she'd touched a nerve. 'Sorry, Rebecca. I didn't mean to pry.'

Rebecca shook her head, sniffed and smiled sadly. 'No, don't fret. I'll tell you about it tomorrow. I'm too tired now. Look, we're here, Spartili Street!'

They argued about who'd pay the taxi before lugging Rebecca's suitcases down the cobbled road.

Rebecca's smile was over bright and again Naomi suspected her sister's life was not as 'fine' as she pretended it to be. Clearly, Rebecca was anxious about meeting Bubba.

219

Heleny rushed out of her house as they approached. 'Rebecca! How lovely to see you again!' She grabbed Rebecca's shoulders and planted kisses on her cheeks.

'Heleny! Gosh, you look good. It's been ten years and you haven't aged a day!' Rebecca said.

'That's your sister's skin lotion, a miracle worker. Everyone loves it.' Heleny walked with them.

'So I was right. You are still mixing lotions and potions, Sis. I must have some of this fantastic cream. I can't have you appearing younger than me.' She laughed. 'Perhaps I can assist with the packaging and promotion, or have you got it all organised?'

'Not my forte, is it? I've done my best, but I'm glad of any help.' They carried on down Spartili Street.

'Does Papas Yiannis still live opposite?' Rebecca asked. When Naomi nodded, she continued. 'Great! I didn't plan to bring gifts, but I noticed an icon of Saint John at the duty free and it reminded me of him, so I bought it.'

They stopped outside Bubba's house. 'Give me a minute, will you?' Rebecca put her hand on her chest. She took a breath and exhaled slowly. 'I have to stay calm. Doctor's orders.' She turned to Naomi. 'No stress, but it's difficult.'

Again Naomi heard alarm bells. She glanced at Heleny.

'Right, I'm off,' Heleny said. 'Come around tomorrow, Rebecca. You know where I live there's always a pot of coffee on the go.'

The cottage door opened. Rebecca's eyes widened. Naomi patted her arm. 'You'll be fine, don't worry.'

'Stupid to be so anxious, Bubba's an old lady.'

Papas Yiannis appeared from the doorway. 'Rebecca! How wonderful!' He held out his hand. She took it and kissed his ring.

'Hello, Papas. It's good to see you.'

'Thanks for coming back,' the priest said. 'Bubba's waiting. I was sitting with her while Naomi fetched you. She's a little anxious.'

Rebecca nodded. 'Not the only one. I'll pop over tomorrow, if I may.'

The priest smiled and nodded.

'Come on.' Naomi linked arms with her sister. 'Leave the suitcases. We'll deal with them later.'

They went through the door together.

After the brilliant sunlight, the room seemed dark and their eyes took a moment to adjust. Bubba sat in her armchair and Naomi viewed her with Rebecca's eyes, realising how pale and wizened she looked compared to ten years ago.

'Oh, Bubba!' Rebecca's tears rose as she dropped onto a footstool beside the overstuffed chair. 'It's so good to be back.' She kissed her grandmother and took her hand. 'How are you?'

Bubba nodded, clearly emotional. 'Thank you for coming, child. I understand it wasn't easy – and before we go any further, I'm sorry for what I said.' Tears trickled down her hollow cheeks. Naomi recalled the first time she saw Bubba cry, on the beach, the day her parents were lost at sea.

'No, no, it's me. I can't apologise enough, Bubba. I was stupid and stubborn, and my behaviour was appalling. I regret everything, with all my heart. But you understand: I *had* to follow the man I love.'

Bubba stuck her chin out and narrowed her eyes. After a long silence, she muttered, 'I've missed you. We should try to put the past behind us.'

Rebecca twisted a length of hair around her finger the way Naomi remembered. A sign of stress. 'You don't know how much I missed you too.'

221

'I've been worried. You should have answered my letters,' Bubba said.

'Letters?' Rebecca blinked rapidly and appeared lost for a moment.

Naomi frowned. Had Bubba's correspondence meant so little to Rebecca that she had tossed them without another thought? Naomi found that hard to believe, yet what other explanation could there be?

Bubba glanced at the door and then at Naomi, who recognised her fear. Naomi shook her head. Bubba sighed and sank back into the chair. Their tension dissipated as they talked about trivia, simple chit-chat, while Naomi filled the table with meze. Courgette balls, calamari, fried cheese, bite-size pieces of salt cod in golden batter, beetroot salad in garlic dressing, and grilled octopus.

'A glass of wine, Rebecca?' Naomi asked.

Rebecca shook her head. 'Erm, perhaps not.'

'Coffee then?'

'Plain water, if you don't mind.'

Naomi frowned; this wasn't like Rebecca.

They sat around the table. 'You got the gun?' Bubba said to Rebecca.

'Well, yes . . . although I didn't realise what it was until the last parcel came.'

'And the diaries?'

Rebecca nodded. 'Two, I found it quite shocking to learn about your childhood, and I'm so amazed by your bravery. I'd no idea what you've been through.' She paused, and glanced at her sister. 'Fritz was astounded too.' She returned to Bubba. 'I hope you don't mind. I decided he should read them. He needs to understand what happened here. Many of the war atrocities were kept from him.' She looked at Naomi, then Bubba. 'He's finished the first one, and taken the other to America to read on the plane.'

'There's two more,' Bubba said. 'But the last one's for another occasion.'

The sisters exchanged a glance.

Naomi changed the subject. 'I forgot your luggage.' She dragged the cases in and Rebecca found the perfume.

'I hope you like this, Bubba. Let me put some on your wrist.'

Bubba grinned her crooked smile as Rebecca sprayed the scent. The old lady lifted her hand and sniffed. 'Oh!' she whispered urgently. 'It's, oh, the cinnamon tree . . .'

'It is. Look, there's even a little cinnamon stick fixed to the lid.'

Bubba touched the thin roll of bark. Her face blanked and she pulled in a sob. 'Oh, Giovanni.' She gazed into the past while fresh tears trickled down her cheeks. 'I waited for so many years.'

Rebecca, alarmed, stared at the fancy perfume bottle and chewed her lip.

Naomi took the scent from her grandmother and returned it to Rebecca. 'Best put it away for now. Don't worry. She slips back sometimes, although not so often these days. She's recalling the past. She'll be fine in a few minutes. Doctor Despina said we should let her work through these things. Just hold her hand.'

Rebecca did, but it was clear Bubba's mind had left the room. 'It was an accident,' she whispered. 'I didn't mean to do it, I swear! Don't leave me, please come back.' Then Bubba was crying bitterly. 'I loved her so much, and now she's gone. I'm cursed to lose everyone I love.' She pulled away from Rebecca and dabbed her eyes.

'How awful! How long's this been going on?' Rebecca asked quietly.

'Since the stroke, she regresses,' Naomi said. 'Suffers through the worst times of her life. There's nothing we can do. It's as if she needs to go through this pain every so often. She'll get over it shortly.' She picked up the perfume. 'The scent has invoked deeply buried memories.' She passed a bunch of tissues to Rebecca, who gently dried the tears from her grandmother's face.

'You've had all this to contend with?' She blinked at Naomi. 'I'm so sorry. I'd no idea. Do you have a nurse that comes in?'

'Don't be crazy. I haven't the money for things like that.' Naomi rubbed a little cream onto Bubba's hands. 'I have a rubber sheet on the bed to deal with incontinence, and the doctor calls three times a week. That's it.'

'This is too much for you, Naomi. You've got to let me help.'

Naomi smiled, but not unkindly. 'Ah, you'll clean her up and wash her down when her bowels misbehave, will you?' The look of revulsion on her sister's face made Naomi laugh.

'Actually,' Rebecca stuttered, 'I was thinking more along the lines of paying for some assistance.'

Naomi doused a surge of resentment and placed her hand over Rebecca's. 'That's kind of you, but Bubba would find it humiliating for a stranger to come in and wash her, clean her teeth and wipe her bottom. It's fine. I can do it.'

'I feel awful, Naomi. I couldn't have done it . . . no way.'

'Let me put it like this: she did it for us, didn't she? All through our childhood not a single thing was too much trouble. Her grandchildren were her first priority; she had no time for friends, or any social life at all. She kissed our bleeding knees, wiped our snotty noses, and applied calamine lotion on our chickenpox. We should have gone to an orphanage, but she gave up everything for you and me. So a few months returning the debt is nothing in the great scheme of things.'

'I've never thought of Bubba like that. To be honest, I took her for granted when I was growing up.'

Naomi hesitated, then said, 'All children tend to do that. Don't worry about it.'

'You're a saint. I'm ashamed that I haven't supported you. Is there anything I can do now?'

Bubba whimpered and stared blankly at Naomi.

'Yes, sure. Bring me a glass of milk from the fridge and her pills off the worktop, while I get her changed for bed.' She turned to her grandmother. 'It's all right, Bubba. You've had a bad dream, that's all. Time for your medication, and a good night's sleep.' She got up and kissed Bubba's forehead.

'Can I do anything else?' Rebecca said, pouring the milk.

Naomi shook her head. 'I'll be an hour. Why don't you get yourself a drink and read some of the third diary? It's on top of the kitchen cabinet.'

Chapter 30

In the villa, I stood before Nathanial and waited to hear what he had to say. He frowned and stared at me.

'I hope I'm not making a mistake.' He lifted the brown satchel. 'We, the *Andartes*, are very short of firepower but I'm giving you your own weapon, little one. It's a 1910 Browning.' He thrust the leather bag towards me. 'I want you to remember that this gun is the same as the firearm that killed Archduke Franz Ferdinand.' He recognised the shock on my face. 'Yes, Dora, a single shot from a pistol identical to this, started the Great War. A conflict that took the lives of millions.'

'I understand what you're saying. A gun can have huge and irreversible consequences.'

'Look after it, use it wisely, and above all, don't let either the gun or the crate fall into enemy hands.'

'I won't, I swear.'

'You will leave before first light. Xanthi is at the hut. She'll mind your sister while Irini takes you to Kapitanos Nikos.'

I nodded, unable to come up with anything to say.

'Now, you're dismissed. I'll send directions in the morning and you'll hear from me again when I've a job for you.'

He turned to Giovanni, who sat by the door. 'Take her back.'

* * *

Giovanni slung the bag with the gun over his shoulder. I longed to inspect it. The crate had a rope handle on either side and together we carried it through the woods.

At the hut, Evangelisa had cooked more potatoes. 'Another amazing job. Well done!' I said, embarrassed by the way she beamed lapping up the flattery. I must praise her more often. I guessed the stranger eating with them was Xanthi.

'We leave an hour before dawn,' I told Irini before sitting to eat.

She threw me a quizzical look.

'You have to give me a riding lesson this afternoon. We must take Zeus with us tomorrow.' I sensed she was unhappy. If only we had some privacy, I longed to tell her all that had happened, but Xanthi and Evangelisa stayed close.

Irini nodded. 'Am I going with you?'

'I don't really know the details. We'll find out in the morning.' Flustered that my best friend had asked me a question I couldn't answer, I continued, 'I guess you'll have to take me this time because I can't ride well enough to control the horse for long.'

'What's in the box?' she said, lifting her chin towards the bed where the crate was stashed.

I shrugged. 'No idea.'

We always shared our secrets. Her face fell, and I got a sinking feeling in my stomach. 'Irini, I want to explain everything, but I can't. For *your* sake. It's dangerous. My only instructions are that we must be ready and wait for Giovanni.'

Xanthi was pleasant enough, and it was obvious Evangelisa liked her. She glowed with admiration, which made me smile. I noticed Xanthi looked more like Evangelisa than I did, both in height and build. Pleased Evangelisa had a new friend, it occurred to me she'd probably been lonely since we left home and her school friends. I must try to be a better sister.

Nathanial told me the best way to establish my authority was to give orders right away, so I did.

'Xanthi and Evangelisa, take care of the dishes and clean up. Irini, saddle the horse. Please.' I said boldly although my insides

227

were shaking. If they rejected my instructions, I'd be left looking stupid and ashamed.

'Giovanni, I'll meet you under the cinnamon tree at sundown.'

Irini flicked a glance of disdain my way.

I'm sorry, Irini!

I found her scorn hard to take and lowered my eyes. She marched off to fetch Zeus.

* * *

'Keep your heels down!' Irini shouted.

I pulled my toes up and pushed against the stirrups. 'Straight back!' she yelled as if she hated me. The atmosphere was dreadful and I didn't know what to do about it.

'Irini . . .' I called.

'Don't talk. Concentrate. Tap his belly with your heels, and squeeze with your knees to urge him on.'

Irini stood in the middle of the clearing with Zeus on a long rope.

Once in the saddle, I tried to remember the things Danial had taught me, but because I had wounded Irini so badly, I found it hard to focus. 'Irini, I'm sorry. Really!'

She lifted her face and, just before she turned it away, I noticed her chin quiver.

Irini was more than a friend – more than a sister. I loved her so much, and now I'd hurt her deeply. My own tears were on the brink.

I wanted to tell her everything, but that would put her in danger. Nathanial warned me, and I understood he wasn't the sort to make an empty threat.

Xanthi and Evangelisa came to watch. Wretched, I realised I couldn't explain anything in front of them.

After the lesson, we ate the last of the potatoes and bread, and a dish of wild greens that Xanthi and my sister had prepared. An awkward silence hung over the meal.

'Delicious.' I said. 'That was the best salad ever!' Evangelisa and Xanthi grinned at each other. Irini stared at the floor, and I recalled she'd made the same food a few days back and I hadn't commented.

'The way your cooking skills are improving, you'll soon be as good as Irini.'

Irini looked up. I touched her arm. 'I have to meet Giovanni and find out about tomorrow.'

'I'll come with you.' She followed me outside. 'You shouldn't be going into the woods by yourself. It'll be dark in half an hour.'

Our eyes met. She was testing me.

'Sorry, honestly, but I have to go alone.' I tried to catch her eye, but she stared at Xanthi and Evangelisa, who were dragging the blanket over the bushes to give it an airing.

'You'll leave me stuck here with them, again?' She sat on the log, her hands between her knees and her head bowed. 'I miss my parents and my sister. I wish I'd gone with them.'

'Stop it! Never say that!' I grabbed her by the shoulders and shook her. 'We have to do everything we can to end the war, then our families will return to Rhodes. You know it. Don't be so childish!' I shouted.

Her eyes filled with pain and her face crumpled. 'We were such good friends, Dora, really close, no secrets, but now I've become invisible. You're more interested in Giovanni. I do everything I can to help, but you can't even say thanks. You've hurt me by taking me for granted and abandoning our friendship.' She sighed, silent for a moment. 'I'm so terribly lonely, Dora, and you are breaking my heart.'

I blinked at her, shocked. Had I really behaved so badly? I considered the past weeks, and realised that she spoke the truth. I stared at the ground, ashamed, then sat beside her and slipped my arm around her drooping shoulders.

'It's true; I do take you for granted, but not in a nasty way. I take you for granted like I take my own heart for granted. It's there, beating away, keeping me going, keeping me alive. I don't even think about it, but without it I'm dust. Without you, Irini, I'm lifeless.' I had to pause, swallow hard and fight to keep my voice steady. I turned towards her and recognised the sadness in her face. It cut me up.

'Please . . . I am so sorry. I didn't realise I'd been so selfish. I've been so wrapped up in the *Andartes'* plans trying to get the war to end. I'm desperate for my family to come back, and I want your loved ones to return too, but without you, Irini, I can' do it. I long to tell you what happened with the rebels, but if I do, they swore they'd kill me and the person I told, in the most horrible way. So, much as I want, I dare not risk it. You're too precious to me.'

She nodded and sniffed hard. 'What's going to happen to us, Dora? Are you in love with Giovanni? I'm so mixed up, confused about my feelings. Perhaps it's jealousy, but I don't want to share you with him.' She shook her head adamantly. 'Whatever it is, when you're with Giovanni, it's so painful for me. Really cuts me up.' She stared at her hands. 'When he kissed me in the woods, I wanted it to be amazing, but it wasn't anything. When I kiss you, it's like my moon goes into orbit. I realise that sounds mad, but I can't explain it any other way.'

I felt terrible because I too was all mixed up inside. 'I don't know if it's love,' I said. 'It is something crazy, and sexy, and insane, and magical. I can't fight it. But it's very different from what we have.' I placed my hand on her cheek and turned her face towards me. Her sad eyes came to meet mine and suddenly everything became clear. 'I love you, Irini. I truly love you, and I will until my dying day. Nothing can change that. Right now, I want to spend the rest of my life with you.' I had to be completely honest with her, even though I understood my words might be hurtful. 'I don't know where this is going with Giovanni. Perhaps it will fizzle out, but I can't ignore it any more than I can explain it. I'm powerless to resist the chemistry between me and him. At times it seems to be swallowing me up, but try as I may, I can't fight it.'

'That's another thing that upsets me, the fighting. You will never end the war by yourself, Dora. Do you really want to risk your life for the *Andartes*? Because that is what you're doing. It's terrible waiting here, wondering if you've been caught committing some crazy sabotage.' She sighed. 'They *will* shoot you if they catch you, Dora. You can't seem to understand the danger you put yourself in.'

'But I have to try, I . . . It's for Papa . . . He gave me life, and I owe him mine.'

'No, you don't! What you owe him is to be safe. You owe him grandchildren, a happy life, a well-kept home for your family — all those things that made his upbringing of you worthwhile. How would you feel if your daughter had herself killed for your sake? You wouldn't want it, not now, not ever, no matter what the circumstances.' Irini sighed. 'I worry each time you leave that I may never see you again, and you can't even be bothered to say goodbye to me.'

Her words touched my heart. I had hurt her so much. 'Oh, Irini, I *am* sorry. I didn't realise how awful I was being. It's just . . . what if the war ends the day after they've all been executed.' I squeezed my eyes closed. 'I go mad worrying about it. I imagine being shot in the head. Do you think it hurts?' She was silent for a moment, then a sob shuddered through her body. I pulled her to me. She pushed her face against my neck and cried, and I held her until she calmed.

'If they do shoot them,' she said,' I hope they're together. I hope Papa is holding Mama and my sister in his arms, the way you hold me.' She started sobbing again. 'Oh, Dora, what can we do? We mustn't let it happen!'

'I wish you could understand, Irini. I would blame myself for the rest of my life if they died. I *can't* allow it. We *must* find a way to speed up the end of the war. I swear to be a better friend and

be with you for eternity. I didn't realise I was being so terrible.'
I leaned forward and turned to look into her face. 'Say you'll
always be my best friend, Irini, that you'll love me forever, as I
love you. Please tell me you forgive me.'

Her eyes, still swimming with tears, met mine. She nodded and
then stared at the ground. 'I want to be more help,' she said.
'Will you ask Nathanial? I have to make sure you're safe and, if
the worst happens, I wish to die at your side.'

'Please don't talk like that,' I lifted her chin. 'We're not going
to get killed, because we're invincible, aren't we, corporal?

She smiled sadly. 'If you say so, *kapitanessa.*'

I promised I would speak to the *Andartes* leader. Silently, we
re-arranged the bed so that Evangelisa and Xanthi slept at the
bottom, and Irini and I took the top, packed like sardines in a
can. The arrangement suited us fine, so long as nobody snuggled down too far so the other end got a pair of sweaty feet
in their face. We made a new rule: everyone had to wash their
feet before they got into bed.

* * *

A long and difficult day has come to an end. Eager to bring
my diary up to date, and desperate for an uninterrupted night's
sleep, I'm writing this at the spring. The sun is setting over the
monastery, a glorious sight to see. The sky was golden when I
arrived. In a matter of minutes, it has turned orange and then
red, washing everything around me in warm light. The air is still,
and the usual woodland sounds have died, leaving me with an
odd feeling that the world waits for something enormous and
uplifting.

I have mixed feelings about leaving my companions, Irini,
Giovanni, and Evangelisa. I will miss them, but I look forward
to having a little time just for myself. The challenge of learning
to shoot excites me.

Friday, 4 August 1944

Dear diary, just a few lines before I leave for the mud tunnels. I woke trembling and afraid for no apparent reason, The air in the hut was damp and stuffy. I lay in the dark trying to recall my nightmare, without success, then I slipped out of bed and sat outside. Being grown-up isn't all I imagined it to be. Suddenly, everything is serious with consequences I had never considered. Responsibility was a weight I hadn't foreseen and was even less prepared for.

Chapter 31

Rebecca traced small watermarks on the cover. Dora had cried over her journal. Then a fresh spot appeared, puckering the paper and slowly spreading. The page blurred as she stared, and Rebecca realised it was her own tears mingling with her grandmother's. She wiped her eyes and looked up from the diary, for a moment confused by her surroundings, like waking from a deep sleep in a strange place. She had her hand on her chest, staring, when Naomi came back into the kitchen.

'Are you all right?'

'I can hardly believe it's Bubba,' she said, her voice thick with emotion. 'Reading this completely changes my perspective of her. Imagine having that kind of friendship, Dora and Irini. They were so close.'

'I've considered that too. I mean, Heleny and I have been best mates all our lives. We started school together, and we've seen each other almost every day since. But recently, I realised she's been lonely for years. It made me awfully disappointed in myself. I wondered why her loneliness had never occurred to me before. Do you have close friends in London?'

Rebecca frowned for a moment, then shook her head. 'I'm in a children's charity group, and a lunch group, and a photography group too. There are a couple of neighbours that will come for a coffee at the drop of a hat, so I have lots of acquaintances but nothing that comes anywhere near Bubba and Irini's relationship. I suppose Fritz is my truest friend – my soulmate. But even though I've known him for eleven years, there are things, innermost feelings, that I'd be reluctant to share with him, and I guess he feels the same.' She stared at the floor, silent, her face stony.

Naomi watched her and wondered if everything was okay between her and Fritz. 'I suspect that changes over a great length of time. Sometimes you see an old couple giving off a certain sense of contentment. Even when they disagree or annoy each other, they're like one person. Do you know what I mean?'

Rebecca nodded. 'As it is with you and Costa.' The silence returned, broken when she looked straight into Naomi's eyes. 'Do you think I'll ever have that?'

Naomi was pained by the sadness in her sister's voice. 'It takes time, Rebecca, and patience, understanding and forgiveness. No marriage is all hearts and flowers.'

'Yours is.'

Naomi chuckled, lifting the moment. 'You believe so? Let me tell you: we've had our ups and downs over the decades. We almost divorced when we were younger, but we hung in there and eventually grew back together again.' Her smile softened. 'A bit like the cinnamon tree, really. A little piece of my heart was taken away, but the scars healed over and now everything appears as it was.'

Rebecca raised her eyebrows. 'Gosh, I had no idea. You mean there was somebody else?' They stared at each other for a moment, then Rebecca broke the silence. 'Sorry, sorry. What an appalling thing to say! Of course there wasn't. None of my business anyway.'

Naomi studied her sister and suddenly saw Rebecca's resemblance to Evangelisa. With this insight came a deeper understanding of Dora's relationship with her sibling, always on the verge of becoming closer, loving each other deeply, yet not really knowing each other.

'Call me old fashioned, but I suspect divorce is too easy these days,' Naomi said. 'When we were young, it still had a certain stigma attached, almost something to be ashamed of. A person got married for life, and changing your mind after four or five years was simply not acceptable.'

'But what if someone made a genuine mistake?'

'Then you'd hope to God there were no children to hurt and unsettle.'

'I long for children.'

Naomi heard such power in the words and, without understanding the reason, sensed heartbreak. Instinctively, she changed the subject. Whatever was wrong, it needed to come out in small chunks. She lifted the diary from Rebecca's lap, wishing she could lift her sister's troubles as easily. 'Shocking, isn't it? The diary I mean. I keep wondering where it's leading, and I have to remind myself of her tender age.'

'Such courage,' Rebecca swallowed. 'And every time she describes a Nazi, she describes Fritz. That part about Nüller? I'm telling you, I shivered. No wonder she was horrified when Fritz walked through the door. Do you remember how she gasped and stared at him, unable to speak? Her past must have come back in one horrible rush.' She pondered for a second. 'You said she gave the diaries and the gun to Papas Yiannis when I was born, when our parents were lost at sea. So, for nearly twenty years the journals had been out of her mind. What a devastating moment it must have been for her when I brought the man I wanted to marry into this room. The most difficult decision I ever made was to walk out of here a decade ago. I took such a hard line. I wish it could have been different, but I can't see how.'

'The bravest thing I ever did was to tell Bubba I was pregnant and *had* to get married. I was terrified she'd disown me.'

They both smiled sadly. 'The point is we had no idea what our grandmother had been through. The diary explains that in her eyes Fritz stood for all that was evil. The Axis had taken everything from her, and then *he* came for *you*. Imagine how she felt. I keep wondering if any of her family returned. What happened to Evangelisa, Giovanni, and Irini? I've tried to remember but I don't think I ever heard any mention of them. Did you?'

Rebecca shook her head and stifled a yawn. 'Sorry, it's been such a long day.'

''Course it has. Come on, I'll help get the cases upstairs.'

* * *

At ten o'clock the next morning, Rebecca stumbled into the kitchen. 'Gosh, I went out like a light,' she said. 'Where's Bubba?'

'Mid-morning nap. Heleny came around and invited you for coffee at eleven. I told her you only drank water or mountain tea.'

'Will you come too?'

Naomi shook her head. 'Lunch to prep. Shopping for dinner and washing to do. And the floors are desperate for a going-over.'

'Do you ever stop?'

They both caught sounds of their grandmother, groaning behind the rug.

'Are you all right, Bubba?' Naomi called. 'Do you need me?'

'Can't a woman have a bit of privacy around her? Leave me be!' she replied.

The sisters exchanged a smile before Naomi continued.

'When I get an hour, I spend it on my lotions and potions. I've always got orders to catch up on. Marina's helping with the Internet stuff, website, Twitter, and so on. She talked me out of considering a shop.'

'Too right. My photography took off online. Very successful. Most photographers closed their premises and went on the net. Such a vast audience at your fingertips. What about accounts?'

'Haven't a clue. I'm hardly making any money yet.'

'My advice is don't wait until you are. Keep a log of everything you spend and take from the start. Then it won't be such a task when you submit your finances.'

'She's absolutely right.' Papas Yiannis stuck his head through the doorway and beamed at the sisters. 'May I come in? Sorry to interrupt your morning but I've got some important information. Good news.'

'Wait for me!' Bubba shuffled in, clutching her new Zimmer and wearing a loose cotton dress and her best cardigan.

Naomi grinned. 'Bubba! You dressed yourself!'

Papas Yiannis smiled, hooked his arm around Bubba's waist and helped her into the chair.

Bubba peered at the priest, her eyes saying *thank you*. 'What are you waiting for, Papas? Tell us this good news,' she said.

'The court sitting has returned to its original date, and secondly, the Jewish Society has funded a lawyer for the Cohen family to help with the legalities.'

'Great to have some people on our side,' Naomi said, glancing at Bubba and thinking of poor Dora and her friends. She dreaded the court case but it was nothing compared to what her grandmother had faced. The first moment she had, Naomi returned to diary.

Chapter 32

Friday, 4 August 1944

I am waiting for Giovanni and try to fill the time by thinking about my family. I'm disturbed that their faces seem slightly out of focus today, as if they're drifting away. A curly feather in a draught, spiralling out of reach whenever I get close.

Mama! Papa!

The feeling that they can hear my thoughts is also fading, and their apparent distance depresses me. What if I wake one morning and the image of my father has disappeared like yesterday's dreams? It would be as if he never existed.

I am trying to strengthen my mind, to shout louder in my head. I squeeze my eyes tightly closed and visualise my family and relations as they were when they got on the ship. Papa with his fingers over his ears, looking around for me.

Papa! It's Dora, at the sheep hut in Rhodes. I'm praying for you.

This sense of panic continues to build until I fear it will give me a migraine. I'm going back to bed for half an hour and plan to record the events of the day later this evening.

* * *

In the big bed, I drifted in and out of sleep as the pain in my head gathered strength. I rubbed my forehead and whispered, 'Papa! You're in my thoughts . . . I love you so much.' Irini turned over and wrapped her arm around me. I guessed she was thinking about her family too because in a moment we were in an embrace, quietly crying together.

Why were they taken from us?!

I held Irini close. With her body against mine the feelings I had for Giovanni rose, confusing me. Dear, sweet Irini. I'd abandoned her and she didn't deserve such treatment. I kissed her tenderly. She hooked her legs around mine and pressed herself against me. The warmth of her body seemed to flow through me, and small ripples of pleasure raced down my spine. We hardly moved, cautious of waking Evangelisa and Xanthi, yet the restraint only heightened a desire that neither of us quite understood.

'I wish we were alone together,' Irini said quietly before kissing me again and slowly sliding her hands over my body.

Overwhelmed by these new sensations, my breath came in gasps. My world was spinning, I floated, drowned, and climbed the heights of new-found pleasure. 'I love you, Irini,' I whispered. 'And I believe that one day we *will* be alone together.' I placed my hand on her cheek and realised she was smiling through her tears.

'Promise me,' she said.

My feelings for Irini were so intense I could not express them in words. My heart and mind were overwhelmed by emotions that transcended any whispered endearments. I guessed she experienced the same. We shared our love, sadness, and worry just by holding each other. It was as if her body soaked up part of my anguish. It was still there but, in an odd sort of way, lifted from me.

Minutes later, I caught a tap on the door and knew Giovanni had arrived with our instructions.

'Come on, Irini. We have to go.'

We slid out of the bed, gulped water, then joined Giovanni outside.

'You ready?' he asked quietly. 'Where did you hide the crate and the gun?'

They were concealed under some scrub near the horse, but I was alarmed to find the dried grass and twigs were now scattered.

'Animals foraging,' Giovanni sounded irritable. 'Don't worry.' He had brought Irini's mule, which her father hired to Giovanni's father at shearing time. The shepherd boy proceeded to tie the wooden crate onto its back.

Evangelisa and Xanthi joined us. Evangelisa was clingy, upset that I was leaving.

'I'm scared you won't return, Dora, like everyone else. What if I never see you again? What will I do?'

'Stop being silly. It's only for a couple of days. We'll all be together again soon.'

'I wish I was as brave as you.' She was so earnest it made me smile.

'I can imagine Mama, right now,' I said. 'Longing to give you a hug. She'll be really proud when I tell her how you've grown up. Just think, with your new cooking skills you'll be able to make us all a nice meal when they return.'

She stared for a moment longer, considering my words. 'When do you suppose they'll come home?'

'I'm not sure, perhaps another week or two.'

'I've written her a letter, like you said. Can you find out where they're staying and post it?'

'Of course. Run and get it, and I'll make certain it goes with today's mail.'

Poor Evangelisa. She misses Mama as much as I miss Papa. I have to keep the terrible truth from her, allow her to believe they are working on Kos.

She rushed back, holding out the letter. 'There might be spelling mistakes, but I hope Mama understands and lets me off. I wrote about our adventure, how I'm learning to cook, and that I can't wait for her to come home.'

'Excellent. She'll be missing you. The letter's bound to cheer her up,' I said as brightly as I could. 'And I've got something for you.' Her eyes lit up. 'Clear the shelf over the fireplace while I get it.'

When she had, I pulled the Babushka dolls out of my duffel and gave them to her. 'Now, line them up, all seven, and think of them as Mama, Papa, Danial, Sammie, Jacob, me and you. The family.'

She threw her arms around my neck. 'Thank you! I'll look after them and keep them safe, Dora. You don't have to worry.'

Giovanni caught my eye with a quizzical frown. I turned my mouth down and shrugged.

Irini saddled Zeus. I kissed and hugged my little sister, and Xanthi too.

'I will take good care of her,' Xanthi said, holding Evangelisa's hand.

'Xanthi's going to teach me the Sperveri, Dora! So when you get married I'll be able to join the women who decorate the bridal bed, and sing about it, and do the dance.' She nodded at Giovanni.

Irini noticed my blush and laughed. 'Planning on getting wed, Dora?'

Eager to leave, I said, 'Enough nonsense. Let's go.'

Not knowing how long I'd be with Kapitanos Nikos, I stuffed a change of clothes into my duffel. I remembered the day Papa sewed my bag together in his workshop. He produced one for Irini too, and I recalled seeing it beside Irini's sister, in L'Aeronautica. I hope she has it with her when she comes back.

Giovanni led the way through the woods.

When we reached the clearing, we aimed for the centre of the island. Giovanni rode the mule, while Irini and I were on Zeus's back. We continued towards Psinthos. Near the outskirts of the hamlet, he tied a leading rope from the mule to Zeus and gave us our instructions.

'Don't turn into the village; go straight on and continue to Seven Springs.' He lowered his voice. 'Hide the crate close to the aqueduct entrance. Cover it well. Then Irini must return to Filerimos before nightfall with the horse and the mule, right?'

I repeated the orders.

'Good,' Giovanni said. 'I have to collect my bike from a friend in Psinthos, so I'll leave you here. Do you know the tunnel?'

I shook my head.

'It leads to the lake. Once you find it, go halfway down, about a hundred metres, and you'll come to an air shaft in the roof. It's built like a well. You can't miss it. Wait there. Someone will meet you and take you the rest of the way.'

'How will I get back?'

'Don't worry. Nathanial's going to organise your return. The crate's the important thing. Whatever happens, make sure it doesn't fall into enemy hands.'

'Why? What's in there?' I asked.

'That information's not for you. Give me your gun.'

I handed him the satchel. He took out a box that contained bullets. I felt sick. He dismantled the pistol grip, which seemed to be a holder for the ammunition. After loading the shells, he slammed it back together.

'If you find yourself in mortal danger, Dora, point the gun and shoot to kill. You don't get two chances. Just do it, right?'

I swallowed hard. 'Isn't there some kind of safety lever?'

'No, it's a safety grip. It won't go off unless you're holding it to fire.' He returned the gun to the bag and slung the strap over my head and shoulder. 'I'll see you when you can handle your weapon. Stay safe.'

I nodded and stepped towards him. He glanced at Irini and turned away.

'Take care, Giovanni!' I called, wanting one of his kisses. He waved without looking back.

While we continued to Seven Springs, I thoughts about the pistol that lay across my chest, would I have the courage to use it? I loved being up on the horse. The world took on a new perspective. I was in command of my surroundings, rather than belittled by them.

Irini spotted a carob tree. We stopped and tested the long, leathery pods. They were ripe, dark brown, and slightly sticky inside. We feasted on them, enjoying the crunchy husks and the sweet, chocolatey flavour. Satisfied, we went on, looking out for a water spring. Irini rode the mule for a while, allowing me to test my riding skills.

Zeus was docile enough until a huge black cyclops bee started buzzing around his ears. I should have shooed it away instead of watching. It appeared too fat to fly and whirred its beautiful iridescent wings noisily. The horse, startled, skipped sideways. Instantly afraid of falling off, I clung on with my knees and hands. I guess Zeus understood the signal to trot on and petrified me by doing so. I leaned forward and gripped the edge of the saddle, but the more I hung on, the faster the horse ran down the lane.

'Stop squeezing his belly and pull hard on the reins!' Irini shouted, cantering up behind me.

Just as we came to a halt, there was a great clatter and I realised the crate had worked free of the ropes and crashed to the ground, startling both animals. Eventually, I managed to dismount. Almost speechless, my knees wobbling and shaking, I cursed the horse.

Irini, hysterical with laughter, fell to the floor and slapped the earth.

'That was the scariest thing, him running off like that.' I rubbed my crotch, which was incredibly sore from the saddle. 'My bits are bruised to hell. My legs have turned into a wishbone. And I swear I'll never walk normally again.' I would have gone through it all over again just to enjoy the sound of her laughter. I fell to my knees and said, 'I do love you, Irini. You know that, don't you?'

'I love you too. I'm going to miss you so much that I might have to kiss your boyfriend while you're away.' She beamed at me, her eyes sparkling as they so often did when we were alone together.

I sighed. 'I wish you were a boy, then we could get married and have babies and live happily ever after.'

She laughed again and got to her feet. 'But that'll never happen, will it?' After a beat she continued, 'Sometimes I want that too . . . Now let's tie that crate onto the mule and get a move on, or I'll end up getting lost in the dark.'

My spirits lifted. When Irini was happy so was I. I tied Zeus's reins to a tree and we backtracked a short way. 'I hope it's not damaged,' I said.

The crate's lid had broken off and what appeared to be another box had slipped halfway out. My first thought was a wireless, like the one we had at home before the Germans confiscated it. Irini found a hefty stone to knock the top back on, and we secured it to the mule once again.

We arrived at Seven Springs and tied Zeus and the mule in the deciduous woods. The area was deserted, silent apart from a breeze soughing through the treetops, and extraordinarily loud birdsong. I glanced around for the culprit. A small grey ball of feathers with brilliant red eyes perched on a bush watching us. It repeatedly flicked its wings as if to say 'Go away! ' while it trilled an amazing song.

'Sardinian warbler,' Irini said. 'Pretty, hey? Little bird with a big voice. Just like you.' Her glance met mine and we laughed. A flash of emerald darted across the water. 'And there's a kingfisher looking for minnows.'

'You know a lot about birds.'

'It's my dad.' Her smile fell and she stared at the ground. 'He's mad about wildlife. I believe he can name every bird on the island.' She paused for a beat. 'Oh, Dora, I hope . . .'

Her sadness was contagious and my mood plummeted too. 'They'll be hanging on, Irini, knowing we're trying to help them. Come on, let's find this tunnel.'

We walked around the lake until we found the aqueduct, which was less than the height of a man and hardly wider than me. I stared nervously at the pitch-dark tunnel. Ankle-deep water ran from the passageway into the lake. The thought of going a hundred metres down that sinister place by myself gave me the creeps.

'Will you be all right?' Irini asked.

''Course. It's only a tunnel, isn't it?' A peacock made its plaintive, mocking, cry. The sound drifted, ghostly, through the trees like a warning. 'Now, let's bury the box,' I said.

We hid the crate under an earthy bank and knocked soil down until it was covered. 'We'd better remember the spot. Imagine if we do such a good job we can't find it later.' I said.

A purple heron flew from a branch and stood, still as a lamp post in the middle of the shallow lake. The water, flat as glass, mirrored the bird, the brilliant blue sky, and the tall trees that surrounded us.

I gazed at the peace and beauty of Seven Springs and decided I'd bring my family here when they returned, when the war was over. But my heart leapt when the silence was broken by the unmistakeable sound of an army jeep.

'Quick, hide!' I said. 'In the woods!'

We scrambled up the bank, dived into the undergrowth, and crouched behind a juniper bush. The vehicle stopped on the road over the tunnel. Two German soldiers went to the tailgate and dragged out a reluctant passenger who was bound and gagged.

The Germans threw their prisoner down the bank and followed on a steep footpath that ran alongside the tunnel. I got a clear look at their terrified captive.

Giovanni! Oh, God help him!

Irini, eyes wide, clamped both hands over her mouth.

I couldn't think what to do!

I fumbled in the satchel and pulled out the gun, my hand shaking badly.

'No! Dora, no!' Irini whispered. 'You don't know what you're doing!'

'I can't let them hurt him, Irini. What if they kill him? I'd rather be dead myself.' The words came out without thought, but they were true. Giovanni had become a part of my life that I didn't want to go without. I hoped to spend the rest of my life with him, and seeing him so badly treated was breaking my heart.

One of the Nazis, pink-faced, white-blond hair, cleft chin, kicked Giovanni in the stomach. He jerked into a ball. They grabbed under his arms and dragged him to a tree between our hiding place and the lake. After they'd tied him to the trunk, they removed the gag.

The Germans had their backs to us. They bellowed questions at Giovanni. When he refused to answer, one of them drew his weapon. He held his gun by the barrel and pistol-whipped Giovanni, catching his forehead, splitting his brow open.

Blood gushed down his face.

One soldier yelled in schoolboy Greek, 'Where are they hiding? Tell us where is the *Andartes* hideout and we will let you go!'

Giovanni's head lolled. He appeared hardly conscious.

Both soldiers continued to yell, and then my heart almost stopped when the German who'd split Giovanni's forehead put the gun to his bloodied temple.

'Last chance!' he said. 'Tell us now, or I'll blow your brains all over that tree!'

I couldn't watch Giovanni's murder. I gripped my pistol in two hands, leapt up and ran at them with all the speed I had.

Then, everything happened fast.

Giovanni saw me before they did. His eyes told me to shoot to kill. I aimed for the middle of the Nazi's back and fired three times in quick succession. The recoil knocked me to the ground and the gun fell from my hand.

In a flash, the other soldier drew his weapon, spun around, and pointed at my head.

'Dora!' Irini screamed.

For a moment, the distracted Nazi glanced her way.

Bang!

An enormous explosion deafened us all, and the second German was blasted off his feet.

I sat on the earth, shaking, poleaxed by horror. The one I'd shot was jerking and twitching as if in the throes of a fit.

'Shoot his brains out, Dora!' Giovanni yelled. 'Quickly! Don't think! Do it now!'

I heard myself whining. 'God help me. God help me.' I grabbed my gun, stumbled up, put the pistol to the Nazi's temple . . . and hesitated. His arm jerked and hit me across my bare shins. My scream escaped as I pulled the trigger. Deafened by the blast and knocked down by the recoil again, I trembled so badly I couldn't get up. Sweat or tears raced down my face. My stomach clamped, rolled, and I threw up carob mush and bile.

Filled with revulsion for the gun still in my hand, I shook it free.

Irini raced out of the bushes and untied Giovanni. They came and sat either side of me. We held each other in a group embrace, the three of us as one body, supporting each other, weeping, physically and emotionally exhausted.

The breeze had died. The air was motionless and heavy. Somewhere, far away, a dog barked. Zeus nickered and whinnied quietly, then silence, as if the world had stopped turning to let us recover enough to do what had to be done.

Chapter 33

Naomi came downstairs with a bottle of bathroom cleaner in one hand, and a mop and bucket in the other. 'How's it going?' she asked her sister.

Rebecca closed the diary and speaking quietly said, 'My God, she actually killed somebody! My grandmother. It's almost impossible to accept that Bubba and Dora are the same person.' Her voice dropped further. 'I can't imagine how lonely and afraid she must have been. I have this constant urge to comfort her.'

Why do I get the impression you are talking about yourself?

'Look, Rebecca, let's drop the show, shall we? You're not fooling me, so you may as well spit it out,' she said kindly. 'Tell me what's up – what's troubling you.'

'I don't know what you mean.'

'Oh, come on. This pretence we've been putting on for Bubba's sake. Why were you nearly in tears on the phone?' Naomi asked.

Rebecca pulled her chin in and blinked at her sister.

'Lighten the load. Spill the beans. Whatever you want to call it.' Naomi continued. 'Then I won't be guessing, and you don't have to keep hiding the thing that's making you miserable.'

'I'd forgotten how blunt you are.'

'When you choose camomile tea over a glass of red? What am I, stupid? It has to be serious, so put me out of my misery.' After a moment's silence, she carried on. 'Will I tickle your feet, or give you a Chinese burn?'

Rebecca's worried face broke into a smile, remembering Naomi's childhood threats when she was being obstinate.

'She needs a poke with a sharp stick!' Bubba's voice came from her room. 'I wasn't fooled either. Wait for me,' she called out.

Naomi jumped up and pulled the curtain aside.

Bubba had managed to sit on the side of her bed and was trying to pull herself up with her new walking frame.

Naomi rushed to help, but Bubba slapped her hand away.

'Leave me alone, child!' She grunted. 'I need to struggle . . . overcome. If I don't, I'll . . . well, I'm not going to fail at this. Not after everything!'

Rebecca saw the anguish on Naomi's face.

Bubba gripped the Zimmer with her good hand and hauled herself up.

Naomi and Rebecca held their breath and leaned forward, mirroring Bubba's struggle. She was almost on her feet when her strength failed and she dropped back onto the bed. Rebecca sensed Naomi's stress as, about to lunge forward and assist her grandmother, she checked herself and simply gripped the top of the walker.

'Come on, Bubba. Make an effort,' Naomi said with mock impatience. 'At this rate we'll be here all night.'

With a mighty grunt Bubba got to her feet. She crabbed into the kitchen clutching the frame and dragging one leg. Finally, she fell into her armchair and slapped a hand against her chest. 'Holy Moses, that was a marathon! I'm doing it again tomorrow, and you can get your fancy mobile telephone out and time me, Rebecca. I intend to enter the Rhodes triathlon next year!'

The two sisters laughed, pulling kitchen chairs up to sit in a triangle around the Zimmer.

'You haven't lost your sense of humour, then?' Rebecca said.

The old lady softened her voice. 'Now, come on, child, tell us what's going on so I can go back to bed and get my beauty sleep.'

*　*　*

Rebecca told them everything, about her endless dream of having children, about the terrible stress it put on her marriage, and about how much she had missed them both when she first arrived in London. Finally, with tears on her face, she disclosed her biggest worry – that Fritz might leave her.

'So, did he give you an ultimatum?' Bubba asked.

'Not exactly. He wants us to abandon the idea of having children. He says he can't stand watching me go through so much pain for nothing.' She wiped her eyes. Naomi ripped off a square of kitchen roll and handed it to Rebecca. 'I thought he'd be thrilled, after all, this is our forth try at IVF, but Fritz is just afraid he's going to see me hurt again. That's why we're having this separation.'

'Separation?' Bubba shook her head. 'Never a good plan. If you have a problem, you should be locked in a room together until you've sorted it.'

'I had started to think he didn't care, Bubba, but before I came here, I climbed up to the loft to find my suitcase and . . .' Tears trickled down her face. 'Damn, I must stop crying!'

'It's your hormones,' Naomi said. 'Make you extra sensitive.'

Rebecca dried her eyes and blew her nose. 'I go to pieces when I remember what I saw. Our attic is full of baby things. Surprises, gifts that my husband purchased for our child. Each time I got pregnant Fritz was so thrilled he went out and bought stuff for the nursery: a train set, a rocking horse, huge teddies, mobiles, baby furniture. Lovely presents, all beautifully wrapped and under various thicknesses of dust. They all had gift tags . . .' She fought more tears and couldn't speak for a minute. 'He'd written the most sweet and loving words.' She sobbed and paused. 'Every miscarriage must have broken his heart anew, but he put on a brave face . . . for me, and I never once considered his feelings.'

'Aren't we forgetting something? You *are* pregnant.'

Rebecca shook her head. 'I am, but all the joy has been replaced by the all-consuming worry that tomorrow I'll lose it. And I have the appalling decision to make . . . what to do with my baby's siblings: kill them, give them away, let them be experimented on, or pay each year to keep them alive.'

Bubba and Naomi stared at her. 'What do you mean?' Naomi uttered.

'There were ten eggs. Four were successfully fertilised to become embryos, and of these four, two were transferred to my womb in the hope that one will continue to develop normally and go full term. What shall I do with the other fertilised pair? They are potentially my children. What if I miscarry but I've had the other embryos destroyed?'

'If you miscarry, you'll get over it, child. Life will go on. Painful as it is . . .' Bubba stared at nothing. 'You're young.' She lifted her lame hand and placed it on the kitchen roll, and then ripped a sheet off with the other.

Rebecca dropped her head into her hands. 'How can you say such a thing? You've no idea!'

'You think not? Here.' She held out the paper towel. 'Let me tell you, I've experienced more loss than you'll ever know, young lady.' She glanced from Rebecca to Naomi and back again. 'Even after the Nazis had taken my darling family away, I went on to lose so much more. I lost everything. The woman I loved, the man I loved, my only sister, and my child.'

Rebecca and Naomi exchanged a glance of astonishment.

'You're reading the diaries, but there are some events I didn't explain fully because they were taboo in those days. I loved Irini,' she said quietly. 'With all my heart and soul. Such things were not talked about back then so I kept it inside me. I never revealed the true depth of my feelings. Irini did the same. What started as childish curiosity and friendship developed into the sincerest love.' Bubba smiled softly. 'Let me tell you what happened. . .

'We were living in the hut: my beautiful sister, Evangelisa; my best friend, Irini; a member of the *Andartes*, Xanthi; and me. It was very sparse. I was helping the partisans to end the war so Papa and my family could come home, but you already know that from the diary.'

Bubba's eyes widened, then glazed over. 'I was sent to the bamboo swamps to learn to shoot. Kapitanos Nikos, my teacher, was a charismatic Cretan who, for some reason, could not go back to his island. He played the *bouzouki*, sang rebel songs, and swore like nothing I'd ever heard.'

Bubba shook her head and produced half a crooked smile. 'He was unique. We lived on fish, sparrows, and bamboo shoots.

'He taught me to use the gun you both held. A weapon that killed eight people by my hand.' Frowning, she stopped to think. 'And one of those was my . . .' Her chest jerked with a sob, and she was silent for a moment. 'But we'll get to that.'

Rebecca realised she and her sister were holding hands, transfixed with a mixture of horror and fascination.

Bubba's gaze rested on Rebecca who had pulled herself together.

With an unexpected glint in her eye, the old woman continued. 'I became a . . . what do they call it these days? A crack pot.'

'A crack shot, Bubba,' Naomi said before biting her lip and squeezing Rebecca's hand.

Bubba nodded and raised an eyebrow. Naomi gave her a 'behave yourself' look.

Before she spoke again, and with a thin smile resting on her lips, Bubba closed her eyes.

Both Rebecca and Naomi guessed she was invoking the past. As the minutes ticked by, they realised their grandmother had fallen asleep.

'Oh, bless her. She's such a darling, isn't she,' Rebecca said. 'I know this seems childish, but I keep wanting to do something monumental for her. I can't explain exactly, but something that shows her worth, her true value. Stupid, really. It sounds so shallow, but . . . do you understand me?'

'That you came back is enough. It's everything she wanted. Come on, help me get her to bed. I suspect we could all do with an early night.'

'She's a cunning old girl. I love her to bits. I mean: "crack pot"?! I ask you!' They both laughed quietly. 'It's all quite deliberate, isn't it? She isn't going gaga at all.'

Naomi nodded. 'She knows exactly where she's at, believe me.'

Once Rebecca had gone up to her room, Naomi glanced around the kitchen. She should wipe the tops, wash the cups, and plan tomorrow's food. Instead, she opened the cupboard, kissed her fingertip and dabbed Costa's photo.

'Good night, my love,' she whispered before picking up the diary and mounting the stairs.

Chapter 34

After some minutes in a huddle on the edge of the lake, Irini, Giovanni and I calmed down. Without looking at the soldiers' bodies we staggered into the water, sat in the shallows, and washed the blood, sweat, and tears away. Giovanni had a gaping wound across his eyebrow. He cupped my chin and peered into my eyes.

'You saved my life,' he said.

I shook my head and answered in a voice still trembling with fear. 'Pure accident. The gun went off of its own accord. Besides, Irini saved my life.' I turned to my friend. 'If you hadn't caused that distraction, I'd be dead.'

She shook her head, mimicking me. 'Pure accident. The scream went off of its own accord,' she said.

Trust Irini to lift our spirits. For a moment, the tension was broken and a smile fluttered between us.

'What happened to the other soldier?' Irini glanced around, fear flashing in her eyes.

Giovanni scanned the woodland surrounding the lake. 'Someone shot him. We're being watched. That was a high-powered rifle.'

'How come they tied you up?' I asked, testing my voice and finding it still ragged and whining.

'I was ordered to follow you as far as the tunnel, where another *Andartes* would take over – probably the shooter. I kept my distance, just watching to make sure you were all right. When you'd eaten the carobs, I thought I'd give you five minutes' start and scoff a few myself.'

'You followed us to make sure we were safe?' I wanted to hug him.

He nodded. 'But after you left, that jeep came down the road. I jumped on my bike and tailed it.' He touched his forehead, stared at the blood on his fingers, and sucked air in.

Irini gawped at him. 'You mean they were right behind us?'

'They'd have caught you too, but they turned onto a track. They've robbed something. I'm not sure if it's valuables from Jewish homes or guns from their stores, but I saw them haul a crate out of their vehicle and bury it near a stone wall.' He held his hand out, watched it shaking, and tutted. 'I thought one of them had gone for a pee, but I'd been spotted. He circled behind me and clobbered me.' He touched the back of his head and winced. 'Next thing, I was in the jeep and you know the rest.'

I stared in the direction of the bodies. 'What's going to happen now?'

'Whoever fired that shot will take over. Don't worry about it. You have to complete your task, and get to Kapitanos Nikos.'

Startled by the sound of a motor, we all looked towards the road over the tunnel in time to see the jeep driven away.

'That'll be the *Andartes* from Psinthos. They'll stitch my head there. Try and forget what happened here, because you *must* go on. Good luck, Dora.' He turned to Irini. 'Are you all right to return the horse and mule to Filerimos?' When she nodded he stood, staggered a little, and scrambled up to the road. A black car pulled up, Giovanni spoke to the driver and got in.

I couldn't take my eyes off him as the car drove away, and suddenly I was crying, my heart breaking. Irini put her arms around me and held me until I could speak.

'He nearly died, Irini. I might never have seen him again. I don't think I can live without him.'

'You have to accept you're in love with him,' she said softly. 'It's all right, Dora. You don't have to fight it for me. I want you to be happy more than anything. I love you with an unconditional love, do you understand that? Your happiness is mine too.'

'Oh, Irini, I love you as well. I'm all mixed up. Don't ever leave me, will you? Promise.'

She smiled, pushed my hair back and kissed my cheeks. 'Promise. Now, come on; we have to get going, *kapitanessa.*'

We returned to the tunnel. So much had happened since we found it. I hugged and kissed Irini, and promised we'd be together soon. I told her to keep an eye on Giovanni as he was prone to taking liberties, and would she make sure Xanthi took care of Evangelisa?

Irini assured me she'd do these things, and watched me enter the aqueduct.

After a short way I looked back. She was still there.

'I'm fine! Leave before it gets dark!' I cried. My voice echoed eerily. I saw her turn and go. 'I love you, Irini,' I whispered. 'Stay safe.'

In the tunnel I was afraid something alive might drop from the ceiling onto my head. Perhaps there were snakes around my feet? The walls could collapse or be covered in millipedes. I clenched everything at the thought. What if bats rushed out into the evening and tangled in my hair, knocking me over? My own breathing grew louder as I waded through the icy water, counting my steps, trying not to touch the sides which were becoming narrower.

Again I turned to looked behind me. The entrance was hardly more than a dot of pale light. I tried to see ahead, but met only dense blackness. I wished Irini and Giovanni were with me.

Papa, I'm afraid of the roof falling in. Send me some courage!

I recalled my birthday wish, to be braver, and so, by reason, I *was* braver. Everything would have been fine, if the wish hadn't reminded me of my birthday and the love and happiness of that day. My darling family.

Overwhelmed by images, my mind became a cinema screen. I recalled the flickering candles on the cake, heard Mama say, 'Make a wish, Dora!' There was Danial with his bottles of ink, granny and her scented bath cubes, and how thrilled I had been to receive the pen that I'm writing with. I evoked my father's smile and his voice, 'Follow your dreams, Dora.'

I turned, but the entrance was now only a spark. In my imagination, that tiny light was my family, constantly behind me, ready to catch me if I fell, there to support me if I needed it. A star in the dark – always there – even if I never saw them again.

Then I told myself I was being stupid. They *will* come home, every one of them.

I waded through the shallow stream, taking deep breaths, letting them out slowly. Just as I started to wonder if I'd missed the air shaft, I noticed faint light ahead. The distance was impossible to judge. Noise from the water seemed extraordinarily loud. My heart thrummed. What if I plunged into a sinkhole? I plundered on, splashing and stumbling, all my faith in Nathanial and his instructions. Was the journey a test? Lately, all of life felt like a trial.

After such a long ride across country, the atmosphere in the tunnel was dank and stilted. But then the air freshened again as the distant light grew stronger. My feet were cold, and I shivered as I walked into the shaft of light. How long before someone turned up?

The vent, round and built of stone, had a rusting metal ladder that reached up to the cobalt sky.

'Hello! Anyone there?' I yelled.

A head, silhouetted in the brilliant sunlight, hung over the top. 'Oy! Dora Cohen?'

Tilting back to shout up the well, I nearly lost my balance. 'Yes, that's me.'

'Climb the ladder,' he shouted.

Oh!

The rusty old rungs reached twenty metres up, and were half a metre apart. Was I capable of this mammoth feat? I grasped the rails and climbed the first few steps. The corroded iron cut into my hands and pain stabbed from my broken wrist with each pull.

'Good! Keep coming!'

By the time I'd reached the three-quarter point, I was gasping for breath and my arms and shoulders burned. *One more step,*

I kept telling myself, forcing my legs to push on, fighting the pain in my arm.

A bar snapped away, clattering and ringing in the shaft until it splashed into the water below. My hands scraped down the blistered metal, and soft skin was grated from my palms. My bare knees hit the next rung and before I could stop myself, I shrieked in pain. The sound amplified in the cavernous space, and the voice above me yelled, 'Hang on!'

I gripped the rail with all my strength while my legs flailed to find a foothold below. Sweat stung my eyes. Hardly able to breathe for the panic gripping my chest, I thought I'd plunge down into the aqueduct below and break my neck. Blood oozed into my stinging palms making my hands sticky. I started to slide down, then my feet found a rung and I put my weight on it. Oh, the relief!

My breath came in gasps. How would I climb over the gap? I rested until the pain eased a little and my heart slowed.

'You all right?' the voice called down. 'Can you move it? We need to go.'

I wanted to punch the idiot!

The effort to get to the top was almost too much. I spanned the broken rung by stepping onto the joints where it met the uprights but without putting all my weight on them.

At the top, I found a thin young man with a sharp nose and frizzy black hair. 'I'm Tassos,' he said. 'Come on, we're late.' He gracelessly hauled me over the wall.

His dilapidated motorbike made a dreadful noise. My body ached and my bleeding hands and knees were whipped by the wind.

We rode a track above the coast, turned inland and followed the valleys and ravines, until we came to a shallow river and a rocky enclave.

'This is where I leave you. You'll find a cave behind the boulders. Wait there.'

Less than ten minutes later, a short man with a miserable face, silver shoulder-length hair and vivid green eyes joined me. 'Dora Cohen?' he said.

I nodded.

'I'm Kapitanos Nikos. Follow me and stay close.'

We continued into a dense bamboo grove that grew from a knee-high delta. We sloshed through water, squeezing between seemingly impenetrable wetlands of bamboo. A small clearing appeared where three string hammocks hung in the vegetation. A rocky area supported a charcoal pit and various cooking and eating utensils.

'Choose a hammock, dump your backpack, and give me your gun. Are you hungry?'

I nodded quickly and he smiled.

'Fish casserole in the big pan. Help yourself. We'll talk once you've eaten.'

While he examined my weapon, I found an enamel dish, filled it with stew, and ate greedily.

'Nice pistol. Just been fired?' he enquired.

I told him about my harrowing afternoon and the mystery shooter. 'That would be Tassos with his rifle.' He lifted his chin towards the cooking area. 'Help me hide this away, then you can get some sleep. We start work early.'

* * *

It has taken ages to record the events of this exhausting day, and it's almost dark now. Kapitanos Nikos and Tassos are sleeping in their hammocks. I am surprised how noisy the bamboo grove is, the water lapping and rippling, and the bamboo stems popping and swooshing against each other. These sounds mingle with odd noises that I don't recognize. I feel quite safe with my hammock slung between the two men, and I'm looking forward to starting work tomorrow.

I hope Irini and Giovanni are okay. I have a bizarre urge to bury my head in the lumpy hammock pillow and cry myself to sleep, and I suspect my Irini feels the same. I wonder where Mama and Papa are at this moment. I wish I could see them.

Sunday, 13 August 1944

Dear Diary, sorry it's been over a week, but I have been so busy with Kapitanos Nikos that I have not had a chance to update my account of life in the bamboo grove. I moved my things to a small cave because I am afraid of my books getting wet, and that is where I am now. The Kapitanos has gone to get fresh supplies and so, for the first time since coming here, I have a few hours off.

Under Kapitanos Nikos's supervision, I practised cleaning and firing the gun. In a narrow mud gorge that was once a river, I spent hours and days at target practice.

Nikos always speaks quietly but forcefully, repeating the same orders: 'Arms straight, Dora.' 'Bend your knees or you'll fall on your behind again.' 'Concentrate on the sights, not the target! The target will go out of focus, but you can still aim for it, or follow it if it moves.' 'Squeeze . . .' 'Breathe, Dora!'

Yesterday, when we took a break, Nikos taught me about the local wildlife, which somehow made me feel closer to Irini. I long to impress her with this newfound knowledge on my return. There are terrapins and fish in the water, and snakes and scorpions in cracks and crevices, dozens of birdsongs to memorise, and insects so bizarre they seemed pure science fiction.

At first, I was afraid and repulsed by many of these creatures, but Nikos's enthusiasm is contagious. 'Each has its place in nature's scheme, and none will hurt you unless they feel threatened. Follow me and I'll show you something special,' he said.

We climbed up, above the 'shooting gallery', which was what we called the deep gorge where I practised. Loosely coiled on a wide flat rock was the biggest snake I'd ever seen.

'She's sunbathing. I call her Jezebel. She's a large whip snake, two metres long,' Nikos whispered. 'Lives on mice, lizards, and small birds. Isn't she magnificent?'

I gulped, both thrilled and horrified at the same time. The snake lifted its slender head and seemed to sniff the air. Aware of our presence, she slipped silently into the vegetation.

Early evening, Thursday, 17 August 1944

My heart is still thudding as I write this. If it wasn't for the quick think-ing of the Kapitanos, I'd surely have been captured by enemy soldiers earlier today, and perhaps I would be dead by now.

I want to go home! I mean really home! Our lovely house in Spartili Street in Paradissi Village. I want things to be the way they were before we had to move into Papa's shop in Rhodes Old Town. I want to play hop-scotch in Spartili Street with Irini until the street lights come on, and then go inside for Mama's rich and wholesome food. I don't want to be an adult! I don't want to have responsibilities, and more than anything, I don't want to be alone and afraid.

I wish I had not written that. I've blown my nose and dried my eyes, and have to say that I'm sorry to sound so weak and pathetic, but the events of the day were exhausting. It all started when Tassos came rushing through the groves. 'Nazis!' he said urgently, 'all around, searching for the two missing soldiers.'

We scarpered, stuffing every trace of our existence into small caves and covering the entrances with piles of vegetation. Nikos led me to a waist-deep lagoon surrounded by thick stems of bamboo.

'Stay underwater. Hold yourself down against the bamboo.' He gave me a short, hollow cane. 'Use this as a snorkel and don't come up until I tell you,' he said.

Petrified, I didn't hesitate and plunged under the surface. I had no idea where Tassos and Nikos were going to hide, but I guessed they'd be doing the same as me. At first, I couldn't see because we'd stirred up the creamy sediment, but as it settled I became aware of dozens of soldiers' boots disturbing it again. The Germans marched past only metres from me. Small fish panicked and darted over my face, flashing slivers of silver quickly hiding amongst the bamboo stems.

A terrapin paddled right before my eyes, lifting its snooty nose out of the water to take air before diving to the bottom. When the minnows emerged again, jostling playfully, I knew the danger had passed. Minutes later I recognised the bare feet of Nikos. He hauled me up.

'Tassos is ahead of the soldiers, but he's gone into the gorge to remove traces of the target practice. It's a dead end; he'll get caught!' Nikos whispered urgently. 'I'm going up the hillside to fire a couple of rounds, cause a diversion.'

Tassos, the shooter, had saved my life. I owed him. I ran towards the shooting gallery. When the backs of the soldiers came into view, I slipped into the water and swam around them. I climbed above the mud tunnel, thinking I might start a landslide so that Tassos wouldn't be trapped by the enemy in the dead end of the shooting gallery. I scrambled up until I was six or seven metres above the troops and the gorge.

The sediment had settled and I could just make out Tassos under the shallow water below my bullet-riddled target. The Germans were about to enter the gorge, heading straight for him. I glanced around for loose rocks but found none. Peering down to the ledge below, I saw Jezebel raise her elegant head. I grabbed a sturdy length of broken bamboo, lowered it, and flicked two meters of heavy snake into the ravine.

Sorry, girl.

There were several screams, a lot of swearing and splashing, then a mass exodus of soldiers from the bamboo groves.

Chapter 35

Naomi made Rebecca's bed, picked up Rebecca's laundry and dropped it in the basket, and wiped Rebecca's toothpaste out of the washbasin. Not in the best of moods, she came downstairs.

'Bubba didn't hold back, did she?' Rebecca said looking up from her grandmother's armchair, her feet on the stool. 'She kept no secrets from her diary. But I guess at sixteen, she never dreamed anyone would read it.' She looked up at Naomi. 'You look tired. Shall I make you a coffee?'

Naomi nodded. 'Although, if you remember, at the start she did record the political situation for her grandchildren. With everything that happened after I guess she forgot about that.'

'Wasn't she totally selfless in her efforts to get the war to end?' Rebecca said. 'I wish I'd inherited a little more of that quality. Being selfless I mean. You've got it, Naomi. You'll do anything for anybody and you've always been like that. I remember that from our childhood.' She thought for a moment. 'Except, to be honest, I always saw you as an adult. I was only five when you were Dora's age, but I remember how much I wanted to be exactly like you.'

Naomi smiled, her mood lifting. 'You were *so* pretty, Rebecca. Whenever Bubba made me a new dress or knitted me a jumper, she would make an almost exact replica for you out of the leftovers. It was like having my own real live doll.'

'I recall being totally heartbroken when you moved over to Crete to study nursing. I was so lonely.'

'You were? I didn't realise I meant that much to you to be honest.'

Rebecca lowered her eyes shyly. 'I still have all the letters you sent me. Do you remember them? I must have been eight or nine. Every time you wrote to Bubba you'd include a little note for me? In one of them you told me you'd helped sew someone's finger back on. I was so proud of you, I took it to school and showed everyone.' She laughed. 'You were my absolute hero.'

'And you kept all the letters? All these years?'

'I wanted to show them to my children . . .'

Naomi's heart went out to her sister. 'How are you now?'

'Okay, I guess. I'm still afraid all the time, and I've become terribly superstitious about talking about it.'

'Okay, we'll avoid the subject for now.'

'Thank you, Naomi. You know, I can't believe how quickly Dora grew up. She seems to have gone from a silly girl obsessed with kissing to a fully blown freedom fighter in a matter of weeks.'

'Don't forget that in her era there was no such thing as a teenager. You were a child, wearing children's clothes and playing childish games, then you were a woman with all the responsibilities adulthood brought with it. Any clue where the story's leading?' Naomi asked.

'Not yet. She's just saved Tassos' life. She dismisses it as nothing because Tassos had saved her life by killing the soldier at the lake.' Their eyes met. 'That's what I mean, Naomi: when someone does something for me, it never occurs to me to repay the favour. I appreciate what they've done but that's it. Was I very spoiled as a child?'

Naomi laughed. 'You were indeed. Very loved too. I think you were all the more special because our parents died a couple of weeks after your birth, and everyone was sorry for you. I was devastated when they were lost at sea and I can't imagine what Bubba went through, losing her only child. So all the cooing and admiration you got lifted our spirits. We all doted on you.'

'I wish I'd really known them, you know. I remember the stories you used to tell me about Papa and his boat.'

'Telling you the things Papa had told me helped me get over my loss. I loved him very much, and the first thing that attracted me to Costa was that he looked a little like Papa.'

Rebecca frowned for a moment. 'I can't remember what made me fall in love with Fritz . . . but I do love him intensely.'

Naomi recognised a cue to investigate another chunk of Rebecca's obvious unhappiness, but after glancing at the clock she ripped off her apron and said, 'Changing the subject, I need to get to the grocer's before all the best tomatoes have gone. Will you listen out for Bubba?'

'Of course. Look, why don't you take a break? Go and have a coffee with Heleny or something. Take your phone and if I can't manage, I'll call you.'

* * *

The moment Naomi closed the front door, Rebecca heard Bubba's TV go on in the next room. She wondered how long her grandmother had been awake, perhaps listening to their conversation. She popped her head into the room that had been the family's lounge when she left for London.

'How are you today, Bubba?' she asked brightly.

'I have to do my exercises. Where's Naomi?'

'Ah, she's slipped to the shops. She'll be back soon.' She stopped herself. 'Why don't you tell me what you have to do and I'll help,' Rebecca said as she sat on the edge of the bed.

266

'That's kind, Rebecca, thank you,' Bubba replied with a twinkle in her eye. 'I need that round cushion under my dead knee, then I have to try to lift my heel off the bed ten times.'

'Simple enough. Let's get going, shall we?'

'Tell me about the diary while I do my gymnastics, child.'

'I'm up to where you're learning to shoot with Kapitanos Nikos.'

'Ah, that man filled me with an uneasy mix of trust and terror.' She stared into the distance, clamping her jaw every time she lifted her heel. 'He took me to a narrow clay ditch about three metres deep, at the bottom of a gorge. The place was a deeply eroded riverbed that contained little more than a stream.'

'That's where he taught you to shoot?'

'That's right. I had to hit his target from three metres, all day long. Then four metres. And five. Until I could get nine out of ten shots at fifteen metres.' She snorted. 'He was such a character, but a good teacher.' She shook her head slowly. 'Poor Tassos. All day, every day he was making ammunition, most of which was fired deep into the mud wall that my target was pinned too. Lead was like gold to us. The *Andartes* stripped the flashing off almost every building in Rhodes Town, stole the lead weights off wheels, and ripped pipework out of unused or bombed buildings — all melted down and poured into bullet moulds by Tassos.'

The old lady groaned.

'Come on, Bubba. Get that heel up. You're doing great. Four . . . five. You're halfway, only five more.' Rebecca held her hand.

'Two weeks later I got back to Mount Filerimos. Something had changed, but I couldn't work out what it was. Then Tassos arrived with a message: I had to meet Nathanial the next morning. Irini asked me if I knew what the bandit wanted.' Bubba shook her head. 'I tried to pass it off as nothing, and told her I didn't know.

'We sat to eat a huge dish of pasta flavoured with wild garlic and leeks. I remember that meal so well. Irini's hand brushed mine under the table and our eyes met. "I hope he's not sending you away again," she said quietly.' Bubba's face turned sad. 'Oh, Rebecca, I really didn't want to upset Irini again. "I don't think so," I said. "But he wants me to take my gun, so I think he wants to see if I can shoot straight," I said.'

Bubba stared at the ceiling, silent with her thoughts as she completed her leg exercises. Rebecca wondered what memories filled her grandmother's head.

'There you are, Bubba. Ten lifts done. Mission accomplished. What's next?'

'I have to spread my fingers and then touch each one with my thumb.'

'Come on. Let's take the cushion away and start on your hand.'

'I can't explain my feelings for Irini. My moon and stars, they say when a person means everything. Irini was more than that: she was my universe. I hated seeing her so upset. "You're not going to kill somebody, Dora? Not again!" she said.'

'The others didn't know that you'd saved Giovanni's life?' Rebecca asked.

Bubba shook her head, staring at her lame hand. 'Come on, move, you useless piece of meat! Oh, there we go.' She spread her fingers.

Rebecca grinned. 'Great! Now touch your fingertips.'

'It's not that easy. I have to try really hard. But that's life, isn't it? You have to keep trying.' She paused for a moment, her eyes flicking up to her granddaughter.

'Evangelisa asked if I had actually shot somebody, and if I had, she thought I was really brave. I just wished she'd grow up, and then I found myself riddled with guilt for being so impatient with her. Sometimes I found it difficult having a younger sister, you know? I was only sixteen, yet I had all the responsibilities of a mother.'

Their eyes met and Rebecca nodded, not sure for a moment what Bubba was hinting at.

'Xanthi stared at me, and asked if I had actually killed somebody. I said no, of course I hadn't. Irini lowered her eyes and stared at her pasta.'

'I feel so sorry for her,' Rebecca said. 'She really loved you, didn't she?'

Bubba nodded, her hand still for a moment.

'Come on, no stopping. Let's keep this hand working. You're doing so well, Bubba.'

She nodded again and stared at her fingers until they moved.

'I told them if killing someone brought the end to the war closer, then I was prepared to commit murder. But to be honest, the very idea filled me with revulsion, and I could see Irini felt the same. Evangelisa asked me how shooting somebody could help stop a world war and I told her that if shooting somebody can start a war, then it stands to reason that shooting somebody can stop a war too.'

'It was only natural that they'd be curious about what you did for the *Andartes*, Bubba, and also worry about you.'

'I found it hard not telling them everything. I mean, under normal circumstances you don't keep secrets from your family, do you, Rebecca? They're the ones you run to for support when you have a problem.'

Chapter 36

Bubba slept, a gentle smile softening the contours of her face. Rebecca smiled too; she felt good about encouraging her grandmother through the exhausting exercises. Although her aim had been to help Bubba become a little stronger, she had an odd sensation of subterfuge, tables turned. As if Bubba had actually put Rebecca through some kind of mental workout. She pondered their conversation as the rug fell between them.

She had just picked up the diary when the phone rang.

'Hi, it's me,' Naomi said. 'Is everything all right? I'd like to take you up on your offer and have a coffee with Heleny and Marina. We're working on a blog for Pandora's Box.'

Rebecca stifled a giggle at the idea of her sister becoming computer savvy. 'Yes, everything's fine. We've done Bubba's exercises and she's asleep again, exhausted, poor love.'

'But she did all her workout this morning. She's not usually so forgetful.'

Rebecca frowned and glanced at the rug. 'Ah well, I guess she had her reasons for wanting to do them again. Anyway, take as much time as you want, you deserve a break. I'm about to have half an hour with the diary.'

'Great, see you later. Bye.'

Rebecca settled in her grandmother's armchair and opened Bubba's journal.

Saturday, 19 August 1944

I arrived at Mount Filerimos, eager to be with Irini and Evangelisa. I'd never been away from them for so long before and needed their affectionate hugs and kisses. Yet, when I returned, I sensed something had changed between us. While they were friendly, they seemed to be holding back. Particularly Irini. An atmosphere of shyness hung over our embraces, and for a short time I saw myself as an intruder. 'Is everything all right?' I asked.

She nodded, her eyes doleful, shifting to the ground and then to me. 'Did you miss me?' she said in a strange way, and I wasn't sure if she was being sarcastic.

'Of course. What do you think?'

She shrugged. 'What's going to happen to us, Dora?'

'I've no idea. I only know that with every day that passes it becomes more crucial for this war to end soon, because irreversible things are happening in faraway places.'

All through our meal, Evangelisa and Xanthi quizzed me about learning to use the pistol.

'Won't you be too afraid?' Xanthi asked. 'I mean, if you have to shoot somebody – end their life. I'd find it terrifying. Imagine who that person might be ... somebody's father or brother. Wouldn't you compare their family to your own? I couldn't do it.'

'Just thinking about it scares me to death,' Evangelisa added.

'Enough! You're not helping me. I really don't want to consider it!' I pushed myself away from the table. 'And you'd better not repeat what I've told you. It's secret!' I stormed out of the hut, turned, and barged back in. 'I must report to Nathanial tomorrow and he said *I* would be shot if I repeated anything to anyone at all.' I stopped to let the statement sink in. Their eyes were fixed on me when I continued. 'And the person I spoke to would also be killed in the most horrible way! You three with your constant nagging have put us all in danger!'

I'd hardly slept the night before, asking myself the same things. Could I kill somebody again? I shouldn't have talked about it, but tiredness and their relentless questions got the better of me.

It's an odd thing, but as I'm bringing my diary up to date, it dawns on me that when you write things down, everything becomes clearer. I realise now, it was wrong of me to talk to my friends about the relationship I had with the *Andartes*. And, I really should have shown more affection to Evangelisa right from the start, as I am all the family she has at the moment and she is still very much a child. Now that I read back, I also see that I have taken Irini's love and loyalty for granted, and I am ashamed of myself.

I can't change the past, but the past can change me. I can and will learn from my mistakes. I will try to be a better person, and give more to my loyal and loving companions in the future.

Sunday, 20 August 1944

Dear Diary, Giovanni arrived at the hut eager to accompany me to the *Andartes* this morning. As always, we made the most of our time alone together and eventually emerged from the woods breathless and blushing. We both needed a moment to recompose before facing Nathanial.

Once we had pushed through the final wall of trees, Giovanni reached for my hand. In the afternoon breeze, we stood and gazed at the mansion that we believed had once belonged to a great sea captain. Mesmerised by the overpowering beauty of the ancient building, I felt Giovanni's hand tighten around mine, and knew he was equally fascinated by the Venetian villa.

The shutters on the upper floor were open and, for a moment, the rising sun was reflected, golden, in the windows, shining like some great, fat, Buda in the depths of the forest, happy to see us.

Then, with a shift in the breeze, slender tree shadows swayed across the dusty pink walls and the building took on a different appearance. Something green, leafy, and fragile had caught hold in the high gutter and trailed its fern-like foliage down the timeworn façade, like the delicate veil of a blushing bride. I was drawn to the cream balustrades of the Juliet balcony and imagined myself up there, gazing upon my beloved Romeo.

'One day, I'll have a house like this. It's my dream,' Giovanni whispered. He let go of my hand and slipped his arm around my waist. 'What's your secret dream?'

I turned to face him, our eyes met and I wanted to melt against his body. 'I think you know that already.'

He kissed me chastely on the lips and nodded. 'We'd better go inside, Nathanial's waiting.'

* * *

We found the leader of the *Andartes* in a pleasant mood. 'I've had good reports from Kapitanos Nikos, little one,' he said. 'You were brave at Seven Springs, and added two more weapons to our cache. Also, in the bamboo grove, I hear you were very quick-thinking. Now, I want to hear about what happened in your own words.'

I hesitated. Was this a test? 'I'm sorry, sir, but I don't know what you're talking about.'

'The shooting? The snake? Kapitanos Nikos?'

'With respect, sir, I don't know anyone with that name, or anything about a shooting or a snake. You must have me confused with somebody else.'

Nathanial roared with laughter. 'Be ready for fresh instructions. I want you prepared to leave in an instant.'

Giovanni walked me back to the hut, always by a different route. Before parting, we arranged to meet under the cinnamon tree that evening. I had dreamed about returning to our special place, and my body tingled with excitement, longing for his touch and his kisses.

I bathed at the spring and removed the splint from my wrist, although it still ached. I held a teaspoon of honey in my mouth for as long as possible, making sure he would never taste a sweeter kiss. Then, I hurried through the trees, eager for his caresses.

He wasn't there.

I was staring at the cinnamon tree, when a pair of hands slid over my eyes.

'Guess who?'

I caught my breath. 'Giovanni!'

He wrapped his arms around me, trapping mine by my sides, then he kissed the back of my neck. 'I've missed you,' he said, turning me and kissing me on the lips.

I stood on my toes and pressed my mouth against his, my legs trembling. He pulled away, sucking his lip. 'Mmm, kisses flavoured with honey. Are you cold? You're shaking.'

I shook my head.

He pulled me into his arms. My body seemed transported on the wings of Eros. I pressed against him, burning with desire to be closer. I held him tightly but then cried out as pain shot up my arm.

'What's the matter?' he asked.

'No, nothing, it's my wrist. I took the splint off.' I clutched it to my chest. 'It still hurts sometimes.'

'Come on. I'll roll you a cigarette.'

We sat together, our backs against the tree, smoking the herb-scented cigarette. As discomfort drifted away, euphoria moved in. He nuzzled my ear. Such powerful urges raced through me. I longed to have his skin against mine.

'Kiss me again?' I whispered.

He half closed his eyes. 'I want more than a kiss, Dora. I can't get you out of my mind. You've managed to take over my heart too.'

274

His words thrilled me. 'Behave, Shepherd Boy,' I said, enjoying his wide smile. We kissed under the cinnamon tree, and my passion found new highs. A glut of emotion, tingling, intoxicating, and urgent seemed to envelop my body. My head buzzed like the air before a lightning strike, during a thunderstorm. Aware that Giovanni was equally excited, I was both afraid and exhilarated by such powerful sensations.

Giovanni took off his shirt and pulled me against his bare chest. My heart pounded.

Momentarily, I sensed the shepherd was also unsure of himself. We both ventured into unknown territory. Passionate about each other, we tried to bridle our desire, but nature tugged at the reigns and we found it difficult to keep our feelings, and actions, under control. We seemed to be kissing for hours. Tremors raced through me, and I loved each moment, becoming bolder and more intimate by the minute.

On our backs, side by side under the cinnamon tree, we took a calming break. He had explored every centimetre of my body, and I, his. I had ached for hands to slide under my clothes, to places that had never been touched before.

I didn't understand my own feelings. I wanted him so badly, yearning to have him inside me, yet scared of reaching that point of no return. Afraid he would hurt me. Afraid he would take my heart and my virginity and leave me alone once more.

I would die if that happened.

We watched the moon slide over the treetops. It passed its zenith and was heading for the western horizon. 'I should go.' I didn't want to. 'It must be around four.'

'Then you may as well stay,' he said, reaching over and pulling me on top of him. His mouth was against my ear, his breath tickling my neck. 'I've had crazy thoughts about you since that first kiss, Dora. Tell me you feel the same.'

In his arms, everything was forgotten. Encompassed by love and happiness, my emotions were soon drenched in passion for

Giovanni. I was hot and wet and insanely burning up with feel-ings stronger than I had ever known. By the time the sun rose, my innocence had flown like a moth in the night, destroyed by outrageous flames of desire. Beneath the cinnamon tree, Giovanni Pastore made love to me, and I made love to him.

I am certain, I will never love another man as long as I live.

Late on Monday, 21 August 1944

I can't get to sleep. Earlier today, Evangelisa's insatiable curiosity about what I was doing for the *Andartes* drove me mad. She's always asking questions and I wonder if Xanthi is prompting her. To be honest, the idea of killing again horrifies me. No matter how evil a person was, I doubt I could coldly execute them. That terrible moment at the lakeside keeps going around in my head, then I think of Papa. If murdering someone evil saves my father's life, as it did Giovanni's, I will not hesitate.

With that sorted out in my mind, I can finally relax, close my diary, and go to sleep.

Wednesday, 23 August 1944

I am in the hut, writing by the light of the oil lamp. My compan-ions are asleep, and I am also very tired, but I want to get this into my diary before I go to bed myself.

This evening, I met Giovanni under the cinnamon tree. Perhaps all the talk about killing had unsettled me, but for the first time since Irini and I fetched Zeus from town, I was spooked. I kept look-ing behind me as I passed through the woods, sure someone fol-lowed; watching me.

Giovanni spread a blanket. We have made love whenever the chance arose, and my days and nights are filled with sweet longing for the shepherd boy. These feelings are in conflict with the love I feel for Irini. I've had no time alone with her since the day I came back from Kapitanos Nikos.

Irini never complains. Occasionally I catch the sadness in her eyes, or the way she swiftly turns away, or her sudden ending of a sentence. I sense she is biding her time, knowing her turn will come, yet I also suspect that she suffers great pain each time I skulk off into the woods to meet Giovanni.

However, earlier this evening I could not relax. I told Giovanni I suspected we were being watched. He marched around the pine trees and, when he returned, insisted we were alone. Still, I pushed him away when he attempted to undo my dress.

'There's someone out there; I sense it,' I whispered and although I could not explain why, I kept thinking of Irini.

'It's your imagination,' he said. 'But if you don't want to love me tonight, you needn't make excuses.' He kissed the side of my neck. 'I'll never ask you to do anything you don't want, Dora.' He gazed into my eyes and I was filled with love and longing. He stroked my back, pulling me against him, and I realised I wanted to be with him always, whatever lay ahead for us.

I whispered into his ear, 'I've fallen in love with you, Giovanni Pastore. I can't imagine life without you.' I pressed my mouth against his.

After a minute, he brushed my hair away from my face, and lifting my chin he said, 'I feel the same way about you, Dora. I can't get you out of my mind. When the war is over, I want to—'

At that moment, I heard movement in the bushes and my body stiffened.

'You were right,' Giovanni whispered. 'Do you have your gun with you?'

'No. What shall we do? I'm afraid.'

'We can pretend we didn't notice anything and see what happens . . . or we can make a run for it.'

'Let's wait. Hopefully they'll go away, then we should hurry back.'

A twig snapped, a rustle of branches, then it went quiet. We could hear ourselves breathing. He counted into my ear. On three, we abandoned the blanket, raced through the woods, and arrived at the hut scratched and panting. I slipped into the room and lit the oil lamp while Giovanni checked out back.

When he joined me, he glanced towards the bed. 'Is everybody all right?'

I nodded. 'Sleeping soundly.'

'There's a leaf in your hair.' He plucked the stray greenery. 'Before I forget: tomorrow you must ride to Kamiros Scala and wait near the beach for instructions. Be there by five in the evening, and remember your gun,' he whispered.

'I want to ask you something.'

We sat together at the low table with our backs to the bed. Giovanni took my hand. 'What is it?'

'Where do you think they are now? Our parents, my family?' He didn't answer. 'They *are* still alive, aren't they? I mean, they couldn't . . .' I could not say more. My pain and dread were overwhelming. Lately, when I tried to talk to Papa in my mind, it seemed he wasn't there at all. Would I sense it, if they had died? *Papa!*

'Please tell me what you know, Giovanni. Don't leave anything out.'

After a moment he said, 'A man escaped from a Nazi work camp in Poland, Auschwitz. He was almost dead, starved. He told the newspapers they were killing thousands of Jews in that place, every day. But he could have been lying.'

'Why would the Poles kill the Jews?'

'No. It's the Austrians and Germans who's doin' the killing.'

'How? Are they shooting them?'

'Shush. You'll wake them.' He nodded towards the bed.

'If they are, I'll go out and shoot as many Germans and Austrians as I have bullets.'

Giovanni shook his head. 'Look, the man also said they had big rooms where the sick were taken. They changed the air and put them all to sleep.'

'What, like a hospital you mean?'

He looked into my eyes for a moment, and then nodded.

I pictured Mama and her bad legs, and old Uncle Levi and his crooked spine. Tears broke free and ran down my face. I imagined Aunt Martha wearing her fine hairnet and red lipstick, and the fox fur around her neck. I could see them in their hospital beds, with starched sheets and fat pillows, falling peacefully asleep without even saying goodbye to each other.

If I believed any of it, I'd go mad from the anguish. Besides, Papa and Danial would discover what was going on, and they wouldn't allow such a thing.

'He probably made it up to get money from the papers.' Giovanni said.

I nodded. 'You must leave. I'll see you when I return.'

At the door, he took me in his arms and kissed me, tenderly at first but then harder until he was trembling. He held me tightly and very still. His breath heaved in my ear and his body pressed against mine.

'I want you so badly,' I whispered.

Evangelisa turned over and opened her eyes. 'What are you doing?' she asked.

Giovanni winked at me before slipping out into the night.

Chapter 37

The three women sat on the patio in the warm afternoon air. Rebecca texting Fritz, Naomi reading the diary, and Bubba trying to lift her lame foot off the floor.

Bubba studied her granddaughters' faces for a second. 'I'm so tired. I need my siesta,' she said reaching for Rebecca's arm. 'In the morning you must visit Doctor Despina for a check-up, child. It will put your mind at ease. Now help me to my bed. My triathlon training will have to wait for another day.'

Rebecca flapped her hand as Naomi stood. 'Stay there. I'll be back shortly. We really should talk about the court case.'

Neither of the women noticed Bubba's thin smile.

* * *

Naomi dozed in Bubba's armchair and woke when Rebecca placed a cup of coffee beside her.

'Lovely, thanks,' she said.

'That's the one I forgot to make this morning, sorry. Look, we can leave our discussion about court until after dinner if you're tired,' Rebecca said.

'No, better talk about it now. Then we'll have more time to plan.'

'To be honest, I didn't quite grasp what it's all about,' Rebecca said. 'Do we have debts, tax, or something; or is it simply about the family property?'

Naomi's irritation rose. She wanted to ask why Rebecca had never read the letters Bubba sent, explaining everything. But she recognised Rebecca's recent resolve to be less selfish, and didn't want to burden her with reprimands.

'It's about our great-grandfather's shop in Rhodes Old Town. Just thinking we need to go through a court case to get it back makes my stomach flip. There's so much prejudice I'm ashamed to call myself a Rhodian.'

'But if he didn't sell it, the building must still belong to our family? I remember from school that Rhodes was first in Greece to make a land registry, though I think Rhodes was Italian at that time.'

'It was. What they forgot to teach us is that they confiscated Jewish property, then changed the names on the property's deeds to suit themselves.'

'I see,' Rebecca said absentmindedly. Then, shaking her head, 'Actually, to be honest, I don't see at all. Can they actually do that?'

'Bubba wrote to you about it. When you didn't respond, she decided to send the gun and diaries to get your attention. She guessed you hadn't read her letter.'

Rebecca stared at the floor. 'I'm *truly* sorry, but I simply couldn't take more stress. I'd started bleeding on the day it came. It was my first attempt at IVF, and there was still a chance I wouldn't miscarry. I recognised Bubba's handwriting so I binned it unopened. Later, I regretted what I'd done, and told Fritz. He said if it was important you'd have written again. But that was eight years ago, Naomi, and not a word since.'

Eight years ago? Naomi remembered Bubba writing many times.

Rebecca continued. 'Surely people tried to claim their property back?'

'They did, but Rhodes was returned to Greece. The bureaucracy, lack of documents, and legal costs meant eventually most realised the futility of the situation.'

'So they're allowing a hearing to put an end to the claims once and for all?'

'Exactly. However, each step is hindered by procedure. The latest tactic? Every benefiting family member must attend court. Bear in mind, many live on the other side of the world, extended families but not rich. The case could take decades. How could they possibly afford to stay here all that time?'

'Dirty tricks?' Rebecca said.

'Precisely. The cases were in alphabetical order, but many families have dropped out. Now, we're first, the Cohens. We set the precedent. That's why it was so important that you came. At the moment we're awaiting instructions from our new lawyer and a definite date.'

Rebecca yawned.

'Boring you, am I?' Naomi joked.

'No, sorry, so tired all the time,' Rebecca said.

'Ah, it's the pregnancy. It will pass after the first trimester.'

'I'm always afraid I won't get that far.'

'I have a feeling you'll be fine. Why don't you go to bed? We'll talk tomorrow.'

'Sounds like a plan.' Rebecca got up and kissed her sister on the cheek. 'Thank you, Naomi . . . for everything.'

* * *

Rebecca plumped a pillow and settled down. Whatever came out of the court case, she was pleased it had brought her back to her family.

She ran her hand over the diary. Her grandmother's revelations were shocking. She wondered what Fritz's grandfather's journal would be like. What were his experiences of the war?

The opposite side of an appalling story, she guessed; but they would never know.

Above all, Rebecca was inspired by Bubba's bravery and self-lessness, and she resolved to try and find that quality in herself.

She opened the diary and started reading.

Chapter 38

Late-afternoon, Thursday, 24 August 1944

Last night, when Giovanni had gone, I pulled off my dress and slid into bed. Irini's body was cold. She mumbled something.

'What?'

'Don't leave me, Dora. I'm afraid I'll never see you again.'

'We'll always be together, Irini. I promise you. Now stop worrying, and sleep.'

We'd had no time alone since I came back from the swamps. I held her close, thinking we needed to talk some more, but dreams of Giovanni overcame me and I fell asleep.

At sunrise, Irini bridled Zeus. I went through the goodbyes again, spending too much time on Evangelisa and not as much as I would have liked with Irini.

'Stay safe, Dora,' Irini said squeezing my hands before she gave me a leg-up into the saddle. 'I can't wait for your return.'

I left for Kamiros Scala, nervous to ride Zeus alone. Irini had tied a rope from under the bridle to his chest. She assured me this would keep his head down and stop him from trotting off. Still, I was afraid and clung to the reins.

I wish I was braver; therefore, I am braver!

Mid-afternoon, after a long and tiring journey, I arrived at the abandoned fishing hamlet of Kamiros Scala. I secured Zeus to the village trough and worked the pump handle. He drank noisily. I stashed my duffel, the gun, and my dress in a crevice, and with my folding knife between my teeth, I ran across the rocks and leapt into the turquoise sea.

Oh, the glorious water!

Air bubbles raced over my body, tickling my skin as I dived. Above me, blinding sparkles of sunlight flashed off the undulating sea. The cleansing taste of saltwater filled my mouth. I swam along the sandy bottom, then searched for mussels on the remains of an abandoned mooring. After prising them free with the tip of my knife, I tucked them into the brassiere I was supposed to grow into, and sprinted upward. On breaking the surface, the muted, swooshing, undersea sounds snapped into crystal clear birdsong and rustling leaves.

I placed the mussels in a shady rockpool and was about to dive for more when I noticed a golden patch of light glimmering on the seabed. After plunging down to investigate, I realised it was sunlight streaming through the chimney of an underwater cave. I thought of Jacob. He would be thrilled to discover this phenomenon. I wondered if the Nazi work camp was near the sea, and if Jacob got the chance to swim after work. I refuse to believe Giovanni's story about the man that escaped from Poland. He must have been misinformed. It didn't make sense to transport people all that way and then not use the manpower to its advantage. Everyone knows a man can't work on an empty stomach.

I dived again, dipping into the cave, and up the funnel to the surface. The low light shone at an angle and lit part of the interior. Bright-red spider starfish clung to the walls. Pipe worms, like exotic dahlias on calcified stems, waved their delicate petals. A baby octopus squirted clouds of black ink before disappearing into a hole.

I came up for air, dived further along the cliff, and found another underwater tunnel that opened into a spacious grotto. My eyes adjusted to the gloom. Devoid of a blue sky above, the water's surface was dark and rolling. Low sunlight filtered through the flooded passageway into the cavern. I was mesmerised until something big and hard banged against my bare legs.

Holy Moses!

I gasped, gagged and spluttered. A large moray eel could take my toes off in a snap. Frantic and afraid, I scrabbled for a hand hold and pulled myself onto a narrow ledge in the cave.

In the cold murky cavity, I shivered, wondering what to do. What creatures might lie in wait for me when I dived into the dark water? I couldn't stay there indefinitely, and if I didn't get out soon, I'd miss my appointment.

My folding knife was tucked into the band of my brassiere. I unfolded the sharp blade and plunged into the sea. I feared the moray's open mouth, sneering rows of vicious teeth, and its wild, lunatic eyes. My heart banged against my ribs. Even when I was clear of the cavern, I swam to shore as fast as I could. Salt stung my eyes as I stumbled and splashed, rushing out of the sea and staring back at the waterline. I shrugged into clothes, my wet skin tugging on the fabric, my heartbeat returning to normal.

At the horse trough, the roar of a motorbike grabbed my attention. I peered at the bend, glad when Tassos appeared. He'd brought two of his mother's freshly baked *tirópita* wrapped in newspaper. Good manners forgotten, I feasted on the cheese pies, flakes of filo pastry messing the front of my dress. Tassos recited orders.

He placed his thin hand on my shoulder, making me feel uncomfortable. 'Connect with a group of British soldiers,' he told me. 'They'll arrive by boat. Be on the shore, watching the sea, at midnight. Lead them up the mountain to the blue and white church in Embona's village square. The door will be unlocked. Tell them to go inside and wait.'

I nodded, eager to execute this important mission. Bringing our Allies to meet, I guessed, with the head of the freedom fighters was a big step towards peace.

'And by the way, thanks for the snake. It saved my life.'

'We're even then; your bullet saved mine,' I said. 'I've got some mussels in a rockpool over the road, if you want them.'

When Tassos had gone, I led Zeus to a grassy area, put him on a long rope, and took off his saddle. After stashing my pistol under the rolled horse-blanket that doubled as a pillow, I caught up with my diary and then slept in the lush grazing.

Friday, 25 August 1944

I am still shaking from the terrifying events that took place last night. I am not out of danger yet, and will not feel safe until I am back at the hut on Filerimos. Although I am only halfway home, I wanted to stop and write everything down while it is still fresh in my mind.

When I awoke in the field last night, darkness had almost fallen. I resaddled Zeus and led him to the water trough. The air stilled and the sea became black and as smooth as oil. At the shore, I crouched and listened. The sounds coming off the water were pure and, as yet, unadulterated by the noise of man or boat. I settled against the rocks until, from the position of the new moon, I knew it was almost midnight.

I sat on a boulder, strained my ears for the slightest sound, and stared into the dark. Stars shone down. Gentle waves lapped the beach and rocks. The silence was unnerving and seemed unnatural, although I couldn't say why. My night vision improved and I saw a wide fissure in the rock face. I squeezed into the crevice, made sure the pistol was ready for action, then I stashed it in the bag across my chest.

I hid there for at least thirty minutes, then I heard a cough, the noise so slight I'd have missed it if I hadn't been on full alert. The hairs on my arms bristled. My eyes were so wide I feared my eyeballs would fall out. Someone was out there, near me! Friend or foe, I had no idea.

A rowing boat appeared around the headland. If this was the British, then who was it that had coughed? I shrank further into the fissure. A man stepped right in front of me, then another; they stood together. I hardly dared breathe or swallow. Surely they could hear my hammering heart.

The dinghy came closer. One of the soldiers before me raised his machine gun. I feared I'd be sick again. My pistol was in the bag, but if I moved, they'd become aware of me, and that would be the end of everything.

Papa! Help me!

The two men with their backs to me exchanged a few words in German. The other lifted his gun too. The rowing boat came closer. I heard oars working the water, then low talking from the vessel – English. As they approached the shore, machine-gun fire flashed from the headland.

'Bloody hell!' one of the English shouted. Three men leapt into the water.

The two Nazis exclaimed, annoyed, then one fired at the Brits. The noise deafened me but I took the opportunity to get my gun out. I was sure our allies couldn't see the Germans in their camo uniforms and so close to the rock face.

The Brits were waist deep, wading straight towards the rocks.

One Nazi whispered to the other, *'Eins, zwei, drei!'*

I lifted my pistol, almost touching the back of a head. The shot kicked my hand up. I brought it down sharply to fire again, but the other soldier had started to turn. I caught the shock on his face. The bullet entered above his ear before the first German had hit the ground. The explosion hammered off the rock behind me, straight into my brain, sharp as a nail. For a second, my adversaries twitched in the throes of death. I doubled up and vomited. I was panting . . . then fighting for breath. My head, spinning, dragged me away from the reality and danger. Blackness invaded the corners of my eyes and I dropped to my knees. The softness of a deceased German beneath me, shocked me into recognising the urgency of the situation.

Back on my feet, I grabbed their machine guns and thrust them into the crevice. From the headland came another flash of gun fire, then a cry from a Brit, followed by splashing and screaming. I leapt over the two dead bodies and raced towards the English yelling, 'Friend! Friend!' as Kapitanos Nikos had taught me to do in a confusing situation.

One Brit floated, inert. The screamer had lost half of his face and now seemed hardly alive. The third clutched his shoulder, his body slumped with pain. I shoved my pistol back into its bag and grabbed him by his good arm.

'Come! Come!' I said.

His knees folded and he collapsed into the sea.

I didn't know what to do! A distant line of silhouettes told me the Germans on the headland were wading straight towards us. We had to hide. I remembered the cave.

Reaching up, I slapped the soldier twice on the cheek, as Kapitanos Nikos did when I wasn't paying attention. He appeared shocked. I grabbed his uniform with my good hand, and hooked the air with the other.

He got the message.

We floundered for the rocks. Machine-gun fire flicked water all around us. When we came to the area where the cave was, I slapped the soldier's cheek twice, and pointed down.

I saw, or rather sensed, he was losing consciousness. Perhaps he'd been shot again. Bullets whizzed by. Sharp, zinging sounds. A fierce sting burned my thigh. Blinding pain. I heaved the Brit on, plunged with him under the water and then started to drag him up the underwater tunnel. He slipped from my grasp just before we reached the cave. If he tried to break through the surface while still in the tunnel, he could drown. The moment was mad, crazy, unreal.

I surfaced in a tumultuous spume, took a breath, and dived back down. He had surfaced too soon and was against the roof of the passageway. I grabbed his hair and pushed my feet against the rock wall to achieve enough forward momentum.

We came up in the cave, gasping and choking.

I hauled myself onto the ledge. The Brit groaned but managed to get out of the water too.

We had no idea how long the air would last, or even how we would know when it was almost used up. Would we fall asleep, or gasp and splutter as if drowning out of water?

I had to check what was happening. The darkness in the cavern was too intense to make signs so I couldn't show the Brit what I planned.

Not knowing the word for 'Stay' in English, I hoped he knew some Italian. '*Rimani qui!*' I said pushing him against the cave wall.

I headed down the tunnel, hoping the moray – or whatever it was – had moved on to a more peaceful residence. When I surfaced, I found I had my night vision.

Silhouettes of enemy soldiers swarmed everywhere. Four Germans carried the two I'd shot towards the road. I had killed again. An irreversible act that I knew would stay with me for the rest of my life.

As I took in what was going on, I heard nearby voices and saw a couple of Nazis in the Brit's boat. They headed my way, pulling themselves along the rocks, searching.

I retreated into the subway and swam back to the soldier.

'Shush,' I whispered after I had surfaced. We sat in silence for a long stretch. Without the moon and stars to guide me, I lost track of time. The air lasted, so I guessed there were cracks in the rock above us.

Sleep was almost upon me, when I noticed light coming through the tunnel. I wondered if it was dawn. I slipped into the water, horrified to realise the Germans were searching the coastline with high-power torches. Their beams shone across the neck of the passageway, silhouetting a barrel shape that blocked some of the illumination. The form inched towards me and I suspected an enemy soldier had found the cave and approached. We had no escape!

Suddenly, I understood. It wasn't a soldier, but a large grouper fish swimming away from the torchlight towards me. I reached out and touched his tail. He darted forward, and I heard the Germans yell.

Thanks, friend!

Not long after the fish incident, sunlight lit the neck of the tunnel. I tried to wake the Brit, but he'd lost consciousness. I couldn't get him out of there alone, I needed help.

I swam out, headed for shore, and raced to Zeus, my wet cotton dress heavy and slapping against my legs. The nasty bullet graze across my thigh stung more intensely as it dried. After untying the restricting leash that kept the horse's head down, I climbed onto the trough, and into the saddle. The nearest assistance was Embonas Village, up the mountain. I whammed my heels against the horse's belly and hung on.

We galloped, my first experience of that alarming speed. The wind dried my hair and dress. Soon, we clattered into the village. I stopped squeezing with my knees and pulled on the reins. The relief when the horse responded was immeasurable. I walked Zeus across the empty square and into the churchyard. The community still slept. As I reached for the bell rope hanging at the front of the picturesque church, the door opened.

'Dora! Get out of here!' Nathanial said. 'The village is full of Germans!'

I gawped at him dressed as a priest complete with cassock and hat.

Chapter 39

Naomi led the way into the surgery. Doctor Despina looked up from her paperwork as Naomi entered with Rebecca.

'Naomi! How are you? How's Bubba today?' She blinked at Rebecca. 'I don't believe it. After all this time! Rebecca, how lovely to see you. What can I do for you both?'

Rebecca explained she was six and a half weeks pregnant through IVF, and simply wanted reassurance that everything was okay.

* * *

Naomi glanced at her watch. Rebecca had been in the examination room for over twenty minutes. What could take so long? She stared at the heavy wooden door and strained to make sense of the muted words that were hardly detectable.

Rebecca reappeared looking anxious.

Naomi caught Despina's eye.

'Don't look so worried, Naomi. Everything's fine. I'm going to the hospital right now, so I may as well take you both with me and get the ultrasound done. It'll save you waiting.'

Someone tapped on the door. A middle-aged woman entered with a plate covered in cling film. 'Spinach pies. I made too many. Help me out, Doctor.' The woman smiled placing them on the desk, and left.

'Delicious. Thank you, Poppy!' Despina called. She went to her filing cabinet and took a square biscuit tin from the bottom drawer, and deposited most of the small pastries into the already almost full container. 'Busy morning. Can I tempt you?' She passed the plate to Naomi and Rebecca.

On the way to the hospital, the doctor dropped the pies off at the refugee centre. 'Another boat of Syrians came in half drowned last night,' she said as they headed for the hospital. 'Poor people, I wish we could do more for them. We've had over two thousand this month alone, and twenty-three that didn't make it.'

'What . . . you mean they actually drowned?' Rebecca said.

'Thrown out before they reach shore, and, of course, most are women and girls who never learned to swim. Can you imagine how desperate people must be to put their families through such terrible risks?'

At the hospital, Despina led the sisters to the gynaecology ward then took Rebecca in to see the specialist. In the waiting room, Naomi fretted about Bubba, on her own for the first time. Both Papas Yiannis and Heleny promised to pop in throughout the morning.

Eventually, the door opened and Despina hurried out. 'Must go. There's an emergency.' She rushed away. Rebecca appeared with the gynaecologist. Naomi's heart plummeted to see her sister in tears.

'Please, sit,' the specialist said. 'First, dry your eyes and stop worrying. The most important thing is to get that blood pressure down. I'm going to give you a list of precautions to take: no cigarettes, alcohol or caffeine, and absolutely no stress. I want you to return to see Despina or your own doctor next week.'

'Apart from that?' Rebecca asked shakily. 'I mean . . .'

'Everything's fine. Relax, Mrs Neumanner. A little high blood pressure is quite common with twins.'

'Twins!' Naomi and Rebecca cried.

The specialist blinked at them. 'You didn't know?'

* * *

Grinning, Naomi hugged Rebecca before they climbed out of the taxi at Spartili Street.

'I can hardly believe it,' Rebecca whispered.

'Wait until we tell Bubba! She'll be thrilled.' Naomi's heart was bursting with joy for her sister.

'Fritz will be ecstatic too. He always wanted more than one child. He was an only child you see – adopted.'

They found Bubba asleep in her chair.

'If you don't mind, I'll take a nap myself,' Rebecca said. 'All that manhandling has worn me out. I'm longing to tell Fritz, but I'll wait until he's home.'

'Go, take a nap,' Naomi said. 'I mean, you'd better get all the rest you can. I'll be hosing the front and catching up on housework.'

In the dappled sunlight on the patio, Naomi smiled to herself.

* * *

Rebecca lay on the bed and stared at the whitewashed ceiling. She gently placed her hand on her stomach. Twins, how remarkable! There was something quite astonishing about dreams coming true. Two babies growing happily in her womb. She wondered if being away, having her thoughts occupied by other things, had helped bring this about. How wrong Fritz was when he said perhaps they weren't meant to have a family. Everything would be perfect, yet in the depths of her mind the seed of uncertainty lurked.

She was dozing when the door opened. 'Are you awake?' Naomi whispered.

'Only just . . .'

'Ah, Fritz is on the phone. Shall I tell him to call back?'

* * *

The kitchen was crammed with Heleny, Georgia, Bubba and Naomi. All eyes were on Rebecca as she put the phone to her ear. 'Hello, Fritz?'

'Hello, is that Rebecca? Sorry, it's a bad line.'

'Darling, it's me. How's it going?'

'Fine. How are you? I've been worried.'

'Good, Fritz. I mean, there's something I have to tell you.'

'No, me first. I've something important to say.' He cleared his throat, the sign of a major announcement. 'Are we still, you know, pregnant?'

Thinking about her great news, Rebecca choked up. A sob escaped into the phone.

'Oh, no. My poor darling Rebecca. I'm so terribly sorry. Listen, I didn't mean what I said. Try and forget it. I was nasty and cruel and selfish. I've missed you so much. I wanted to tell you that I don't care if you want me to go to the IVF clinic a thousand times – I'll do it for you. You're more important to me than anything else. Being apart has brought it home.' His words came out in a breathless rush.

Now, Rebecca was crying hard. Everyone in the kitchen stared at her.

'Oh, Fritz! I love you so much! But there's no need. Listen to *my* good news.' She accepted tissues from Heleny. Staring straight into Bubba's eyes, she said, 'Fritz, darling, we're having twins!'

Heleny and Georgia clapped and hugged each other, and Naomi and Bubba squeezed hands.

'Twins?' He gasped. 'Rebecca, please come home. I want to look after you.'

'No, Fritz. I'm here for another two weeks.'

'Can I speak to Bubba?' he said. 'If you think she's strong enough.'

Rebecca held the receiver out. 'Can he talk to you, Bubba?'

Bubba's smile fell. She considered the request, then reached for the phone. 'Yes,' she said. After a long silence on her part, she said, 'Yes, I see', and handed the receiver back.

Rebecca told Fritz she loved him, hung up, and then returned everyone's smiles. 'If you'll all excuse me, I'm going back to bed.' She kissed Bubba on the cheek. 'Far too much activity down here.'

* * *

Rebecca drew the curtains, lay on the bed, and did her breathing exercises. *Twins.* Suddenly, she longed to be home, rummaging in the attic, planning the nursery, holding Fritz in her arms. How long would it be before she knew the gender of her babies?

She fell into a restless sleep, her mind filled with images of drowning refugee children, Nazi death camps, and her grandmother emptying her pistol into the head of a young man. She woke with a start and realised she had flung her arm out and knocked the bedside lamp over. The clock said she had slept for less than half an hour. From the sounds drifting up, the kitchen was still overcrowded. She plumped her pillow and reached for Bubba's journal.

Chapter 40

In the churchyard I quickly explained to Nathanial that the British soldier needed a doctor urgently. He'd lost a lot of blood and might have more bullets in him. To get him out of the cave we required a couple of strong men and a long rope. I rode back to Kamiros Scala at a steady trot.

After securing Zeus, I raced to the shore and pulled off my frock. A tamarisk tree grew on the beach, so I looped my dress onto a branch. The Embonas rebels would see it if they arrived while I was underwater.

I dived, hoping the grouper fish hadn't returned. Harmless he might be, but I didn't want to play chicken in the passageway. My luck was in. The soldier was barely conscious. The sun, now up, no longer directed light into the tunnel.

I felt the soldier's face, patted his cheek twice, then gently pushed him against the cave wall. I hoped he got the idea to stay there. I swam out of the tunnel and saw four men riding mules towards the shore. One was Nathanial. There was no sign of the enemy or the dinghy. Two Brits floated in the eddies, arms and legs spread like starfish.

I put my thumb and forefinger in my mouth and whistled as Giovanni had taught me. Despite the grim situation, I smiled to remember the shepherd boy. Just thinking about him gave me strength.

Nathanial and the Embonas *Andartes* secured their mules at the trough alongside Zeus. The beasts nodded and blew as if having a heated conversation. The men dumped a rope and a medical bag under the tamarisk tree. I tied a circle in one end of the coil, and then led the *Andartes* to the rocks. Once inside the cave, I struggled to get the loop over the soldier and under his arms in the dark. Back in the water, I reached up and pulled on his arm. He cried out, but got the idea and dropped into the sea with a splash.

I yanked three times on the rope, at which the Embonas men heaved so hard the Brit's head cracked against the roof of the tunnel. He went under spluttering. I swam after him, glad to break surface on the other side of the passage. To add to the soldier's injuries, I saw a nasty gash on his forehead. A bullet had gone through his shoulder, and another was lodged in his leg.

The graze across my thigh hurt like hell. I struggled into my dress and bid goodbye to the Embonas men, who were dressing the soldier's wounds.

As I turned to go, the soldier yelled weakly, 'Oy!' He thumped himself in the chest, winced, and said, 'Sergeant Tommy Bloomberg!' then he pointed at me.

'Rhodes Freedom Fighter Pandora Cohen,' I said. I stood tall and saluted him.

He flicked his hand to his forehead, smiled wearily, then held out his good arm and we shook. Nathanial grinned, and I sensed the men's eyes on my back as I climbed to the crevice. After retrieving the two machine guns, I placed them in Nathanial's lap, saluted him, and walked away.

With the sergeant in capable hands, my job at Kamiros Scala was done. I seemed more adept at handling Zeus each time I rode and as I sat in the saddle, I contemplated all that had happened. I had killed again and with all the stress of the night, I hadn't considered my actions until that moment. When I recalled pulling the trigger, my emotions got the better of me and I trembled so violently I feared I would fall out of the saddle.

I walked Zeus off the road, leaned forward, and hugged his neck. He stood perfectly still while I cried. Although this sounds perfectly ridiculous, I sensed he understood what I was feeling, and his placid sturdiness helped me to recover my senses.

When I urged him back to the road, he made a quiet snicker, as if to say, 'Better now?'

I wondered if my actions really would help to end the war. Would there be a chain reaction that led to the release of Papa and all my family? I imagined someone unlocking Papa's door and saying, 'You're free to go. You can thank Pandora for this.' My heart soared as I evoked Papa's wide smile and his reply. 'I always believed she'd come to our rescue.'

I could see his face again but it only made me cry once more.

I recalled Giovanni's words, *They's killin' them all*, and I crushed that sentence to dust in my mind. Even the Nazis couldn't simply kill all the Jewish people. It wouldn't be allowed.

Friday, 25 August 1944

My diary is up to date. I am in the hut, exhausted, but eager to hear Irini's voice. I long for her embrace. On the last stretch of my journey up Mount Filerimos, with the wind in my hair and the sun warming my shoulders, I realise I want to spend the rest of my life with Irini at my side, and I was going to tell her the moment I saw her. Just because I loved Giovanni, didn't mean I loved Irini any the less. She would understand that.

But Irini wasn't at the hut. Xanthi told me she had gone out shortly after I left for Kamiros Scala and hadn't returned.

Evangelisa rushed up and hugged me. 'Will you tell us everything that happened, Dora?' she said, her eyes sparkling. 'Did you have a real adventure? Did you shoot anybody?'

She wore her best dress and red ribbons in her hair. I understood this was in my honour and I was touched.

'You look beautiful, Evangelisa.' I kissed her cheeks and hugged her. She held her skirt out and twirled.

'Dora, you *can* borrow any of my dresses or ribbons whenever you want. I wouldn't lend them to anyone else, but you are so special, and I'm sorry to say so but you've been looking a bit dishevelled lately.'

This was an honour indeed. 'That's so generous! Wait until I tell Mama what a fine young woman you're turning into with your cooking and housekeeping. She'll be so proud. You'll make some handsome boy a very lovely wife one day.'

Her cheeks flushed and her eyes sparkled, and I loved her so very much.

'Come on, Dora, I'll find a really nice frock for you.'

'Evangelisa, will you forgive me if I go for a sleep first? I'm so exhausted.'

She took my hand and led me into the hut. 'You get some sleep, Dora, and don't worry about a thing,' she said. 'I'll sort you out with some fresh clothes when you wake, later.'

When I woke, I refused one of her flamboyant party dresses and I settled for a simple blue gingham frock with little puff sleeves and white buttons down the front. Evangelisa also insisted I took a pair of her pristine ankle socks.

Giovanni turned up, took in my appearance and smiled. I longed to fall into his arms, but he told me I had to report to Nathanial immediately.

* * *

I left my sister with Xanthi. Giovanni led me to the villa, once again by a different route. And once again, I sensed we were under observation. The *Andartes* leader seemed moody. While recounting the events that led me to the little church in Embonas, I became dizzy and my knees buckled.

Next thing, I was carried upstairs by a burly rebel who deposited me on a huge four-poster bed. I opened my eyes and found Giovanni staring into my face, his concern very apparent.

'You fainted. Here, drink some water.' He slid his arm under my shoulders and sat me up.

'I was scared,' he said.

'What, in the woods?'

'No, silly, when you blacked out like that.'

We returned downstairs, and I apologised to Nathanial, explaining that apart from the cheese pies, I'd hadn't eaten or drank anything in forty-eight hours. He ordered Josie, his woman, to fetch soup and bread.

'Now start again. I want to hear everything that happened at Kamiros Scala in your own words, little one.' I left nothing out. 'You were brave,' he said finally. 'From what you've told me, I realise it wasn't a chance encounter, the Germans were waiting for the British. Clearly, someone had informed the Nazis that our allies planned an insurgence. This means we have a traitor.'

Finding the information difficult to grasp, I said, 'Perhaps the traitor was connected to the British soldiers.'

He shook his head. 'No. It's someone here.'

'I can't believe it. Who would do such a thing?'

'Yesterday, the Gestapo stormed the bamboo groves again. This time they tortured and killed Kapitanos Nikos and confiscated the radio.' He narrowed his eyes. 'Who saw the radio, Dora?'

'Kapitanos Nikos. Oh, no!' This shocking news made me dizzy again. I shook my head and shrugged. 'What radio?'

'The radio that was in the box I gave you for Nikos. The person responsible for Nikos's death knew about it. Are you telling me you never looked in the crate?' I stared at him. 'Dora?'

'He was so full of life.' I tried to grasp what Nathanial implied. 'The lid was nailed down. I had no idea what was inside.'

Nathanial narrowed his eyes as if he had realised I was lying. 'We've lost important equipment, Dora.' He rubbed his hand over his mouth for a moment. 'Even worse, the Kapitanos is dead. He glared. 'We *must* discover who the traitor is before more lives are taken.'

Only Irini and I knew about the radio, and Irini had disappeared.

Josie, a good-looking fair-skinned woman about twice my age, stuck her head into the room and called, 'Food!'

'Get Giovanni, Josie. They can eat together. In fact, it's getting late; they can sleep here tonight.'

Josie ladled two bowls of chicken lemon soup thick with rice. Nathanial and his woman left the kitchen, and moments later Giovanni entered.

'Are you all right now?'

I nodded. 'You've got some food. Let's eat. I'm starving.'

Despite the upsetting information, I ate ravenously. We both licked our spoons when the bowls were empty. 'I'm worried about Irini,' I said.

'Don't fret. She'll turn up with an explanation. You were brave yesterday, Dora.' His voice was soft. 'You killed our enemies and you saved a man's life.' He seemed distracted, then he took my hand. 'Nathanial said you can stay here tonight.'

He gazed into my face. I understood his thoughts, lowered my eyes and shook my head.

'Why?' he said. 'I want to sleep with you in a real bed. Spend the night in each other's arms, all the way until morning.'

'No, Giovanni. That will be the most precious night of my life, and I want to save it for . . . you know.'

'But we won't be able to' – he swallowed hard – 'until after the war. I've got no money for a wedding now.'

'Wedding? You mean we will be married?' I was shocked, happy, and sad all in the same instant. Somehow it set an appointment. An event for my family to come back to. A wonderful time in the future when this war could be forgotten and happiness would rule the day.

'You will marry me, won't you, Dora?' He lifted my face, his slow-blinking eyes gazing into mine. 'I love you, Pandora Cohen.'

Filled with emotion and unable to speak, I nodded.

He cupped my chin and kissed me tenderly. 'Then I must make arrangements.'

Giovanni left the kitchen and returned minutes later. 'Come with me.'

He led me up the red marble staircase, and out onto the Juliet balcony. A million stars twinkled in an ebony sky. An owl hooted. Crickets trilled their monotonous song and the warm air was laden with the scent of wild honeysuckle.

Nathanial joined us. He smiled and said, 'Stand together.' We did. 'With the power vested in me as Capitano of the *Andartes*, I ask if you, Pandora, take Giovanni as your husband, to love and honour for always?'

I may have gasped, I'm not sure, but when I found my voice I looked into Giovanni's eyes and said, 'I do.'

Nathanial said, 'Do you, Giovanni, take Pandora for your wife, to love and honour for always?'

Giovanni continued to gaze at me. 'I do,' he said softly.

'Then place the ring on her finger.'

Giovanni pulled at a leather thong around his neck and as it emerged from under his vest, I saw a ring glint in the starlight. Nathanial cut the thong and Giovanni slipped the simple band of gold onto my finger.

'I now pronounce you man and wife. Kiss the bride,' Nathanial said. Giovanni took me in his arms and kissed me tenderly.

A great racket of clapping and whistling came from inside, and I realised the rebels knew what was happening. Someone struck up an accordion, *raki* was handed out, olives and bread on the table, and a party whooped into full swing.

By midnight everyone was a little drunk. Giovanni whispered, 'Let's escape.' And we rushed upstairs. In front of the bedroom door I'd been in earlier, he picked me up, carried me over the threshold, and placed me on the bed.

I took the wedding ring off. 'I'm afraid of losing it, Giovanni; it's too big.'

He pulled the thong from his pocket, slipped the gold band onto it, and tied it back together. 'Then wear it like this until I can have it made smaller. It belonged to my mother.'

We abandoned our clothes and for the first time slept naked, all night long in each other's arms. The happiest night of my life.

Afternoon, Saturday, 26 August 1944

I am back at the hut, and write this while Evangelisa and Xanthi are clearing a new kitchen garden at the edge of the woods.

Before I left the villa this morning, Giovanni and I ate eggs and bread with olive oil in the big kitchen. Nathanial came in and said I was to have a break for a week or so.

'But I don't want any time off, sir. We must end the war. I have to help my family return home!' I cried. 'Tell me how to get the radio back!'

But he was insistent.

Sunday, 27 August 1944

Where is Irini? She's been gone for two days. I fear for her safety and miss her terribly. I wanted to keep our wedding a secret until I had told Irini about it myself. At midday, I met Giovanni under the cinnamon tree but I couldn't relax.

'I'm sorry, Giovanni. I'm so worried about Irini. Where can she be?'

'It looks bad,' he said. 'That night, when I came to tell you where you were going, when you suspected we were being watched, you're sure it wasn't Irini? And are you certain she didn't know about the radio?'

'Of course!' I lied. 'How could you say such a thing!' I turned and stomped back to the hut. He realised there was no point in following me.

I couldn't believe Irini was an informer, but it didn't look good. Her body was cold when I got into bed that night. She was the only one who had seen the radio and knew I was meeting Kapitanos Nikos. She also knew I was going to Kamiros Scala.

There was a simple explanation for these things, and I had to find it. Irini would never betray me – not ever – as I would never betray her. I felt sick at the thought of someone assisting the enemy when the lives of our families depended on the war ending.

* * *

Dear Diary, it is afternoon now and there is still no sign of Irini. With every hour, my concern deepens. After meeting Giovanni, I was sitting on the log outside the hut, contemplating all that had passed, when Evangelisa brought her hairbrush and started untangling my long hair.

'I don't know how you manage to get so much grass and twigs in the back of your hair, Dora,' she scolded. 'You really should wear a scarf when you go into the woods.'

She was full of questions: Where had I been? What happened? Had I received more orders through Giovanni? Did I think the Germans had captured Irini?

That very thought horrified me, and I decided I had to talk to Nathanial about my fears.

My sister was growing quickly, taking on responsibility for our comforts. She and Xanthi had dug a patch in the rich soil and planted tomato pips, and she'd cut the sprouting ends off the potatoes hoping they'd grow too.

'I'm proud of you, Evangelisa. You're doing a wonderful job,' I told her as we went inside.

'Xanthi's teaching me so much, Dora,' she said. We're baking bread tomorrow.' Clearly delighted, she fussed around the hut. She had even placed a jar of wild flowers on the table.

'Where's Xanthi?' I asked.

'She's gone to meet one of the *Andartes*.' She leaned forward, her eyes shining. 'Don't let on, but he's her boyfriend.'

'What makes you say that?'

'The other day, while you were away, she met him and came back with a love bite on her neck.' Evangelisa nodded rather like Zeus. 'I'm sworn to secrecy, but right after the war, she is going to get married and I'll be her bridesmaid!'

'That's lovely.'

'I wish I had a boyfriend,' she said. 'I watched you and Giovanni kissing. I want a boy to kiss me too.'

I remembered how Irini and I would study lovers kissing at the port. 'When did you watch us?'

'Ah, that would be telling.'

Monday, 28 August 1944

I hardly slept last night for worry about Irini. I plan to speak to Nathanial this very morning. His men might have heard something. Xanthi has gone to collect pine cones for the fire, and Evangelisa is arranging fresh wildflowers for the table.

Giovanni appeared in the doorway. 'Can I speak to you outside?' he said.

We sat on the log. Evangelisa followed.

'Evangelisa, you realise this is the very best time to water tomatoes?' I said. 'If you're hoping for really big ones.'

'Oh, right.' She grabbed the bucket and headed for the spring.

Giovanni smiled. 'She's cute, isn't she?'

'What did you want to tell me?'

'Nathanial wants to see you. He said they've discovered who the traitor is.'

'Who?'

He shrugged. 'I have my suspicions, but it's not for me to say.'

'Is he still at the villa?' I asked. Giovanni nodded. 'Then will you stay with Evangelisa, while I go? I can't leave her alone if there's a traitor watching.'

* * *

All the way through the forest, I fretted. Who was the informer?

I sat with Nathanial on the stone wall outside the Villa. When he answered my question, I was speechless, I snapped my mouth shut and stared at him.

'I can't believe it,' I managed. 'Why would Xanthi betray us to the Nazis? She has *nothing* to gain.'

'We have learned that her lover's a Nazi. She'll do anything for him, even give him information. You really had no idea, little one?'

I shook my head. 'Would I leave my sister with her if I suspected Xanthi was capable of treachery? It's too awful! I thought someone was following Giovanni and me the night before I left Kamiros Scala.'

I knew it couldn't be Irini!

He nodded. 'Xanthi will be dealt with. Is there anything else you want to talk about?'

'I'm worried sick about Irini. She left without a word three days ago. It's not like her. Something's terribly wrong, I sense it. I don't understand. We *never* have secrets, apart from what passes between you and I, *capitano*.'

'Ah yes, now we come to Irini.' Nathanial stared at the ground as if searching for words among the wild flowers and blades of grass. He rubbed his hand over his beard. 'There's no easy way to say this. I'm sorry, little one. Your friend Irini . . . her body was found this morning.'

Chapter 41

Naomi closed the diary. As the sun rose, she had caught up to Rebecca's bookmark. She twisted her wedding ring. A family heirloom Bubba had said when she slipped it off her finger and gave it to Costa, before their marriage.

'It belonged to my husband's mother and then to me, Costa,' Bubba had said. 'Naomi's mother, Sonia, wore it on her wedding day, and now it must go to her first-born daughter, your wife to be.'

Naomi regarded it as the most special thing she owned.

'How come it wasn't lost at sea, Bubba?' she asked later.

'Because the fates played a hand, child. Sonia's fingers swelled when she carried Rebecca. When they went fishing for the very last time' – her lips trembled and she took a moment – 'that night, she oiled her finger and pulled it off, because of the discomfort. She intended to get it stretched a little.' The old lady dabbed her eyes. 'I found it by her bedside the next day and I've worn it ever since.'

Despite Naomi's questions, Bubba had refused to talk about her wedding or about Naomi's grandfather, who she now suspected was Giovanni.

She opened the diary and continued reading, eager to discover the reason for Irini's tragic death.

Nathanial's news escaped my logic. 'Sorry, I didn't understand you,' I said, his words swimming around in my head, jumbled in my mind, impossible to comprehend.

His eyebrows bunched and a small vein throbbed on his forehead. His eyes flicked up to meet mine and stayed there. 'The girl – your friend, Irini – from the hut. We found her in the valley. She's dead. I'm sorry, little one.' He lowered his voice, his right fist opening and closing.

'The traitors – whoever Irini passed her information on to – tortured her and threw her body off the mountainside, and they're going to wish they hadn't.'

Nathanial's words seemed delayed in the air between us before arriving in a nightmare of comprehension. My screams came in single file, straight from my heart, piercing the sky and ripping through everything sacred.

'Irini!' I shrieked. 'No! This can't happen. It's impossible!'

Nathanial clasped a hand over my mouth and bundled me into the villa. 'Shush, little one.' He gave me a glass of *raki* and ordered me to drink it.

Irini . . . dead! I feared it, yet denied it to myself. She would never stay away from me, not for any reason on earth. Now, I couldn't tell her the whole truth – that I *truly* loved her, that although I had secretly married Giovanni, our love was entirely different. How mean were the fates to keep that from us?

I don't know how long I vented my distress in the villa, but gradually the hysteria left me. With my heart nothing but splintered shards, I continued to hear the echo of Nathanial's words, 'Your friend, Irini, she's dead.'

Oh, Irini, what you feared so much would happen to me has happened to you! Why is life so unjust? I was the one who had killed, yet you suffered torture and murder. Is this my punishment for killing?

I found Nathanial sitting on the wall outside.

'Where is she? I must go to her,' I said, my voice thick with emotion.

'We buried her. You shouldn't see her, believe me.'

I ran at him, pounding my fists violently at his chest. 'Please, I have to! You don't understand, Nathanial. I loved her with all my heart and I never told her! I pretended we were only the closest of friends, and now I can't tell her at all.'

He stood firm, taking my blows until I collapsed, sobbing, into his arms.

'Nathanial, please, take me to see her.'

'Like I said, they tortured her, little one. They blinded her.'

'Blinded?! Please, I'm begging you!'

Nathanial sighed. 'All right. We'll go together.'

We walked side by side, his hand on my shoulder, through the woods, up towards the Catholic Cloisters of Mount Filerimos. The wind howled through the pines above our heads, like miserable ghosts watching us mourning the death of my true love. Outside the walls, between the trees, a patch of freshly turned ground marked Irini's grave. The nightmare that so far had only been words now became real. My skin shrank over my body.

Irini, sweet Irini!

'I want to look upon her face for the very last time,' I said in a whisper.

He shook his head. 'No, you don't, little one. The bastards were cruel to her. It would break your heart, I promise you. Better to remember her as she was.'

'No! Will you listen to me? I *have* to see her. I *have* to,' I insisted. 'You can help me or not.' I fell to my knees and raked at the earth with my bare hands.

He knelt and helped me dig, until we came to a white sheet, about half a metre down. 'Turn away for a moment,' Nathanial said.

I did, guessing he closed her eyes. I think I appeared calm on the outside, almost comatose – yet inside, I exploded with grief, regret, and the most terrible sorrow. Had my whole life been lived on a journey to this moment? The greatest part of me lay dead in the ground. We shared everything, our most secret thoughts and feelings.

Nathanial got to his feet. 'I'll wait by the building while you say goodbye.' He walked away.

311

I unfolded the corner of Irini's shroud. Her eyes were closed, and her face pale as porcelain. After brushing her raven hair back, I kissed her forehead and then hugged myself recalling her cold body the last time we slept together. Nothing I could say would change what had happened but as my grief mounted, I sensed her presence in the air around me.

'Irini!' I howled into the wind. 'It wasn't supposed to be like this. You tried to tell me, but I wouldn't listen. Now, this is my punishment!' I stared about wildly, expecting a sign that she understood. 'You're taken from me but I'll always love you, Irini, until the day I die; and then we'll be together again.'

I knew she could hear me. She'd understand my tears; my grief mirrored hers because Irini had been my life and soul.

A climbing rosebush, heavy with white blooms, hung over the cloister wall.

'I'll be back in a moment, my dearest friend,' I whispered, getting to my feet. I ran to the shrub, held out my skirt, and gathered the petals off every flower.

After returning to Irini's side, I surrounded her head with the virgin-white rose petals, their scent as sweet as her breath when she laughed. 'You'll be in my heart as long as I live. And I swear on my life, I will kill the person who did this to you.'

Leaning forward, I kissed her lips before I lifted the corner of the shroud and placed it gently over her. Tears streamed down my face as I scattered a handful of earth upon the sheet.

I turned to the sky. 'Irini!' I cried out, and gripping the hem of my dress, I tugged at it with all my strength, welcoming the pain in my wrist, wanting more than I was able to bear. The cloth tore apart and I ripped it all the way to my waist. I started to say the words that go with the Jewish tradition of rending the clothes of life, 'Blessed are You, Our God, Ruler of the Universe, the True Judge.' But it was impossible to disguise my anger at God and His angels. He'd stolen Irini from me! My punishment because I'd killed three soldiers? They were Nazis who'd taken my family away and Irini's loved ones too. What God would consider this as just? What sort of God allowed such a diabolical imbalance of fairness?

'Irini! Irini! Irini!' I cried to the heavens.

A hand fell gently on my shoulder. I looked up to see a visibly upset Nathanial. He sniffed hard and said, 'Come on, little one. Let's cover her now.' He folded back the shroud, brought two coins from his pocket and placed them on her eyes.

'Why are you doing that?' I whispered.

'To pay Charon who will ferry her across the river Styx to Hades. When it comes to religion, best to play safe. After all, the only person here who knows where death leads us is Irini.'

Oddly enough, his words calmed me. I imagined Irini on a journey to the Elysian Fields. A final resting place for the souls of the heroic and the virtuous. A land to which I'd travel myself one day. I knew she'd wait for me and I envisioned her standing on the riverbank, arms wide, eyes sparkling as they so often did when we were alone together. I placed my hand on her cold cheek. 'If Nathanial's right, don't pay the ferryman until you're safe, Irini. We don't know where his loyalty lies. I'll join you soon, my dearest friend. I'll see you on the other side.' Fresh tears blinded me. I wiped them away and took a long, last look at the woman who had taken my heart. Sadness dragged me down as I placed the white cloth over her sweet face, and replaced the earth.

* * *

Nathanial and I walked towards the villa in silence. My cheeks were stiff with dried tears. Each step further away from Irini became more grudging and leaden. I had nothing to say, the pain in my throat so intense I doubted I would ever speak again. Irini's words were ringing in my ears.

Don't leave me, Dora. I'm desperately afraid I'll never see you again.

My cold bones ached for her.

'Nathanial, was Xanthi responsible for Irini's death?'

He nodded. 'Xanthi guessed you were on a mission. She informed the gestapo, and we think she also said that Irini probably knew the details of your assignment, or at least the whereabouts of our hideout, the villa.'

'In that case, I must be Xanthi's executioner.'

He stared at me for a moment, then nodded once more. I swung around and raced back to the hut.

I needed Giovanni's comforting words. Desperate for him to hold me tight and tell me everything would be all right, as he did when he fixed my broken wrist. Giovanni could take some of my pain away.

I broke through the bushes and there he was: Giovanni with Evangelisa in his arms, and his lips against hers. 'What are you doing?' I ran at them.

Evangelisa squealed and dived into the cabin.

Giovanni raised his hands to avoid my blows. 'Stop! Stop!' he yelled. 'She wanted to know what a real kiss felt like; that's all!'

I snatched the hoe and ran at him, hurling it javelin style. He startled, dodged the missile, and tried to take me in his arms. I punched and slapped him while screaming abuse, until exhausted and in tears, I cried, 'Irini's dead!'

'What?! What happened?'

'Xanthi's the traitor. She had Irini tortured and thrown off the mountain. I'm going to kill Xanthi! I swear it. Then, I come back and find you *kissing* my little sister! You're unbelievable, you dog! You bag of stinking shit! Get out of here. I never want to see you ever, ever again!'

I stormed into the hut, slammed the door, and hurled abuse at Evangelisa. 'You want the shepherd boy? You're welcome to him because I can't stand to have you, or him, near me at this moment.' I hauled the door open. 'Go on. Get out! I've had enough of traitors for one day!'

She started crying. I didn't care.

Giovanni stood in the clearing. He stared at the hut. I pushed Evangelisa in the back. 'Go! The pair of you, get out of my sight. Do your kissing somewhere else!'

'Dora, I'm sorry!' Evangelisa cried.

'Don't waste your breath, I'll never forgive you. Get away from here!' I threw myself into the hut and slammed the door so hard the cabin shook.

They finally left. With everyone I'd ever loved gone, my life seemed empty and without direction. I didn't know what to do. Mentally and physically exhausted, and completely alone in the world, I cried more tears. Nevertheless, I needed to draw a line under this appalling chapter, and perhaps, who knows, start again – or simply end it all.

At that moment, I desired nothing more than to join sweet Irini. To imagine life without Irini was impossible. As I wept bitterly for my friend, noise outside caught my attention. I thought Giovanni or Evangelisa had returned to apologise, and suddenly I wanted to hold them, share my grief, hear them tell me it would be all right. Filled with remorse for my vicious outburst, I needed them badly.

Tassos came through the door. 'Nathanial said, "Tonight, if you can."'

He didn't need to explain.

'Yes, tonight's fine.' Then I would leave this cruel world having kept my promise to Irini. Her death would be avenged.

'Here's the instructions.' He gave me a folded note, turned and left the hut.

The small village of Marietta, near Filerimos, was the home of Giovanni's family. At this place, I was to execute Xanthi. I read Nathanial's orders over and over before I burned them. I had two hours to prepare.

Chapter 42

Rebecca fell into a deep sleep and woke refreshed. Her first thought: she was having twins! Fritz loved her! Life was truly wonderful. She tossed the covers aside, pulled on her clothes, and headed for the beach. When she reached the old cement pillbox, she sat on a rock with her back against the gun-shelter and gazed out to sea. Everything had changed since the terrible day of her departure so long ago.

She recalled taking Fritz home to meet Bubba. She'd met him at college in Athens and it was love at first sight. Yet the moment he walked through the cottage door, Bubba had gone ballistic. She jumped to her feet and stared at Fritz. He stepped towards her, smiling, with his hand stretched out, but before he could speak, she said coldly, 'Get out of my house. You are not welcome here.'

Rebecca was confused and embarrassed. 'But, Bubba, this is Fritz. We want to get engaged.'

'What?!' Bubba cried. 'No granddaughter of mine will marry a Nazi!' She rushed at Fritz.

Naomi grabbed her and said, 'Bubba, calm down! What's going on?'

'Get him out of here!'

'I'm leaving,' Fritz said, then turning to Naomi, 'I'm sorry.' He touched Rebecca's arm and said, 'I'll see you later.'

When he'd gone, Rebecca said she couldn't believe the terrible thing Bubba had shouted at Fritz. He wasn't a Nazi. Her grandmother was consumed by rage and hatred the likes of

which she had never seen. Naomi managed to calm Bubba a little, and Rebecca was so upset, but then her own anger flared and
she retaliated. She called Bubba a small-minded Jewish bigot.
And it was Bubba's turn to shed tears.

Despite Naomi's effort to sooth them both, trying to put each
point of view to the other, things escalated over the next few
days until Bubba, refusing to explain the reason for her animosity, forbade Rebecca to see Fritz. If she did, she was no part of
Bubba's family.

With that ultimatum, Rebecca retaliated with words she had
regretted ever since. Then, she packed a bag and left.

Thinking about it on the Paradissi shore, she realised how difficult the situation had been for Naomi, living in the same house
and loving them both.

Memories of her childhood returned, Naomi, always there,
looking after her.

*Put your clothes higher up the beach. Don't go in too deep. Put
your sandals back on, as there might be broken glass between the
pebbles.*

Good old Naomi, she'd been sister, mother, and friend; and
nothing was ever too much trouble.

* * *

Naomi had found the diary and caught up to Rebecca's bookmark again while she had her morning coffee. Poor, poor Dora.
With such a lot to do, Naomi reluctantly closed the journal
and traipsed upstairs to make Rebecca's bed. She folded back
the sheet, smoothed the pillow and stared at it, imagining her
grandmother's emotions when she uncovered the face of her
most beloved friend, Irini in her earthy grave.

'Phone!' Bubba called.

'I've got it,' Naomi replied, rushing downstairs.

'Hi, Mama!' Angelos, her eldest son calling from Cyprus. Instantly alarming.

'Angelos! Is everything all right?'

'Yes, don't worry. Just to let you know we'll be home tomorrow.'

'Lovely . . . but . . . why? What about your jobs? Are you sure everything's okay?' Both sons worked for a dive centre in Cyprus during the university's summer break.

'We're fine, Mama. The water sports shut down for a fortnight. There was an explosion but we're fine. We'll see you soon, bye.'

'What? Wait! An explosion? What happened?'

'The dive centre's short-staffed, Mama. Konstantinos was filling dive tanks when he was called away to give a windsurfing lesson. I was out with the boss and a paraglider. Nobody turned the compressor off so eventually the cylinder exploded.' He paused to laugh. 'Took all the legs of the wetsuits. Blew one of the walls out too.'

Naomi thought of Konstantinos's legs and clutched her stomach. What if he'd returned to the hut at that moment? 'Was anyone hurt?'

'Nah! Don't worry. See you later.'

'Bye. Love you,' she said, but he'd already hung up. An explosion! She stood, scratching her head and staring around the kitchen. Where would her boys sleep? Rebecca occupied their room. She glanced around the four-by-four-metre kitchen. If she slept in the kitchen, the boys in her room, Rebecca in the boys' room, and Bubba in the lounge, they could manage. At least until Costa came home for the court case.

Everything seemed a problem lately. Perhaps she should have listened to the builder and had the new bathroom built at the back, instead of taking up the third bedroom. But Naomi hadn't wanted to lose space in her yard where an ancient grapevine and her pots of tomatoes flourished. Anyway, too late now.

Naomi had not laundered her own sheets for a month. She hardly had time to straighten the bed, never mind change the bedding. At night she fell in, exhausted, and before dawn she tumbled out with a mental list of urgent tasks. She suddenly rushed upstairs and dragged the white bedding off. She should vacuum. Her heart thudded – palpitations – she flopped into the mattress clutching the bunched-up sheets to her chest.

The musky scent of Costa rose from the bedding. She buried her face in the linen and inhaled. How she missed him. The sweetness of making love in the dark returned to her. The comfort of Costa's arms and sweet dreams without a care. Naomi smiled and her heartbeat slowed. In less than a fortnight he'd be home for the court case. In the bathroom, she shoved the laundry onto a quick-wash cycle.

In the kitchen, Naomi stared at the back wall. A two-metre-long stone banquette, used in the old days as a bed or seat, was covered in clutter. Bubba's old sewing machine, Angelo's mandolin and music books, a stack of cushions, and an ancient contraption for spinning wool. At the other end stood Costa's metal toolbox, Konstantinos's plastic fishing box and a couple of collapsed beach casters.

Naomi glanced at the cheap clock hanging over the banquette. Time to prepare some food. She'd placed a kilo of beef to marinate in red wine the day before, and now she set about peeling tiny onions. Once the ingredients for *Kapamás* were in the casserole, she had to get Bubba to bed for her mid-morning nap. The old lady laughed at something on TV and Naomi regretted not having spent more time with her grandmother.

Rebecca waltzed in. 'Gosh, I'd forgotten how lovely the beach is,' she said breezily. 'If I were you I'd be there every day, Naomi. It's not good for you to be cooped up in here. I'm absolutely famished, must be the fresh air . . . and the twins.' She grinned, squeezed Naomi around the waist, and Naomi felt happy for her. 'What's for lunch?' Rebecca asked innocently.

Naomi blinked and returned to the drudgery. 'I have no idea. I've still got the washing to hang out, the beds to make, the plants to water and Bubba to see to. Aromatic beef in red wine and garlic potatoes with juniper berries for dinner okay?' she quipped sarcastically.

'Delicious! But, you really do have to get organised, Sis. Let me look after the lunch. Where's the nearest takeaway?'

'Top of the street turn left, four doors down.'

'Back in a moment.' Rebecca rushed out.

Ten minutes later she returned. 'Right, Papas Yiannis and Heleny are coming to eat with us. What's the phone number of the takeaway? I'll order some food.'

'I have no idea. You'll have to walk round there.' Naomi tried to keep the sarcasm from her voice. ''Scuse me while I empty the washing machine, peg out, make the beds and peel the potatoes. I hope I've got enough plates and cutlery for everyone. I don't suppose you could water the tomatoes?'

Busy thumbing her iPhone, Rebecca wasn't listening. 'Ah, here it is! I'll place an order. Is there anything you fancy?'

Naomi shook her head.

'Right. Pork giros, Greek salad, tzatziki, garlic bread, baklava and ice cream, okay?'

Naomi nodded. 'Just getting the washing,' she said going up to the bathroom. 'Back in a moment.'

'Naomi, you really should take it easy. Now, I'll sit with Bubba and watch TV with her for a bit. Could you set the table ready for lunch? That would be great!'

She's pregnant; her head's in the clouds, Naomi thought. Breathe in and count to ten.

Papas Yiannis and Heleny arrived just before the food. Rebecca made a fuss of the delivery boy, but then asked Naomi for help when he wouldn't accept Rebecca's credit card. Fifty-three euros, almost all the money Naomi had in the house – what was left of Bubba's pension and all Naomi's money from Pandora's Box.

Everyone enjoyed themselves and said how lovely it was of Rebecca to do this. Naomi caught a look from Bubba and sat by her side.

'Remember: she'll be gone soon, and then you'll be sad,' Bubba said quietly, understanding and patting the back of Naomi's hand.

Papas Yiannis was leaving. He turned in the doorway. 'Thank you, Rebecca. That's the best food I've had for a long time.'

'Me too,' Heleny agreed.

Bubba patted the back of Naomi's hand again. 'They're just being nice.'

'Yes, it was lovely, Rebecca,' Naomi said, heartbroken that all the money she'd made from the products had gone.

Rebecca beamed. 'My pleasure.' She turned to her grandmother. 'Come on, Bubba, let's watch some TV and de-stress.'

Naomi gathered the dishes, avoiding the urge to make a clatter or throw something. The room emptied. She heard Rebecca and Bubba giggling at the TV with a backdrop of canned laughter. Alone with the chores once more, Naomi experienced a wave of exhaustion.

'Could you stick the kettle on, Sis? We're parched,' Rebecca called from behind the rug that hung over the archway.

Clamping her mouth shut, Naomi pulled her hands out of the dishwater, wiped them down her skirt and marched out of the front door. Suddenly finding herself without direction or purpose, she headed for the beach. When did her sister become so thoughtless? She told herself to calm down, that Rebecca meant no harm, that she was simply too happy to think straight. Still, nobody liked being taken for granted.

Five hundred steps and she would turn around. She paced, hard and fast, wishing with all her heart Costa was home. He'd be serving afternoon tea to guests right now, the cruiser moored at Mykonos.

Naomi sat on a rock and gazed out to sea. She recalled her honeymoon on that island and wondered if it had changed much. In each other's arms, they'd watched from the top ferry deck as it approached the harbour.

The small island had shone, a jewel in the turquoise Aegean. Square white houses clustered around the port, like sugar cubes thrown at the landscape. They visited blue-domed churches and expensive gift shops, drank coffee on a Juliet balcony that hung over the sea, and walked up to the pristine, thatched windmills which stood to attention in a row.

That week was filled with love and happiness. Both thrilled to have a baby on the way. With that memory, her heart went out to her sister. She must have suffered terribly. To miscarry, to have her dreams shattered over and over again. Slightly ashamed to have got in a tizzy about Rebecca's thoughtlessness, she abandoned the walk and returned home.

The problem was that since Rebecca's return, Naomi had felt strangely invisible, and as lonely as she'd ever been. She loved Rebecca very much, yet somehow her sister seemed to sap Naomi's lifeblood. She should get back and produce some candles and cream, as that always lifted her mood, but there were so many other jobs to be done first.

She arrived home refreshed, telling herself not to be so silly.

Rebecca was making a drink. 'Ah, there you are. I wondered where you'd gone,' she said.

'I need a hug.' Naomi wrapped her arms around her sister. 'It was kind of you to get food for everyone, Rebecca. Thanks.'

'I'll give you the money back tomorrow, Naomi. Sorry about that. How embarrassing!' She handed a mug of tea over.

'Thanks. It wouldn't matter but I am a bit short this month. Big phone bill. You know how it is?'

Rebecca shrugged and blinked, bewildered. 'Do you need some help?'

'No, no. I'm fine really. Costa's wages will go in the bank next week,' Naomi said quickly.

'Tell me what you want to cook tomorrow and I'll do the shopping,' Rebecca offered.

'Great, that would free up an hour. I have some orders to take care of.'

'I hope you don't mind; I've put my laundry in the machine, but I'm not sure how it works. Would you do it for me?'

Naomi took a breath. 'Yes, of course.'

'Could you be careful ironing the pink blouse though? It cost a fortune.'

Naomi's self-control snapped. 'What?! You expect me to do your ironing too! You're taking advantage now. What do you do at home?'

'I have an ironing lady. Please, Sis. I'm useless.'

'No! I'm not your bloody servant, Rebecca! It was different when we were kids, but you're an adult now. Do your own laundry. The ironing board's in my wardrobe, okay?'

'Right then. I will.' Rebecca stuck her lip out and rushed upstairs.

While she finished washing the dishes, Naomi heard Rebecca clattering about above her. Suddenly aware of a long silence, she called up, 'Did you find it? Are you all right?' No answer. She hurried upstairs. A whimper came from the bedroom. 'Rebecca, is everything okay?'

Rebecca's head was buried in her hands. 'I'm so sorry, Naomi. I can't think straight. It's as if I have to be horrible to block out whatever's happening at home.'

Naomi sat beside her and slipped an arm around her sister's shoulders. 'And what exactly is going on at home? You used to tell me everything, Rebecca. What's changed that's making you so unhappy?'

'It's Fritz. I don't know what's going on. He's deceiving me.'

'What?! You mean there's another woman?' she said softly.

'No. At least, I don't think so. But I'm not sure about anything these days.' She was silent for a moment. 'Tell me: did you and Bubba send more than one letter?'

Naomi nodded. 'Bubba wrote to you over and over again, but she never received a reply and I'm sure you'll understand how much it hurt.'

'That's it, you see. I only ever got one letter. And now there are these Mondays.'

'Mondays? Sorry, you've lost me.'

'Every first Monday of the month, Fritz goes to the office before daybreak and doesn't return until near ten in the evening.' She wiped her eyes and faced Naomi. 'Last month I called his office, which is something I don't normally do. They told me he never works on the first Monday of the month. Where does he go, Naomi? I'm frantic, all sorts of things are going through my head.'

'Did you call his mobile?'

Rebecca nodded. 'Turned off.'

'Why don't you ask him about it? Talk it through.'

'I'm afraid, Naomi. I'm such a coward. Every day for the past month I've thought about asking him, but he must have a reason for not wanting me to know. I couldn't bear to lose him. What can be so important that he thinks he has to deceive me for so long? Now I find out about the letters. Fritz must have taken them; there's no other explanation. To top it all off, I'm hopeless at confrontation. I keep fretting about it and also about the lives of our children growing inside me.' She sighed. 'No stress, it's so easy to say.'

They sat in silence for a while, then Naomi said, 'Do you want me to speak to him?' This was the wrong thing to do. She shouldn't interfere, but she couldn't stand to see Rebecca in such a state.

'Would you?' She faced Naomi. 'I can't do it. Just can't. Whatever's going on, I suspect he might prefer to tell you instead of me and let you break it to me gently. I know Fritz. At least I think I do. He won't tell me anything over the phone.'

Naomi chastised herself, she'd done it again. Rebecca should stand on her own two feet and take care of her own problems, yet it broke Naomi's heart to see her so distressed. 'Give me your phone and I'll call him.'

Bubba looked up as Naomi came downstairs. 'Is she all right?'

'She wants her husband. Would you let Fritz come, Bubba?'

Bubba stared at the wall for the longest time and then finally nodded.

Naomi sat at the kitchen table, scrolled through Rebecca's numbers, and called Fritz's mobile.

'Rebecca, darling,' he said, his voice thick with emotion.

'It's Naomi, Fritz. I need to talk to you.'

'She hasn't. . . Rebecca and the babies, are they all right?'

'Yes, fine. Don't panic. It's about Rebecca I'm calling. She's upset, Fritz. She needs some explanations.'

'Oh, Naomi.' From his subdued voice, she understood he too was distressed. 'I need to talk to her, but not over the phone. I'd like to come over? Some things have happened, and right now I probably need her as much as she needs me.'

'I'll book you both into a local hotel, so you have some privacy. When will you come?'

'I can be there this evening, if that's okay?'

'Text your arrival time, and we'll meet you in the airport lobby.'

'Thank you, Naomi.'

Naomi hung up and realised Bubba was staring. 'No, before you ask, I have no idea what this is all about.' She glanced at the small picture of Filerimos over the phone. 'You had a really hard time in the war, didn't you?'

Bubba nodded. 'Not as awful as some.' She spread her fingers and then touched her thumb and index fingers in an okay sign. 'Look at that! I'll be playing the piano before you can shake a baton.'

Naomi grinned. 'You won't need me. I'll be redundant.'

'Pity I don't have my old Remington anymore. I was good at touch-typing. I'd like to write more songs and poems too.'

Naomi recalled Bubba as an attractive woman, typing out school reports, wearing nylons, and beads, and a slide in her hair. 'How long did you work at the school?'

'Ha! You remember? For three years before Rebecca made an appearance. When I was a child, I wanted to be a reporter, and that was the nearest I got. The teachers gave me their end-of-term reports, and I was supposed to type them out as they were but I used to elaborate a little.' She giggled and watched her spreading fingers again. 'It's all very well the school telling parents about their child's failings, but I believed their achievements should be commented on too. I'd look for the subjects that got high marks and add a comment, for example: 'A talented artist', 'Exceptional music skills', 'A born sportsman'. I think the students, and their parents, got something from that.'

'I'd almost forgotten those days.' Naomi frowned for a moment. 'Do you remember the poppets?' Bubba shook her head. 'Heleny and I had bought little plastic beads that pop into each other, and I made you a multicoloured necklace. One day the teacher gave me a note to take to the office; you were typing and I saw you were wearing my poppets over your twinset. I was so proud!'

Bubba smiled, and Naomi realised how much she had been loved.

'Time has a habit of repeating itself,' Bubba said.

'How do you mean?'

For a moment, she stared ahead. 'Irini and I . . . one day, we found lots of shiny fat beans under a tree. They were so beautiful, striped, browns and creams. We decided to make necklaces for our mothers, and I took a spool of button thread and a needle from Mama's sewing box. We sat there, poking holes in those seeds all afternoon. I was so happy with Irini. At dusk, we were tired, rubbed our eyes, and parted, each with her lovely jewel-lery gift.' Bubba chuckled. 'Mama went crazy when I gave the necklace to her. She marched me around to Irini's house, and then we were hauled off to see the doctor.'

'I don't understand. Why?'

'They were the seeds from a castor oil tree. One of the most poisonous plants in the world. You see them all over the place now, but kids have more sense than to play with them. The next day, we couldn't see. No school for a week, and we had to lean over a chair while Mama put drops in our eyes.' She smiled softly. 'The eye-drop bottle came in useful when Irini found an abandoned baby bird a while later. We fed it mashed insects and milk, squirting them into the back of its gaping mouth, hoping it would grow into a fantastic peacock and follow us everywhere. It died of course.' Her face fell. 'Poor Irini, I'd forgotten those childhood days. We were so happy together.'

'I'll bet you have great stories to tell, Bubba. If you want to write again, you can always use my laptop. Just tell me when, and I'll set it up for you.'

'I'd like to try it sometime, but I'm tired now.' She let her lame hand fall into her lap. 'Too many exercises. I have to recuperate in my bed for an hour.'

* * * *

Naomi washed up. The house was eerily quiet, as if waiting for something important. With the diary in her hand, she stepped outside and took a deep breath of fresh air. Her thoughts returned to darling Costa, Mykonos, and their honeymoon. They were standing on a veranda, watching the sunset, when their baby moved for the first time. She almost fainted with delight, took Costa's hand and placed it on her tummy. Silent, they'd gazed into each other's eyes until Costa said, 'Wow! He's a footballer. Naomi, I've never been so happy in my life. Thank you, darling.'

Poor Rebecca, cheated of so much more than she can imagine. Her children dying in her womb. All her hopes and prayers pinned on this pregnancy. And poor Bubba, to have those awful memories of killing people. How could she get to sleep at night? Naomi shook her head, the thought too horrible to contemplate. She sat on the patio and opened the diary. Dora, she remembered, was going to execute Xanthi.

Chapter 43

Late at night, Tuesday, 29 August 1944

Why am I still alive after such a terrible day?! I should be dead. . . I want to be dead! Why are these horrid things happening to me? Yesterday was the worst day of my life, everything went wrong, even my own execution! I am in such despair I no longer want to live.

With all my heart, I have longed for my family to come home, but now I hope they never see me again. I hope I am dead before they return and they fail to discover my awful deeds.

I had Nathanial's instructions and I carried them out perfectly, but to no avail. Death, death, and more death! The people I love may have already gone to God, and me on my own, such a failure, and now I can't even manage to take my own life!

Irini, I want to join you, but they have taken my gun away. For my own good, they say. Wait for me, Irini, please!

Last night, the light was fading fast. I knew I hadn't much time and went over my plan again: wait in Marietta village; shoot the traitor; wrap the gun in the oilcloth that lay to my right; drop my pistol into the hole next to the fence post and cover it with earth; shake my hair out and, with an enormous cabbage in hand, skip back into the village by the longest route, as if returning from one of the many vegetable plots that surrounded the houses.

I lay on my stomach in the dirt between two rows of brassicas, hidden by the massive leaves, watching Xanthi talking to a soldier. My heart hammered.

The sun was setting behind them. Shafts of light dazzled between the buildings' windows, making me squint. The traitors huddled together mauling each other. The German grabbed Xanthi's bottom and kissed her hard on the mouth. I truly hated Xanthi for what she had done. How could she kiss a German when she knew they'd interned our families in camps of horror? But Xanthi had proved she was capable of anything. Filthy treacherous Nazi-loving whore. Torturer! Murderess! Xanthi was responsible for Irini's death. For me it was as if she had committed the acts of torture and murder herself.

I trembled like Giovanni's dog, my body saturated with loathing. I thought of sweet Irini, how much pain she had suffered, and how much I loved her. Now she was gone, thanks to Xanthi.

I pulled up a giant brassica, stripped the outer leaves and rolled the vegetable into the centre of the rut in front of me, to act as a gun rest. Gripping the pistol in two hands, I placed them on the cabbage, my elbows supported on the soil irrigation mound either side of me. Squinting into the sun, my eyes started to water.

Come on, Xanthi! In a few minutes' time I wouldn't be able to see clearly enough for a clean shot.

The conspirators parted, turning in opposite directions. Xanthi glanced over her shoulder, before being hidden from view by a house. The German didn't look back. I pointed the pistol at a narrow gap between the next buildings. The moment Xanthi appeared, I would fire. The space between the dwellings was only a couple of metres, leaving no room for hesitation. I was seeing spots from the sun's glare, but in a minute or two, the sun would have dropped behind the houses.

I could hear Kapitanos Nikos's instructions in my head: focus on the sights, not the target, line the bead with the notch on the barrel, squeeze the trigger until you feel the slightest resistance, hold it; wait for the target.

Evangelisa would never have the courage to do this thing. Yet, I had decided to believe Giovanni about the kiss and forgive Evangelisa. I loved them both, and right now they were all I had left. If only I hadn't been so awful to them earlier, but it was too late now, and I hoped they would understand that I was too upset to think straight.

Had I the guts to take care of Xanthi? Yes, certainly! I would kill her for what she had done to my dearest Irini. I wavered – more killing. I took a breath and held it. Any second now.

I screwed my watering eyes closed to get rid of the tears and, as I opened them, there was a girlish figure with long hair about to disappear behind the next building. Xanthi! I focused on the sights and fired. She dropped like a rock. My nostrils filled with the stink of carbide. The explosion cracked, hammered into my brain so violently I couldn't breathe.

I shook all over. Work through the plan! Suddenly traumatised, I let go of the gun, and fumbled for it among the cabbage leaves. Panic rushed through me but I followed instructions. At the edge of the plot, I plucked a cabbage from the ground and raced around the outskirts of the village to the far side.

Who would take any notice of a kid with a cabbage?

Someone shouted in the main street. People passed me quickly. I tagged along as if part of the group. I had to see that Xanthi, hateful daughter of the devil and killer of my beloved Irini, was dead.

My pulse thrummed in my ears. Our shadows stretched out ahead of us and I felt as though I walked into darkness.

'A girl's been shot!' someone yelled.

Ahead, a group stood in a circle, bent over Xanthi's body. I reached them, my breath coming in gasps, my mouth dry as sand. She lay face down, the back of her head bloodied and mashed. I trembled as they turned her over.

'Don't look, child,' a woman said, taking hold of my shoulders and trying to twist me away.

I shrugged free of her grip. Xanthi would have known nothing, unlike poor Irini who suffered horribly and died in terror and pain.

Someone brought a sheet to cover the body. Although still quaking, I was proud of what I'd done. One of the men rolled the dead girl onto her back. I saw her face—

Oh, God! Evangelisa, no! No!

I screamed. 'My sister! Evangelisa!' My world went crazy. I had shot my sister! She couldn't be dead. I felt myself sucked into a nightmare like dirty water in a storm drain, my heart breaking, my head pounding. I couldn't speak, or even think, then rage filled every part of my body. What possessed me from that moment was pure vendetta. I raced back to the cabbage patch, retrieved the gun, and returned to the hut. I waited in the bushes on the edge of the clearing.

Xanthi arrived after dark. She must have heard what had happened, yet still she called out, 'Irini! Evangelisa! Dora!' When nobody appeared, she slipped inside and a flickering light told me she had lit a candle. Every sound seemed amplified in my heightened state of nerves. The door was ajar. Xanthi washed her body and changed her clothes. She came outside, sat on the log and brushed her long hair.

The hoot of an owl sounded from the woods.

Xanthi giggled, dropped the hairbrush, and hurried down a track that led to the cinnamon tree.

He was there, sitting on a boulder, waiting. His dark civvies set off his white-blond mop and pale skin, making him luminous in the moonlight. They kissed. He had a blanket over his shoulder.

I watched him spread the rug, then lean against the tree and unbutton his trousers. Xanthi threw off her top and her brassiere and squirmed lewdly before him, giggling and touching herself. He pulled her to him and lifted her skirt while kissing her. In a moment they were on the ground and he was at her, his bare bottom alabaster in the moonlight. I waited until his thrusts picked up speed. I stepped up close, with my feet either side of Xanthi's head. She opened her eyes.

333

Before she could react, the first bullet entered the back of his head. Blood spattered Xanthi's face and the roots of the tree. Her lover's head fell to one side. I could see the vein pulsing in Xanthi's neck. Her mouth made an 'O'. The next bullet left a red dot between her eyes, and her surprised expression froze into death.

'That's for Irini and Evangelisa, you bitch of Satan.'

'Irini, wait for me,' I whispered, turning the gun towards myself and holding it to my temple, thinly aware of my knees hitting the ground. Sobbing, I tried to pull the trigger before encroaching blackness enveloped me.

*   *   *

Dear Diary, now you know everything. I am ashamed and broken hearted. Poor Evangelisa. Poor Irini. Both dead because of me. If I had boarded the ship with my family, they would both be alive now. I learned that Tassos, who was instructed to watch over me, carried me back to the Villa. They tell me I am ill.

Friday, 22 September 1944

I could not update my journal any sooner. Apparently, I was sick with malaria and they say I was in fits of delirium that kept me talking gibberish. For my own safety, and for the safety of the *Andartes*, it was decided that I should not be taken to hospital.

At the Villa, Josie looked after me. By the time I began to recover, Giovanni had signed for the army. He came to say goodbye, but our meeting was not a happy one. I was devastated that the war was taking somebody I loved once again.

'I have to ask: did you shoot your sister because I kissed her?' he asked quietly.

'No, of course not. It was a terrible, terrible mistake, Giovanni. Can't you understand how I feel? I killed my own sister. She was all I had left. I thought she was Xanthi – she was supposed to be

Xanthi! I don't know how it happened; one moment Xanthi was there, so I fired, and Evangelisa was killed. By me. I'll never forgive myself. Please, please believe me!'

'How can I, after the things you said? You hated her, all because of a kiss.'

'You don't understand, Giovanni. I'd been to see Irini.' My voice fell to a whisper. 'I was devastated, angry, and then I saw you two kissing and said things I didn't mean.' With that, I broke down.

'But she didn't know that. She idolised you. She was going to the hut to beg your forgiveness.' His eyes tearing up, his voice ragged. 'I told her to go and talk to you in the evening because I knew you wouldn't turn her away in the forest at night. I'm the reason she went down that street when she did.' He put his hands over his face. 'It's my fault she's dead. She was a child, and she died believing you really hated her and never wanted to see her again.'

I could not speak for crying.

He seemed to hesitate. 'I don't know what to think anymore.' He came towards me, and I was sure he was about to take me in his arms, but he pulled the catapult from his belt and thrust it at me. 'Keep this until I come back. I have to come to terms with all this.' He started to leave, picking up my duffel on his way. 'I need this.' He turned and looked me in the eye. 'One day I'll return it.' With that, he left for the army.

Sunday, 1 October 1944

Although I am recovered from the sickness, I can't get over killing my own sister, or the murder of Irini. The details of both deaths remain a secret between Nathanial, Tassos, Giovanni, and myself.

My strength came back slowly, although my heart was broken and pure misery coursed through my veins. I told Josie that I wanted to return to the hut. Nathanial gave his permission, so long as I took Giovanni's dog with me. In the villa's opulent bathroom, I bathed and washed my hair in warm water pumped up from the wood stove. I dressed, made sure my weapon was ready for use, and placed it in the bag slung across my chest.

'I'm going, Josie. Thanks for taking care of me. You saved my life.'

She hugged me. 'Stay safe, little one. I'm always here if you need me.'

The men were busy in the big room, planning their next espionage, so I slipped out of the rear door. I tied a rope to Kopay, and together we set off through the dense woodland.

The paths through the woods had overgrown and I soon lost my way. Kopay found everything interesting. She tugged on the rope, vacuuming scents from the ground, snuffling and muttering her analysis. Tired of being pulled by a dog that weighed as much as me, I let her off the leash for a run-about. I lay on my back, staring up, wondering what would become of Pandora Cohen.

The treetops towered above me, and from my supine position it looked like they painted white fluffy clouds on the deep-blue autumn sky. Mesmerised, I watched the changing cloud shapes until men's voices interrupted my fantasies. All the horror of Seven Springs came back as I realised they were Germans.

I rolled onto my knees, crawled into the dense scrub, then unbuckled my gun bag. Kopay returned, sniffed around and, discovering where I was, lay in a nearby patch of sunlight. I hardly dared to breathe, my ears alert to every noise in the forest. The soldiers were ambling about with no apparent purpose. They talked quietly and, horrified, I realised they were heading straight towards the villa. Kopay stood, her ears up, alert. I stuck my arm out of the bush and drew a line in the air. She lay in the sunlight once more, deathly still, only her big eyes darting here and there. As I crouched between her and the enemy, I knew she sensed danger, or perhaps my fear.

What to do?

336

I decided to wait and make sure they were alone before following at a distance. If they missed the villa, then best to let them go, but if they found it, I had no choice but to take action.

A flock of migrating starlings crashed into the treetops, their boisterous chatter loud as hail on a window, breaking my concentration on the soldiers. Kopay leapt to her feet, nose in the air. Afraid she'd bark, I said, 'Ssh!' and drew a line again. She hit the ground. The birds took off in one swirling, shape-shifting formation which threw a shadow over everything. I took advantage of the chaos and rushed forward to my next cover where I strained to hear the soldiers.

In the distance, one of them laughed good-humouredly. Instantly, Danial came to mind, then Xanthi's words: *Imagine who that person might be . . . somebody's father or brother. Wouldn't you compare their family to your own?*

Overcome by cowardice, I wanted to shut my eyes and make it all go away. My attempt to end the war, alone, was futile. Hunched under the scrub, I faced my own private battle. Was I a deserter? Was my only purpose on earth to have children and keep a clean house, like my mother whom nobody took seriously? No!

Poor Mama.

I listened again, oriented myself once again, and rushed quietly from bush to bush. I caught up with the soldiers near the wall of trees and, staying low, I slipped the pistol out of my bag. They stopped, sat on their haunches and smoked a cigarette. I didn't move a hair until a rustle behind me made my skin shrink. I spun around.

The dog's eyes met mine. I drew a line again and she dropped to the ground without a sound. One of the Germans urinated against a tree, but as they were about to skirt the wall of trees, a noise came from the villa. Somebody shouted, 'Josie!'

Alert, the soldiers swung their machine guns forward, and one unclipped a grenade from his belt. They pushed through the dense vegetation, squeezing between tree trunks, until they stopped with the villa in full view.

They exchanged a few quiet words. One pointed to the left, while turning to the right. They were going to split up, in which case I'd have no way to shoot them both.

Two clean shots were required, I wouldn't get a second chance against their machine guns. I focused on the one with the grenade. After a steadying breath, I squeezed the trigger.

Before my target had hit the ground, the other soldier dived into the wall of trees. I fired blindly, running. Kopay burst through the trees and we both gave chase. The grenade exploded. *Andartes* rushed out of the house and I could hear them behind me. Being smaller than the soldier, Kopay and I had an advantage through the scrub. We closed rapidly, but then a branch knocked the gun from my hand.

Defenceless, I raced on. Thorns scratched my face and arms and tore my dress as I punched through the undergrowth. The dog bounded ahead and attacked the soldier's ankle, unbalancing him. He fell, firing his weapon as he went down. I dropped to the ground. Fearless, Kopay attacked his wrist. The soldier let go of his machine gun and tried to beat off the dog. I grabbed the firearm. When I leapt up and aimed at him, the soldier appeared astonished.

'Kopay, off!' I ordered after stepping back, keeping the machine gun trained on the soldier. The German lay on his back, his wrist a mess of ragged flesh, bleeding heavily, his other hand raised in defence. Kopay danced with excitement. I stood my ground until the *Andartes* caught up.

Chapter 44

Adrenalin pumped through Naomi's veins as she turned the page. She wondered how her grandmother ever survived. A sheet of newsprint, carefully folded into quarters, lay between the next pages. She teased the layers apart and read the front cover of a Rhodes newspaper.

> *The child, fatally shot on Sunday in the village of Marietta, has not been identified. The girl, aged between twelve and fourteen years old, and believed to be called Evangelisa, will be buried in the cemetery of Filerimos tomorrow. Police are asking for anyone with information relating to this tragic death to come forward. Seventeen-year-old Xanthi Streusel, a young Rhodian woman, found fatally shot on Mount Filerimos, was buried in the town cemetery at 11 a.m., yesterday.*

Naomi flipped the newspaper and scoured the reverse side but saw nothing about a murdered German soldier. Some mother's son, how tragic. Perhaps simply another naive idealist eager to end the war, or a white supremacist on a witch hunt, or just an army boy with no choice but to follow orders.

'Naomi!'

She looked up from the diary to see Marina running across the road. 'Naomi, you'll never guess what I've found! Grandpa's wetting himself; *he* wanted to tell you himself but had a little job to do at the church.'

'What is it?'

'I was surfing, looking for angles on your products and, as Bubba is Jewish, I hit on a Jewish website out of curiosity.' She gulped, beaming. 'It's the official papers that prove you own the property in town. It looks like they've been found!'

Naomi thought for a second. 'Sorry, Marina, but you must be mistaken. In Bubba's diaries, she said they had to hand their documents to the Nazis in L'Aeronautica. They confiscated and destroyed everything.'

Marina could hardly speak for excitement. 'No, no! This is what I've just read. You know the big police station in town, the headquarters?'

'Opposite the fire station?'

'Right on. Well, according to this website, decades back, a former employee of the Greek bureaucracy – I forget his name – kept pestering to have a storeroom in the police station unlocked, but they refused permission. Nobody wanted to reveal the contents of the sealed room. Finally in 2002, out of frustrations, he began writing to people higher up.'

Naomi wondered where this was leading.

'This guy, well, he claimed that Rhodes police headquarters contained a locked vault full of old files and records, all of the utmost importance to historians. One of his letters landed in the archives office of the Dodecanese Islands.'

'And . . . did anyone do anything about it?' Naomi asked.

Marina shook her head. 'No way. At least not for the next ten years. In 2012, a new boss, a woman, got appointed as director of the Dodecanese State Archives. Now, here's the cool bit: at the same time, an *Italian* historian carried out research on the island, because Rhodes used to belong to Italy, remember?'

Naomi nodded.

'The historian had also come across rumours about the same locked room. He wondered what could be in there. Finally, the historian and the Archives' director got together, and in 2013 they managed to get permits to have the vault opened.'

'A search warrant for Rhodes police headquarters? That must have been difficult.'

'Exactly,' Marina said.

'What on earth did they find?'

'Some records had rotted away with the damp, but around ninety thousand documents from the years between1912 and 1946 were rescued.'

Naomi blinked at her. 'What an incredible discovery!'

'Well . . . yes, it is.' Marina beamed.

'I'm finding all this hard to take in,' Naomi said. 'Such an important historical find. Why didn't *we* know about it? Why wasn't it on TV, splashed all over the national news, or at least in the local papers?' She had a vague recollection of Georgia and Heleny gossiping about a secret door on the day she posted the first gun part to Rebecca. Was this what they were prattling on about?

Marina shrugged. 'Grandpa said we have to come to our own conclusions about that.'

'Iced tea?' Naomi asked, reaching into the fridge.

'Yeah, great, thanks. So, with the documents being found, Grandpa says we stand a chance, as long as the papers we need aren't among the ones that rotted away.'

'I'll have one of those too,' Bubba called, shuffling into the room on her Zimmer.

'Did you hear all that, Bubba?'

'I did. It sounds promising.'

'Naomi! Ah, there you are.' Papas Yiannis hurried into the kitchen. 'Good news, hey?'

'But, Papas, didn't you say the Rhodians changed the names on Jewish property deeds in the land registry?'

'They did, but these papers are from the Italian census, long before that. The survey was locked away after they shared the information with the Nazis. It consisted of land deeds, business, bank accounts, vehicle documents, houses, loans. Everything! Also, it recorded religions. It has the names of all the Jews, the lists of the possessions of the families that never returned, and the addresses of buildings in Rhodes Old Town and all over the island that belonged to the thousands that left or were forced off Rhodes.

'Several important people didn't want this news to get out. Apart from everything else, think of the effect it would have on tourism. If the rest of Europe learned that the happy, fun-loving Rhodians assisted with the deportation of the Rhodian Jews to Auschwitz and then stole their property, the world heritage site would be seen in an entirely new light.'

'Yeah, just imagine,' Marina said thoughtfully. 'Who could enjoy a meal in a taverna if they knew it had been a house stolen from its real owner? If that owner had starved to death in a concentration camp, after their children had been thrown into the furnaces alive?'

Naomi's stomach cramped. The young woman had an unapologetic way of expressing the truth. 'It's amazing news, a miracle . . .' She recalled Georgia saying as much, and Naomi had laughed, not taking her seriously.

Papas Yiannis nodded. 'The historian said the room contained the largest collection of records for that era, outside Italy.'

'But how does all this affect us? I don't understand.'

The priest smiled triumphantly. 'What happened to all the property that belonged to the Jews? Not only the ones sent to Auschwitz, but another two thousand that left before all that transpired? The Nazis used that census to round up the Jews that remained in Rhodes and they made them bring all their papers with them, to be confiscated, so nobody could ever prove what was theirs.'

'Right, I'm getting you. So, the documents that the historian uncovered tells us who owned what?'

'Basically, yes, we're hoping so. The Rhodians are worried because they invented a law that made it legal – and easy – to change the name on the deeds of any buildings. All you had to do was get a witness to sign a paper that said you'd lived in the property for fifteen years, and nobody could object. A regulation that still stands today. At the beginning of the war, the Jewish community counted almost four and a half thousand people. Let's not forget that these were Rhodian citizens – families who migrated here from Spain many generations earlier. Jews lived here even before the Christians and, until the war, they were respected members of the community. Their only difference was religion: they believe in the Old Testament, while the Italians and Greeks follow the New Testament.'

'But a lot left the island, didn't they?'

'Yes, that's true. They applied for visas to other countries. These application letters were also kept, but in July 1944 the Germans used the list of the remaining Jews to round them up and deport them to Auschwitz. Eighteen hundred Jews were taken from Rhodes and Kos. Only one hundred and sixty-three survived; more than half of those died before returning to their island, and the majority of the survivors stayed in Italy or left Europe altogether.'

'Jacob lived in Italy,' Bubba said quietly, her eyes glazing.

Naomi recognised the look. Bubba was away with her memories. She caught the priest's eye and mouthed, *Jacob, Bubba's brother?*

'Played the violin at your mother's wedding.' He nodded, then shook his head. 'Best leave it for the moment.'

'It's uncanny that all this should come out now,' Naomi said. 'Easy to understand why the Greeks are keeping quiet. Must be a legal minefield with the island having belonged to Italy.'

'The papers contained data on a hundred thousand people that lived in Rhodes,' the priest said. 'Information about their economic and social life, their friends and foes, their political leanings, their faith, and so on. Under Italian dictatorship, the "Enemies of the State" were black-listed. The Carabinieri, a division of the Italian army, kept records on spies, fanatics, partisans, and their religions: Muslim, Catholic, Orthodox, or Jewish. The files concerning the Jewish race came to the attention of the Germans when they took over the island.'

'And you hope these documents will help get our property back?' she asked again.

'I'm not sure, but they can't harm our case. The main problem is that they've all been taken to Italy. Getting the relevant papers in time for court will be near impossible. We have to think things through. See what we can do.'

Naomi said, 'So, the local government of Rhodes were aware of the census being found, knew about our case to reclaim family property, and they chose to keep quiet about the documents.'

'A little underhand, perhaps,' the priest said.

'A little?!' Marina cried. 'Grandpa, it's disgraceful!'

* * *

'Will it help?' Bubba asked when the priest had gone.

Naomi shrugged. 'I guess we'll have to wait and see.'

'Will you give me the diary? I'd like to read some. I can't recall much of what I wrote.'

'It's pretty powerful stuff, Bubba. I don't want you getting upset. I've just read about you shooting the German to save the *Andartes* in the villa. My heart's still thudding. Can you hang on until you are a little stronger?'

Bubba's eyes glazed for a moment, then she nodded and quipped, 'Perhaps you're right. I'll sit outside and do my gymnastics for a while.'

Chapter 45

The *Andartes* surrounded me, Kopay, and the wounded soldier. One of them took the machine gun from my hands. Trembling, I sank to my knees. Nathanial lifted me onto his wide shoulders.

'She saved our lives, men. And thanks to the little one, we add more firepower to our arsenal. That's six machine guns she's brought us! Come, we must honour our hero!' he boomed.

The rebels clapped and whistled in admiration as I was carried shoulder-high to the villa. Josie painted the German's wrist with iodine and then bandaged it before he was tied to a chair in the cellar. Two men went out to bury the dead soldier. Nathanial poured *raki* for everyone, and we slammed our glasses down and knocked it back. I kept glancing at the door in the hope Giovanni would appear, but he didn't.

'He's gone, little one,' Nathanial said quietly, guessing what was going through my head. 'He'll be back, don't worry.' He dished out more *raki*, but I told him I wanted to return to the hut on Mount Filerimos.

'Then Tassos will also go, and stay with you tonight.' He caught my nervous look. 'Don't worry, little one, you'll be perfectly safe. Go now, before it gets too dark.'

One of the rebels put a record on an old wind-up player. The men sat in a circle, hitting the *raki* hard and watching Josie perform *Tsifteteli*, the sensual Greek belly dance.

As I passed through the front door, I turned and gave them a wave. They were true friends who had looked after me when I needed them. Nathanial had buried Irini and helped me with my grief. There had always been someone in the background, keeping an eye on me, making sure I was safe. The

Andartes leader had married me to Giovanni. I was sad to leave them all.

Tassos, Kopay, and I squeezed through the wall of trees. I looked back at the villa once more, remembering the first time I had seen it, then we set off, up through the forest to Filerimos. My heart went out to Giovanni. Such a weight of guilt he carried. I hoped he would stay safe in the army. After all that had happened, even if I never saw him again, I had to know that he was alive and I prayed he would find happiness when the war ended.

Most of all, I hoped he would come back to me.

The three of us walked in silence, our surroundings silver in the full moon.

Tassos heard it first. He stopped, rested a hand on my arm, and turned his eyes towards the sky. Then I recognised it too, the drone of a distant plane. As it neared, anti-aircraft fire rocketed from the airport viewing tower. We both leapt when an explosion ripped open the night and illuminated the top of the hill.

'Here!' Tassos yelled, dragging me behind a fallen tree. 'Get down!'

The whine of a falling bomb had me petrified rigid. Memories of the Levi's house rushed back. Tassos threw himself over me, knocking me down. There was a second of silence, an explosion that deafened me, and terrible pain in my ears. In the same moment, a rush of air blew dirt and grit and forestry detritus through the trees around us. A thick branch crashed to the ground right in front of the tree trunk. I curled up against Tassos, sure we were going to die.

When I put my hands over my ears, I felt warm, sticky blood. In a few moments, the whistling in my head stopped and I heard a cacophony of explosions chasing each other down the mountain. Then an entirely different hit; not the dull noise of bombed earth and splintered forestry, but a hard, yet shattering, sound that pulsed through me.

'Dear God! It's the villa! Run! Run!' I screamed.

347

We leapt to our feet and raced back the way we had come. Even before the wall of trees that hid the villa, there were chunks of pink masonry scattered about the forest floor. Motes swirled in the air like smoke. We pushed through and, where the villa had stood, there was nothing but an enormous pile of rubble, dust rising in clouds, and the silence of death all around us.

Then, a moan so horrible it made my flesh crawl.

I raced towards the sound and stared at the head of Nathanial. Oh! I thought he had been decapitated, but as I dropped to my knees, his eyes flicked open. Pleading. Half of his face had gone. His jawbone and strong teeth had been stripped bare and the bone shone pink in the moonlight. The Juliet balcony had crushed his chest, and below that was nothing but a mountain of rubble.

Hardly moving his lips, he said quietly, 'Shoot me.' With each breath, blood bubbled from his mouth and nose.

Oh! Tears raged down my face as I drew my pistol.

'It's an order . . . shoot me, little one.'

My hand was over my mouth, and I sobbed air in through my fingers. There was no hope for him. And he was clearly in agony. I placed my hand over his eyes and closed them, bent forward and kissed his forehead.

'Now,' he whispered through his teeth.

I squeezed the trigger. And he was gone. Oh!

I threw my head back and howled into the night. Tassos raced to my side, understood the situation and nodded.

'It's called a mercy killing,' he said. 'You did right.'

Tears raged down my face. 'He ordered me to do it.' I sobbed helplessly.

Then we both heard a muffled cry coming from the rear of the house.

'That's Josie!' I jumped to my feet, hope rising in my chest. I glanced at Nathanial and remembered how he helped me to come to terms with Irini's death. Poor Josie, her heart would break.

We raced around the debris, following the pleas for help, until I realised they were coming from the cellar grill.

Kopay sniffed and scrabbled in the wreckage, looking up occasionally with an excited bark.

'Josie! Are you there?'

'Help us, we're in the basement! The ceiling's collapsing and we can't get out.'

Kopay whimpered, twisting in agitated circles.

An explosive crack of masonry splitting apart, followed by more dust billowing out of the vent.

'Quickly!' Josie cried. 'It's crumbling around us.'

Tassos and I lobbed great chunks of sandstone off the small iron grill until Tassos managed to drag it free.

We hauled Josie out, and then the German, whose hands and feet were still tied. Josie told us she had gone down with food for the soldier when the bomb exploded and I realised that trivial kindness had saved her life.

She sat on the ground, her head in her hands, then looked over the demolished building. 'A direct hit. Is anyone else . . .?'

I shook my head. 'Sorry, Josie.'

'Nathanial?'

'Sorry, Josie, he's gone. We must leave. We'll return in the morning. I just need to speak with Tassos, then we'll go to the hut.'

The full moon had passed its zenith. Pine trees swayed in the breeze, their long, thin shadows moving back and forth across the pale dust and rubble. Ghostly fingers of death caressing the final resting place of the *Andartes* of Rhodes.

My friends were buried together in a mass grave. This was what war did. It destroyed lives, families, homes, and the children's future. My own family came to mind. The German was around the same age as Danial.

'I'll shoot that Nazi bastard,' Tassos said viciously, drawing his pistol from its holster.

I shook my head. 'No! He's hardly more than a boy, Tassos, younger than you. Haven't we had enough killing? I'm sick of it.

We've seen too many lives lost here. Think about it. What difference will it make if we let him go?'

'We have to kill him to avenge Nathanial! A life for a life.' He raised the gun level with the soldier's head.

I pulled my pistol out of the saddlebag and pointed it at Tassos's head.

'I said NO! Nathanial's struggle was for peace, not murder. Our fight isn't about killing as many of the enemy as possible.'

Tassos stared at me. 'It's not?'

'No, of course it isn't. It's about saving lives and ending the war as soon as we can. I won't be party to senseless acts of barbarism, but if you shoot him, I swear, I'll shoot you. As you said, a life for a life.'

'But he'll tell them about us.'

'You really believe so? What do you think he's going to say? A little girl crept up and shot his partner, a dog got his machine gun off him, and a beautiful woman fed him home-made food while he was tied to a chair?'

The soldier spoke in Italian. 'I won't make trouble for you. I swear on my mother's life.'

'What's your name and how old are you?' I demanded.

'Gustave Merkle. I'm eighteen, from Berlin.'

Tassos lowered his gun. I lowered mine. Everyone sighed.

Before Josie untied his feet, I patted him down, until I recognised the jingle of money in his pocket. I retrieved the coins, took two, and put the rest back. I returned to Nathanial and placed the coins over his eyes.

'Goodbye, sir,' I whispered, standing to attention and saluting him. 'I'll see you in the Elysian Fields.' I covered his face with rubble and rocks to protect him from vultures and foraging animals.

I returned to the back of the building. When the young German was out of sight, we checked the debris again for signs of life but found none.

We three, along with Kopay, moved into the hut on mount Filerimos. Over the next days, Tassos taught me to use the catapult and we became friends, although our relationship was purely platonic. Josie mothered us, cooking and cleaning. Because my old dress was in rags, she made me a sort of uniform with trousers out of a brown blanket that was going spare.

I continued to wear Evangelisa's pretty dresses to commit petty acts of sabotage, and I found that particularly painful. Sometimes I'd try to analyse all that had happened, and I came to the conclusion that Evangelisa had saved Giovanni's life. If my sister hadn't been shot, Giovanni would not have signed up for the army, and therefore would have been in the villa at that fateful moment.

As the months slipped by, I realised Tassos avoided giving me missions that could put me in any actual danger when we tried to disrupt the Germans.

'Is this the best I can do?' I asked Tassos. 'Cut phone wires and poison wells? I have to stop the war, for my family! Why are you suddenly afraid I can't handle more serious action?'

He stared at me for a moment and then called Josie. 'I don't think she understands her situation,' he said. 'You'd better tell her.'

She took me into the hut and explained.

I was pregnant.

Chapter 46

Bubba placed her hand on her tummy and stared at it. Poor Rebecca, she thought. A mother never gets over the loss of a child. At least Bubba had shared thirty years of her beautiful daughter's life, and now she knew the joys of caring for Sonia's children and grandchildren.

So unfair that Rebecca has not experienced any of those pleasures yet. However, things were looking good, and Bubba had a feeling this time Rebecca's dreams would come true. She looked up to see Papas Yiannis on his patio. She lifted the diary. He nodded and smiled sadly.

Bubba's mind went to Sonia's father, Giovanni. He had missed out on so much too. Not a day passed when she didn't think of the shepherd boy and wish for the strength of his arms around her. Yet, life seemed to have evened itself out somehow. The court case was bringing everyone together, and that was all she wanted from it.

The truth was, Bubba was tired of living. She found herself thinking of Irini more often, and in her vanity, hoped her friend would see her as the young girl she'd been when they parted. She closed her eyes and saw a vision of Irini standing on the banks of the river Styx, waiting for her.

'You're always late, Dora!' Irini said, and they laughed and kissed and walked hand in hand through the Elysian Fields.

* * *

Naomi, ironing, stopped for a moment to check on her grandmother. She stuck her head outside. Bubba had nodded off with a smile on her face and the diary in her hands. She decided to leave her in peace. About to return to her chores, the phone stopped her. She put the iron down, squeezed around the board and picked it up. It was Fritz with his arrival time.

'That's wonderful, Fritz.' She hesitated. 'Look, it's unfortunate what happened. We got off to a bad start ten years back, but I want you to know that I regret what happened. I hope you understand and we can start again. I'll see you later.'

She hung up and phoned *Rent Rooms in Paradise* to confirm a double room.

The day had been long and stressful. She still had ironing to finish, beds to make, and Bubba to see to. She heard a noise outside and stepped out onto the patio.

'How are you doing out here, Bubba?'

'I nodded off. It's a beautiful sunset. Where's Rebecca? She's been helping me with my exercises.'

'She's shopping in town. Fritz is arriving this evening. I'm booking them into Paradise. How do you really feel about him coming over?'

Bubba paused, and then said, 'I can't say exactly. Just the mention of his name brings back the darkest hours of my life and all I lost. Nevertheless, I never thought I'd be able to read the diaries, and I can. It was difficult at first, remembering Irini and everything, but I managed to come to terms with it. Don't worry, I'll do my best to behave myself. They've enough on their plate without me being cantankerous.'

Naomi hesitated. 'I wonder . . . but, no, nothing.'

'Go on,' Bubba said. 'Tell me.'

'I can't help wondering what he said on the phone to bring about this change of attitude.'

Bubba flashed her crooked smile. 'The man should be a politician, the way he manages to soothe troubled waters. He told me he'd read the first two diaries and was saddened by the tragedy, but I was in danger of losing my granddaughter if I couldn't move on from the past. He asked whether it wasn't racism that took everything from me in the war. Yet there I was, being racist myself – hating him only for where he came from.'

'I've never thought of it like that before.'

'Me neither, child. Anyway, he asked if I could try and overcome my feelings of animosity towards him for Rebecca's sake. Because whatever our differences, he knows we both love her, and would I allow him to visit at some point in the future.'

'And can you, Bubba, accept him as he is?'

She stared at the floor for a moment. 'I don't know, but I'll do my best.'

'Go on,' Naomi encouraged.

After a minute with her thoughts, Bubba continued. 'You see, I don't understand what it's like to have a husband. When I see you and Costa together, still in love after all these years, and your lovely boys, it only reminds me of Giovanni and all that was taken from me. Sometimes I wish the past would go away and leave me in peace. Yet, at the same time I hate to forget all those I loved and lost.'

Naomi felt her heart break. She took Bubba's hand.

'Now I realise I shouldn't try to take that happiness from Rebecca. I should be pleased that she has found love too. It's so difficult, Naomi, but I am trying to change my attitude towards her husband.'

'That's a relief. Come inside for a wash and some dinner.' She helped Bubba up and into the cottage.

'You know what, I'll give the ablutions a miss, child. Those wet wipes are just fine for my craggy bits. And a simple sandwich would be perfect. Let's have a big glass of red wine with it, yes?' She paused for a moment and then placed her hand on Naomi's cheek. 'I love you, you know that? I appreciate how difficult it's been, how hard you've worked since I had my stroke. I don't believe anyone would have taken such good care of me.'

'Bubba . . .' Naomi blinked back tears. 'What a lovely thing to say. Thank you.'

'Where are you up to?'

'Laundry and beds—'

'No, the diaries?'

'Oh, Josie tells you you're pregnant.'

Bubba nodded. Lost in thought for a moment she shook her head. 'Sonia, oh how I loved that child.' Then she returned to the present. 'Look, nobody cares if their sheets are ironed. Let's give up everything that isn't essential for a few days. Now, come on, a sandwich please, then I'll get out of your way. I'm desperate to watch the TV quiz, test my brains, and I'm eager for you to learn more of my experiences from the diary.'

Naomi kissed her cheek. 'Thank you.'

* * *

'I love you, Fritz,' were Rebecca's first words to him when he answered the phone. She went over everything that the specialist had said. They were heading for parenthood.

355

He said all the right words, yet she sensed something was amiss, as if he wasn't quite grasping the situation.

'Fritz, what is it? Is something wrong?' she said.

'I'm on speaker in the car on my way to the airport. I'll tell you when I get to Rhodes.'

'You're coming to Rhodes! How wonderful, when?'

'As I said, I'm on my way now.' He paused. 'I know you've been through a lot, darling, but, well, we'll talk when I arrive.'

'What do you mean? Tell me.'

'I can't. I'm driving and it's lashing down. I need to concentrate on the road. I'll see you in a few hours.'

The call ended. Rebecca stood outside the shop where she'd just bought her first maternity dress. Afraid of learning what Fritz had to say, she wondered where he had gone to on the first Monday of every month. The worst possible news came to mind: he was leaving her; he had cancer; they were bankrupt because of the IVF; his merger had fallen through. Then she told herself to stop being stupid. Whatever she was about to learn, they would deal with it together.

* * *

Marina cupped Bubba's chin and peered into her face. 'There you are, all done. You look fab! Short hair suits you, Bubba, and with the lip gloss and your new cardi, the boys won't recognise you.'

Naomi watched as Bubba patted her soft curls and grinned her crooked smile. The phone rang and she picked up.

'I'm just waiting for a taxi to bring me back, Sis.'

Naomi remembered her boys would be there soon too. 'Did you have a good time shopping?'

'Yes, lovely. Naomi, I hope this will be all right. Fritz is arriving in a few hours, and I'm worried about Bubba. Shall I keep him away from her? I'd never forgive myself if, you know, seeing him upsets her again.'

'Don't worry, he phoned. Bubba's okay with it. I've booked you into *Rent Rooms in Paradise*. I imagine you'd want to spend some time alone with him. Of course, you'd be welcome to come here first. Whatever you choose is fine.'

'Naomi, you're so thoughtful, thank you.'

Naomi hung up, rushed upstairs, and started packing her sister's things. The diary was on Rebecca's bedside table. She sat on the bed and opened it, deciding she deserved ten minutes for herself. Also she felt that, to better understand her grandmother, she needed to read as much about Bubba's past as possible.

Chapter 47

Friday, 4 May 1945

Dear Diary, months have passed since my last entry. There has been little to write about, except\that I am heavy with child and not much use to anyone. We have not heard news of my family, or the other Jews that were taken from here ten months ago, but every day I hope.

I'm still living in the hut on Mount Filerimos with Josie and Tassos. This morning, as I gathered our second crop of tomatoes from the plot Evangelisa had started, I heard Josie scream. My heart seemed to leap into my throat, and I waddled cautiously back to the hut, afraid of what I might find.

Josie and Tassos were hugging each other. They both grinned at me.

'What's going on?' I asked.

'I have it on good authority from the *Andartes* in Crete that the war will end within the next three days,' Tassos said.

'We can go home, Dora!' Josie cried. She was already stuffing things into a bag.

We had been together through winter and spring, and each of us longed to return to our homes. With the glorious news, we planned to part company the following morning. Tassos, who was also a shepherd, agreed to take Kopay and Irini's mule, and keep them on form until Giovanni returned. Josie took Zeus as she was a competent rider and I felt I owed her so much. In my advanced condition, I was safer on my own two feet.

Saturday, 5 May 1945

Once my friends had gone, I sat alone in the sparse room, thinking about all that had happened since my family boarded that rusty ship. Heavy with child and afraid of giving birth, I walked through the forest, wanting to see the cinnamon tree before I left.

Undisturbed for six months, the place had grown lush, the path hidden. The white flowers of wild cyclamen hung their heads like shamed virgins in the deep shadows of surrounding trees. In the clearing, grass had risen calf-high. My mind was full of Giovanni, the only man I have loved.

I waded through the vegetation and reached out to touch the tree. 'Hello, old friend,' I whispered. 'Remember me?' I rested my forehead against the bark, my fingers tracing the rectangle where Giovanni had taken a piece of her heart.

'He stole my heart too. I hope your wound's not as painful as mine, dear tree.' Tears rolled down my cheeks. 'He doesn't even know I'm having his baby. I pray God keeps him safe, for his child's sake.' I stroked the bark, remembering the first time I collected cinnamon with Giovanni's hand covering mine. Earlier memories flooded back: how I had watched him singing in the choir while my darling family believed I was doing schoolwork.

I lifted the penknife from my pocket and cut the outline of a heart into the bark. Inside, I engraved our initials. I smiled to think of him, and gently sliced the arrow of Eros right through the heart. 'Make sure he sees this when he returns from the war, dear tree, and send him to find us.'

I wiped my eyes, patted my belly, and returned to the cabin. I started packing for my return to Paradissi. Quite unexpectedly, I felt energised and had an urge to clean the hut before I left. I folded the bedding, polished the windows and swept the floor. Mama would be pleased. With my few belongings stuffed into a net bag, I wondered where my duffel bag was at that moment. About to leave, I noticed some fabric poking from the junk cupboard.

I climbed on the mattress and yanked the door open. Evangelisa's clothes tumbled out. Unbalanced, I fell back onto the bed. I couldn't deal with it. That I had shot my own sister. I had blocked her and the appalling event from my mind. I carefully folded the pretty dresses, remembering her in each of them, twirling, holding the sides out, curtsying, tap-dancing, which she was very good at. She had loved looking beautiful.

I'm so sorry, Evangelisa. So sorry.

My family were gone; my best friend had been tortured to death; I'd killed my own sister; and the man I married had left me. Why was all this happening? Racked by remorse, I didn't want to leave the place. I lay on the bed crying for all the people I'd loved and lost, until dusk eventually fell. I got up and lit the fire, boiled the last of the rice and greens, and decided to sleep in the hut for one last night.

Saturday, 6 May 1945

I was ready to leave when my attention was drawn to the cinders in the grate. If a strong wind caught the chimney, the ashes would blow all over the hut, my hard work wasted. Using our home-made besom and the shovel, I cleaned the hearth.

Outside, I noticed the scent of charcoal. I sniffed. There it was again, the smell of woodsmoke. A distant glow above the trees caught my attention and the sickening reality hit me. I hugged my enormous belly. A forest fire raged uphill, heading straight for me and my baby.

In the centre of the Filerimos forest, the hut offered no protection against fire. I had to escape, and quickly. I grabbed my bag and waddled as fast as possible down the track.

The smoke became thicker, my eyes stung and the back of my throat burned, but there was no other way off the mountain. I prayed I'd get past the fire before it reached the road. I hurried on. Flames licked the trees on my right, they seemed to leap from one to the other, following me like a pack of blazing wolves, waiting for a moment to pounce. I tried to run, but found it impossible. The wind shifted, parting the smoke. Down the hillside, heading my way, a row of soldiers beat the smouldering vegetation.

Where could I go? I turned, but knew I would not make it back up the mountain. The wind changed again. Smoke enveloped me. A tree, only metres away, cracked open with an explosion of flames. 'Help me!' I screamed, falling on my knees onto the road, sure the flames would reach me any moment. Heat rolled over me in suffocating waves. My throat burned raw with each breath, and my eyes stung so badly I couldn't see where I was going.

I gave up the struggle and lay on the road.

Moments later, I became aware of strong arms lifting me and running, German voices, distant, shouting. Water on my face. Someone patting my cheeks, then everything rushed away.

I resurfaced prostrate on a blanket at the side of the road. A young German soldier I recognised instantly lifted my head and held a cantina to my lips.

'Drink, drink,' Gustave said.

I gulped the sweet water.

Someone called him. 'Leave here as soon as you can. Do you understand?' he whispered.

I nodded, an odd feeling that Nathanial was looking down and smiling. *A life for a life*. 'Thank you, sir,' I whispered.

As soon as Gustave returned to his troop, I got to my feet. My legs were shaky. My baby seemed heavier than ever and I walked in a most ungainly way. I had to escape before someone asked for my ID.

I continued down the hill, hiding in roadside shrubbery whenever a vehicle approached. Nearing the village, my back ached so badly my knees buckled and I had to squat until the pain eased.

The journey seemed endless. I arrived in Paradissi Village in the early hours. Spartili Street lay in darkness, deathly quiet. Our home was boarded over and that broke my heart. The house was the symbol of my beloved family even though they were all gone. I sensed the essence of them, lingering there to comfort me. In reality, I found only shutters and eerie silence.

Fumbling blindly, I tried to remove the planks, but they were firmly nailed down.

A door across the street opened and I recognised the priest's voice. 'Who's there!' he called.

I cowered, but there was nowhere to hide and in my condition running wasn't an option.

'It's me, Pandora Cohen,' I said as loud as I dared.

The papas scurried over.

'Child! Oh, glory to God! I thought you'd been taken to Auschwitz with the others. Where's your family?'

'They're gone but I escaped. I want to go home, please, that's all. I won't be any trouble.' My heart was breaking with sorrow. To be so close to our home and my bed, and be thwarted.

The priest sighed. 'Sorry, child, the house is closed. I did it myself to keep the vultures out. I hoped one day somebody would return.' He hugged me and, in doing so, recognised my condition.

'Oh, Dora.'

I broke down right there in his arms. He held me for a while, muttering 'It will be all right. Don't fret now. Trust in God; He'll take care of you.' When I regained control, he steered me across the street into his own house.

As I stood in the priest's living room, his wife, Mrs Spanaki, came downstairs in her flannelette nightgown and a hand-knitted cardigan that was buttoned up wrong. Her long grey hair, plaited, hung down her back. She was a homely woman with a kind face.

Mrs Spanaki and the priest seemed to have aged a lot since I'd left Spartili Street. Her eyes flicked down to my expanded belly. 'Oh, my poor child, let's take care of you.'

She fussed, making me drink mountain tea and eat her homemade bread drizzled with olive oil, which was so delicious it satiated my hunger.

'Sleep on our sofa tonight, Dora,' the priest said. 'Tomorrow, we'll sort out your house. Good night, God keep you safe.'

'When's your confinement, Dora?' Mrs Spanaki asked.

I shrugged, 'I hope it's soon. The walk down the mountain has given me a dreadful backache.'

'Goodness me. You look engaged and about to drop the baby. Do you have anything ready for the mite?'

I shook my head. 'It's been difficult, hiding all these months.' I leaned forward and rubbed my lower back. 'The *Andartes* told me the armistice will be announced in the next day or two, so I thought I'd take a chance and come home.'

'You did right.' She paused and stared at me. 'Is that really true? Peace at last?'

I nodded, winced and rocked forward again.

'I'll get the midwife at first light.' She pulled cushions off her sofa and piled them on the stone floor. 'Kneel over those,' she said, taking off her woollen slippers. 'Put these under your knees for a bit of comfort.'

I did, and the pain eased immediately. 'Thank you, that's much better. Such a relief.'

'Mmm, takes the pressure off your spine,' she said.

A weight lifted from my mind too. Mrs Spanaki was caring, and seemed to know about childbirth. I knew nothing, except I had seen a lamb being born once.

'I'm sorry about this,' Mrs Spanaki said. 'But I'm afraid if your waters break, you'll ruin my sofa.' She pulled an oilcloth off the table and spread it over her settee.

'Waters?' I asked.

She stopped making my bed. 'How old are you, Dora?'

'Sixteen.'

Mrs Spanaki straightened and crossed herself. 'Oh dear. It's going to be a long night.'

The next day, the priest and his wife helped me move back into my Paradissi home. It had changed little since our move to my father's shop in the city. I wondered if the choirmaster and his wife were still living there, in our town house behind the shop, but to be honest I didn't care. With the onset of labour, I had enough to think about.

* * *

363

Peace was announced the next day: 8 May, 1945. That evening, in my own home, I gave birth to Sonia Phoenix Cohen. She rose from the ashes of war. A new life that came into the free world with the sound of a fanfare.

Outside, Paradissi erupted with joy. Church bells rang. Someone blew a tuneless trumpet. Music blared. People shouted, 'No more war! It's over!' I heard laughter and the explosion of firecrackers. A jubilant accompaniment to the moment was when the midwife placed Sonia Phoenix Cohen in my arms.

My beautiful baby girl was born into a safer place, our planet free of conflict. A place of peace and harmony where we'd accept people of different religions and cultures. A perfect world.

With her little clenched fists, Sonia Phoenix Cohen boxed an invisible foe, and pride welled up inside me. This was my child! A born fighter, a survivor, the same as her mother. I called her Sonia after my grandmother who, like my father, always told me to follow my dreams. Also, I knew the name 'Sonia' came from the Greek for wisdom.

I imagined Papa's homecoming. Run, little rabbit. And I would, right into his arms. I could feel that first hug. Then, I would present him with his granddaughter, Sonia Phoenix Cohen. How I loved the sound of her name.

These thoughts tumbled through my mind as I held my tiny baby. What sort of life would she have without her father? Perhaps Giovanni would come back now the war was over. Just one look, that's all the shepherd boy would need, and he would commit to being the best father in the world. He hadn't meant all those things he said. Like me, he was upset, shocked.

Sonia's life would be perfect; of that I was sure. I swore an oath; 'I will protect you, Sonia Phoenix Cohen, from harm for all the days of my life.'

'She's tired. Let's swaddle her and let her sleep.' The midwife took Sonia from me.

I waited for news of my family, my parents and my brothers. They'd been gone for ten months. Surely the war had ended in time to save them. I'd done my best, and like me they were fighters, survivors.

I learned our Jewish friends and families on the three ships were taken to the concentration camp of Auschwitz. Rumours trickled back. We heard how some prisoners endured the most horrific circumstances, yet survived. Those people were held in Italy, until they were strong enough to travel. Awful pictures appeared in the newspapers of living skeletons staring bleakly ahead, too horrible to believe.

Sonia was two months old when I tied her onto my back and walked to the monastery. I came across a grave bearing only a date and the name 'Evangelisa'. In the shade of a nearby oak, I spread the blanket and put Sonia down. She was no trouble, content to feed and sleep her days away. As she lay gurgling and boxing, I picked wild flowers and laid them on Evangelisa's grave.

Remorseful that I hadn't been a better sister, I cried. All she wanted was to be like me. Why did her life have to end that way – with a bullet from my own gun? I fell to my knees, sorrow exploding in my heart once again.

Evangelisa would have loved Sonia and made a wonderful aunt. Why shouldn't she have a kiss from Giovanni? I had so much from him. I thought about the shepherd boy every day, praying he'd come back and find me. I hoped he would come to accept that shooting Evangelisa was an awful accident, and forgive me. I went to bed each night with a broken heart, and woke each morning filled with hope for Giovanni's return.

Chapter 48

Rebecca returned from grocery shopping in town. 'How do you feel about Fritz coming over?' Naomi asked when they hugged.

'I'm thrilled. He's landing at six. Can you come to the airport with me? Will Bubba be all right on her own for an hour?'

'Of course I'll come with you. I'm just waiting for the boys to arrive.' The pain in Rebecca's eyes told Naomi there was more going on than her sister had revealed.

'I'm not a damn invalid! I *can* manage by myself you know.' Bubba called as she emerged from her room.

'The stroke didn't affect her hearing then,' Rebecca said quietly, and they both laughed.

'Mama! Mama!' The door burst open and Angelos and Konstantinos rushed at their mother.

'My boys!' Naomi leapt to her feet, arms wide. Reaching up, she pulled them both to her, kissed their cheeks, stroked their hair, and kissed their cheeks again. 'Oh, it's so good to see you both. Are you okay?' She glanced at Konstantinos's legs. 'Good job you weren't in that room when it happened. I was horrified when Angelos told me.'

'Wait here,' Angelos said. They nipped outside, and returned immediately, one holding out chocolates, the other a bunch of roses.

'For the best mother in the world,' Konstantinos said.

'Oh, I'm touched. How thoughtful.' Naomi beamed at them both.

Angelos grinned. 'Don't be too happy, there's also a sack of washing outside.'

'*Yiayá*,' he said, giving Bubba the Greek title for grandmother while stooping to kiss her. 'You look younger every time we come home! Have you been stealing Mama's cream again?'

Bubba's eyes sparkled, her smile as wide as it could be.

Rebecca sat at the kitchen table, watching the glut of love and celebration that seemed to fill every corner of the room. Her heart exploded with happiness. To be part of such a wonderful family was one of the most important things to live for, and she deeply regretted staying away for ten long years.

Rebecca had never had parents, or children, so this was her first experience of a room bursting with the love and kinship that came with a complete family. She thought about Bubba, and the diaries, and realised this atmosphere was the day-to-day norm in her young life; and it had been all so cruelly snatched away from her. Amidst the hugging and laughter, she caught Bubba's eye and felt her tears rise. Bubba clearly under-stood Rebecca's emotion and, smiling softly, nodded as if to say, 'Your turn will come.'

In the cramped kitchen, Konstantinos turned and cried, 'Look who's here! Aunty Rebecca, just as gorgeous as I remember you!' The boys came either side of her and planted a great kiss on her cheeks.

'Do it again!' Naomi cried, grabbing her phone and taking a picture when they did. 'That's one for the cupboard door.'

'I hear you're giving us some cousins at last, Aunty Rebecca, you clever old thing,' Angelos said.

Rebecca sniffed. 'Less of the old, if you please.'

Konstantinos grinned. 'Any time you want a babysitter in London, I'm available for a very modest fee. Just send the flight tickets.'

At which Naomi clipped him around the ear and wagged her finger, which led to more giggles.

'Hungry?' Naomi said, already knowing the answer and starting to set the table. 'Beef in red wine and garlic potatoes?'

Angelos turned to his brother. 'Why did we ever leave home?'

'Must have been mad!' Konstantinos replied, and everyone laughed.

* * *

At seven thirty, Rebecca had a bout of nerves. Fritz had landed, and she and Naomi were waiting in the arrivals foyer. He had already left for America when she found the cache of baby gifts in the attic, and the discovery had a lasting impact. She recalled some of the tags: 'I love you and our baby more than life itself', 'To the woman who made my dreams come true', 'My precious wife and child, you are more than I could have ever wished for', and so on. Dear Fritz, a rigid businessman but a real softie at heart. She stood on her toes and peered over the latest gaggle of tourists, desperate to meet her husband and find out where he disappeared to on the first Monday of every month, and why he had to keep it from her.

Naomi took her hand and squeezed it. 'Stop fretting. He'll be here any minute.'

Suddenly Fritz was there, sweeping Rebecca into his arms. 'My darling, I love you so much that I couldn't stand another day without you. How are you? How are the twins? Did they treat you well at the hospital?'

'Fritz! You came for me, I can't tell you how happy that makes me.'

Naomi smiled, soaking up the scene. Fritz noticed her, let go of Rebecca and held out his hand.

'Thank you for taking care of my wife,' he said cautiously.

'We both love her, Fritz. At the moment it's the only thing we have in common, but I hope we'll get to know each other a little better.' Fritz met her eyes and nodded. Naomi continued. 'Would you like to go straight to your rooms?'

'I wondered if I could have a few minutes alone with Bubba? I've brought her a gift and I need to say a few words. Clear the air.'

Slightly alarmed, Naomi peered into his ice-blue eyes, but she saw only kindness, maturity, and a depth of sadness that pulled at her heartstrings. She stepped forward. 'How about a hug for your sister-in-law first?'

* * *

Fritz waited in Spartili Street while Naomi and Rebecca entered the cottage.

'Where are the boys?' Naomi asked. 'They haven't left you on your own?'

'Don't fret, child. They've gone to the café for an hour.' She turned to Rebecca and then nervously glanced at the door.

Rebecca sat on the footstool by her grandmother's chair and took her hand. 'Bubba, Fritz is outside. He wants to speak to you, but if you're not up to it, we'll go straight to our rooms.'

Bubba dropped her head to one side and thought for a moment. 'Send him in,' she said, her eyes narrowing.

Rebecca stepped outside and Naomi followed her. 'Be gentle, Fritz,' Naomi said.

He nodded, pulled a shoebox out of his overnight bag, and entered the cottage. The top half of the front door swung open as he closed the bottom half. Naomi slipped her arm around her sister's waist and they watched their grandmother.

'Mrs Cohen, may I speak with you?' Fritz said.

'No need to be formal. You're family now.' Bubba's words had such a venomous edge Naomi feared this would not end well.

'Pandora?'

'Bubba will do just fine.'

'I read the first two diaries, and now I understand why you dislike me so much. I represent all the evil that came into your young life, don't I?'

Bubba nodded.

'It's a miracle you survived, but it's another miracle that I found your granddaughter and that she fell in love with me.'

'Sit down. You're making me uncomfortable looming over me like that,' Bubba said flatly.

He sat on the footstool next to the chair. 'I'm mortified to come from a country that, in the past, was shamefully cruel to so many people, and I'm sorry beyond words for what they took from you and what they did to millions of others. But it wasn't me – and I can't change history. Nevertheless, I'm asking you to accept me for who I am. I don't want to come between you and the woman I love. Do you think you can you do that, Bubba?'

Silence hung in the cottage. Naomi watched, tightening her grip on Rebecca, hoping her grandmother could find it in her heart to let the past go. Time seemed to go on hold, the world and millions of Jewish souls waiting for Bubba's reply.

Bubba reached out, her fingertips touching Fritz's white-blond hair. She stared for a moment longer, her lips trembled, and her eyes glazed over.

'Don't take my papa,' she whispered. 'I'm begging you.' Tears spilled onto her cheeks.

Naomi stepped into the cottage. 'Don't worry, she'll come back in a moment. She turned to Bubba and patted her hand. 'Come on, Bubba. You're having a bad dream. Wake up, now.'

Naomi noticed Fritz's shoulders slump and realised how tense he was. He turned to her and said, 'There's more. Will she be all right, or should I stop?'

'Why shouldn't I be all right, young man? Don't talk about me as if I wasn't here,' Bubba said.

'I'm sorry, Bubba, but I have an appalling secret,' Fritz said turning back to her. 'It concerns your past, and I don't know if you are strong enough to hear it . . . or if I am strong enough to tell you.'

Bubba nodded and thrust her jaw forward. 'I was right, wasn't I?'

She recalled the oath she had made all those years ago. A frightened girl under a lorry watching her world being taken away from her and the man responsible, arrogant and satisfied with his work.

One day, Frick Hendrick Nüller, I will find your family and I will take them from you.

Fritz sighed deeply. 'As a baby, I was adopted by the most wonderful Austrian family. I never knew my real parents or grandparents, and when the law changed and the "right to know" came about in Austria, I had no interest in finding out about my roots.

'However, Rebecca was deeply upset when she left you ten years ago. I wanted to prove you were wrong about me and my family, so I tried to trace my birth-mother.' He paused, and seemed to struggle with his thoughts. 'I discovered she was

German, unmarried when she had me, and that her father had disowned her. She died of lung cancer before I got the chance to meet her.' He swallowed. 'Her surname was Nüller.'

Bubba's jaw thrust forward again and her hand flew over her mouth to stifle a whimper.

Rebecca clutched Naomi. 'Oh, God!' she whispered. 'Bubba was right all along.'

After a moment's silence, Fritz continued. 'I was shocked and horrified and decided to try and find her father. It took me five years, but eventually I discovered he was in a residential home in Switzerland. My plan was to hand him over to the authorities, but before I did, I wanted to see him for myself. Three months ago, I went to the residential home and found a ninety-five-year-old man close to death with advanced Parkinson's disease.'

Fritz looked up at Rebecca. 'I'm sorry I deceived you.' He turned to Bubba again. 'It's the only secret I've ever kept from my wife, partly for her sake and partly because I was so ashamed to have come from him, his bloodline.'

Rebecca entered the cottage. 'Is that where you go on the first Monday of the month? Switzerland?'

Fritz stared at her. 'You knew? I'm sorry I deceived you, darling. You said you needed absolutely no stress. I thought it better not to tell you, even though I was desperate to talk about it. You see, I had to decide what to do. Like keeping the letters from you, it was a mistake I made because I thought it was in your best interest.'

'You had no right, Fritz. You can't control my life, no matter what you think is best for me. It was up to me to decide if I wanted to read the letters or not.' She placed her hand on her stomach and paused. 'We'll discuss this another time, but I can't help wondering what else you've done *in my best interest*?'

Naomi interrupted. 'And about your grandfather, Fritz. What decision did you come to?' she asked quietly.

He glanced from one sister to the other, seeming unsure for a moment. 'Last month, when Rebecca thought I'd gone to America, I returned to Switzerland to meet with Nüller for the last time. I told him that I, his grandson and only heir, had married a woman of Jewish descent, then I read him Bubba's diaries.

'He begged me to stop, but I wouldn't. He swore he had only carried out orders, but I said I didn't believe him and neither would the war-crimes tribunal. He had escaped death by disappearing fifty years ago, but I would make sure it wouldn't happen again. The diaries of an innocent sixteen-year-old girl were proof of the pleasure he got from his persecution of the Jews of Rhodes. He would be exposed for who he was and what he had done. He became deranged and fell into an epileptic fit. I informed the medical staff that he did not wish to be resuscitated and then I told the police my grandfather's true identity.

'Frick Nüller is dead.'

Bubba stared into space. 'Then the world is a better place. May he be damned to burn in hell for eternity.' The room was silent, everyone with their thoughts, then Bubba spoke.

'And the letters I wrote to my granddaughter?'

Fritz sighed deeply. 'I *am* so sorry. I have them all bar one. When we go home I'll give them to Rebecca and she can decide to read them now or keep them until after the babies arrive. I was simply trying to protect her, Bubba. I realise now that I had no right to take matters into my own hands. I should have let her deal with them. My mistake.'

After a long silence, Bubba said, 'It took some courage to come here and tell me this.' Naomi realised that Bubba could not look at Fritz. 'You could have kept it to yourself and nobody would have known, except for me of course. And do you know why that is?' She turned to face him, blinked hard and shivered. 'Because you, Fritz Neumanner, are the absolute double of your grandfather. I cannot look at you without remembering that day on the dock.

'When you walked through that door and said you were going to take my granddaughter for your wife, it's a good job my gun was with the priest because I wanted nothing more than to kill you.' She sighed deeply, glanced at each of them in turn, and said, 'But the past is in the past and it's finally time to move on. Let's try to put this behind us.' She almost smiled. 'And will you get up and sit on a chair?'

'First, I've brought you a gift.' Fritz opened the shoebox and folded back layers of red tissue.

The scarlet velvet slippers had lily-of-the-valley embroidered over the fronts and were edged with tiny white pearls. They had a luxurious, oriental appearance. Gently, Fritz removed Bubba's brown-check footwear and slid her feet into the flamboyant slippers.

'How do they feel?' he asked quietly.

'They feel expensive,' Bubba replied, and for the first time, Bubba and Fritz exchanged a cautious smile.

* * *

It had been a long day with a satisfactory result. When the kitchen was finally empty, Naomi, bone-tired, climbed the stairs with the diary in her hand.

Chapter 49

Today is my birthday, and I sit at the kitchen table and remember my last celebration, when we lived behind the shop in town and everyone spoiled me with so many fine gifts, only days before we were parted. So much has happened since that time, it's hard to accept it was only a year ago.

Sonia is ten weeks old, healthy, and incredibly beautiful. The doctor says she is going to be tall, and I am pleased about that. We are dependent on handouts. The kindness of my Paradissi neighbours knows no limits and I'll always be in their debt. They have given me baby clothes, toys, a crib and a pushchair. I confessed to the papas most of the events that took place with the *Andartes*. Nobody has said anything, but I suspect he told people that I'd worked with the Resistance, and this is the reason for their charity.

I didn't tell the papas, or anyone else, what had happened to Evangelisa, only that she'd died. I'm ashamed and so very sorry, and I beg her forgiveness in my prayers each night.

There were questions about Sonia's father. I wore my wedding ring on the leather thong around my neck over my clothes. I said that it was my husband's mother's, a family heirloom that I would have altered to fit when I had the money. I am sure rumours circulated but I told the truth: Sonia's father was a soldier who had not yet returned from the war.

Times are hard now, with little food and no money. I live on herbs, snails, and anything I can get my hands on. I keep a yeast culture going in a jar on the windowsill and make bread with it twice a week. I collect driftwood from the beach and salt from the rockpools. Bags of pine cones from the forest fuel the stove. If I have flour and olive oil, I manage. Mrs Spanaki unravelled her blue bed jacket and knitted a matinee coat, a bonnet, and bootees for Sonia to keep her warm. Sonia's first cradle was a drawer on two upturned crates, next to my bed.

One afternoon, while Sonia slept on Mrs Spanaki's porch, I held a skein taut for her, while she wound the wool into a ball.

'What's happening to your father's shop, Dora?' she asked.

'I don't know. I was thinking I'd like to go into town and clean it, ready for his return.'

Her eyes met mine and she turned away quickly. After a long silence, she said gently, 'Have you heard anything from your family?' She knew I hadn't, and I should have realised what she was trying to tell me, that they might not come back. Hope was all I had. I shook my head and stared at the floor.

'I'll see what I can find out. At least you should get some money for the shop.'

My life revolves around my baby and there is no time for anything else. I spend every spare minute sewing for us or knitting for the winter, and I do some cleaning in the neighbourhood to put food on the table. Sometimes, I find a box of vegetables, fruit, or eggs on the doorstep. People are kind. They continue to give me their children's outgrown clothes, and we survive.

Wednesday, 8 May 1947

Sonia is two years old today! I made her a rag doll with button eyes and yellow woollen plaits and she loves it. She's fit and healthy and started walking at twelve months. Everyone says she looks like Mama, but I see Giovanni.

Recently, the newspapers announced that our beloved island of Rhodes, together with the other Dodecanese islands, is to be reunited with Greece. Since World War One, we have belonged to Italy, and everyone born between the wars has

Italian citizenship. But now, we are about to become Greek once again.

I read the Jews who are still in Italy have the choice of an Italian or a Greek passport. They are able to choose their nationality. Out of almost two thousand people taken from Rhodes, hardly more than a hundred have survived Auschwitz, and many of those simply died of starvation or exhaustion days after their rescue.

The government said anyone choosing Greece would be returned to their island. Very few chose to return to Rhodes, and after what had happened, who could blame them? Almost three years have passed since my family were taken, and although there is still no news of them, I know they will be re-grouping in Italy. Now there is real hope that the Italian government will repatriate them soon.

I am so glad to have Sonia; a mother couldn't wish for a more beautiful child. Her huge brown eyes gaze at me as I breast-feed her in the morning. The time has come to break that habit, although many mothers continue to feed their children for another year.

Mrs Spanaki gave me an aspirin bottle. She told me to put honey and water in it, and a teat with a small hole to pacify Sonia and help wean her off the breast. I tied her hair in ribbons and strapped her into the pram. She wanted to walk, but I had neither the time nor the patience to hang on to leather reins while she tugged in every direction. Proudly, I pushed her through the village to the general store.

'Dora! Dora!' A neighbour stood in the post office doorway, waving at me.

'You've a letter from Italy!' she called. 'Come, quickly!'

Me? A letter? All the hopes of three lonely years welled up inside me. My family! Papa! It *had* to be them! They were coming home at last! 'Hold the pram!' I cried to a passing friend, thrusting the brake down then running towards the post office.

Papa!

They handed me a flimsy airmail, grey-blue with red stripes around the edges. I would always remember this gloriously happy moment. The stamp was a pinkish picture of a hand planting an olive tree, franked by a rectangle of wavy lines like a flag, free as the wind. The address: Pandora Cohen, Paradissi, Rhodes.

I ran my fingers over the shaky handwriting, amazed that thoughts could travel from the brain to the fingertips and then spill out of a pen onto a sheet of paper. In a rush of happiness, I pressed the correspondence against my chest. This meant they were alive and safe! What would Papa have to say?

Papa! Papa! Papa!

A hand rested on my shoulder, I realised I was sobbing. 'I've been alone for so long, hoping,' I cried.

I opened the mail, unfolding the delicate envelope to read the lines inside. Blinded by tears, it became impossible to read. I dragged my cardigan sleeve over my eyes. Word spread quickly. Friends and neighbours squeezed into the post office.

'Read it out, Dora!' someone shouted.

I nodded.

1st May, 1947

My Dearest Pandora,

I hope this letter finds you well. Sincere apologies for taking so long to write, but I have not been too good. However, I am on the mend now, and I want to let you know that you were in our hearts throughout the time of our separation. While we were in Auschwitz, thoughts of you and your escape kept us strong in our darkest hours.

If you are reading this letter, then you really did manage to stay safe on that fateful day, when we were taken from our beloved island.

I hope sweet little Evangelisa managed to avoid capture too, and you are both content and happy.

You must be nearly nineteen now, but being grown-up is no protection for the terrible news I am about to give you. I am so sorry to say, dearest Pandora, that as far as I know, I am the only one who survived the deplorable ordeal of Auschwitz.

My heart plummeted to new depths. I clasped my hand over my mouth to stifle my cry of despair as I scanned down the page. The writing became smaller and smaller, until I struggled to read the last line.

At the end of that unforgettable letter, my question was answered.

Your loving brother,
Jacob

A great howl escaped from me. 'NO!'

Several hands grabbed me as my knees buckled and I crumpled to the floor. Danial and Samuel; Papa, my dearest, darling, father; Mama and her bad legs; my proud and upstanding grandparents; Aunt Martha in her fine hairnet and perfect makeup, and dear Uncle Levi who wouldn't hurt a fly. All dead?!

I remembered every detail from the time I watched them so carefully in L'Aeronautica, and finally when they boarded the ship. My entire family, and all my other aunts, uncles, and cousins, had been killed in the atrocious gas chambers I had read about, or starved to death in the unholy Nazi prison camp.

'Why?!' I cried. 'They've murdered my papa! My mama! Danial and Samuel! I've waited every day for news, longing to hear from them, and now I learn they're dead!' Somebody brought me a chair, and someone else a glass of water. 'I wanted to present them with their granddaughter. What will I do now?'

The letter was taken from me. I stared, my mind blank, tears streaming down my face.

Two women linked arms with me and walked me home. My neighbour followed with the pram.

In the cottage they gave me strong tea thick with sugar. Sonia cried. Someone took her away to feed her. I wasn't to worry.

Friday, 24 May 1947

Some days after I received Jacob's letter, Doctor Michalis came to the house with pills. Lithium bromide, it said on the label. He told me they were proved to help depression, and were sure to make me feel better, but I could no longer breastfeed. Traces of the medication in my milk would harm Sonia.

Nobody seemed to understand that I didn't want to feel better, and I didn't care about Sonia, and in truth, I was a bad person who had killed many people, and here was my punishment. I deserved this mental torture. My penance for killing my sister was the awful knowledge that the rest of my family had suffered horribly. They were taken from me, and each other, forever and there was nothing I could do to change these facts.

I cried for Irini's help, but in truth, I knew I did not deserve her loyalty. She had also suffered a terrible death, rather than betray me. And I had been selfish, enjoying her love, and yet giving mine to Giovanni.

Apparently, Mrs Spanaki sent for the doctor when she found Sonia crying, hungry, and in need of a nappy change. It seems I was unaware of my daughter's needs. She told me later, I was completely distressed and depressed, surrounded by the newspapers with pictures of concentration camps.

I don't remember much, only that my mind was spinning with the images I'd seen in those papers. Mass graves, starved humans, living skeletons. I stared at the gaunt faces. My family was there, amongst them, somewhere! I could not face food with those scenes at the forefront of my mind, and I had no inclination to wash myself, or change my clothes. What did it matter how I looked? Hours blurred into days, sleep and wakefulness merged. Nightmares and reality were indistinguishable and the only sounds in our house were Sonia's plaintive crying and my own sobs.

The following days were a fog of pills, friends, and whispers.

Sonia was brought to me for short periods, but all I did was stare at her. My little girl seemed like someone else's child. When she cried of hunger or thirst, I had no compulsion to nurture her. The kind and generous people of Paradissi took my child away and cared for her.

I asked for the letter, to read it properly, but it was kept from me. 'When you're stronger,' they said.

One tranquillised day drifted into another. I had stopped caring for myself, stopped writing my journal. Sonia faded into insignificance. Life lost its value and nothing seemed important.

I asked for Jacob's letter every day. 'The doctor has it, Dora,' the local nurse told me. 'He'll give it to you when you're strong enough.' She put her arm around my shoulders. 'If you don't improve soon, he'll insist on electric shock treatment at the hospital.' She shook her head. 'It's awful, Dora, quite unpleasant.'

'Then why would he send me?'

'Because it makes you lose your immediate memory. He reckons if you forget what happened to your family, you'll get better.'

Her words had a profound effect. The last thing I wanted was to lose the memory of my loved ones. Recollections of them all before their departure on the ships were so precious. Memories were all I had. My mother's food, my father's stories, my brothers and the games we used to play. Danial and his riding lessons, Samuel, the brainy one who helped me with school work. Jacob who played the violin so perfectly, and he was only a year older than me.

Since his letter, I had heard the sad, mournful sound of his violin in my head while recalling newspaper pictures of atrocities beyond imagination.

I tried to be like Jacob, practising my vocal scales to perfection. I dreamed that one day we would stand together on the stage, him playing and me singing. He'd take my hand and we would bow and curtsy. My family in the front row clapping crazily, the applause magnificent.

The doctor must not rob me of these dreams and memories!

I bathed, washed my hair, and cleaned the house, which had become dirty and unkempt. I collected Sonia from a friend who'd been kind and understanding, and I went to see Doctor Michalis.

I left Sonia's pram outside, and carried her in on my hip.

'What's come over you, Dora?' he said smiling, taking in my fresh appearance. 'I'm very pleased with your progress.' He examined Sonia and then returned her to me. 'You seem to have recovered. Promise me, if you ever feel depressed like that again, you'll pay me a visit?'

I gave my word and asked for my brother's letter. He chewed his lip and for a moment I thought he would refuse. From his desk drawer he retrieved a bundle of mail, each with the blue and red border.

'These arrived for you, Dora. I took the liberty of collecting them. I'm going to give you the first one. Return in a couple of days and I'll decide if you're strong enough to deal with the rest.'

The moment I was outside, I sat on a low wall in the shade of a grand walnut tree, opened the letter, and skimmed down the lines until I came to the sentence that had torn me apart. I read on.

I am twenty now, Dora, but I'm not as strong as I was. I was poorly when the British rescued me from Auschwitz, weighing twenty-six kilos and too weak to walk. Another day in that place and I would have perished. We were down to one kilo of bread every three days, and water that turnips had been boiled in.

I believe everyone else in our family has gone to God, apart from you and Evangelisa. Please tell me I'm mistaken! Tell me you have heard from somebody else! I thought about you often, and dreamed I would return to Paradissi and sit with you at a table laden with mountains of food.

I listened to your wonderful singing in my head, and remembered your laughter when Papa tickled you until you couldn't breathe. Those dreams kept me alive. Thank you for that. You saved my life.

I'm too tired to go on, but I'll write again soon.

Your loving brother,

Jacob.

My poor dear family. I had been cheated by hope. They were gone, snatched away when they had full lives to live. And I never hugged them. And I never told them how much I loved them. And I never said 'Goodbye.'

Sonia fell asleep in the pram as I pushed her home. I parked her in the shady courtyard. Tears were streaming down my face and I didn't care who saw them.

Why was life so cruel?

A pair of swallows had started building a nest under the tiles over the front door. I watched them for a moment flitting in with beaks full of mud, plastering their cup-shaped nest in the eaves.

The priest's wife came over with a bowl of soup. 'They're dead, Mrs Spanaki! All but Jacob! I wish I was dead too, then I'd be with them in heaven.'

'Now, now, Dora,' she said, 'that's not the way. You must be strong for Sonia, and you have to represent all your family to your child. She needs grandparents, a father, aunts, uncles, cousins. You have a big role to play and your loved ones would expect nothing less. Don't let them down. If you do, they will have died in vain.'

At first, I was angry. I wanted to spit some clever quip back at her, but as her words sank in, I realised she was right.

The swallows returned and continued their nest building, preparing for a family – preparing for the future.

* * *

'I'm better, Doctor, thank you,' I said. 'I replied to Jacob's letter, but I think it's time I read the rest of his correspondence.'

Doctor Michalis pulled my lower eyelids down and peered into my eyes. 'Are you sure, Dora? Perhaps it would be advisable to wait a while.'

'I'm starting to fret, Doctor. Withholding them is doing me more harm than good. I don't want to get poorly again, and I promise you that if they're too awful, I'll put them aside until I am stronger.'

His eyes flicked to the desk drawer. After a pause, when the antiseptic smell of his surgery had become almost unbearable, he said, 'All right but only if you give me your word you'll be cautious.'

'I will, I swear.' I laid my hand on my heart.

He handed me the mail, warning me to take it slowly.

I rushed to the bakery for a loaf, then continued home. After feeding Sonia, I settled her down for a nap.

My stomach growled, but the letters seemed to call my name. I made a strong coffee, remembered the bread in the pram basket, and broke off a chunk.

My insides trembled as I tore open the second letter, understanding that Jacob's words would probably break my heart.

Chapter 50

A week before the court case, Naomi opened the top half of the door. Morning sunlight streamed into the kitchen. Bubba dozed in her chair. Rebecca and Fritz had returned to London but were due back in Rhodes any day. Naomi longed to hear all the baby news. She put the boys' washing in the machine, and started mixing a new batch of cream. Orders had risen dramatically, thanks to Marina's blog, and Naomi was having trouble keeping up.

'Yoo-hoo!'

She looked up to see Heleny's beaming face peer through the top of the front door. 'Shush . . . Bubba's asleep. Come in, Heleny,' she said. 'Sorry, I can't stop stirring.'

Heleny glanced at Bubba resting in her chair. She unlatched the bottom of the stable door and sidled into the kitchen which immediately felt cramped. 'Sounds interesting. What is it?'

'Neck cream.'

'I just wanted to tell you, the perfume worked. Fannes says the magic has died; he still likes me a lot but only as a friend. No more nights of rampant sex. It's such a relief!'

Bubba snored, her grin so wide that if she'd worn dentures they would have fallen into her lap.

Georgia appeared at the door. 'May I come in? I've brought you your mail, Naomi.'

'Of course,' Naomi said. 'Will somebody put the coffee on? And, Bubba, you can stop pretending to be asleep.' She studied the brown envelope of officialdom before tearing it open. 'It's about the court case.'

She read the letter twice. The court could not accept anything in the Italian census as it had been taken out of the country, and the information about the Rhodes property was unlikely to be found in time.

'That's that, then. A dead end. So bloody annoying. I'll just pop over to Papas Yiannis while you two make the coffee.' Naomi pulled her cream off the stove.

The priest, obviously disappointed said, 'Let's not fret about what we can't change. I'll scan the letter and send it to your lawyer.'

'What's going on?' Naomi stared at a mound of furniture with rugs and pictures piled on top in the centre of the room.

'Marina's boyfriend offered to do the painting, which reminds me, the sooner you take my old sofa, the better, though I wonder where you'll put it.'

'I've a plan. The boys can earn their keep while they're here and knock out the banquette.'

* * *

Naomi wondered if her boys could make any more mess. She scooped up another bucket of debris and tipped it on the patio corner.

'Just going for a coffee in the square,' Angelos called. 'We can't do any more until that rubble's out of the way.'

'You're not going anywhere until the job's done!' Naomi shouted. 'Rebecca will be back in a couple of days and the wall needs to be plastered and painted. Now shift that mound of rubble while I get *your* washing out of the machine, prepare *your* food, and make *your* beds!' She stomped upstairs, only halting for a massive dust sneeze.

She snatched the diary and a pillow from her bedroom, locked herself in the bathroom, and got comfy on the floor in the corner. She found another two airmail letters between the pages, and opened them carefully.

1st June, 1947

My Dearest Pandora,

I can't tell you how much your letter has lifted my spirits. I am weak and have pain in my joints, and after what I have seen, sometimes I think I don't want to live any longer. I've prayed for death. Now, YOU have given me new life. I must get better and stronger. Oh, the joy I felt when I received your letter, to know I wasn't the only one left.

I'm determined to recover enough to come home.

You asked me to describe what happened to us. Dear sister, it is too difficult for me to recount it all at once. I will write as often as I can bear to recall the days after we left Rhodes.

We were about six hundred people to each ship. I was separated from the others and forced into the hold where we were crammed, unable to sit down. When that space was full, they filled the upper deck. I don't know which was worse, to suffocate below or fry up top. We had no toilet or water.

We left the port on the 23rd of July. It was over one hundred degrees Fahrenheit, and the rusting old ship was burning hot. In the dark hold, I thought I would die, and feared for the rest of our family up top in the blazing sun.

I don't know how they managed up there with no food, water, or toilet. In the hold, we all had to press even closer together so that there was a corner where people could relieve themselves. The old women and the young children cried a lot, and soon the stench and the heat were choking.

The sea was rough. Urine and excrement swam about our feet. Exhausted and cramped, many of us became seasick, vomit adding to the intolerable conditions. One of the old men near me died. He made a whimper, clutched his chest, and then his knees buckled. We managed to get him over to the door, where he lay at our feet in the filth. That poor old man was our first fatality. Little did we realise the number of deaths ahead of us.

In the morning, we docked at the deserted island of Piscopi. Two of our men were allowed to take the body off the ship and bury it at the foot of one of the nearest mountains.

On the second night, still on our feet, we berthed at Kos, where another group of Jews, between ninety and a hundred of them, were forced onto our boat.

We had been three days without food or water when we anchored at the island of Leros.

Later, I learned from those on the open deck, that the other boats were also moored up in that port. There, the captain of the fleet hired to take us to the port of Piraeus, an Austrian national, refused to continue after seeing the atrocious conditions we were forced to travel in. Unless they gave us food and drink, he would not set sail for Athens.

We were given a little bread and water. The piteous crying from the children was the only sound in the hold. The stench was intolerable. Three more old people died, their bodies thrown overboard.

We arrived at Piraeus, the port of Athens seven days later. Lorries waited at the quayside. After ten days in the dark, the light was blinding. We were filthy, foul-smelling, and desperate for water. I felt sorry for the mothers, unable to console their weeping children. You could see their hearts breaking.

They separated men from women, loaded us into trucks and transported us to the camp of Haidari. We were forced to sit in the middle of a field, surrounded by armed soldiers. There I found Papa, Uncle Levi, and my brothers, their faces and necks blistered and peeling to the flesh, but being united after such an ordeal lifted our spirits. Grandpa was missing. We guessed he was a casualty of the ship.

We prayed for him.

From the field, we saw the trucks full of women and girls entering the barracks. Papa worried about Mama and about Grandma. Mama's legs had swollen after standing for so long. Naively, I hoped there'd be a doctor in the barracks.

We stayed in that field for three days, until finally we were reunited with the women and children.

Dearest Dora, I'm tired of this misery. I want to tell you my good news. I am living with an Italian nurse who looks after me very well. I am in love. Her name is Lucia, and one day I intend to marry her. She's beautiful and kind, but bossy. She tells me to stop now. It's time to eat and sleep. I'll write again in a few days.

All my love, dear sister, from your brother,

Jacob, XXX

Naomi realised Jacob would be her great-uncle. So, Dora had written to him in Italy. She wondered what had become of him as she unfolded the next letter.

14th June, 1947

My Dearest Pandora,

I hope you received my previous correspondence, which told of our journey to the prison camp at Haidari, outside Piraeus.

389

They gave us bean soup, which was sour with maggots in it, but being so hungry and thirsty, we all got some down.

We had to strip completely to be searched. The women too. Their shame at being naked in front of children and other men was heartbreaking. The soldiers were brutal to the young girls, prodding and taunting them, and we all thanked God that you and Evangelisa were spared that humiliation.

When the guards had finished degrading us, we were crammed onto lorries and transported to Athens, then packed into cattle trains, over seventy to a wagon. They sealed the doors. Moving was impossible. Ventilation consisted of a small window in the roof that didn't let in enough air for everyone. We almost suffocated in the heat.

The wagons remained locked for fourteen days while we travelled over land. We had nothing but a drum of rancid, undrinkable water and dry bread. At one stop, they gave us a few onions and a handful of raisins to share. We cried for people to give us water, but our guards threatened anyone who went near them. There was so much suffering!

We crossed Bulgaria, Yugoslavia, and headed towards Austria. When we entered Czechoslovakia, the local people recognised our distress. When we stopped, people brought us fruit, bread, and sweets, but the Germans confiscated everything. Exhausted, we lay on top of each other in the filth of the wagons that had been our prison for the previous two weeks.

The children and babies didn't even have the strength left to cry.

We arrived at Auschwitz on the 16th of August 1944, but that was not the end of our journey.

It is, however, the end of my story, Dora. Separated from the others, I never saw any of them again. We made a pact that *should any of us survive, for we accepted that most of us would probably not, we would write to you.*

I still hope so badly, Dora, that I am afraid to ask.

Did anyone else contact you?

Although I didn't see any of our family again, I believe that, like me, they thought about you and Evangelisa every day. You gave us light in our darkest hours, and hope for the future.

Please write back and answer the question that has haunted me for so long. Did you hear from Mama? I miss her more than anyone. I dream about her, and I'm afraid for her.

You are in my heart, Dora. My darling Lucia's very pleased with my progress. I've gained a little weight since hearing from you, and I am all the better for it.

All my love, my dearest sister,

Jacob, XX

Naomi carefully flicked through the diary, and wondered what had happened to the rest of the correspondence? Perhaps the priest still had the letters.

16 October 1947

Dear Diary, I am so excited! Jacob is coming home. I received a telegram at noon, which he had sent on his way to the port this morning. Right at this moment, he is on the ship sailing from Athens. I'm thrilled but also terribly sad; my family should be with him, but they're not. I recall Jacob's words: they've gone to God.

17 October 1947

It is 6 p.m., and I write this as I sit at the end of Spartili Street, gazing out to sea. I am waiting to catch a glimpse of the Athens Ferry as it approaches the island. It takes the ship about an hour to get from here to the deep port in Rhodes Town. Memories surface.

Irini and I watching lovers kiss goodbye. Me, dressed like a child, stabbing packets of pumpernickel. Nathanial sitting in the café, watching me. So much has happened in the past three years.

Sonia is asleep in her pram, and I will leave her on Mrs Spanaki's porch when I go to meet the ferry. Doctor Michalis has offered me a lift to the port to fetch my brother. He wants to keep an eye on me, in case I have a relapse.

I see the ferry, a spec on the horizon, and my heart is racing. I'll slip my diary under Sonia's mattress and update it this evening, when everyone is asleep. The plan reminds me of how I would slip out of bed in the hut, to write my journal, while Irini and Evangelisa slept. But there is no time to reminisce now, I must take Sonia to Mrs Spanaki and then hurry to the doctor's.

* * *

I had never been in a car before and became very excited about it. I took in every detail of the fine vehicle. Inside, it smelled of wood polish and new leather. I wore my best clothes, and red lipstick that a neighbour had lent me. I also put a dab of her '4711' eau de Cologne behind my ears because Mama wore it, and Jacob and Mama were close.

The journey to the port took half an hour. I watched people waiting for the ferry. An air of excitement surrounded me, everyone talked too loudly. I felt the presence of Irini beside me and wanted to reach out and hold her hand.

Oh my darling Irini, how I miss you.

In my letter, I told Jacob that Evangelisa had died in a shooting accident. I knew I would have to explain more fully, but I feared how he would take the news that I had killed our sister.

The ferry came into view. Everyone surged forward, staring at the passengers pressed against the ship's rails. I searched the sea of faces for my brother. I thought of Papa and Mama, Danial and Samuel. I had a man's handkerchief somewhere in my handbag. I fumbled, sniffing.

Oh Jacob!

I glanced over to the doctor's car. He stood with one foot on the running board, his elbow on the roof, posed elegantly as he smoked a cigarette. He lifted his trilby, nodded, and smiled.

Passengers disembarked. They lugged brown suitcases with worn corners, bulging canvas bags, crates of chickens, a horse, bicycles, coach-built prams, pushchairs, and motorbikes.

People shouted and whistled. Pandemonium grew as travellers tried to board while others continued to disembark with their goods.

I waved my big white hankie and called, 'Jacob! Jacob!' whenever a young man went by. The man who stopped and stared looked too old to be my brother. His pallid skin stretched across the bones of his face, eyes sunken with dark circles beneath.

'Dora,' he gasped. 'Dear, sweet, Dora!' He dropped his bag and hugged me.

I recognised my brother's voice, but I didn't believe the decrepit, wizened creature that approached could possibly be Jacob. I battled to hold my tears, seeing the gauntness of him, so old before his time. What had happened to the chubby, bright-eyed brother that was taken from Rhodes only three years ago? His wide smile had gone, his strong, broad body was wasted and stick-like, and the alert twinkle in his eye dulled to nothing.

I recalled unforgettable photographs in the newspapers, mountains of naked bodies, starved to death, skin and bones. My heart broke with love and grief for my departed family.

Jacob cried too, his bony ribs shuddering against me, our heads pressed against each other.

I don't know how long we held each other.

We both looked up, sniffing and blinking away tears. The doctor said, 'Welcome back, Jacob,' then reached out and shook his hand. 'Let's get you home.'

* * *

'Do you mind if I take a siesta, Dora?' Jacob asked. 'I'm so tired. The ferry took fifteen hours, and I found it impossible to sleep on the deck. Horrid memories.'

'Of course. Your bed's ready, but before you go, I must tell you something.' I hesitated, worried.

'Go on,' he said.

I pulled on the string around my neck and held my wedding ring. 'I have a daughter, Sonia; she's two years old. She'll be here when you wake, but I wanted to explain now.'

'What! You had a baby . . .' He stared at me, shook his head slowly, and then stared at the ring while digesting my news. But . . . the father?' he said after a moment.

'There's no father, Jacob. He went off to war and didn't come back. She's mine, and that's all that matters. I'm heartbroken that her father never saw her.' I spoke the truth; there was nothing else to say.

'Did you marry him, Dora? Does she have her father's name?' he asked urgently.

'How could I officially wed him, Jacob? I was a Jew in hiding. However, we were joined in matrimony by a *capitano* who had the power to conduct such a ceremony. We exchanged oaths and he gave me this wedding ring. We are married in the eyes of God. Sonia's father saved my life on the day you were taken. He took care of me, and I loved him with all my heart – a heart that's broken now, a heart that will never love another man. Sonia is all I have left of our love, so she's doubly precious to me.'

He nodded slowly. 'I see. It must have been difficult, alone with a baby.'

'Difficult, yes, but I discovered the true worth of people. I came home alone and went into labour the night before the war ended. The old priest across the road and his wife helped deliver my baby. He was the nearest thing to a father since—' Thinking of Papa, I filled with emotion and could not say more.

'The priest . . . the *Orthodox* priest?!' He looked aghast.

'Without their help, I don't know what I'd have done. They've been so kind to us both, and so have many of his parishioners.'

'They're Greeks, Dora. They hate us Jews. They sold us to the Germans and helped ship us off to Auschwitz. Never forget it!'

I shook my head. 'They're not all the same, Jacob. I promise you.'

'I find it hard to believe. Nevertheless, it's not for me to judge. If ever you want to talk about what happened, or need help, just say, Dora.'

I lowered my eyes, unable to look at him. 'Thank you.'

25 October 1947

Dear Diary, today Giovanni came back! What am I to do?! Jacob and Sonia are asleep now, but I cannot rest. Over the years, I have found it helps me to cope if I write down my greatest problems and sorrows, so here I am again, pouring my heart into my journal.

Sonia scrambles onto Jacob's knee at every opportunity. She adores him. I also love having him around, and I enjoy the freedom his presence gives me. This morning, he was out on the front courtyard, playing with Sonia, when I took the opportunity to escape to our small backyard. I had tomatoes to plant.

'Dora!' Jacob called through the house. 'You have a visitor.'

My hands and fingernails were caked in mud. I gave them a thorough scrub under the outside tap. Jacob appeared in the yard with Sonia on his hip.

'There's a soldier out front. Wants to pay his respects.'

'A soldier?' My heart leapt! 'Who is it?' I dried my hands hurriedly. 'What's his name?'

Jacob shrugged. 'No idea, he didn't say. He asked for you. Sonia told him, "Mummy's busy, so we have to be a good girl." She wagged her finger at him, so funny.'

I rushed to the front of the house and peered up and down the street. 'What did he look like, Jacob?'

395

'Tall, strong, handsome. Dark, army-cut hair. He had a wide scar across his left eyebrow.'

'Giovanni! Oh, Giovanni! Alive! Where is he?!' I couldn't say any more. From Jacob's expression, he clearly understood.

I ran to the end of the street, but Giovanni had disappeared. Customers and shopkeepers were startled when I launched myself into one shop after another.

Where had he gone?

'Giovanni, come back!' I cried.

I raced home, put Sonia in her pushchair and hurried to the airport, a distance of three kilometres. The sun blazed down burning my bare arms, but I didn't care. The pushchair hood shaded Sonia. My child had spoken to her father without realising it.

I believed Giovanni had the wrong impression; he had never seen Jacob and couldn't know he was my brother. Nor did he know I had his baby. I'd dreamed of the day we'd be together again, prayed at night that he'd find me. My heart ached to place his baby in his arms, but that chance had passed. Sonia was growing quickly.

Each meal I cooked, I imagined Giovanni at the table. Everything I did, I wondered if Giovanni would approve. His ghost existed in my everyday life, and at night he filled my dreams and helped me to block the horrors of the war. With no chance of more family members returning, or Evangelisa, or sweet Irini, all my prayers lay with Giovanni. For him I always had hope.

Chapter 51

Naomi looked up from the diary. The banging had stopped. *Damn, they've snuck out for a beer*, she thought, but they hadn't. 'It's too quiet down here,' she said, coming down the stairs. 'What's going on?'

'There's something at the bottom of the banquette, Mama.' Angelos leaned on his lump hammer. 'Metal, it might be an old electrics junction box.' Konstantinos scraped around the rusty rectangle with a bolster chisel.

Horrified, Naomi cried, 'Wait! Don't electrocute yourself, I'll turn off the power.' She rushed to the fuse board.

'No, it's not connected to anything, just a box. Pass me the crowbar.'

'What's going on in here?' Papas Yiannis called as he came through the door. 'Bubba's asking if she can come home yet.' He stood for a moment and surveyed the chaos. Rubble all over the floor, and thick grey dust blanketing every surface. 'Goodness me, what a mess!' he said. 'I'll get the kids to help clear up.'

Naomi dropped her head into her hands. 'This was a mistake. Rebecca and Fritz arrive tomorrow, and Costa on Thursday! Your father will go mad when he sees this mess. What am I going to do?'

'Mama, stop fretting! We'll be finished and plastered before midnight, promise!' Angelos said.

'There, that's done it,' Konstantinos lifted the box. 'Looks like somebody lost their toolbox.'

The priest's eyes narrowed. 'That's not a toolbox. Put it on the table.'

Naomi's mind flashed back to the diaries. Her pulse raced as she recalled the words: 'Smashing the floors and ripping out cupboards, greedily searching for the secret cache of Jewish wealth'.

'Get a knife,' Angelos said. 'See if we can break the rust.'

The knife bent. They tried a fork, but that bent too. 'Spoon handle,' Konstantinos suggested.

'At this rate, I'll have no cutlery left!' Naomi cried. 'Use the blade of the shears.'

The rust cracked, the lid moved, and everyone held their breath as Angelos prised the box open.

Inside the tin, they found an old waxed folder, tied with string and sealed with red wax. Inside that, was a fat envelope stuffed with documents, but none of them written in Greek.

Papas Yiannis returned to Bubba on his porch, while Marina, her boyfriend, Jason, and Heleny came to help clear up.

'Clean the kitchen table and chairs and lift them onto the patio,' Naomi said. 'Bubba can sit out there and try to make sense of the papers while we get finished.'

'What do you think they say, Mama?' Angelos hefted another bucket of rubble.

Naomi shook her head. 'No idea. It's in Hebrew, but I saw a date of 1929.' She picked up the oil-cloth packet that had protected the papers.

'There isn't room for all of us in here,' Heleny said. 'Why don't I go home and cook eggs and bread for everyone?'

'You're a saint!' Naomi said.

An hour later, the kitchen was reasonably organised. 'Leave the plastering,' Naomi said. 'Bring the rug from my bedroom for the floor, and we'll put the sofa against the wall. Job done.'

Outside, Bubba and the priest were talking excitedly.

'Any joy?' Naomi asked.

'Bubba thinks it's her grandfather's will. We're finding the translation difficult because some papers are in Hebrew and others in Ladino.'

'Ladino?' Naomi asked.

'The language your ancestors spoke when they migrated to Rhodes from Spain. I doubt we'll get them translated before the court case.' Seeing her frown, the priest added, 'There's been a Jewish community living on Rhodes since before Christ, before Christianity – before my religion was ever *invented* if you like.'

'Internet!' Marina cried. 'Bound to be an official website somewhere. We can scan or photograph the papers and email them to an expert. They'll love dealing with such historical documents. Leave it with me.'

Naomi remembered the card Despotakis gave her. She retrieved it from her handbag and reached for the phone.

* * *

Naomi ran her finger down Costa's itinerary. Athens. She hadn't been to the big city for decades, and promised herself another trip once the court case was over and Bubba had made a substantial recovery. She loved Athens, especially the museums, and she recalled her favourite sculpture of all time: Boy on a Horse.

Now, the life-size bronze in full gallop with a wind-whipped child hanging on to its mane made her think of Dora and her incredible bravery at Kamiros Scala. She had an urge to google more information about the figure that she knew was correctly called the *Jockey of Artemision* but with a hectic day ahead, she didn't have time. Nevertheless, the sculpture seemed to put meat on the bones of Bubba's diary.

Memories of Athens stayed with her as she washed the breakfast dishes.

In an empty carriage on the funicular railway up Mount Likabettus, she had told Costa they were having a second child. She recalled her embarrassment when they reached the top, still locked in an embrace. People on the platform seemed to sense their happiness and beamed.

At sunrise, outside the blue-domed chapel of Saint George, they held hands and watched a soldier raise the Greek flag. Another soldier played a military tune on a trumpet. Blissfully happy and overwhelmed by the view, they gazed over the city with the magnificent Acropolis at its heart. Later, they'd seen the change of the guard at the tomb of the unknown soldier where they had both been proud of their country.

Now, Costa was at the Athens port for two days between cruises, disembarkation and embarkation, and he usually phoned her around mid-morning. Rebecca and Fritz had returned, thrilled to tell Naomi all their good news about the twins. But today, Fritz and the boys had gone into town for some 'man time'. The annual rally of top spec cars was about to parade through the city streets, and Konstantinos longed to get up close to a Ferrari.

With so much going on, Naomi was glad to take a break from the chores when Georgia and Heleny arrived for coffee, gifting her an enormous box of honey-soaked baklava.

* * *

Rebecca found it difficult to drag her thoughts away from her babies. In no mood for gossip, she made an excuse to escape.

'I've missed reading the diaries so much. Would you mind if I have a quiet hour on the patio with Bubba, to catch up?'

'Go right ahead,' Naomi said, passing the journal over.

Rebecca kissed Bubba's cheek, sat beside her, and opened the diary. Her bookmark, a folded Lidl receipt, was still where she had left it.

Chapter 52

I raced towards the airport, searching for Giovanni and trying not to cry. I practised my words. 'Giovanni, say hello to your daughter, Sonia. Isn't she beautiful?'

Inside the terminal, several groups of soldiers stood around piled kitbags. Laughter. Back slapping. Fake punches to the bicep or chin. The camaraderie was obvious. Some appeared startled when I rushed up and peered at their faces.

'Giovanni, Giovanni, where are you?' He must have gone to the port; the bus ran every hour from the airport into town. I stared at the big clock in the foyer and realised I'd missed it by ten minutes, but still, I had to check. Sonia had fallen asleep. I rushed outside with the pushchair. There was a taxi, but I didn't have money. At the bus stop, a soldier with an enormous kit bag stood with his back to me. Could that be Giovanni? My heart was nearly leaping out of my chest.

I had never hoped for anything more intensely. I raced around him, peered into his face, and saw a stranger.

I could not get to the port before the ferry left for Athens and so I returned to the village, dragging my feet on the hot pavement.

'He's gone,' I said to Jacob. 'I didn't see him, never gave him his child to hold.'

'What's that?' Jacob pointed to a bag on the chair.

'My old duffel that Papa made!' Inside I found a large dried pomegranate, the skin hard and polished as old bronze. A sliver of skin had been carefully pared away, leaving the cream pith exposed. I stared at the pale heart, below it were the words, 'This is yours, Pandora Cohen.' Was my darling Giovanni referring to my bag, or his heart?

I recalled our last day together, in the villa, when he took my duffel and left me his precious catapult.

I turned and stared at the window sill. The catapult had gone.

Devastated to have missed falling into his arms, presenting him with his daughter, and planning a life together, my tears were dangerously close. 'Will you help us to the roof, Jacob? I want to watch Giovanni sail by.'

We climbed the metal steps from the courtyard and sat in the shadow of the water tank. The sun was sinking and warm golden light bathed our faces. Distant Turkish mountains paled, mauve against a pinkish sky. I peered towards Rhodes Town. The Blue Star Ferry sailed towards us.

'I wish—'

'No point,' Jacob said. 'I learned that a long time ago.'

Sonia scrambled into my lap and pointed. 'Big boat, Mama!'

'Your papa's on that blue ship, baby. The man that came today, he's your papa and he loves you more than he knows.'

The ship neared. 'He'll be at the railings, looking our way, baby. He'll see the cross at the top of Mount Filerimos and he'll think of you and me. Look, Sonia, here he comes, sailing past the airport and Paradissi.' The ferry was too far away to see any people, but I knew Giovanni would be gazing in our direction, perhaps his heart as broken as mine.

Jacob reached over and rubbed my back. 'He'll return. Love always finds a way.'

I longed to say so much, but the words stuck in my throat, so I stared at the vessel and rocked Sonia. She snuggled against my breasts and fell asleep.

Blinking away tears, I said, 'I recall the day; the ship's railings. . .' and I couldn't say more. Jacob squeezed my shoulder and I turned to see his face crumple.

'I remember it too,' he whispered. 'They saw you duck out from under the truck and wave at the ship. Just a fleeting moment, but when they told me a little misery was lifted. My first job at the camp was to pull dead men off the electric fence. We were all dying, but some chose to end their lives rather than continue suffering. I considered it myself but then I'd remember you were at home waiting for us, so I tolerated the abuse.'

'When you were in Auschwitz, did you come across any of the others?'

He stared at the sky. 'A few months later, I was forced to throw the bodies into the furnace – all day, every day.' He placed his hands over his face, as if to block the images. 'Most of the time, they were dead.'

'Oh, no. Who?' Afraid of his answer, I hugged Sonia even closer to my chest.

After a long silence, he swallowed hard. 'Danial. He was my favourite of everyone. I admired him so much, wanted to be like him – and there he was, skin and bones, his face twisted in pain, starved to death. I didn't want to let go of him. Thin, thin skin stretched over bones. Dear Danial, my dear brother.'

I stared at the ferry that took Giovanni from me and Sonia. Danial's last words returned with such clarity I sensed he was there on the roof with us.

A riddle for you, Dora. What falls into the sea every day, but never gets wet? A bag of caramels for the right answer.

I gazed at the sun sinking into the Aegean. 'You owe me a bag of sweets, Danial,' I whispered, my heart breaking.

Sonia snuggled up, blinked at me, then closed her eyes again. My brother and I sat on the roof, silent with our private thoughts and memories until the moon came up. 'Why do you think all this happened to us, Jacob?'

He just stared into the dark, his eyes wide and a look of complete horror fixed on his face.

* * *

404

Two weeks later, I stood on the quayside with Sonia on my hip, waving goodbye to Jacob. He would be happy in Italy, married to the nurse he'd fallen in love with. He promised they'd come to Rhodes for their honeymoon and I looked forward to meeting her.

1 July 1965

Dear Diary, the years have flown. My Sonia has grown and gets married tomorrow. The last month was filled with preparations, but now I have an hour for myself and my diary.

Jacob arrived from Italy this morning with his lovely wife and their two girls. He has become a music teacher, and plays the violin very well. We are going to perform at Sonia's wedding.

Sonia has asked me to sing *O Mio Babbino Caro*, because she has never known her father, yet in an odd way, she feels it will make Giovanni part of her wedding ceremony.

The song will be excruciating for me because my heart still aches painfully for my family – especially my own father – who gave me the pen I'm writing this with just a few days before he was taken away. The words of the song turn over in my mind.

O my dear Papa. I love him. He is handsome. He is handsome.

I recall the choir singing outside my father's shop. I was a child in love with a curly haired boy. I am afraid I will break down in the middle of the melody and embarrass Jacob.

Sonia's going to marry a local fisherman, Zorba. They are in love. My daughter was baptised into the Greek Orthodox Church by the old village priest. I found that hard to take. My own child, a Christian!

It was the Christians who slaughtered millions of us simply because of our religion. It was the Christians that herded us, young and old, rich and poor, into the gas chambers and crematoriums, burning old women and babies alive. For what reason?

I feel I have betrayed my family and my roots by allowing it. But then I remember Sonia's father. Giovanni, the shepherd boy. He was a Christian.

Before his retirement, the old papas visited me. He was a kind and understanding person who said, 'We must learn tolerance for other religions if the world is to become a better place.'

I haven't met the incoming priest who will marry Sonia and Zorba tomorrow. His name is Papas Yiannis Voskos, new to the area and living with his wife and child in the next village until the house opposite is refurnished and painted.

Sonia told me that Papas Yiannis is open-minded and in my honour and out of respect to Jacob, some Jewish traditions will be incorporated into the wedding.

The Breaking of the Glass is a Jewish tradition that means a lot to me, although I never had the opportunity myself. It comes at the end of the Jewish wedding, and the interpretation's left to the bride and groom.

I wonder what Sonia and Zorba will say.

Sonia has done the most unusual thing. Her dress is heavy white lace, fitted but flaring out at the knees down into a fabulous mermaid's tail that lengthens into a train at the back. The narrow sleeves are unlined lace and come down to a point that covers the backs of her hands. The neckline is a scalloped boat-shape that highlights her perfect shoulders but is at the same time modest.

I thought of Evangelisa's blue gingham dress with puff sleeves and white heart-shaped buttons that I wore for my wedding.

At the dressmaker's, I helped her into the gown and then cried. I couldn't help it. So much has happened in my life, and there I was standing before this vision of beauty, my daughter. I wished Giovanni could see her. Even after all these years, I can't forget the shepherd boy that I married on a Juliet balcony. Beneath the cinnamon tree with its hidden scars, he gave me the greatest gift of my life, my beautiful child.

I see him in Sonia's eyes and I explode with love. I also remember Irini, and then my heart breaks even more.

Sonia works at the local bank and brings home a good wage. She gives me a little money each week, and she has paid for half of her wedding with her savings. I wish I could have done more, but Zorba's parents understand my situation and have helped.

My daughter had my dress made from the same white lace as her wedding gown. The style's similar in that it's fitted, but it finishes just below the knee. The neckline is less dramatic, and the sleeves are three-quarter length. I have a huge white hat. The brim is so big I can hardly see past people's chins.

At first, I was shocked and said, 'Sweetheart, I can't wear white at my daughter's wedding.'

'Mama!' she cried, 'You are going to wear white, hold my bouquet, and have rice and rose petals thrown over you. You've been mother and father to me, and I want you to have a little of the fancy wedding you never had. And you can give me that ring from around your neck, because I'm having it altered to fit your finger in time for my wedding.'

At that point, I thought my heart would burst with pride. 'No, child, you must have the ring made to fit your finger. It belonged to your grandmother, and it must go to your firstborn daughter. That's the way it is.'

Sonia smiled. 'I'll be proud to wear it, Mama.'

Giovanni, how I wish you'd known her.

'Besides,' Sonia said, 'Zorba had better understand; if he marries me – he marries my mother.' She laughed at my shocked expression. 'You know what I mean, Mama.'

Sonia's going to walk down the aisle between me and Jacob. And I'm to stand next to her throughout the service, holding her bouquet. It's my daughter's big day, but I'm secretly thrilled and excited by the role I will play, and I believe tomorrow will be one of the most special days of my life.

The new priest came over and introduced himself. Although he's a bear of a man with a big hairy face, he seemed nervous. I did my best to relax him and made him coffee. After some chit-chat, he asked me about Sonia's father. He had touched a nerve and I turned away, reluctant to tell him anything, save that her father was the only man I ever loved, a shepherd boy by the name of Giovanni.

* * *

The ceremony was wonderful. The new priest did an amazing job. He has one of those voices that you feel you know, like an old friend or a brother, and I warmed to him immediately.

At the end of the service, Sonia and Zorba sat in two high-backed chairs to the side, and Jacob, holding his violin, joined me in the central aisle. We turned to face the congregation, the priest standing behind us.

Full of emotion, I concentrated on my breathing while Jacob played the beautiful introduction on the violin. As I sang, *Oh my dear father*, I saw Papa before me, his fingers wiggling over his head. *'Run, little rabbit, run!'* I felt his presence in the church. I was a little girl again, with his arms around me, his face smiling and his eyes shining with love. *'Follow your dreams, Dora.'*

My voice waivered as I battled against emotion, and then I heard Giovanni, 'Be brave, Pandora Cohen!' His voice was so real I almost turned, expecting to see him right there behind me.

I recalled the night I wrote the words to a song, and then Giovanni and I sang it together. We made love by the light of a full moon. The first time for me – I suspect for both of us – under the beautiful cinnamon tree. Memories drifted through my head and filled my heart with renewed energy. In that Greek Orthodox church, I sang like I had never sung before.

When the music finished, I closed my eyes and took a shaky breath. There was a moment of complete silence in the church, and then the congregation burst into applause.

Sonia came to my side and kissed my cheek, almost knocking my hat off. She slipped her hand into mine and squeezed it, and immediately Evangelisa came to mind.

My pretty sister. If only she could have been with us today. It occurred to me, for the first time, that at least Evangelisa never knew the horrors that befell our family. She believed they would return soon. Evangelisa had no notion of the appalling things they were forced to endure before their lives ended. I could never forgive myself for what I had done, yet with that thought a little guilt lifted from me and I felt light-headed.

'Thank you, Mama,' Sonia whispered. 'I'm sorry my father isn't by your side. He would have been proud.'

'Honestly, darling Sonia, I feel as though he is here,' I said. It was true. I had a sensation I wasn't alone. For a moment, I was lost in a time long gone, when I gave myself to Giovanni. The pain of what had been taken from me by the enemy, started to heal. I could smell the rosemary in Giovanni's hair, the red wine on his breath, and the sheep's lanolin on his strong, soft hands.

But to imagine he was actually there was a stupid idea, and I dismissed it immediately. Yet my heart ached to share this special moment with the shepherd boy.

Jacob stood next to the priest. He carried a fine wine glass and a white napkin. 'Ladies and Gentlemen, I am proud that my niece wants to end this joyous ceremony with an old Jewish tradition, and I thank Papas Yiannis for allowing it.' He gazed over the curious congregation. 'The breaking of the glass symbolises many things; each couple have their own interpretation.' He placed the glass in the cloth and passed it to Zorba.

Zorba said, 'I believe this is a very good custom. It made me think carefully about what this day means to me. Shattering the glass signifies how irreversible my vows are. I can't go back on my promise to Sonia, to love and honour her always, just as the glass can never return to its previous state.'

Sonia placed her hands over Zorba's, her eyes met mine, and she smiled.

'For me, the shattered glass is a reminder of how fragile love is. A single action or thoughtless act, or breach of trust, can shatter a marriage. Life is delicate and may come to an end suddenly. We should remember when glass is broken, it can't go back, like a lost life or a broken heart. From this day on, my life will never return to the time before I met and fell in love with Zorba.'

They threw the bundle down and, holding hands, stomped on it.

We all clapped. A small part of me was sad. My daughter had left me for the man she married. He was a good person and there was no doubt he adored Sonia, yet I felt a little abandoned. But doesn't every mother on their child's wedding day?

Hopefully there will soon be children. I long to be a grandmother!

Chapter 53

Rebecca closed the diary. She wished she had known her parents. Naomi was lucky to have memories of them. She recalled starting school and realising her classmates had a mummy and daddy and she hadn't. Naomi would sit on her bed and tell her stories of her father and their fishing boat, *Elevtheria* . . . *Freedom*. There would be mermaids and sea monsters, and always a safe haven in a storm.

She glanced towards the sea, which she could not actually see from the cottage but, looking up, there was a special light over the water that confirmed the presence of the Mediterranean. She decided to walk to the small harbour where her father would have moored his boat. Perhaps she would meet an old fisherman who had known him.

Naomi's friends were leaving. When they came onto the patio, Rebecca sniffed hard and wiped the backs of her hands over her eyes. 'Sorry. It's so sad.' She closed the diary.

'You're welcome to come to the church any time you want, Rebecca.' Georgia patted her shoulder. 'We always need extra help with the polishing and the flowers.'

'Thank you, that's very kind.' Rebecca shared a glance with Naomi.

'By the way,' Heleny said. 'Did you get all those packages Naomi was posting?'

Rebecca nodded.

'And was everything in order when you received them?' Georgia asked.

'It was.'

Heleny said, 'You understand it cost her a fortune? Week after week.'

Rebecca smiled, enjoying the game.

'She worried about those parcels. We could tell, couldn't we, Heleny? We were concerned for her.'

Heleny nodded. 'Very concerned.'

'Ladies, don't worry. I got all the gun parts and snapped the weapon together in seconds. It's ready for use.'

Georgia and Heleny stared at each other.

'It was a gun!' Heleny stuttered.

Georgia's eyes were wide, her face astonished. The two women turned and scuttled up Spartili Street muttering to each other.

Naomi grinned. 'You monkey! That'll be all around the parish in an hour. You coming in?'

Rebecca nodded. 'It's great to be back, Naomi.'

* * *

After dinner, Naomi and Bubba sat at the table outside, a mound of sultanas between them.

'You sort them, and I'll de-stalk them,' Naomi said. 'You're getting a lot more control in that hand, aren't you?'

As Bubba smiled her crooked smile, Naomi noticed the left side of her grandmother's mouth twitch. Such a small thing, yet Naomi's joy was immeasurable.

'That will be Costa,' she said when the phone rang. She dashed indoors and picked up, eager to share her elation. At last, Bubba was well on the road to recovery and her husband would return home soon.

'Bubba's mouth moved just now,' she said into the phone.

'That's great news, love. You've worked really hard with her. We're all so proud of you,' Costa said.

'When will you be home? We're worried sick about this court case, so many people depending on us. I'll feel much better when you're here.'

She glanced at her laptop, the inbox crammed with emails from Jewish diaspora around the world. Well-wishers, people begging for help, holocaust stories, and all of them hoping that the Cohen family case would set a precedent.

'One young couple have sold their house in Canada and given up their jobs to fly over to try and get their great-grandparents' place back. It's not just about Bubba's father's shop anymore. Such a tragedy if we lose the case.'

'Naomi, love, I have to tell you that I can't come home. I'm truly sorry but I'd risk losing my job for next year.'

Naomi felt her world collapse. 'It's so important to me, Costa. Surely, the company must understand. We're setting a precedent, and the entire Jewish world is watching. I was certain *The Royal Sapphire* would make an exception.'

'You never can tell how people will react when it comes to anything based on religion,' he said. 'And you know how it is – everybody has cousins on the islands. It'd be just my luck for someone in personnel to have Greek relatives owning property in Rhodes Old Town. I would never work on a cruiser again. Have you any idea how many people want my job? I guess at least two hundred just on this ship. I'm so sorry, love. I really am. I would love to be at your side. I understand how important it is to you, darling.'

'But the case isn't about religion, it's about injustice, Costa. It's about our family.'

'Don't be naive, Naomi. Of course it's about religion,' he said softly. 'I really do want to support you, but the risk is too high. If I lost my job, we'd have to pull our sons out of university. How would you feel about that? They've got their entire lives depending on these qualifications, and we would put an end to their plans and dreams. They would end up as hotel waiters in the summer, and olive pickers in the winter.'

'Costa, the boys are back from Cyprus and Rebecca's arrived from London. We'd be a united force in court, the whole family together. Please try again. It's *so* important to me, to us all.'

He sighed into the phone. 'I'll see what I can do, but don't depend on me being there, okay? I love you, Naomi, and I can't wait for the end of the season.'

* * *

Naomi opened the kitchen cupboard and studied the itinerary. *The Royal Sapphire* had arrived in Mykonos at sunrise. After disembarkation, Costa would take the Blue Star Ferry that berthed in Rhodes that evening, in time for the court case the following day. *The Royal Sapphire* would continue to Santorini without him, and Costa could catch up with his ship at its next port of call.

She longed to have his arms around her. With Costa by her side she could deal with anything, but right now, on her own, Naomi's nerves were shot to hell. So much depended on the impending judgement.

Nobody sat on the fence. She only had to look into people's eyes to see what they thought. She had been sneered at, and recognised

414

looks of disdain, but no one actually had the courage to stand up and state their opinion, or even discuss the imminent trial.

A swastika had been drawn on the Spartili street sign, and another under the bridge into the next village. She had heard that similar graffiti had defaced the Jewish Martyrs' Monument in Rhodes Old Town. She didn't doubt it was the cowardly behaviour of new Nazi Greeks who had big boots and even bigger mouths. Naomi thought too many Rhodians forgot their past, or didn't know their own history.

However, many people were kind beyond words, stopping to shake her hand in the street. 'Good luck, Naomi. You're a brave woman,' they said.

Naomi understood her fellow Rhodians, after all she was one herself. Their incredible generosity and freedom of spirit, which came from being Greek, was counterbalanced by other traits, born through many centuries of occupation and oppression.

She glanced at the clock. Her husband would be off duty in an hour. She waited for his call.

* * *

'I'm so sorry, Naomi,' Costa said. 'There's no way I can leave the ship. As I said, I'm not risking my job when the court case doesn't even involve me.' He sighed. 'Can't you see, we can barely afford the university fees and accommodation for the boys as it is? I didn't want to tell you this but I had to take a loan out to pay for their costs. It puts me in a terrible position and I feel I can't push my luck here by asking them again. I understand how much you want me there and I'm terribly sorry. I did try to explain.' He sighed again. 'I know you'll be disappointed, darling. I've dreaded having to tell you, but it's impossible . . .'

415

His voice was determined and Naomi realised she had no chance of changing his mind. Tired, exasperated, and stressed, all her worries seemed insurmountable at that moment. The pressure of the emails, the swastika under the bridge, setting the precedent for so many people who had been wronged, all these things exploded in her mind in one great rush of anger.

'You're afraid to ask, you mean!' she shouted. 'You always were a coward when it came to facing up to authority! Well, damn you, Costa. If your job's more important than your family, you can go to hell!' She slammed the phone down, her whole body shaking. Then, instantly regretting it, she burst into tears.

Bubba shuffled into the room clutching her Zimmer. 'What's the matter?' she said. 'Why were you shouting? Why are you crying?'

Naomi turned away and dried her eyes. 'Costa can't make it to the court. I lost my temper, sorry.' She clenched her fists.

'Relax, Naomi. It's not a problem. He has other priorities. Don't worry about things you can't change, Naomi.' Bubba limped over to the table and sat. 'Why don't you light one of your nice candles? Come into my room and watch the TV with me for a while.'

Naomi tried to smooth the furrows from her forehead and let the tension go. 'Sorry,' she said again. 'I'm all het up; I can't get my mind off the case. I wish I hadn't been so horrible. Poor Costa.' She took Bubba's advice and lit a vanilla and cinnamon candle.

Bubba closed her eyes and inhaled. 'Mmmm, my favourite,' she whispered.

Naomi helped her grandmother back into the bedroom where they settled in front of the TV. 'I can't believe how well you've improved lately, Bubba.'

'Once I manage the stairs, you can have the living room back. I realise how hard it's been, only having the kitchen to live in for all this time.'

* * *

Sitting next to Bubba's bed, Naomi lost herself in the antics of a long-running TV soap, glad to have her mind taken off the court case. Her boys were at the local café-bar with friends. Costa, she had to accept, was not coming home; and Rebecca, who always made excuses for an early night, was sleeping at *Rent Rooms in Paradise* with Fritz.

Why had she yelled at Costa like that? She had hurt him, and he didn't deserve it. The moment he called again, she would tell him how sorry she was.

Naomi dozed vaguely aware of Bubba's snores and a National Geographic documentary on TV. Too tired to move, she flicked the TV remote off and allowed herself to drift into a light sleep.

Pandemonium exploded through the half-open kitchen door, waking her with a start.

'Mama! Mama!' Angelos and Konstantinos sounded breathless.

Naomi's heart hammered, and Bubba jumped from her sleep too.

'What? What's the matter? I'm in here!' Naomi sensed an emergency. She turned to her startled grandmother. 'Go back to sleep, Bubba. It's a big day tomorrow, with the court case and everything.'

She slipped into the kitchen. Angelos hooked the air and nodded to the door. 'Come outside, Mama. We don't want to wake Bubba.'

'A bit late for that with your racket. What on earth's going on?'

She stepped onto the patio and saw Rebecca and Heleny rushing down the street towards her. Papas Yiannis, Marina, and her boyfriend, were already halfway across their patio. Everyone wore a horrified expression and foreboding gathered in the pit of Naomi's stomach. She looked from one to the other, waiting for an explanation.

'Will somebody tell me what's happening?!'

'Dad's ship's sinking!' Konstantinos cried.

'*What? Costa!*'

Angelos nodded. 'A newsflash in the bar five minutes ago. They think the cruiser struck an uncharted rock as it entered the Santorini caldera, but nobody's sure. We came straight home.'

Chapter 54

Naomi watched TV through the night, jerking herself out of sleep whenever she realised she had nodded off, afraid of missing something. They were reporting live, covering the demise of *The Royal Sapphire*. When they had nothing new, the same footage played on a loop. She had vague recollections of various family members taking it in turns to sit with her through the night, but now she was alone, and glad of it. She could concentrate on the screen, and not miss anything.

Be safe, Costa!

A helicopter hovering over the scene offered a fresh perspective. Naomi dragged the chair closer and sat on the edge of the seat. People were sliding down yellow inflated chutes into orange lifeboats metres below. Passengers at lifeboat stations clutched the rails and peered into the churning sea far below. Everything seemed organised with no sign of panic from the guests.

But where was Costa, and why hadn't he called? She had phoned him, but the number was unavailable.

A cascade of water, pumped from the stern, shot out like an enormous waterfall, plunging thirty metres down into the sea. Presumably, it came from lower decks, already flooded. The dining rooms and kitchens were down there. Watertight doors would be closed, sealed.

Oh Costa!

Black smoke billowed from the funnel. Naomi wondered if there was a fire, or had there'been an explosion?

The Royal Sapphire listed to port. Helicopters circled, their distant shadows flitting like water nymphs over the sea. Queues of small vessels, water taxis and trip boats waited their turn to transport passengers in a mass evacuation. Pale-faced people in fluorescent life jackets were helped onto excursion boats. The TV showed new footage garnered from tourists' phones. Naomi scoured the faces for Costa.

The news returned to the studio. The anchor man asked the Greek correspondent, 'Can we confirm that the lower decks were cleared of travellers *and* staff before they were sealed?' Naomi held her breath. The reporter stood on the deck of a trip boat that was taking on cruise passengers. He shook his head, his voice drowned by the thrum of a nearby helicopter.

Back in the studio, the anchor man said, 'In a statement from *Royal Cruises*, we read that at this moment they can't confirm there've been no injuries or that everyone is accounted for, but the safety of the passengers continues to be paramount. Concerned family and friends will find more information on the *Royal Cruises* website.'

With an acute feeling of helplessness, Naomi broke down. She grabbed her phone and found the website, but there was no news that she didn't know already. She peered at the kitchen clock: 4 a.m. She then turned back to the screen, unable to think of a reason why Costa wouldn't call her.

The loop played through again. High on the cliffs of Santorini, she saw picturesque whitewashed buildings with azure water sparkling from infinity pools with underwater lighting,

Softly-lit blue-domed churches with arched bell towers seemed to add to the drama. Despite the unearthly hour, rows of tourists continued to stand on rooftops and balconies. Everyone stared down at the tragedy. Naomi wanted time to stand still, but the news–loop started again with yesterday evening. On the TV dusk descended, fairy lights winked and glinted from the scene. TV cameras zoomed in on the holidaymakers: it wasn't a vigil. They were staring at their phones held at arm's length, recording the disaster.

Back to the live streaming, searchlights played over empty decks and doorways, the pristine paintwork turning yellow in artificial light. Was anyone still inside? The vessel, almost a hundred thousand tonnes, as Costa had often told her, turned slowly onto its side.

Costa, please don't be in there!

The sea spat out luminous lifeboats that bobbed on the surface in a bed of foam.

The numbers ran through her head. Over three thousand passengers, two thousand crew, one husband.

When the camera pulled back, taking in the whole scene, it was clear the ship had listed into a critical position.

The Royal Sapphire turned as slowly and definitely as the arms of the kitchen clock. A vessel destined to turn into turtle. A thought Naomi did not want to contemplate.

Suddenly she realised that everything had changed up a gear. Blurred images from someone's Go-Pro showed desperate people crawling along a corridor floor, the angle making walking impossible. Furniture skidded over the carpet at bone-breaking speed, bowing to gravity, a chandelier shattered, a piano waltzed across a dance floor, men and women teetering drunkenly. Passengers scrambled, sliding, rushing, frantic now. At the escape slides, holidaymakers in fluorescent life jackets clung to railings. The waterfall pumped from the stern ceased. What did that mean? Had they given up? Naomi's stomach rolled. She didn't want to watch, yet couldn't tear her eyes away.

There were still people at the rails! People inside! Where were the crew? Were they forbidden to leave until all passengers had reached safety? Where was Costa?!

Suddenly, she realised Rebecca was at her side.

'He'll be all right, Sis. I promise you. Go to bed for a few hours. I'll sit and watch, and wake you if anything new comes up. They won't let anything happen to their staff, believe me.'

Naomi shook her head. 'Look, people are still inside and on the decks! The whole damn ship's about to flip! They'll be sucked down with the vessel.' She struggled to hold it together, but couldn't. 'I wish I hadn't told him to go to hell. Why did I do that? Stupid fool!'

She lost track of time. Rebecca placed a mug of coffee in front of her.

'Let's make you some breakfast. It'll help I promise,' Rebecca said, sitting on the arm of Bubba's chair, rubbing Naomi's back gently.

Naomi shook her head. 'I've heard the caldera's bottomless, the centre of a four-thousand-year-old volcano. Once the ship goes under, there'll be no chance for anyone left on board.'

Papas Yiannis came into the cottage. 'Any news of Costa? They say three thousand have been taken off, but Santorini can't cope with the communication overload. They've asked everyone to post information on Facebook.'

Naomi shook her head. 'Costa hasn't got a Facebook page. Look! There are people still on the upper decks! How could this happen? If he's safe he'd have called. He'll know I'm frantic.' She fought another sob. 'If anything happens to him ... I can't *live* without Costa. Why did we have to fight? I hate myself...'

She stared at the screen. A helicopter transmitted from above the listing ship. Tables, cushions and chairs suddenly raced across the vacated sundeck. They would have knocked anyone over the side or broken their backs if they had been caught at the rails. Dozens of sunbeds hit the banister and flew into the air like a cloud of emerald butterflies, before plunging into the Aegean. All three swimming pools emptied at the same time; turquoise water cascading all the way down to the sea.

Rebecca's arm slid around Naomi's shoulders and suddenly it was all she could bear. She had fought with Rebecca and it had cost them ten senseless years apart. Now this had happened. It was Naomi's fault that her last phone call with Costa had ended with angry words.

She turned to her sister. 'I'm sorry we fought, way back. I know what it's like to love someone above all else.'

Rebecca squeezed her shoulders. 'Let's concentrate on Costa.'

'Why hasn't he phoned? He'll know I'm out of my mind.'

Papas Yiannis said, 'I understand you're distraught, Naomi, who wouldn't be? But trust in God and, of course, the cruise company. They won't let anything happen to Costa. Have you been up all night? You must be exhausted and the taxi will be here in an hour to take us to the court.'

'No way!' Naomi cried. 'I can't leave here. What if Costa calls and I'm at the court? What if someone phones the house with news? I want to go over to Santorini on the next flight.'

'I understand how you feel but...'

Naomi butted in. 'How can you?! My husband's in great danger. I have no idea where he is right now or what's happened

423

to him, and there's nothing I can do to help him. He might be dead!' She stopped, gasped, bit on the knuckles of her bunched fist.

Naomi was petrified Costa had drowned, all alone. If he was sinking in that bottomless sea, she wanted to be with him, to comfort him. When she had drifted into a light sleep, Naomi had visions of holding him in the dark swirling waters of Santorini's caldera.

'Don't let him die, Papas.' Her tears welled. 'Pray for him with everything you've got. Tell your God I need him, his boys need him.' She leaned against the priest's chest and he held her until her tears stopped. She broke free, snatched the kitchen roll and dried her face. 'Sorry,' she said.

The priest rubbed his forehead. 'Believe me, I do understand, Naomi. But I must remind you that these people who have so generously funded your court case are not rich. They've spent all they have and more in order to set a precedent. Some of them have actually sold their houses for this. We can't let them down now.' Papas Yiannis patted her hand. 'Nothing we do will alter Costa's situation, but everything we do today will have a profound effect on the lives of thousands of people, of all the descendants of the Jews of Rhodes.'

Naomi dropped her head into her hands. 'I'm incapable of thinking straight, Papas, how can I stand up in court? I'm sorry but it's hopeless. I can't do it.'

'Of course you can.' He lifted her chin. 'Look to your grandmother for inspiration. The Cohen women are strong in the face of adversity. They rise and fight for the rights of others, regardless of the odds. They're at their best when needed, when oppressed. Haven't you learned that from Bubba's diaries, from her bravery and selflessness?'

As his words sank in, Naomi's shame rose. Bubba had fought for those who didn't fight for her or her family. She fought for the Rhodians who not only looked the other way when the Nazis took two thousand Jews off the island but the worst of them pillaged the property of the oppressed like greedy vultures and changed the laws to make it legal.

Those people were no better than the Nazis – yet Dora still risked her life for them in an effort to end the war. The injustice of it all hit Naomi and she realised, wherever Costa was, he'd want her to stand up in court.

Chapter 55

The courtroom buzzed with an atmosphere of expectancy. All seats were taken, and the sides and back aisles were packed with people standing. The air already smelled of sweat, cigarettes and cheap perfume. A strip light flickered. Someone had an irritating cough. A ragged butterfly fluttered repeatedly up the dusty window then fell exhausted to the sill.

A panel of three judges sat on the bench. Only the central one, a mature woman, spoke to the claimants. Naomi, wiped out by tiredness and worry, stared blankly at the dais. The lawyer, Bubba, and Rebecca sat next to her, and in the row behind, Papas Yiannis, Naomi's sons, and Fritz. All eyes were on her as she was called to stand.

She took an oath and answered all the questions asked, but her head was filled with nothing but the cruise ship.

'Madam!' the judge said sharply when she didn't respond to a question but stared blankly into space.

'I'm sorry, Your Honour. My husband works on *The Royal Sapphire*. I haven't heard from him and I am sick with worry.'

The judge raised her eyebrows. 'Very commendable that you attended court given your circumstances.'

A man in a silver-grey suit asked to speak. The judge allowed it. He took the stand.

'State your name and occupation.'

'My name is Lord Elijah Bloomberg. I own a chain of retail stores.'

The magistrate nodded. 'And what would you like to say, Lord Bloomberg?'

'I've come here to question the integrity of a system that rewards theft and condemns bravery,' he said calmly. 'The matriarch of this family risked her life, again and again, in a heroic effort to rid this island of the Nazis. And Rhodes rewarded her, not with a medal of valour, not with a statue in the town centre or any kind of recognition, but by stealing her property, by defiling the Jewish war monument, by continuing to bully and oppress her and any people of her religion.'

He paused to allow his words to sink in. 'If it wasn't for Pandora Cohen and the other members of the *Andartes*, you might all be speaking German today. Pandora Cohen is a person who should inspire us all. To fight for your rights and your beliefs is an act of bravery we are all capable of, but few of us undertake.' He gazed around the courtroom. The silence was absolute.

'I came over from America to speak to you. Unfortunately, I'm not from this beautiful island. If I were from Rhodes, I would place this woman, Pandora Cohen, on a pedestal, build her a statue, and ensure she was recognised as a hero throughout Europe, certainly in Greece. I would be exceedingly proud to have her as a citizen of Rhodes.'

Lord Bloomberg sighed and turned to the bench. 'But, at the risk of alienating myself from this court, I must speak the truth as I find it. Here, we have a fine example of the age-old problem not only of Greece but of the world over. Greed and Jealousy. Grasping at grants and chattels. Aristotle would turn in his grave if he knew what his great nation had fallen to.'

He turned back to face the courtroom. All eyes were on him and complete silence reigned. 'To quote Aristotle, if I may: "At his best, man is the noblest of animals. Separated from law and justice, he's the worst."'

The judge spoke. 'What's your point, Lord Bloomberg?'

'My point is Aristotle's point: justice. We become "just" by performing just actions. Property that was taken from the Jewish population should be returned to them. That's just. That's in *your* power. As the philosopher said, "We are brave by performing brave acts. What it lies in our power to do, it lies in our power not to do." You have the ability to give this family its property back. That choice is yours. Pandora Cohen had the option to fight for your people. She didn't hesitate. She was prepared to sacrifice her life for the freedom of this island. What will you do to reward her? I ask you to return to Pandora Cohen what is rightfully hers.'

'Thank you, Lord Bloomberg. I would like to know if you have claim to any property in Rhodes, indeed, in Greece?'

'None at all.'

'Then why are you here?' the judge asked, peering over her half-glasses.

'Because in 1944, Pandora Cohen committed an act of incredible bravery. She risked her life to save a wounded British soldier from the Nazis, at Kamiros Scala. That soldier was my father: Sergeant Tommy Bloomberg. Later, my father was awarded the highest honours for bravery from the British Army. Although I owe my life to Pandora Cohen, as do many people on this island, she received no recognition from the Greek government. Instead, her home, the only thing she had left, was stolen from her. Some people have tried to claim their property back, but the deliberate system of delaying tactics implemented by an overbloated bureaucratic system means that most cannot afford their mounting lawyer's bills.'

Lord Bloomberg held his hands out, palms up. 'The majority of the property owners were murdered, entire families wiped out, leaving no living relatives. Over one thousand properties were taken away from Jewish Rhodians. We are requesting only a tiny fraction, less than a hundred, of those places to be returned to their rightful owners.'

'You may step down,' the judge said. She glanced at her watch. 'We shall break for lunch. Please be back in the courtroom at two.' Everyone stood as the three judges left the bench.

'I'd forgotten about that,' Bubba said. 'The soldier at Kamiros Scala. Isn't it odd that his son turns up here?'

'Quite a coincidence,' Papas Yiannis said, but Naomi caught his eye and guessed the priest had more to do with Lord Bloomberg being in Rhodes than he was admitting.

'We're all so proud of you, Bubba,' Naomi whispered before she faced the priest and mouthed, *Thank you.*

He turned his mouth down dismissively and held his arms out, like a stained-glass saint displaying the pierced hands of a stigmata.

*   *   *

Naomi spent the break on her phone, trying to obtain news of Costa. By the time she returned to court, where all mobiles had to be turned off, she felt light-headed and sick. She stared at the judge but her mind was in the Santorini caldera. Papas Yiannis squeezed her hand. 'Have faith,' he whispered.

The judge was summing up. 'We're not here to discuss the war or the holocaust. This case has nothing to do with the Nazis. We are not here to "make good" atrocities that happened in the war or to reward our heroes. As Aristotle said, "Law is reason, free

429

from passion."' Her eyes flicked to Lord Bloomberg for a second before she continued. 'I want to make clear that the issue we have come here to resolve must be devoid of historical context.

'What we have to do is find resolution to a case of injustice. Yet, the complexity of the situation is exacerbated by the length of time that has passed, and the fact that at the time of the acquisition of the claimant's property, this island belonged to Italy.

'However, with the documents recently discovered in the city police station, new evidence has come to light regarding the lost Rhodes census. Also, the last known will of Pandora Cohen's grandfather has come to light, which states that the property be left to his grandchildren, and clearly shows the property's history and boundaries. I am going to rule that a committee be set up to instigate the restitution of Rhodes property to its rightful proprietors, where those owners or their direct descendants are still living.' She banged her gavel.

There was a second of silence, then uproar. All around Naomi, men and women were clapping and shouting, 'Bravo!' The decision was all that they'd hoped for.

The courtroom emptied. Everyone spilled down the wide stone steps. People grabbed her affectionately, hugged her, called 'Congratulations!' Rebecca and Naomi's sons shielded Papas Yiannis and Bubba, but Naomi was jostled. She checked her phone. Seven missed calls! A reporter rushed through the crowd and pulled on Naomi's arm. Everyone grinned and shook hands. She thumbed redial. Someone took her hand, shaking it boisterously. Someone else slapped her back, unbalancing her.

'Bravo! Bravo!'

Naomi's phone fell to the floor, bouncing down the steps between people's feet. She lunged, desperate to rescue the device before somebody stepped on it. Breathless, she snatched it up, sat on the bottom step, and returned the call. A well-wisher congratulated her, grinning, the gleeful face only inches from hers. She turned her back.

'I'm replying to your call,' she said shakily. 'My husband works on *The Royal Sapphire*.' She pressed her free hand over her other ear so she could hear over the tumultuous throng. Her heart hammered. The spin of vertigo dragged her away from the building and everything solid. She recalled her dream, holding Costa as he slipped into the dark depths of Santorini's caldera. Reality took a step back. Naomi was alone with the voice in her ear.

Chapter 56

'Thank you,' Naomi uttered, ending the call. The air of celebration and jollity morphed into a monotonous buzz in her ears like a high-volt battery, or a pylon on a damp day. Darkness hovered at the corners of her eyes, then spread rapidly. She tried to stand, but her knees buckled and the real world shrank away.

Angelos and Konstantinos were at her side. 'Mama!' They lifted her off the pavement. Someone brought a chair. Someone else wafted a document folder over her face, and yet another person tried to give her a glass of water.

Naomi pulled back and dropped her head into her hands. 'Costa is safe,' she sobbed. 'Your father, they found him. He was knocked unconscious, taken to hospital, but he's fine now. He's in the airport, arriving home in a couple of hours.'

'What a relief, Mama!' Angelos said, spreading his arms and enfolding his mother. 'How is he?'

Naomi, trembling, couldn't speak. Angelos was as tall as Costa. She pressed her head against her son's chest and felt the strength of him around her. 'He's fine,' she whispered.

'Thank goodness. We've all been out of our minds with worry. I've been desperate to speak to him. What happened to his phone?'

'I don't know. Are you all right now?'

Angelos nodded. 'Konstantinos is refusing to accept anything bad could have happened. He kept saying there must be a simple explanation. It's his way of dealing with it, that's all.'

'It's such a relief, I can't tell you,' Naomi said.

Rebecca joined them and hugged her sister tightly. 'It's been an awful strain, hasn't it? Bubba's stroke, me, the court case, and Costa going missing. I just don't understand how you've coped.'

Naomi struggled to keep it together. Their eyes met and she nodded.

Rebecca gently coaxed her sister. 'Come on, the time has come to step away for an hour, walk around the city, and let everyone look after themselves.'

'I can't do that. Costa will be home soon. The boy's laundry needs to go in the machine, so it's dry for Cyprus. There's Bubba to settle. I haven't even organised the food for this evening.'

'Come on, relax Naomi. They're adults. They'll be fine without you for an hour, trust me. Your absence won't make much difference in the big scheme of things, but if it does, you'll be appreciated all the more when we get back,' she said softly. 'I'm so proud to be your sister, Naomi.'

'Give me a hug, will you?' After a few moments, Naomi straightened. 'Sorry about that.' She escaped Rebecca's arms, sniffed, and scrabbled around her handbag for a tissue.

'Not a problem at all. Now, when was the last time you were in Town?'

'I don't know, six, maybe nine, months back.'

'Well, come on then. Let's get an ice cream and walk for a while.' She turned to their group of supporters. 'Look at your friends and neighbours. They are all fine people, and as for Angelos and Konstantinos, they're your sons, I'm sure they'll take control of everything.'

'We certainly will, Aunty Rebecca. Go on, Mama, have a break,' Angelos said. 'You deserve it.' He kissed Naomi's cheeks and gave her another hug. 'You're amazing. We're very proud of you.'

Konstantinos peered at his mother as if seeing her for the first time. 'Sure, relax, Mama. I'll book a table for supper, and *we'll* take care of Bubba and Papa. If there's a problem, we'll text you, so go, and don't worry.'

* * *

Rebecca linked arms with Naomi and they walked across from the courthouse to the seafront. Colourful boats bobbed side-by-side in Mandraki harbour. To their left stood the gothic cathedral of the Annunciation, and to their right, the cause-way to St Nicholas lighthouse. On the pavement, under giant ficus-ficus trees with their smooth wide trunks and shiny leather leaves, handsome young men and women sold boat-trip tickets.

The sisters bought one-euro ice creams from a small prom-enade stall, and then sat on a bench to people-watch.

'It was good of Fritz to come to the court. It can't have been easy for him to sit there, knowing that his grandfather was responsible for so many deaths. Even though all this is nothing to do with him, he must have felt awkward.'

Rebecca nodded. 'I can't imagine how I'd feel in his situation, but I was pleased that he came to support us.'

The glass-bottom boat came in. Tourists in sundresses and shorts, with sun-burnt shoulders and wide smiles, queued to get off. 'I've always wanted to do that,' Naomi said.

Rebecca grinned, 'Then before I go back, we shall go on a boat, Cinderella!' They laughed together. 'Come on, let's walk into the old town. I should buy something nice for Fritz. And you know what, I'd like to see where our great-grandpa had his tailor's shop.'

They entered the Old Town by Freedom Gate, and walked though imposing walls that were forty-feet-thick in places, and dated back to 1330.

'I can hardly believe we own a piece of this world heritage site. It's absolutely amazing, isn't it?' Rebecca said.

Naomi nodded. 'And stunningly beautiful, don't you think?'

They took in the Temple of Aphrodite on their left, the decorative Arts Museum on their right, and opposite that, the Byzantine Museum. They turned into the Street of the Knights, treading the cobblestones and admiring the inns and residences of the Knights of Saint John. Carved sandstone architecture, clearly influenced by various countries such as Spain, Italy and France, lined their way. At the top of the street, they stopped to stare at the Palace of the Grand Masters, then carried on to browse souvenir shops and café-bars that lined the tourist's way.

They passed the dusty-pink domed building of Suleiman's Mosque. Naomi nodded at it. 'Remember the Turkish Consul, all the lives he saved? What a brave man.' They continued in silence, each with their thoughts of Bubba's diaries, until they arrived at the Gate of Saint John.

'Dora and Irini came through here with their belongings, didn't they?' Rebecca stared at the road over the moat.

Returning to Freedom Gate, they stopped in Jewish Martyrs' Square. 'Look, I don't want to rush this,' Naomi said. 'I can imagine many hundreds of women and children gathering here, the whole wretched situation. The Rhodians hiding behind their shutters, watching Jewish families leave.' She peered at the buildings, all tavernas or tourist shops now. 'I'd like to go into the Jewish Museum and the Synagogue and find our family's property, but I need to get back to Costa. It's been lovely, Rebecca, but I'm starting to fret.'

'No, that's fine, don't worry. It will be interesting to see how everyone's coped without you.'

They both laughed.

* * *

Spartili Street was deserted, Naomi's house empty. Suddenly afraid her grandmother had suffered a relapse, she called Angelo. Bubba answered. 'Where are you?' Naomi asked.

Bubba giggled. 'I'm in one of those pop bars, drinking beer and eating a burger, child. But I'll get Angelos to bring me home for a nap before we go for dinner. Costa's here. Do you want a word?'

'Naomi, love. Are you feeling better? They told me you needed a little space after all that happened. I can't wait to see you,' Costa said. 'I'm coming home right away.'

'I'm so relieved you're okay, darling; the boys are too. Are they both with you? Wish I was there, but . . . Bubba's in a bar?' Naomi stuttered.

'And loving it. I can't wait to have you to myself, Naomi.'

'You sure you're okay, Costa? I mean, concussion, should you even be drinking?'

'Don't worry, we'll be back in ten minutes.'

Naomi hung up and turned to her sister. 'Bubba's in a bar, swigging beer and eating burgers with your husband, my husband, and our sons, I can hardly believe it!'

'Before you know, she'll be smoking pot,' Rebecca quipped.

'She's already done that, right?' Naomi said and they both laughed.

Chapter 57

Bubba was sleeping, the boys still in the bar, and Rebecca back in her rented room with Fritz.

Naomi allowed Costa to lead her to the bedroom. He sat beside her, both of them silent, thinking of all that had happened over the past twenty-four hours. She turned and peered into his eyes and saw so much; fatigue, the remnants of fear, a spark of wildness that had attracted her to him decades ago. She found it impossible to be this close to him, and not marvel at the handsomeness of him. That a man of such beauty had fallen in love with her remained a mystery.

'I thought I'd lost you,' she whispered.

'You're not *that* lucky.' She loved his gentle smile. 'Come here, woman,' he said tenderly taking her into his arms. 'How many nights I've dreamed of being right here, with you. We have some catching up to do.'

* * *

That evening, family and friends gathered at Antonis Restaurant, in the nearby village of Trianda. Halfway through the meal, Marina rushed in. 'Naomi! I have great news. Lord Bloomberg wants to talk to us about Pandora's Box! We have an appointment with him next Monday. I can't believe it.'

Naomi stared at her. 'How did that come about?'

'I took the opportunity to have a word with him after the court case, you know, thank him and all. I told him Pandora Cohen had started a family business of pure, natural, lotions and potions, and we were looking for funding. He's interested in Pandora's Box!'

'Well done you! Can the day get any better? Why don't you and Jason join us?' Naomi said, waving the boy in the doorway over.

Bubba beamed and nodded, as if her plan had come together. She was on form, her first evening out since her stroke. After the meal, she drank a little wine and said to Naomi, 'Child, I'm so happy to have all my family around me. I feel that even my Sonia's here in spirit.' She looked towards the ceiling and smiled. 'I would like to sing something for you all. I haven't had the urge to sing for a long time. Do you think I could?'

Naomi remembered how Bubba would go down to the beach and sing when Naomi was just a girl, before her parents were lost at sea. She hadn't heard her sing since that tragic day.

'Of course you can, Bubba, we would love it if you did, wouldn't we, people?'

'Rip it up, *Yiayá*!' one of Naomi's boys shouted, and everyone laughed.

Bubba grinned and gave him a shaky thumbs-up. 'I'll do my best, son.'

Naomi helped Bubba to the music area in the corner of the taverna.

'What music would you like?' Antonis asked as he fiddled with his iPad.

Bubba thought for a moment. 'Have you got the music for *I Dreamed a Dream*?' Bubba asked. 'Just the music. I've got my own words.'

Antonis nodded. 'Anything you want.' His eyes met Naomi's with a question.

'Don't worry,' Naomi said, sensing his concern. 'She can do it.'

'Would you like a chair?' Antonis asked, adjusting the microphone.

'No!' she replied indignantly, clearly forgetting her age and fragility.

Naomi supported her grandmother behind the microphone and, for a moment, she was overwhelmed by the love she felt for this remarkable woman. Lord Bloomberg was right, Pandora Cohen should be placed on a pedestal. The intro came through the speakers. The old lady surveyed the room, looking into the faces of her family, smiling and nodding to each of them in turn. The taverna stilled. Bubba closed her eyes, her shapeless bosom rising and falling as she concentrated.

When she started her song, the notes were clear and strong.

Naomi smiled to see Costa's jaw drop. Like most of the people there, he had never heard her sing before.

When Bubba opened her eyes, they were glazed, her expression blank and distant, and it became obvious to them all that she had slipped into her memories of past times. It was sixteen-year-old Pandora Cohen on that small stage.

Naomi remembered the line in Bubba's diary: *I was holding the last note with every ounce of energy I had. I thought I'd suffocate with the need to breathe in before I got all of the note out.* Then she realised, the words that Bubba sang were not *I Dreamed a Dream*. She recalled Bubba's songbook, on the shelf over the sink. These were her *own* lyrics, her *own* song.

Naomi listened carefully.

I knew a time when life was fine
With songs to sing, their words uplifting.
I searched for love, a heart divine
Then war broke out, all hell existing.
I lost them all, it went so wrong. . .

She waivered, took a breath, and continued.

My precious dreams they all flew by
My hope was lost, life at its bleakest.
I'd dreamed my loves could never die
And prayed to God for strength when weakest.

Bubba's voice broke and her lips trembled. Papas Yiannis heaved himself out of his seat and took Naomi's place. He slipped his arm around Bubba's waist and supported her.

Papas Yiannis whispered into her ear, but the microphone picked up his words. 'Be strong, Pandora Cohen. We'll sing it together. Remember?'

Naomi wondered when they had sung together.

Bubba turned her glazed eyes to the priest and her face glowed with a memory. 'You came back for me . . .' she said, touching his cheek.

Papas Yiannis sang a few lines, encouraging her to continue.

I was a boy so bold and brave
And women's hearts I went a stealing.
You had no need to be afraid
We sang our songs, you started healing.

440

Bubba continued with renewed strength, her voice clear and strong.

> *You'd spent the autumn at my side*
> *My heart was filled with such emotion.*
> *A child no more, yet not a bride,*
> *But then you left with my devotion.*
> *My dream remained, you'd come to me . . .*

Papas Yiannis seemed moved. He closed his eyes and pinched the bridge of his nose, then joined Bubba, singing the next lines together.

> *In happiness, we'd live together.*
> *Yet sometimes dreams aren't meant to be . . .*

At the end of that line, on one long harmonising note they stopped. Bubba turned her face into Papas Yiannis's chest. He closed his eyes again and held her for a few seconds.

Naomi and Rebecca hugged each other, both women let their tears fall.

Clearly, Bubba was tired. She looked up to the priest and said, 'I can't go on.'

Papas Yiannis, still holding the old lady, spoke into the microphone, 'I suspect our star needs to sleep. I'm going to take her home now.' His voice was shaky and Naomi realised he too was exhausted.

Everyone clapped, whistled, and called, 'Bravo!' as the elderly couple walked from the small stage to the door. In the doorway, Bubba turned and studied her family and friends. Her awareness had returned, and pleasure beatified her face. She gave her loved ones a final wave.

Naomi collected Bubba's shawl and, with Rebecca, accompanied her grandmother and the priest to a waiting taxi. She offered to go with them, but Papas Yiannis said she should stay with the family, the celebration must continue, but would she please help them into the vehicle?

They both kissed Bubba. 'Hey,' said Naomi. 'You know I love you, Pandora Cohen.'

Bubba's eyes sparkled, and she nodded.

Then they kissed the priest, which was not the appropriate thing to do, but he seemed pleased and, for a moment, Naomi thought she glimpsed a tear in his eye.

'Are you all right, Papas?'

'You won't believe how weary I am, Naomi. So terribly tired.' He offered her a weak smile. 'God bless you both.'

Naomi slipped her arm around Rebecca's shoulders and they watched the taxi drive away.

'*You* made all this possible, Rebecca,' she said. 'I'll always be in your debt. I know it wasn't easy to come back and make peace with Bubba. Thank you.'

* * *

The party continued. An hour after the old folk had left, Antonis called taxis for the jubilant family and their neighbours.

At the top of Spartili Street, the men drifted towards the tables outside Manno's kafenion where they ordered final drinks. The women grinned at each other and hummed Bubba's song as they strolled down Spartili Street. Naomi and Rebecca linked arms with Heleny who had promised them all hot chocolate and cookies to end a perfect evening.

They chuckled about their good fortune. The case was going to committee; they stood a real chance of getting their father's property back.

On the patio, relaxed on the new sofa, Bubba lay in Papas Yiannis's arms. Their heads were together, eyes closed. Their peaceful faces, lit by moonlight, were turned to face the stars.

'Look, they've fallen asleep,' Naomi whispered. 'What a beautiful sight.' They all stopped, silent for a moment, enjoying the lovely tableau.

'I'll get a blanket, so they don't catch a chill,' Marina said.

But before she returned realisation hit Naomi. 'Rebecca, would you stall Marina for a moment?'

'Why ... what's ... Oh no!'

'I think so,' Naomi said. For a weird moment, she sensed she had lived her entire life to reach this moment. Like recalling a far-distant dream or the peculiar electricity of *déjá vu*. She rushed onto the patio, placed her hand on Bubba's forehead and felt it deathly cold.

'No,' she sobbed quietly, and then tried to get a pulse under Bubba's jaw. Her grandmother's flesh was already stiff and lifeless.

She turned her attention to Papas Yiannis's wrist, still flaccid, but also unresponsive. Bubba had died in the old priest's arms and he had continued to hold her, until he too passed away.

'No ... oh no,' Naomi sobbed uncontrollably. Tears flowed freely as she stared at their faces; transcendental, loving, content.

* * *

443

The tragedy affected them all. They hardly spoke the next day, everyone fighting emotions, hugging, worn out by poignant memories of Bubba, the woman they all loved.

Marina, distraught by her own loss, blamed herself for not accompanying her grandfather home.

The next day raced by in a fug of officialdom and funeral preparation. Naomi heard that in many European countries, there were several days, sometimes weeks, before the funeral, but in Greece, it was practically the next day. Life moved quickly on with hardly any time for the family to comprehend their loss, to grieve, or to contemplate the life of their loved ones. All of that came in the thirty days of official mourning after the funeral.

Rebecca went to the synagogue to make arrangements with the Rabbi, then she met with Georgia at the church to help organise things for Marina, who seemed to be in a daze.

Costa and Fritz had taken the boys out to eat, sensing Naomi wanted some time on her own. Rebecca was still at the church when Marina brought her grandfather's documents over to Naomi, so she could arrange the death certificates.

'Are you all right over there on your own, Marina?'

She nodded. 'I've got relations coming to stay for a few days, then . . . do you think it's all right if Jason moves in for a while? We were going to ask Grandpa if we could get engaged, but now we have to wait a year out of respect, you know how it is.' She broke down and threw herself into Naomi's arms. 'I'm going to miss him so much, Naomi.'

Naomi felt her own tears rise. 'Your grandpa loved you very much, you know, despite the four o' clock ladder.'

Marina pulled back, blinked at her and sniffed. 'The four o' clock ladder?'

'He would stand in his dark kitchen and watch the reflection of his own house in my windows, waiting for your safe return in the early hours.'

Marina stared. 'You mean he saw us? He knew? He never said anything.'

'You were his world. Do you remember how proud he was at our brainstorming? And did you see the look on his face when you walked into the taverna last night? I'm telling you, he grew ten centimetres in his chair. Didn't you notice that it was *you* he was looking at as he sang with Bubba?'

'You mean he really loved me? And all the time, I thought he was just looking after me because of what happened to Mama. Like he was stuck with me and had no choice. I never realised. . . thought I was a burden. . . Oh, Naomi, I never told him I loved him! Never, not once! I'm so sad that he's died and it's too late now.'

'Some people aren't very good at showing their true feelings. Believe me, he loved you very much. I'm sure he would be happy with whatever makes you happy, and of course he knew you loved him, it didn't need saying.'

'Thanks, Naomi.' She nodded at the battered shoebox on the table. 'They're Grandpa's papers. I haven't a clue what to look for. To make it worse, all the old ones, like his birth certificate and his army documents, are in Italian.'

'Don't worry, I'll sort them.'

There was no order to the priest's documents, simply dropped into an old shoebox for years.

Naomi paused for a moment to recall the shocking car crash that took Papas Yiannis's wife and daughter. Unexpectedly snatched away in one brutal minute. The tragedy left the priest's granddaughter, Marina, strapped in the baby seat, virtually unscathed.

She remembered how Bubba helped at the funeral. Although reluctant to enter a Christian church, she had attended the service.

Sorting Papas Yiannis's papers was difficult. Rhodes had been under Italian rule when the priest was born, and didn't return to Greece until after the last war so, as Marina had noticed, many of his papers were in a language she didn't understand. Lining them up in chronological order, she slowly unravelled the priest's life.

He had entered the priesthood in 1948, his first parish located on the other side of the island, in the area of Lindos, where he had married and later had a daughter. He took over the parish of Paradissi the week before Naomi's parents were married.

She lined the documents like a game of solitaire with one large stack for papers that didn't apply to the priest, mostly belonging to parishioners with no next of kin. Halfway down the box, she took another handful and started dividing them out between the relevant piles. Naomi came across an old 1940 identity document, written in Italian, which again was quite normal as Rhodes belonged to Italy until 1947.

Nationality: Italian

Name: Giovanni Pastore

'What!' Naomi blinked at the name. 'Giovanni . . .' She stared at the photograph of the good-looking youth with a scar across his left eyebrow. She checked his date of birth and discovered him to be six months older than Bubba. Her mind raced. Why was the document in Papas Yiannis's box? Then, with terrible sadness, she realised there was only one explanation: Giovanni Pastore had died.

Giovanni must have come back to Paradissi. Did he see his daughter, Sonia? Naomi was both excited and sad. Her hands trembled and she rushed through the documents looking for clues. Papers slid to the floor. She dived down to gather them up, wondering if Giovanni had seen her and Rebecca too. Maybe he discovered Sonia was his daughter? Perhaps when he heard she died so tragically, he decided to attend the memorial service which was held seven years later. She hoped he came back sooner. Naomi had so many questions and wondered who could answer them.

Naomi was eighteen and Rebecca, eight when Papas Yiannis organised the seventh-year memorial service for her parents. Their bodies were never recovered after the storm, so there was no funeral. For the memorial, she wore all black and cried in the church. Costa, then her boyfriend, stood beside her, awkward with the emotion. Bubba and the priest had comforted her, although Bubba was also visibly broken-hearted.

Naomi remembered there were some strangers in the church, but she didn't recall anyone paying special attention to Bubba.

Did Bubba see Giovanni? Why didn't he stay? Where did he go? Naomi wanted to stop everything and read the last diary. Surely it would answer her questions.

Bubba's words came back to her. 'The last diary is for later, another occasion.' Then deep sadness fell over Naomi as she realised, once again, the priest would only have Giovanni's identity document if Giovanni had died. Perhaps his death certificate was also among the papers. She continued to search, desperate to know more and hoping to have her questions answered.

Chapter 58

Naomi studied the sepia photograph of Giovanni, stuck in the top corner of the Italian ID. A handsome boy, as she imagined when reading the diaries. Although his black curly hair tumbled over his ears, the scar across his left eyebrow was clearly visible in the picture. The event at Seven Springs came back to her. The first time Dora killed someone, and the only reason she did it was to save a life, that of the young man she loved.

Naomi held the document to her cheek and whispered, 'My grandfather, I wish I'd known you, Giovanni. You were hardly more than a boy, yet you were incredibly brave too. Prepared to give your own life, rather than disclose the whereabouts of the *Andartes*. I wonder what happened to you.'

The poignant moment was broken when the door opened and Heleny stuck her cheerful face into the room. She had been in and out all morning, and although Naomi realised Heleny was simply concerned and wanted to help, her constant interruptions and efforts to make her friend feel better were, in fact, driving Naomi insane.

'For God's sake, Heleny, not now!' Naomi barked.

Heleny's grin fell and she withdrew.

Instantly regretful, Naomi dropped Giovanni's ID and dashed outside.

'Heleny, sorry! Please come back!' she called up the street.

Heleny returned with a basket of hot cheese pies.

'Please, tell me you forgive me,' Naomi said. 'I don't know what came over me, yelling at you like that. I'm ashamed of myself. I'm sorry, really sorry.'

Heleny nodded. 'It's the grief. Don't worry about it. I thought you might not have time to cook, with all you have to deal with. So I baked these for you.' She placed the mountain of small pastries on the table, her wild grin reduced to a nervous smile. 'If you're cramped for space, some of your family can sleep at mine.'

'I'm overwhelmed. I'm sorry I snapped. I don't know what's the matter with me. It's just, oh Heleny, I loved her so much. So many things I wish I'd said, places I could have taken her, times I could have shown her how I appreciated what she'd done – given up – for me and Rebecca. Now it's too late and all I'm left with is terrible regret. I can't imagine life without her. It's as if she's taken part of me with her. I'm in pieces. Why wasn't I more considerate?' She realised she was crying now, and she had never felt so miserable.

'Shush! Enjoy the pies.'

Naomi looked up and smiled. Trust Heleny to think food was the answer to everything.

Heleny gave her a hug, then glanced over the papers spread across the table top. 'Not very organised, was he?' She picked up Giovanni's ID. 'Such a sad loss,' she said.

Naomi's jaw dropped and she blinked away her tears. 'You knew him?'

Heleny shrugged. 'As well as anybody, I guess.' She scanned documents and picked one up. 'Here's the one you want.' She passed Papas Yiannis's ID card to Naomi.

'Thanks. I was looking for it.'

'The earlier one's no use, but Marina might like to keep it as a momento.'

'What?' Naomi frowned, wondering if Heleny needed specs. She stared at the priest's photograph, his hirsute face and glasses, and then read the words.

Nationality: Greek

Name: Yiannis Voskos

The sensation Naomi experienced was similar to the seconds before she opened her eyes after sleeping, wondering if dawn was about to break. Voskos, the Greek word for shepherd. *My family have been shepherds since Byzantium*, Giovanni had said to Dora. Naomi's skin tingled. Could the shepherd boy and the priest be one and the same? If so, Papas Yiannis was her grandfather, her *Papoú*. She recalled the night before, when too much wine had prompted her to kiss the old man affectionately. She touched her lips, so glad of that intimate moment with him.

Naomi fell into the chair, her hand over her mouth, her mind racing through the diaries.

'Are you all right?' Heleny asked. 'If there's anything else I can do, just say.'

'Could you clarify something?'

'Happy to try.' Heleny set about making them a coffee.

Naomi gulped, forcing her emotions down. 'How do you say shepherds in Italian?'

'*Pastore*, why?'

Naomi gasped. 'I see. It was the priest's Italian name before Rhodes became Greek. I hadn't made the connection. What about "Yiannis" in Italian?'

'That's easy. Yiannis in Greek, Giovanni in Italian, Hans in Dutch, Iain in Scottish, John in English . . . do you want me to go on?'

Stunned, Naomi understood. The priest was Giovanni. All those years he'd watched over her family, quietly taking care of Bubba, supporting each of them when they needed it. Her mind went back to the diaries. Giovanni Pastore in Italian translated into Yiannis Voskos in Greek.

She had read the journals while the shepherd boy Bubba loved and lost, Giovanni Pastore, lived right across the street; the elderly priest that Naomi had known all her life.

This meant that Naomi's mother, Sonia, was the priest's daughter. Giovanni was already married with a child when he took over the parish of Paradissi, just before her own parents' wedding. She wondered how he felt to discover Dora had waited all those years for his return.

Giovanni – Papas Yiannis – performed the wedding ceremony of Sonia and Zorba in the local church. How his heart must have broken when his daughter was lost at sea. So terribly sad. She picked up the priest's latest identity card and stared at it.

'Can I do anything before the God Squad arrives?' Heleny asked gently, breaking her thoughts.

Despite her shock and grief, Naomi smiled, knowing how her friend referred to Georgia and the church ladies. She shook her head again.

'Then I'll leave you in peace.' As Heleny left, she passed Marina in the doorway.

'I've come to thank you for dealing with this. There's no way I could have handled it. I'm hopeless with paperwork, Naomi.'

'It's no problem,' Naomi said. 'Sit down, Marina. Would you like a cheese pie?'

'Wouldn't I just, thanks.' She sat at the table and placed a carrier bag in front of Naomi. 'I brought this over. It's the last diary. I know Grandpa was giving them to you. Also, there's a china ornament he was very fond of. He said Sonia gave it to him after he'd celebrated her wedding. It meant a lot to him, in fact he treasured it. As it came from your mother, I thought you should have it.'

Naomi touched Marina's hand, suddenly realising they were related, her grandfather was also Marina's grandfather. 'Thanks, it's very thoughtful of you.' She pulled the figurine out of the bag.

A china figure of a shepherd boy, a lamb under his arm and a sheepdog at his feet.

Naomi glanced at the other ornament, which had always stood at the end of the bookshelf. The china figure that Bubba cherished because Sonia had given it to her on the day of her wedding to Zorba. A dark-haired girl, singing, her eyes turned up to a blackbird on a branch, as if in duet with the bird.

Naomi wondered if her mother knew that Papas Yiannis was her father as she picked up the final diary.

Chapter 59

7 February 1977

It's been so long since I wrote anything in my diary. After Sonia's wedding she went to live with her husband's family, as is the custom. She comes to see me every day. Their house is on the other side of the main street of Paradissi, only a few minutes away.

Sonia's old bedroom has become a junk room, cluttered with useless stuff that mostly needs to be mended or thrown out. I came across my diaries in there. How time has flown. The journals were in a box that used to contain six wine glasses but now holds all the special bits and pieces one collects over a lifetime.

Pandora's Box.

I also found the childish drawing of a horse that Sonia made in her art lesson. It won a gold star that is still stuck in the corner. I touched it and smiled to remember how proud we both were. I discovered her school reports, a necklace she bought me with her first wages, a baby tooth from my first grandchild, Naomi, an envelope of dried rose petals from Mount Filerimos, and a lock of curly hair that belonged to the boy I loved.

I sat in my armchair and read the journals from start to finish. I didn't realise how dark it had become until I reached the end. My eyes were sore from the dim light and the tears for my dear departed friends and family.

My dream has come true, I have two grandchildren, ten-year-old Naomi, and Rebecca who was born only one week ago. They are both beautiful, but not alike. I can already see that Rebecca will be the double of Sonia, fine-boned with almond eyes and full lips. Naomi looks a lot like her father, square-jawed and an aquiline nose. But Naomi also has the round heavy-lidded eyes of Giovanni, and his mouth that was always quick to smile. Sometimes, when the light catches her in a certain way, I'm so shocked by the likeness that my heart leaps.

I often think of him. It's been thirty years since the clean-shaven soldier with an army haircut came looking for me. I wish I'd seen him, and I often try to imagine what he lookes like without his curls. I wonder, if I hadn't chosen to plant tomatoes that day, how different my life might have turned out. Unfortunately, we can't change the past. I go on alone – yet not alone.

After she was married, Sonia stopped working in the bank. The sedentary work gave her dreadful headaches, migraines, so Zorba taught her to fish with him on the boat. The fresh air seems to help. She had a break from fishing for her confinement, but tomorrow she's going out with Zorba again.

They fish at night, and until baby Rebecca was born, I went to sleep at their house on the other side of the main street, to take care of my granddaughter. Zorba's parents are too elderly to look after young children. The problem is that I share a bed with Naomi and, although she's only ten, she's already as tall as me and sleeps like a starfish.

Sonia's going to bring the children to me this time. My suggestion. Then Sonia and Zorba will get a few hours of uninterrupted sleep after work, and I'll send Naomi off to school. Sonia has looked pale lately and the headaches have come back. I persuaded her to return to the sea, night fishing with Zorba.

9 February 1977

I'm frantic! Sonia and Zorba haven't returned. Why in God's name did I encourage her to go with him?! Last night, an urn blew over on the patio and smashed, the noise woke me and I heard the unrelenting wind. A horrendous storm raged, turning into a hurricane. Rhodes' radio station announced that an earthquake, deep below the sea and forty kilometres off shore, had triggered turbulent seas and steep waves over four metres high. Winds were gusting at more than fifty knots, and the Coastguard and Search & Rescue have been out since midnight.

. I tried to call *Elevtheria* on the ship-to-shore radio but got no reply. I tuned to channel sixteen, the emergency and distress frequency, and kept it open all night. There were calls for help from local fishing boats but nothing from Zorba and Sonia. Perhaps they turned back and are waiting it out in some sheltered bay or the harbour. I can only pray for that.

When daylight arrived, I sent my granddaughter to school and fed Rebecca the bottle Sonia had left. By the time Naomi returned at two o'clock, I was beside myself with worry. Papas Yiannis came over and sat with me, assuring me they would be fine. Zorba was a good sailor and not one to take risks. Yet, I could see the concern in his eyes too. He loved Sonia.

And the wind blew.

Ever since he moved in, the priest had been a good friend. His wife, who is ten years younger than he is, has also grown close to Sonia and Zorba, almost like an older sister. She sent food over. A thoughtful gesture but I couldn't eat for the worry; nevertheless, it saved me cooking for Naomi.

My granddaughter has not grasped the seriousness of the situation. Naomi's positive her mother and father are safe in some distant cove. I hope she's right, but I am unable to believe it myself.

1 March 1977

This morning I found my daughter's wedding ring on her bedside table. I hadn't been in her bedroom since she brought the children to me on that fateful evening. I slipped the ring onto my finger, and remembered those minutes on the villa's Juliet balcony, when Giovanni took me as his wife. Then I recalled Sonia's wedding, when Zorba slid this gold band onto my daughter's finger.

I wished with all my heart Giovanni could have seen his mother's ring go on his child's finger.

One day, the ring will go on Naomi's finger, and I wonder if I will still be here to see it.

Sonia and Zorba's wedding was the new priest's first in our parish. I remember there was an embarrassing moment after he'd blessed the gold band when he seemed to lose his place. The priest pinched the bridge of his nose and closed his eyes. Everyone stared at him until he recovered and said, 'Apologies, a sneeze coming,' and we all smiled. I'm crying as I write this. The memory of that wonderful day brings back so much happiness.

These have been the hardest three weeks of my life. I must accept that my dear, darling, daughter is not returning home. I am heartbroken. Why is God so cruel? It seems everyone I love is snatched from me and I am destined to suffer alone. Is this my punishment for shooting my sister? Poor Evangelisa. They say hell is on earth, and in my darkest hours I believe that's true. I spend a lot of time talking to Irini in my head. I'm unable to say why, but she comforts me and I often feel she is near me, standing behind me, or in the next room, or holding me in the dead of night as I cry myself to sleep. Sweet Irini.

Jacob would like to come over from Italy and support me, but his health is not good. He never returned after Sonia's wedding, the strenuous journey was too much for him. Perhaps one day I'll go to Italy. He writes often, tells me about his wife, who's having their second baby. I always get a lift from his correspondence and write back immediately.

10 February 1984

How could I know all those years ago the things I'd be writing in my journal today?

I've fallen in love with the most wonderful man. This sweet agony and ecstasy is tearing me apart, for this is a forbidden love than can lead nowhere. He's happily married, with a child. What's more, he's Greek Orthodox.

I look out for him every day and dream about him at night. My lonely heart longs for him to take me in his arms, and my pulse races as I write this just from the very idea.

Papas Yiannis, the priest across the road. When I think of him, my emotions go crazy, sawing and breaking in the same instant.

After I lost my beloved daughter, the priest and his wife were a comfort, although Papas Yiannis always seems to keep his distance. Now, seven years after their tragic death, it is time to arrange the memorial service for Sonia and Zorba. Yesterday, Papas Yiannis came over to run through the church details. The priest understands that the situation is difficult for me, as I am Jewish and the memorial service will be in a Christian church.

We talked for some time, and then I'm afraid I got over emotional thinking of Sonia. I broke into tears. We were sitting on the banquette, and as I cried, the priest placed his hand on my shoulder and said something comforting. It was all too much for me. I turned towards him, threw my arms around his neck, and cried on his shoulder.

I felt his body tense. He lifted his hand away from my shoulder, but I was overcome with emotion and wept heavily. After a moment, he slipped his arms around me and held me tight. I had not been in a man's arms since the morning Giovanni said goodbye in the villa.

Oh, Giovanni, how I loved him, how I missed him, how I longed to be in his arms again. I think I may have whispered his name, I'm not sure, but something made the priest pull away from me. I blinked at him, wiped my tears away and apologised. Then I could see that he was full of emotion too.

The priest got up and sat at the kitchen table, and I sat opposite him.

'I'm so sorry, Papas. Please forgive me,' I said. 'It's just. . . I've lost so many people that I loved . . .'

He nodded sadly, pulled off his glasses and pushed back his wild curly hair.

I stared at my neighbour, Papas Yiannis, Orthodox priest of Paradissi. No two people could have exactly the same scar across their eyebrow.

Images of the pink-faced Nazi returned. The shepherd boy with a gun held to his head, blood streaming down his face. The horror of Seven Springs. My dearest, darling, Giovanni.

I was sitting in the kitchen opposite the only man I'd ever kissed, ever loved.

I wanted to fall into his arms! I longed to be naked against him, desperate to taste his kisses just one more time.

'Giovanni,' I whispered.

'No! No!' he exclaimed, realising his mistake, thrusting his glasses back on. 'I'm Papas Yiannis, Orthodox Priest of Paradissi. I have a wife and a child. Pandora Cohen, they know nothing of my past. Listen to me for their sake: I am Papas Yiannis, shepherd – soldier – priest. Never forget it.'

That night, I cried myself to sleep.

1 September 1989

It's been such a long time since I picked up this beautiful pen that my dear papa gave me all those years ago. The ink had dried up, and that seemed symbolic somehow, although I am not sure of what. They found a dusty bottle of India ink for me in the post office and I'm delighted to use Papa's birthday gift once more.

Tomorrow, young Naomi is getting married. Naomi's more like a daughter to me, and I cannot take my mind away from her mother's wedding. Bringing up Rebecca was hard work, her being little more than a newborn when my Sonia perished, but Naomi, ten years old at that time, practically brought herself up.

She was no trouble; in fact she shared many of my responsibilities and I love her with all my heart.

Her husband-to-be is the steady sort. Costa will never be captain of the cruise ship he works on, but he'll always have a job, and won't drink or gamble his money away. I haven't long to wait before I see my first great-grandchild. They have the process in hand already.

Chapter 60

The rest of the pages in the diary were blank. Naomi closed it and realised she was crying again. She lifted the ornament from the shelf and placed it beside the figurine of the shepherd boy.

The funeral parlour brought Pandora Cohen and Papas Yiannis home for burial the following morning. As was the Orthodox tradition, the priest's ornate coffin lid stood outside the house, telling everyone they could come and pay their last respects to the deceased.

Naomi walked across the road and asked Marina if she could have a moment alone with the priest, before she let his parishioners in.

'Of course. It's the least I can do,' Marina said. 'I'll close the door and stand outside until you leave. Take as long as you want.'

In his coffin, on a trestle in the centre of the living room, Papas Yiannis Voskos, shepherd, freedom fighter, father and friend, lay in a bed of white chrysanthemums. Only his face and hands visible in the sea of flowers. Naomi went to his side. It seemed the priest was about to smile.

'Dear Papas,' she said shakily. 'I don't know your beliefs, but I hope your soul lingers until after the funeral and you are here in this room, able to hear me.' She glanced around. 'My grandmother loved you. She never loved another man. I believe you knew that. I would have buried you together, but although religion unites us, it also divides us. Besides, your place is with your wife and daughter. Thank you for being a wonderful grandfather. Rest in peace, Papas Yiannis Voskos. Rest in peace, Giovanni Pastore.'

Naomi reached into her bag, pulled out the ornament of the singing girl, and tucked it deep under the white carnations. They would, in a way, be buried together. She left the priest's house, bowed her head, and walked past his congregation who stood in a line that reached down the street, ready to file into the room and pay their respects. Mourners would kiss the icon of Saint John that lay on the priest's chest before leaving the house and gathering in groups on the street.

Across the road, in respect for Bubba's religion, Naomi had placed boiled eggs and small dishes of cooked lentils and chick-peas on the table around a large dish of apples and oranges. All 'round' food, in keeping with Jewish tradition – symbolising that life is a circle.

Later that afternoon, Naomi and her family stood at Bubba's graveside with her friends and some of Costa's relations. She placed the china shepherd boy in Bubba's grave, followed by a branch from the cinnamon tree and a handful of earth.

'Rest in peace, Pandora Cohen, freedom fighter, daughter, sister, mother, lover, friend, grandmother, and great-grandmother,' Naomi said quietly. On the horizon the sun slipped into the sea, and overhead a brilliant explosion of fireworks lit up the dusk sky.

* * *

A little more than two months later, Rebecca and Fritz returned to Rhodes. The cruising season had finished, and Fritz enjoyed helping Costa with the olive harvest, coming back exhausted and satisfied with the manual labour. Rebecca made use of Naomi's

461

creams, rubbing balm into her husband's tired arms, before he massaged cream to fight stretch marks on her belly.

'Shall we go for a walk up Filerimos tomorrow, Naomi?' Rebecca asked.

Naomi nodded. 'I'd like that.'

They left the men with the harvest and drove to the top of Filerimos. After walking the stations of the cross between tall pines and strutting peacocks, they came to the imposing crucifix, a landmark that was visible for many kilometres. They gazed down over Paradissi and out to sea, each recalling parts of the diaries.

'Let's go around the other side of the monastery, and see if we can see any signs of the hut, or the cinnamon tree,' Naomi suggested.

They walked for over half an hour, but found nothing relevant and eventually sat on an ancient log in a small clearing. 'I wonder where Irini is,' Naomi whispered, glancing at the lush ground dotted with wild orchids.

'I was just thinking . . . could this possibly be the log, you know, outside the hut?'

'I'd like to think so but who knows!? Shall we go back to the car?'

They passed closer to the convent on their way back, and Naomi spotted a flash of white. She stopped and touched her sister's arm.

'Look, roses.' They both glanced around. 'Irini must be near. Let's scatter a few petals for her.' They did, careful not to step on the wild flowers. Satisfied, they stood perfectly still in the shade of the building and observed a minute of silence in memory of the young woman whom Dora loved.

Naomi's eyes widened and she slipped her hand into her sister's. They stared at a small bundle of grey feathers. The bird with bright red eyes flicked its wings at them, before trilling its heart out.

'Little bird, big voice, remember?' Naomi said quietly.

'Do you think it's . . . near Irini's . . . no, it's impossible. I don't believe in that stuff, do you?' Rebecca whispered, and although her words were dismissive, she turned to Naomi with her eyes brimming. 'I wish . . .'

And Naomi heard Jacob's voice in her head. 'No point in wishing.' Her phone rang, and Costa asked where they were.

'Will you meet us at the harbour taverna, Naomi? I could murder a moussaka and a cold beer. We've finished at the olive factory, delighted we'll have a hundred litres of prime olive oil!'

Naomi hung up and told Rebecca what the men planned. 'Why don't we take some petals down to the port, for Bubba's family while we're there,' she said.

The sisters filled their handbags before returning to the car.

They found Costa and Fritz with a beer at an al fresco table, and Rebecca told them what they planned to do.

'Let's walk over together,' Costa suggested, 'I was fond of the old girl.'

Fritz stood tall and squared his shoulders. 'I admired her more than anyone I know. She was a most remarkable person.'

The sisters smiled at each other. They stood on the quayside, both wondering if that was where the rusty ships had moored. Together, they threw the rose petals on the turquoise water. A moment later, Rebecca began to sob, her knees buckling.

Fritz caught his wife, who was staring vacantly in the mid-distance, and Naomi suddenly realised what was going on.

Her face broke into a wide smile as she took her brother-in-law's hand and placed it on Rebecca's tummy.

Rebecca covered her husband's hand and found her voice. She whispered, 'It's our children moving, Fritz.' They gazed at each other, their happiness blatant.

Costa slipped his arm around Naomi, and as they watched the petals float away, he mischievously muttered, 'Have those two lovebirds ever experienced a sleepless night? Because I still remember ours.'

'I love you,' Naomi said.

* * *

In the maternity ward, five months later, a nurse placed a baby boy, John Phoenix, in his father's arms, while Rebecca held Pandora Sonia. She smiled across at her darling Fritz.

'Are you all right with our son, Dad?' she quipped.

'I'm doing okay. How are you coping, Mum?' he replied, his grin as wide as it had ever been.

FACTS THAT INSPIRED
VILLA OF SECRETS

Villa of Secrets is based on a true story: what happened to the Jews of Rhodes, the confiscated Jewish property, and the recently discovered archives kept behind a locked door at Rhodes Police Headquarters for over seventy years. However, the court case at the end of the story is pure fiction. The Jews of Rhodes have not, to date, February 2018, had their property or homes returned to them. You can read more at:

http://primolevicenter.org/printed-matter/the-secret-of-the-last-jews-of-rhodes/

http://www.jpost.com/Jewish-World/Jewish-Features/Rhodes-A-decimated-Jewish-community

I was inspired to write this novel when I came across the story of fifteen-year-old Sarika Yehoshua and events that took place in Greece, 1944. By all accounts, Sarika was a precocious Jewish child who insisted on going to school. She lived on the Greek island of Euboea in the Aegean Sea.

The island, although occupied by the Germans, was used as a gateway out of mainland Europe and the war by soldiers, politicians, Jews, and freedom fighters in danger of capture.

Sarika ran away to the mountains to join the resistance, the *Andartes*, expressing a wish to become a freedom fighter herself. Eventually she gained permission to establish her own group of twelve Greek girls whom she taught to shoot, to defend themselves and their honour, and to defend their country.

Sarika's cousin was brutally tortured and killed in mistake for Sarika. Her commander gave young Sarika permission to find and execute the collaborator responsible, which she did.

The nationalistic spirit of this famous *kapitanessa* is captured in a quote, '*This is my country. I was born and raised here. The Greeks are my people, their fight is my fight. This is where I belong.*'

It seems the feeling was not mutual. Despite risking her life in a selfless struggle to defend Greece against the Axis, Sarika found herself close to being arrested by the Greeks for her services to ELAS (the Greek resistance). However, she was warned by the local police chief and fled from Greece.

After the war, Sarika Yehoshua became a teacher in an Israeli school, and a wife and mother.

More here:
http://www.jewishpartisans.org/partisans/sara-fortis

Acknowledgements

I would like to thank Samuel Modiano for sharing with me his terrible experiences when he was transported on one of the ships from Rhodes in July 1944, and later his tragic internment in Auschwitz. Samuel, one of the few Jewish survivors of Rhodes, weighed only 26 kilos and was close to death when he was rescued in 1945. Also thanks to Karmen Cohen, director of the Jewish Museum in Rhodes Old Town, for answering all my questions with remarkable patience. Without their help, I could not have written this story. However, I want to point out that any mistakes in the facts are entirely of my own doing.

Thanks also to the people of Paradissi especially Mike and Mama for their local war stories and fabulous Sunday lunches, Anna Oripoulou for helping with translations, Katarina Sparti for her heart-breaking revelations. Ron Jefferies for his fire-fighting expertise, Antonis Taverna, Tony Fyler, and all the team at Bonnier Zaffre especially Eleanor Dryden, Caroline Kirkpatrick, Sarah Bauer, Divia Cowley and Federica Leonardis. And last but not least, my superb agent, Tina Betts.

If you enjoyed *Villa of Secrets*, you'll love Patricia Wilson's debut novel, *Island of Secrets*. Order now.

Can you escape your past in paradise?

Island of Secrets

FOR FANS OF
Victoria Hislop
A PERFECT SUMMER READ

Patricia Wilson